The Garden of Heaven

ALSO BY MADHULIKA LIDDLE

The Muzaffar Jang Series

The Englishman's Cameo (2009)
The Eighth Guest & Other Muzaffar Jang Mysteries (2011)
Engraved in Stone (2012)
Crimson City (2015)

Short Stories

My Lawfully Wedded Husband & Other Stories (2012)
Woman to Woman: Stories (2017)

The Garden of Heaven

A Novel

Madhulika Liddle

SPEAKING TIGER

SPEAKING TIGER BOOKS LLP
125A, Ground Floor, Shahpur Jat, near Asiad Village,
New Delhi 110049

First published by Speaking Tiger Books in 2021

ISBN: 978-93-5447-208-4
eISBN: 978-93-5447-209-1

10 9 8 7 6 5 4 3 2 1

Typeset in Sabon LT Std by SÜRYA, New Delhi
Printed at Chaman Enterprises, New Delhi

For Ramya. Thank you.

Contents

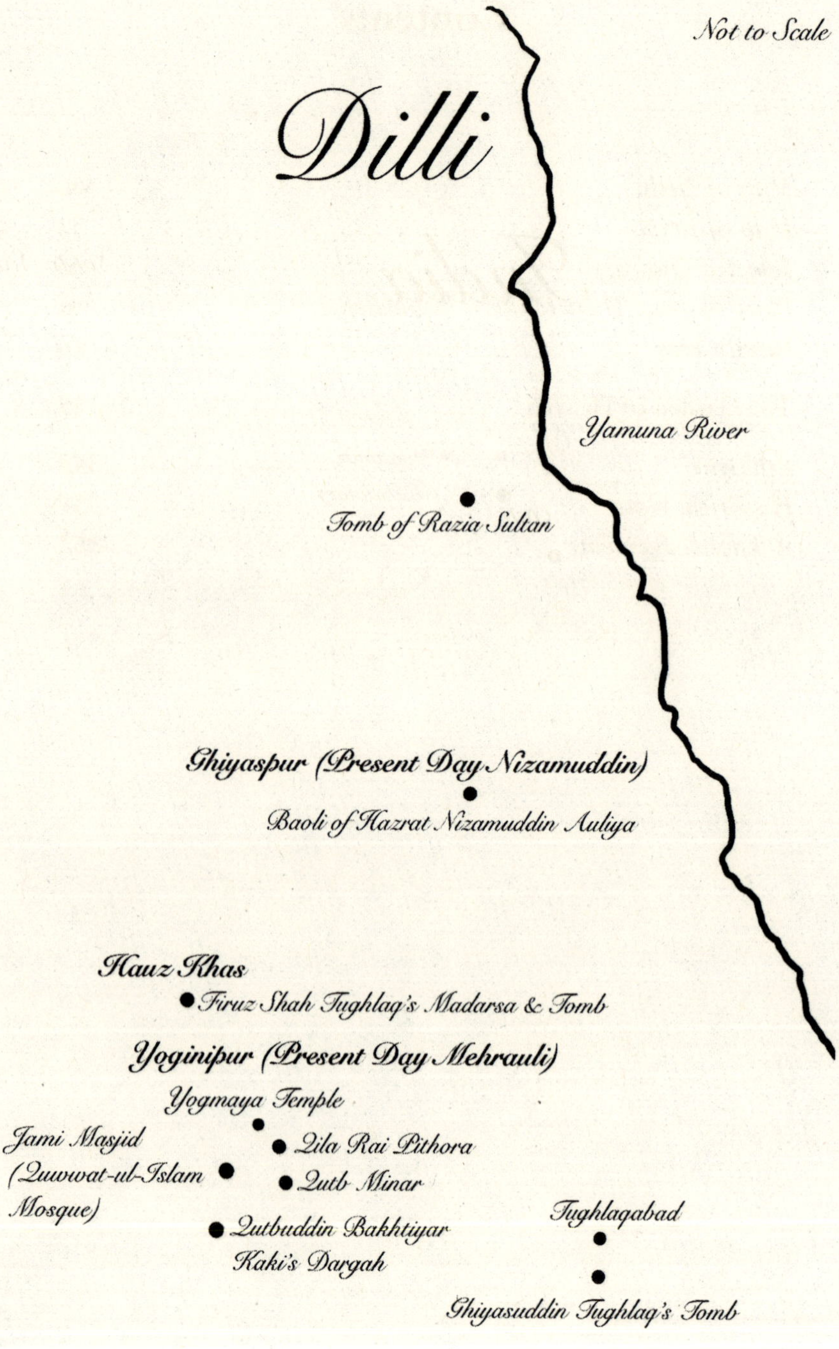
Not to Scale
Dilli
Yamuna River
Tomb of Razia Sultan
Ghiyaspur (Present Day Nizamuddin)
Baoli of Hazrat Nizamuddin Auliya
Hauz Khas
Firuz Shah Tughlaq's Madarsa & Tomb
Yoginipur (Present Day Mehrauli)
Yogmaya Temple
Jami Masjid (Quwwat-ul-Islam Mosque)
Qila Rai Pithora
Qutb Minar
Qutbuddin Bakhtiyar Kaki's Dargah
Tughlaqabad
Ghiyasuddin Tughlaq's Tomb

India

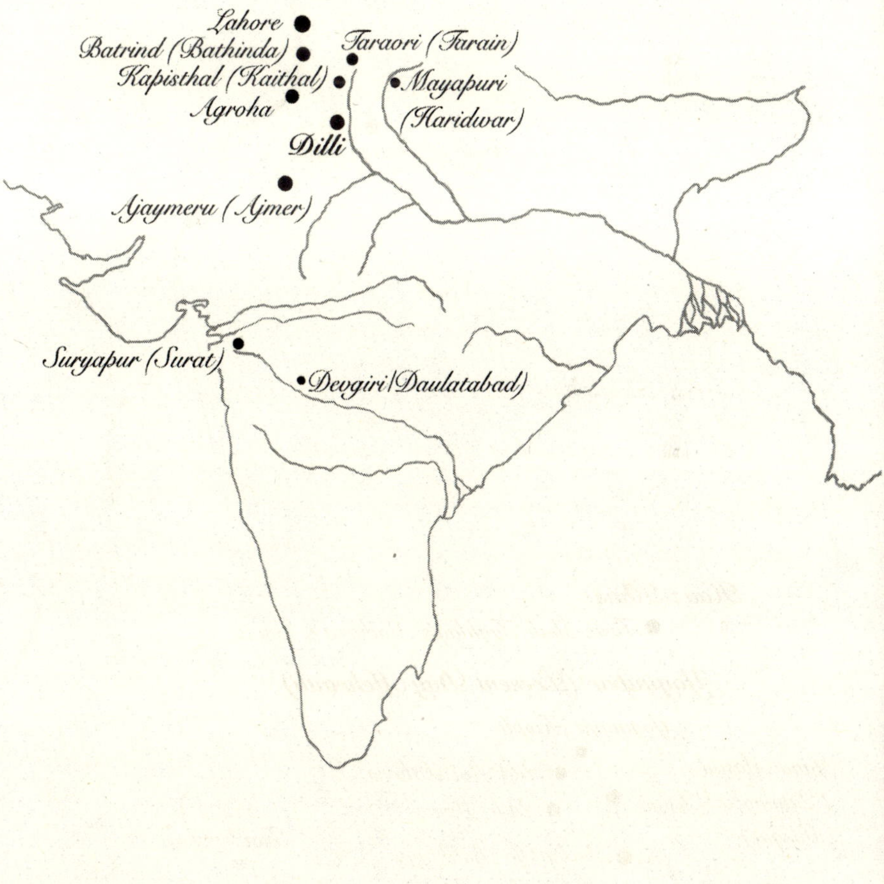
Not to Scale
Lahore
Batrind (Bathinda)
Taraori (Tarain)
Kapisthal (Kaithal)
Mayapuri
(Haridwar)
Agroha
Dilli
Ajaymeru (Ajmer)
Suryapur (Surat)
Devgiri(Daulatabad)

Selected Glossary

Hauz	Water tank, pool
Jarool	*Lagerstroemia speciosa*. A flowering tree, also known as pride of India or queen crape myrtle
Jital	A coin commonly used in various parts of India
Kanju	Indian elm, *Holoptelea integrifolia*. A tree native to the Indian subcontinent
Khirni	Ceylon iron wood, *Manilkara hexandra*. A tree native to the Indian subcontinent
Madarsa	In medieval India and elsewhere, a term used for a school of higher education, a university
Makoi	*Solanum nigrum*. A wild plant of the nightshade family, bearing berries that look like miniature tomatoes
Peelu	*Salvadora oleoides*, also known as toothbrush tree, or *misvak*. A tree native to Delhi
Shilp Shastra	A collection of ancient Indian texts that deal with the principles, rules, standards and descriptions of various arts and crafts
Yojana	A measure of distance. One yojana was about four kos, a distance approximately between 13 and 16 kilometres

Place Names: Their Modern Equivalents

Agroha	A town in Hisar district, in Haryana
Ajaymeru	Ajmer, in Rajasthan
Batrind	Bathinda, in Punjab
Daulatabad	Also known as Devgiri. Near Aurangabad, in Maharashtra
Kapisthal	Kaithal, in Haryana
Mayapuri	Haridwar, a town on the banks of the Ganga in the foothills of the Shivaliks
Ranasthambhapura	Ranthambore, in Rajasthan
Sthanishvar	Thanesar, in Haryana
Suryapur	Surat, in Gujarat
Taraori	Tarain, near Thanesar, in Haryana

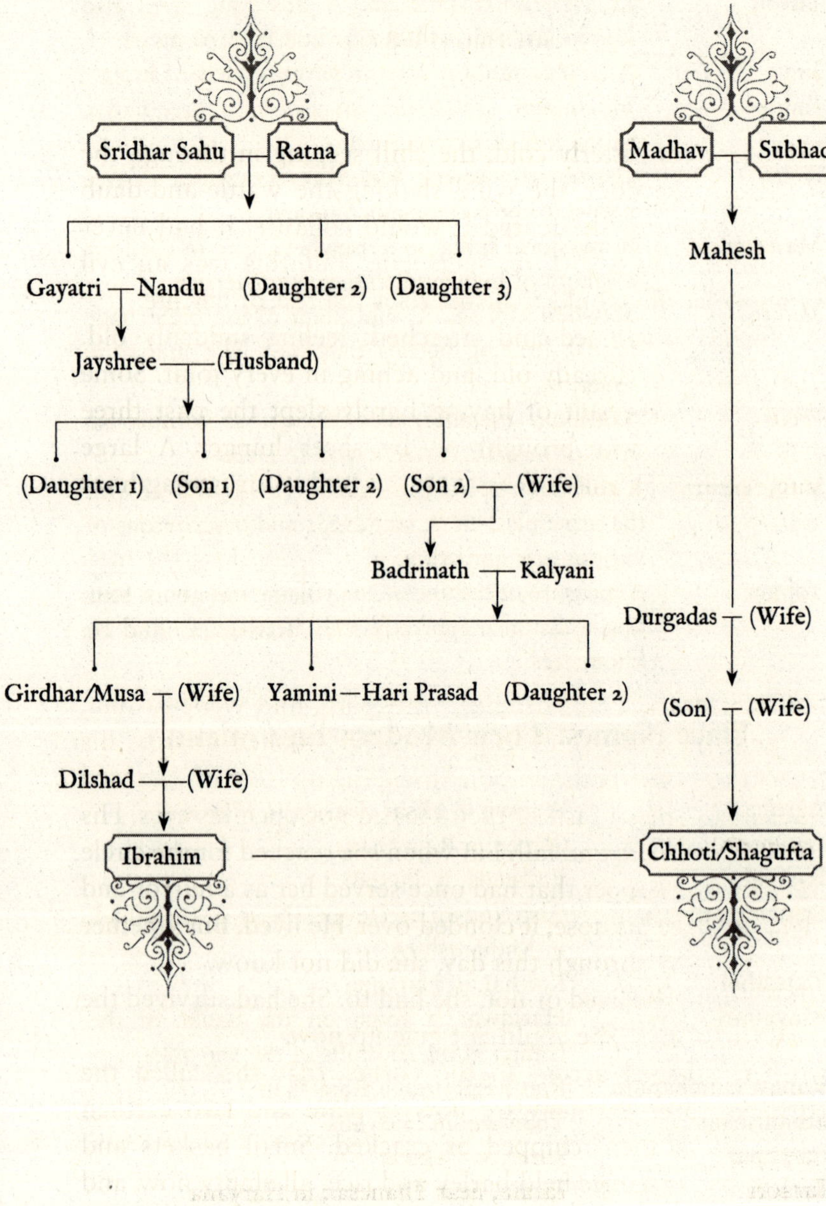

Sridhar Sahu
Ratna
Madhav
Subhadra
Gayatri
Nandu
(Daughter 2)
(Daughter 3)
Mahesh
Jayshree
(Husband)
(Daughter 1)
(Son 1)
(Daughter 2)
(Son 2)
(Wife)
Badrinath
Kalyani
Durgadas
(Wife)
Girdhar/Musa
(Wife)
Yamini
Hari Prasad
(Daughter 2)
(Son)
(Wife)
Dilshad
(Wife)
Ibrahim
Chhoti/Shagufta

Prologue

Dilli

801 Hijri (1398 CE)

It was cold. Bitterly cold, the chill seeping in through the gaps in the door, the wind shaking the wattle-and-daub of her hut until she feared it would collapse. It had never seemed so flimsy before, so fragile. But this was an evil winter, one she would remember for the rest of her life.

Shagufta yawned and stretched, feeling suddenly old. Just thirty, but already old, and aching in every joint. Some of that was a result of having barely slept the past three nights. Some was brought on by sheer hunger. A large part of it was misery. Nothing sapped your strength as misery did.

She looked across, her eyes swollen and red, at the man huddled under the ragged quilt on the floor. He was still. Alive? Or dead, despite all the energy she had expended on keeping him breathing?

Shagufta got up, wincing with pain, and went to him, to pull the quilt from off his face. He looked ghastly, his cheekbones sharp, the stubble spreading up from his bearded chin in an unruly rash of grey. He did not open his eyes. His chest did not rise and fall. But when she reached for the circle of tarnished copper that had once served her as a mirror and held it before his nose, it clouded over. He lived. But whether he would live through this day, she did not know.

Whether he lived or not, she had to. She had survived the past three days. She could not give up now.

She stepped across to the corner that she called the kitchen: three earthenware pots, a plate and two earthen cups, all of them chipped or cracked. Small baskets and sacks that had once held barley and rice, all empty now, and a few withered vegetables. Shagufta took stock for the sake of it, though she knew well enough what she possessed. A handful of parched gram. Two of millet. A little salt. A small beaker of water, set beside the wounded man's bed.

She sighed. She would have to go out, like it or not.

Another glance at the man, a hand on his forehead—the fever was abating, she thought—and then she drew her shawl closer about her, pulling it up to cover her head before she unlatched the door and stepped out.

She nearly reeled back with the stench. It filled the air, hung over everything. The smell of death and decay, so putrid that it brought the bile rushing up to her throat. Shagufta swallowed, willing herself to stay upright, to not duck back into her home.

There was mist all about, the fog of the winter and the smoke of the houses that had been burned. She had heard, on the day Taimur's armies had appeared on the far horizon, that the Sultan had ordered that people burn their houses and flee. But why would the Sultan order something so craven, she had wondered. Why would he not exhort his subjects to stay and fight instead? And they had fought, only to have the Mongol hit back—hard. For three days, his maddened troops had gone on a rampage; for three days, Dilli had burnt, thousands had been killed, their corpses strung up at prominent places across the city as an example to others.

Shagufta moved away from her door, her path taking her from one house to the other. These were not burned, not even singed, but they were empty. Empty of people, empty of belongings. The families she had known had all fled. Gathered up their clothes, their utensils, their children, their memories, their sorrows, their joys, and left—gone like the mist that would disappear when the sun was full.

They were not all gone.

Lying in the drain along the alley was a man with his stomach slashed open, his entrails spilling out. Beyond, on the low platform surrounding the peepal tree, she could see a pair of dogs worrying at a heap of something dark. Their snarling, the crunch of bones, drifted to her ears. Above, with a flapping of heavy wings, a pair of vultures alighted on the bare branch of the old tree.

Shagufta closed her eyes.

She returned a quarter of an hour later and unlatched the door with trembling fingers. She was clawing off her shawl, pulling it, shaking it, even before she had quite managed to close the door. Throwing it aside, frantically wiping her worn sandals on a tattered rag she used to block up the chinks in the door. Grabbing the damp rag with which she had been cooling the sick man's brow, using it to scrub at her hands, her face, any part that had been exposed to the filth outside.

When she looked down, the man's eyes were open.

Watchful grey eyes regarded her with an unblinking stare as she lifted his shoulders to let him sip from the cup she held up to him. When he had drunk, she offered him a handful of small translucent reddish-pink berries to eat. His eyes narrowed in suspicion, but he ate. She did, too, savouring the burst of sweetness followed by the distinctive peppery aftertaste. The man frowned, but in puzzlement, she thought, nothing more.

'It is peelu,' she said softly, slowly. Did he understand Persian? What did the Mongols speak? Turkish? Persian? Or some other language she knew nothing of? 'There are a few trees nearby.'

Not Persian, at any rate; he did not seem to have understood her.

Then he spoke. 'You speak Persian?' His accent was strange, but not jarring. 'I did not think the people of this land spoke Persian.' He lay back, exhausted by the effort of sitting up. Beads of perspiration appeared on his forehead despite the chill. Shagufta reached across and wiped them away with the frayed edge of her shawl. 'Not everybody does,' she said. Not the common people, she thought silently.

He would wonder how someone like her—her clothes threadbare, her home one-roomed and ramshackle, her food foraged and meagre—could set herself apart from the common people. She was common. That was the truth, even if she refused to accept it.

'How many days has it been?' His voice was a whisper.

'Three.'

There was a long silence. The man swallowed. She thought he might be thirsty, and offered him the cup again, but he shook his head weakly. His eyes remained open, red-rimmed, bloodshot. The fever had abated, but the weakness would take a long time to go. If it ever did.

'Speak to me,' he said.

'What?' Shagufta frowned.

'Speak,' he repeated. 'Say something.' The words were a susurration, a hiss so low she might have never heard them had she not been leaning so close. She stared at him. What did he want her to say? To tell him who she was, where the city gates lay, how his fellow invaders had rampaged and pillaged and raped over the past three days? How many corpses lay piled up in the streets outside?

No. She would not tell him that now. There would be time enough for him to discover it for himself when he had recovered.

'The silence. Speak.'

She realized then what he had meant. Yes, there was utter silence, the distant cawing of crows the only sound of life. She had become used to the silence over these years, even grown fond of it, enough to cherish the solitude. But this soldier, accustomed to living every moment in company with hundreds of others, was not used to it. For him, it would begin to pall.

'Would you like to hear a story?' she asked hesitantly.

She had to be certain. Noting the almost imperceptible nod, she allowed herself a small smile of satisfaction. Yes, a story. She knew many stories.

She shuffled forward, moving closer to him, settling herself so that she could rest her back against the wall. It gave her a few moments to think. To decide what she should tell him. The stories Meera had told her when she was small she dismissed; they were too childish, too innocent. Something, perhaps, of the anecdotes that Ibrahim had recounted. Salacious, she had thought them back then when she had been young. Entertaining, but far too scandalous to be spoken.

No, she thought. Those were best kept tucked away in the far recesses of her memory, along with Ibrahim.

Then ... what?

Only one thing came to her mind. It would be a long story, she thought. Long enough to keep her talking through the rest of the day and into the night, if he allowed it and she was able.

She cleared her throat. 'Two hundred years ago,' she said, 'a man came to Dilli from Agroha.'

1

Agroha

Vikram Samwat 1244 (1188 CE)

Sridhar Sahu, one hand resting on the carved wooden handle of the cradle, asked, 'She is three months old today, is she not?' His youngest, the third of three daughters, was at her mother's breast. Two plump ankles, each adorned with a string of black and gold beads to ward off the evil eye, were all that could be seen of the baby under a fold of Ratna's sari.

Ratna looked up, her eyes filled with dread. Six years of marriage and four births—their first-born had left the world within a week of entering it—had taught her Sridhar's belief: that a woman needed three months of rest after giving birth. Then, alongside her duties as a mother, she had to go back to fulfilling her duties as a wife. He was reminding her. Tonight she would be in his bed.

'Good,' he said. 'Then you will be strong enough to begin packing. We are leaving Agroha.'

Ratna froze. The sound of the baby's vigorous sucking filled the room.

'Leaving?' Her voice was a whisper; this was a surprise. An unpleasant surprise. 'For—for how long?'

Her husband turned away, his starched dhoti and tunic limp with the sweat of a long day in the marketplace. Sridhar Sahu, wealthy merchant and one of the most respected citizens of Agroha—an Agrawal worthy of the name he bore—did not lift heavy loads or crush stones, or do any of the many menial tasks that helped most people keep body and soul together. All he did was use his mind, and the experience of not just thirty years of his own life, but the accumulated experience of his forefathers too. They had been merchants, dealing for generations in cloth and silk and occasionally, gemstones; men of worth, who could sniff out a profit in the most unlikely of opportunities. Men who could negotiate, who could sell a broken bowl to the very man who had thrown it into the gutter. Astute men. Ruthless men.

And Sridhar Sahu—said those who knew him well—was the most astute of them all. There were some who said, only half in jest, that the infant Sridhar had emerged from his mother's womb ready to whittle down the price the midwife asked for her services. His business acumen was bred into him.

He frowned now at Ratna, irritated at her question. 'Forever,' he said in a brusque voice as he walked to the small niche in the wall. An earthen lamp flickered there, its flame reflected in the pool of oil that bathed the fat wick. A moth was hovering, its wings creating the minutest of breezes. Sridhar Sahu's fingers half curled. Then, with one swift, sure move, he caught the moth and crushed it between his thumb and forefinger.

He turned back to where Ratna, watching him with huge eyes, had shifted the baby to her other breast.

'We are moving to Suryapur,' he said. 'Agroha has nothing left to offer. It is time to try for a better life.'

When Ratna was a little girl, too little even to really know what it meant to be married, her mother said, 'Remember, Ratna. Your husband is always right. Even if you know he is not, pretend he is. Men do not like to be told they are wrong.'

It had been too much for a girl so young to comprehend, but the important part had burrowed its way into Ratna's head and stayed there. She was never to question her husband, never to say nay. It had been constantly repeated to her long before a bridegroom had been found.

Sridhar Sahu, nine years older than her, had intimidated her from the beginning, and she had never questioned him. She did not question him now.

A week passed. Her days went in sorting through their belongings, packing all that needed to be taken along. The more fragile things—the earthenware pots and plates and bowls, the intricately carved wooden household shrine and the lamps that burned both before it and in all the rooms of the house—had to be wrapped carefully in rags, cushioned with cotton. The rest: the low stools, the heavy wooden trunks and chests, the beds, the metal utensils and tools and dozens of odds and ends had to be wrapped, too, to prevent them being scratched or getting dusty. She did not have to do it herself; there were servants for that. But it was tiring, frustrating. And there were the children, too. Gayatri, now nearly five years old, could be left to herself, but her younger sister was only two, and a handful. The baby was, as all babies are, always in need of attention.

'Why are we going to Suryapur?' Ratna asked in a hesitant whisper as her husband ate his dinner one evening.

Sridhar Sahu paused in the act of ladling melted ghee into the bowl of lentils on the large, flat metal plate. He glanced up at her, his eyes watchful. 'Why do you ask?'

His evasiveness did not surprise her. She continued to swing the little circular bamboo fan she was holding. 'I have lived in Agroha all my life,' she said. 'I know no other life. No other people, no other places. It will be so new.' With her free hand, she slid forward the pot of spinach, prompting him wordlessly to help himself. 'I fear the newness. The unfamiliarity.'

He took a generous spoonful of the greens. It was a favourite dish of his, and she knew it. He helped himself, too, to the pickled raw mangos in the glazed earthenware jar beside his plate. He took the topmost chapati from the small plate and tore off a piece.

It was not until he had dipped the chapati in the spinach

and eaten the morsel that he replied. 'Every place is new to begin with.'

He did not understand. Or even if he did, he would not admit it. Ratna sighed inwardly.

'Suryapur has more trade than Agroha does,' Sridhar Sahu said between mouthfuls. 'Ships travel from Suryapur all the way to where the sun sets. And to where it rises. Silk, cotton, spices, porcelain, gemstones. Do you know how much money I can make there? I could buy all of Agroha after working in Suryapur for just five years.'

She did not believe that. No matter how naïve he thought she was; no matter how naïve she knew herself to be.

'Suryapur is so far,' she said, after a few minutes had passed. Her voice sounded wistful; she could not help it.

'Ninety yojanas,' he agreed.

'It would take nearly three months to get there,' she said in an awed whisper. 'The baby would be old enough to be rolling over perhaps, by the time we arrived.'

He shrugged in response. 'If we moved faster than a yojana a day, there is no reason for the journey to take that long. But why do you worry? Your maid will look after you and the children. There will be other servants too. And there are travellers' inns aplenty along the way. It is not as if you have to walk the distance with your children on your back.'

Ninety days, she thought as she watched him eat. Ninety days of sitting, perhaps ten hours a day if not more, in a rattling, shaking bullock cart. In weather like this, already hot. And with the rains not likely to arrive for the next couple of months, certain to get hotter still. The very thought made her feel sick. It did not matter if she had a hundred servants to wait on her hand and foot. No matter what, she was the one who would have to make that journey.

A thought struck her. 'Is it because of Shantinathji?'

'Shantinath? My partner in the trade?' He frowned in response to her nod. 'Why should it be because of Shantinath?'

'Did he not go to Suryapur too? Less than a month ago—no, was it a fortnight? I remember you telling me. You go to join him, is it? The two of you will work together again?' Her brow furrowed as she recalled something someone had said. 'But that cannot be, can it? You had said Shantinathji was going to Suryapur for some work. Not that he was shifting to Suryapur. And his family is still here—'

'He may have left his family behind because there is no need for every man to drag his wife and children about all over the land,' Sridhar Sahu replied. 'I prefer not to leave my family in one town while I live in another.' He lifted the earthenware beaker of water to rinse his hands over the empty plate. Then, having wiped his hands on the thin cotton napkin she held out, he rose to his feet. 'Whether I trade alongside Shantinath or not is up to me. Do not worry yourself about such matters. We leave in four days' time, no later. Make sure we are ready.'

And she was ready. Ready in the sense of having everything packed and waiting to be loaded on to the bullock carts that would transport them to Suryapur. But not ready to leave. Not ready in her heart.

She never would be, Ratna thought, as she stared out of the window, the baby in her arms. She had been to her parents' home to bid them farewell. She had visited her sisters in their homes, met her few friends and an old aunt. Of all she had begged leave. Ninety yojanas, a journey of three months, her aunt had wailed. How often did one accomplish a journey such as that in a lifetime?

They would not see her again, they had said in despondent voices, and Ratna had known that was very likely true. This might be the last time she would see Agroha, for who knew how long she would live? She may not even survive the journey to Suryapur.

At the threshold, a maid coughed, trying to catch Ratna's

attention. They would be leaving before dawn, to get as much of their travelling done before the sun rose too high in the sky. It was already well past midnight. This girl would be wanting to sleep, Ratna realized. But there were instructions yet to be given. Reminders to check that the pickles, carefully packed in massive jars, were well sealed so that they would not leak. Questions about the water pots, the quilts, the rugs. So many details.

Her husband was asleep in his own room. Ratna looked in on him and resented his peaceful sleep.

'Shush,' she whispered, whirling away when the baby let out a whimper. It would not do for Sridhar Sahu's sleep to be disturbed. It did not matter, she thought half an hour later, as she tossed and turned in her own bed—with the two older children beside her and the baby in her cradle—that she should not be able to sleep. That was her duty as a mother. As it was her husband's duty to provide for his family.

She wished, though, that things were different. That she could have a say in where they lived, for instance.

❧

'I don't understand,' Gayatri wailed. 'Why are we leaving home? When will I see my friends again? And what about that baby goat I feed? What will happen to it? It'll die!'

Ratna closed her eyes, weary. They had been travelling in the bullock cart for two days now. She had not realized just how painfully the cart would lurch and rattle along. How, within a couple of hours of travelling in it, her body would be able to feel every pebble the cart went over, every rut its wheels traversed. She had not known how dusty it would be, how the dust would work its way in through the thick cloth that covered the curved bamboo ribs of the cart's roof. How it would get into every fold of clothing, into their hair, forming a thin layer on every single thing.

Most of all, she had underestimated the effect the journey would have on her children. The baby had wept herself into a state of such fatigue that she had finally fallen asleep, but the two older girls had been too overwrought to sleep. Initially there had been excitement; the novelty of going on a journey, the sights to be seen, the newness of everything around. They had stared, wide-eyed, as the town houses, with their mud-plastered walls and thatched roofs had given way to fields, and then to scrub and patches of forest. They had seen the crowds thin, the bustle of the marketplaces retreat, until all that was left was the occasional village, quiet and sleepy.

But the excitement had lasted only so long, revived only briefly when the little caravan had stopped beside a stream to let the bullocks drink. The girls had played by the water, watched by a maid while Ratna stretched her legs. Then they had climbed back into the cart to resume their journey. Now, more than a day later, even such delights as a bright blue bird perched on a branch, or the whitened skeleton of some unidentifiable animal lying beside the road, failed to evoke any emotion. Ratna shuddered to think how they would survive three months of this journey.

'Nothing will happen to the goat,' Ratna said, recognizing that worry as an important one; Gayatri had loved the little animal. 'You have seen its mother, haven't you? She will feed it.'

'How? Where will she get rice for it? And jaggery?'

'Goats don't eat rice and jaggery—'

'Mine does.'

'Only because that was what you fed it. Its mother will give it milk.'

Gayatri made a face. 'How dull. I hate milk.' She saw there was no more to be got out of that subject, and switched to her other complaint. 'And what about my friends? Mala and Vidya. And Chitra? When will I meet them again?'

'We've only just left, Gayatri. You played with them the evening before.'

'Yes, but I play with them every day! And today's almost

over—will I see them tomorrow? Will we go back home tomorrow? Ma?' She was growing increasingly agitated, petulant and angry and anxious all at the same time.

Ratna's temper, already frayed, fell to pieces. 'Oh, be quiet! Didn't I tell you? That is not our home any more!' She saw her daughter's face crumple and suddenly felt guilty. 'Come here,' she murmured, pulling the child into her lap, unmindful of the way Gayatri's weight pressed down on her aching legs. She pressed a kiss to her daughter's forehead, wiped away the child's tears, whispered reassurances. There would be more friends in Suryapur. They would play with her.

'And goats? Baby goats?'

'I suppose so.'

'And they will eat jaggery and rice, not just drink milk?'

At that moment, before Ratna could respond, the cloth flap at the back of the bullock cart was lifted. The bullocks had been trudging along so slowly that the maid had decided to walk a while. She climbed back in now, and crawled to the other end of the cart, making for her usual place next to the odds and ends stored there for easy access. A reed basket which held the girls' toys, their little clay dolls and tiny wooden drums, bells, a cart with wheels that rotated, little animals carved from wood and painted in bright colours. Jars of snacks, both sweet and savoury. A full water pot, nestling in a coil of wet, twisted cloth to keep it upright and steady.

The maid undid a knot in the end of her bright red odhni and took out a handful of pebbles. 'Look, Gayatri,' she said, holding them out. 'Aren't these pretty? Look, this one is pink, and this is almost green, is it not?' She tipped them into Gayatri's cupped hands, and watched with fondness as the child began sifting through this unexpected gift. Then she looked up at Ratna.

'Didi,' she said in a low voice, 'we are travelling away from the sunset.'

2
Yoginipur

Later, Ratna wondered how she could have been so stupid. How did she not understand the implication of what the girl had said? Or had the heat and the exhaustion numbed her brain? As it was, she had just mumbled a 'Yes,' and gone back to staring into space.

The maid had sensed that her mistress was not paying attention. She repeated her words, and added, 'Is not Suryapur south of Agroha, didi? Why are we travelling away from the sunset, then? The sun should set on our right, not behind us.'

'Only birds fly straight,' Ratna retorted. 'People follow roads. Roads are rarely straight.' They would be moving, she thought, towards an inn. A wayside resting place with a well, rooms for the people, troughs from which bullocks and horses could be fed and watered.

She had not, therefore, paid any heed. And, over the following days, the sun continued to set behind them. Every day, the maid would point it out. Every day Ratna would say that they were merely following the road. Every day it grew worse, the children more irritable, the weather hotter, the road more dusty. The bullocks walked ever slower.

Then, suddenly, one day, after what seemed an eternity of travelling—though she knew it was perhaps just over a week of having left Agroha—she discovered the truth.

They had stopped for their midday break under a spreading banyan tree beside a partly dry streambed. Around the base of the massive tree trunk, earth had been piled up and shaped into a platform, smoothed by generations of travellers sleeping and sitting on it. Even now, it was crowded, with people sprawled on the ground as well. Under the heavy curtains of roots hanging from the branches, reed mats and sheets had been spread, bundles of food opened. People ate, dozed. Some men had gathered around a chaupar board and were engrossed in the game.

Ratna, the baby in her arms and her two older children running on ahead, sat on the mat the maid had spread on a relatively secluded piece of ground. Sridhar Sahu would come by later, she knew, after he had assured himself that the bullocks had been attended to and that the manservant deputed to act as guard was at his station. He would return to them later, at unexpected intervals, to check. No wonder he was such a successful trader, she thought with pride and bitterness. He was well aware of what was his, and guarded it with a possessiveness that was both praiseworthy and frightening.

The girls were playing, swinging from the hanging roots of the banyan. The maid was setting out the food she had cooked that morning. Ratna tugged her voluminous odhni well over her head and settled herself to feed the baby.

'Are you going to Dilli, or coming from there?' asked a voice. It was a rotund, formidable-looking woman of about forty years, clad in a faded orange sari. 'Going to Dilli, I would suppose,' she answered herself, with a shrewd glance at them—the mother, the maid and the children. 'You've certainly been travelling more than just a couple of days.' Without waiting for an invitation, she sat on the mat opposite Ratna.

'Dilli?' Ratna shifted the baby to her other breast and looked up, puzzled. 'Does this road also go to Dilli?'

The woman stared, her eyes narrowing. 'Also?' she echoed. 'In this direction, it goes only to Dilli.' She chewed meditatively for a few moments before turning her head aside, leaning forward and spitting, sending a stream of red arcing through the air to land in the dust behind her. 'Of course,' she added, 'you could be going further—Braj?'

A strange foreboding gripped Ratna. There was

something wrong here. 'Suryapur?' she asked. Her voice emerged somewhere between a gasp and a croak.

The woman's forehead crinkled. 'Suryapur? Suryapur—isn't there one—' she broke off. 'Oh, of course. You are not Hindu, but Jain, isn't that so?' Ratna barely had time to nod agreement before the woman barrelled on, triumphant at having solved the mystery. 'You mean the Shri Suryapur Teerth, then? The temple to Neminath Swami? He was born in Suryapur, wasn't he?'

Ratna shook her head vigorously. The baby was being burped, and the sudden movement made her yelp. Ratna patted her and looked over the baby's head towards the woman.

'No,' Ratna whispered, when the baby had calmed down. 'No, not the Suryapur where Neminath Swamiji was born.' She could hear the rising panic in her own voice, and struggled to control it, afraid of what would happen if she suddenly burst into tears. How humiliating that would be. Her husband would never forgive her. 'The Suryapur that is far away to the south, near the sea. Ninety yojanas from Agroha.'

The woman's eyes widened. 'Ninety yojanas? That must be far indeed. I have never heard of that Suryapur.' She chuckled. 'But who am I to say? I have lived my entire life within two days' travel from Dilli, in Yoginipur.' Her eyes twinkled. 'Not like you. Wealthy. Privileged.' There was no trace of malice in her words, just a statement of fact.

She undid a large square of cloth to reveal her frugal lunch, two chapatis and some cooked vegetables. She did not seem to notice the consternation on the face of her new acquaintance; perhaps she was not especially observant about such matters. Or perhaps she was being diplomatic.

She ate, and she chatted between mouthfuls, pelting Ratna with questions. What did Ratna's husband do? When had they set off from Agroha? Why were they going to that faraway Suryapur near the sea? And she offered information about herself. She was a widow. There was nobody to look after her, and so she looked after herself by running a small food stall. 'These same things I'm eating. It may not be fancy, but it's a good enough meal for the poor.' A lot of workers, men without womenfolk to cook for them, without home or hearth where they could cook for themselves, came to her stall.

The woman impressed Ratna. She was so different from all the other women Ratna had known: so outspoken, so blunt, so brave. A little frightening, somewhat crude. But there was also something solid about her. She looked and sounded as if she could withstand any storm that blew her way. And that, if you happened to be beside her—and if she liked you—she would shield you from the storm too.

'Yogi Maiyya,' she said, in response to Ratna's hesitant query. 'That's what everybody calls me. My mother named me Yogmaya, you see, after the goddess.' She saw the bafflement in Ratna's eyes and explained. 'Yogmaya was Krishnaji's sister. Krishnaji's uncle Kansa tried to kill Krishnaji when he was a baby, you know, and to fool Kansa, Yogmaya was put in Krishnaji's place. When Kansa tried to kill her, she disappeared—but she predicted that Kansa would be killed by Krishnaji.'

She tugged at the waist of her sari and pulled out a small drawstring pouch. Untying it, she tipped a few pieces of areca nut into her palm. The pouch went into her waistband, the areca in her mouth. 'There is a large temple dedicated to Yogmaya next to my house. Yoginipur is named after the temple, you see. I was born in that same house, a week after my father died of cholera. My mother thought I wouldn't survive either, I was so puny. So she named me after the goddess in the hope that Yogmaya would keep me safe.'

Ratna smiled. 'And she did.'

'She did,' Yogi Maiyya agreed, getting to her feet. 'I must go now. I have spent more time here than I should have.' Ratna remembered she had mentioned that she was on her way to attend a distant relative's wedding. Her nephew had come to Dilli to fetch her.

She paused for a moment. 'If you come to Yoginipur, let me know. I can help you find servants. I know people.' She smiled, a broken-toothed, red-stained smile that was attractive because it was real. 'If you go to the Yogmaya Temple, ask anybody outside for Yogi Maiyya; they'll tell you.'

'This road leads to Dilli,' Ratna said quietly.

They were alone under the banyan tree; the maid had taken the baby and the children to play near the streambed. There was nobody in sight, and hopefully nobody within earshot.

Sridhar Sahu looked up from the somewhat rudimentary meal he was eating. 'So?' His voice was sharp, his eyes watchful.

Ratna felt a surge of fear, but she tamped it down. She had to know.

'Are we—are we going to Dilli?'

Her husband gathered up a morsel of cooked vegetable in a piece of the now dry, cold chapati. He put it in his mouth, chewed, swallowed. Reached for the bulbous little copper vessel of water. Drank. Put the vessel down.

'Why do you want to know?' He looked at the morsel he was shaping in his fingers.

Ratna was too exhausted to be cowed any more. But habit had shaped her behaviour; she could not snap at her husband and tell him that there was nothing illogical or unnatural in her wanting to know where she might be going to spend the rest of her life. 'Please,' she whispered. 'Tell me.'

Sridhar Sahu glanced at her. 'Yoginipur has far better prospects than Agroha.'

'I thought Suryapur had better prospects—'

'Where would you rather be?' he demanded. 'Ninety

yojanas from your beloved Agroha, or just about thirteen? For someone who complained so bitterly about travelling for three months at a time, you do not seem to appreciate that simple fact!'

He pushed the plate away, leaving the rest of his food. When he had gone, his dhoti flapping angrily about his ankles, Ratna got up and scattered the remains of his meal near the banyan tree. The squirrels would eat it, she thought. Or the birds.

That night, in the quiet of their musty room in an inn, he apologized, in the only way Sridhar Sahu knew: by answering the question she had asked hours before.

The two older girls slept beside the maid in the tiny room next door; the menservants—the cart driver and the odd-job men—slept outside, under the mango trees. Ratna envied them; the open air was cool and fresh. Earlier in the evening, she had noticed the men dig a small shallow pit and fill it with handfuls of neem leaves. They would have burned it, letting the smoke rise up around them, driving away the mosquitoes.

There were still mosquitoes inside their room, though, and much of Ratna's night would be spent in trying to shield her baby from them. She swung her handheld fan rhythmically, shooing away the less persistent mosquitoes and bringing a breath of a breeze to the stuffy room.

'You will like Yoginipur, Ratna,' said Sridhar Sahu through the dark. They had put out the lamp before opening the window; the only illumination was the moonlight that filtered in, the paleness of watered milk. 'It is a far better place than Suryapur. Or Agroha.'

Far better in what way, she wanted to ask. Would she find by some miracle that all her family and friends were there? Would there be all the places she held dear? The mango tree, its trunk perennially home to nesting parrots? The swing, suspended by sturdy ropes, on which she and her friends flew high up into the sky, touching the clouds with their feet? The lanes she knew so well, the sweets her mother's maid made, rich with ghee and jaggery?

His ever-fragile patience would snap, shatter into sharp-edged fragments, each more hurtful than the last, if she were to say any of that. 'Yes,' she murmured.

He must have heard the scepticism in her voice. A sigh of exasperation escaped him as he stood at the window, looking out. An owl called, a low mournful hoot. It was answered a moment later by an identical hoot, further away. Sridhar Sahu reached into the strip of cloth wound about his waist and drew out something that glinted gold in the moonlight when he turned it over in his hand. A flat disc, bright and glittering.

'This,' he said. 'Look at this, Ratna.'

She did not need to look closely at what he held; she knew. A gold coin, with a bull engraved on one face, its rump emblazoned with a trident. And on the opposite face, alongside the figure of a horse rider bearing a lance, the name of the man who had issued the coin. Sri Prithvi Raj Deva. Also known as Rai Pithora, or Prithviraj Chauhan, the ruler of the swathe of land that stretched from the town of Ajaymeru to Dilli. Though he did not usually live in Dilli, that was the city where Prithviraj Chauhan had built a fortress and named it after himself: Qila Rai Pithora. Yoginipur abutted Qila Rai Pithora; that a bustling and wealthy trade centre should mushroom beside a hub of political power was hardly to be marvelled at.

It was for this coin that her husband looked towards Dilli. As a centre of trade, Dilli was formidable. Even she, illiterate about the affairs of business, knew that much.

'You know men who will put you in the way of business?' she whispered.

Sridhar Sahu shrugged. 'I do not have it in so many words from any one man I can name,' he admitted. 'But Yoginipur is the city of Nattal Sahu. There will be place for yet another Sahu in it.'

Nattal Sahu, yes. She had heard of him. Which Jain of the trading community—even if merely married into that trade—did not know of the legendary Nattal Sahu, who had lived some fifty years ago? Not just a merchant, but *the* merchant, his trade stretching from where the Ganga rose to where she spilled her holy waters into the blue of the sea, from where the sun rose to where it set. Nattal Sahu, whose stature in the world of trade was such that he had risen to be a minister in the court of Anangpal, the Tomar ruler of Dilli.

Looking at her husband's firm-jawed profile as he gazed out of the window, his fingers still turning the coin over absently, Ratna wondered. Just as Anangpal Tomar had made a minister of Nattal Sahu, did Sridhar Sahu hope to be a minister to Prithviraj Chauhan? No. That could not happen, since the Chauhan ruled not from Dilli, but from Ajaymeru. Only one of his sons, Govindraj, ruled in Dilli on behalf of his father.

It did not matter, she reflected later that night, long after her husband had fallen asleep. That she would now be only within about half a month's journey of Agroha was comfort enough.

3

Near Taraori

Four Years Later

Vikram Samwat 1248 (1192 CE)

In the space of just one day, Madhav went from being the runt of the litter to the head of the household. He didn't have time to wonder what to do with the corpses of his father and brothers before he had run home to find that his mother and younger siblings had been—what? Carried away? Burned beyond recognition, one of the many charred heaps in the smoking remains of the village? He stared, tears trickling down soot-stained cheeks, at what had been, till that morning, a home. Mother, father. Three sisters, four brothers. All gone.

Madhav closed his eyes. His palms were a mass of blisters from his frantic attempts to rummage through the burning debris of the hut, to find someone to rescue. He dimly remembered someone, a neighbour perhaps, shouting to him to run. He remembered standing, the wind blowing soot and embers and dust all about him, the smoke rising high and thick enough to obscure the ruins of the village. It had been all so bewildering, and he had felt so alone.

The terror had come later, when the hopelessness of it all dawned on him. That had happened only when he had found a bit of space in a passing cart. It was a runaway cart, the bullocks racing madly through the burning villages before they were brought under control by a passerby strong enough, desperate enough, and unscrupulous enough to eagerly snatch another's property. The man had commandeered the cart to escape from the blazing countryside, and other people, similarly left bereft and alone by the disaster that had struck, had joined him. Madhav was one of them, having heaved himself up onto the edge of the cart on the outskirts of his village. He now sat huddled against one side, knees drawn up and throat hurting with all the smoke he had swallowed.

'Will Dilli be any better?' asked an old man, his voice high with panic. Madhav, startled out of his grief, looked up. 'After all,' said the man, 'Prithviraj Chauhan is defeated, dead—' a chorus of voices drowned his out, refuting that assertion as mere rumour. No, said one man, louder than the others. No, Prithviraj Chauhan could not possibly be dead, for everybody knew how very brave he was. And what a fine army he had. Hadn't Prithviraj Chauhan led the Rajputs into battle against this same invader—this Muhammad of Ghur—just the previous year? And at the very same battlefield, too? Taraori, near Sthanishvar. Prithviraj Chauhan had defeated him then.

'But he has been defeated this time,' pointed out a quiet voice. It was an old man, who had introduced himself as Balram. One of his legs was withered and one eye clouded with cataract, but he seemed less shaken than the others, more resigned, perhaps, to what was happening. 'And if he is defeated, it matters not if he is alive. He must still bow to the invader.'

A glum silence greeted his words. The only sounds were the low, monotonous trundle of the bullock cart's wheels and the jingle of the bells tied around the animals' necks. From a nearby clearing, a couple of lapwings rose into the air, flapping and calling to each other, their distinctive tee-tee-hee-ree ringing out loud.

The air was cool, and the breeze had erased most of the stench of smoke from his clothing. If he closed his eyes, thought Madhav, the silence and the calm would make it seem like it was yesterday again. A day like any other.

'It is quiet here,' someone said, almost as if he had read Madhav's mind. Or were all of them thinking the same thing? These people—two dozen of them, a ragtag bunch, bloodied and wounded and burned, but somehow alive—had been left adrift in the world. Children who had lost their parents, parents who had lost spouses or children or both. People bereft of everything except what they stood up in. They were all, more or less, like Madhav. One or two of them were better off than the others, having escaped with something: a piece of jewellery, a few coins. A relative.

'Why are we going to Dilli, after all?' asked the old man who had wondered if they would be safer in that city.

'What would you do in your village?' asked Balram. 'Does your home still exist? Do your people still live there? Do the crops still stand in your fields? Is the well not stuffed with corpses?' That last remark ignited a howl of rage and sorrow from one of the women. She was all alone, her belly big with child. It had taken three men to prise her off the charred corpse of her husband, and the combined efforts of those already in the cart to hold her in it.

They should have been prepared for it, thought Madhav with bitterness. After all, it was not as if the battle had come out of the blue. For days, they had been hearing reports of troops gathering at the battlefield where last year the Ghurid army had been trounced. Travellers spoke of warhorses and elephants, of thousands of troops, both on foot and on horseback. They said, with fear in their eyes, that Prithviraj Chauhan and his allies appeared far outnumbered.

But Madhav's father, looking at the crops in his fields, had dismissed it. Yes, there would be a battle, but why should it affect them? Muhammad of Ghur had been trying for several years now to extend his range from the western half of the land of five rivers into its eastern half, over which Prithviraj Chauhan held dominion. The previous year's battle had been part of that attempt, and it had proved unsuccessful. This too would go the same way.

'The Rajputs know this terrain,' Bapu had said, quietly confident in the might and military prowess of the ruler he had never seen. 'The invaders are foreigners. What do they know of this land, of how to fight here?'

'And they are from the mountains,' Madhav's eldest brother, sixteen years old to Madhav's ten, had added, eager to show off. 'They will not be able to bear the heat.'

And so they had assured themselves and gone back to their work. Secure in their belief that the battle being fought less than three hours' walk from their village would be a mere ripple in the air. Fought, won by their side. A calm victory.

Instead, what had come to be was this. Death. It had begun as a dull roar approaching from the direction of the battlefield, and Madhav's father had looked up, straightened, squinted, with one hand still clutching a handful of weeds. The sound had swelled, turning from the dull rumble of thunder to the frenzied galloping of hundreds of horses, the pounding feet of thousands of men.

By the time the first soldiers had crested the low ridge that overlooked the valley, Madhav, his brothers, and their father were already running. Running back homewards, racing to save the rest of the family. And themselves. There were others, too, converging into one panic-stricken mob that ran out of their fields, leaping over ditches and the low verges that divided fields, trampling standing crops without a thought. In the few years of his life, Madhav had never seen anything like it.

Then, as they neared the village—they could already see the bright clothing of the women, swarming about outside the mud-daubed walls of the huts—someone had barrelled into Madhav. He, in turn, had stumbled and fallen, rolling to the edge of a ditch. And over its crumbling lip, screened by a dense growth of scrubby bushes. Into the damp, fetid depths of the pit.

'I'm hungry.'

No one said anything. The cart went on, its progress slower now, the bullocks exhausted.

'Ma. I'm hungry.' The statement had become a whimper. He could not have been more than three years old, the tousle-haired little boy clad only in a dirty strip of cloth knotted about his waist. Dried tears had left clean streaks on his sooty cheeks. 'Ma!' The whimper became a cry of anguish.

No one said anything. The boy began to cry. His little body shook, the line of knobs that was his spine bent over, quivering. His sobs grated on Madhav's nerves. He wished someone would shut the boy up. All these women, all these adults. People who were supposed to look after little children.

He bore it until he could bear it no longer. 'Your mother's dead!' he shouted, clouting the boy, throwing himself half across the cart. Losing his balance and coming down with a thud, his own body sprawled across the laps of three people. The breath knocked out of him, tears of frustration and misery springing from his eyes. His injured hands—he had forgotten about them in the heat of the moment—aching as if they were on fire.

A woman gathered the toddler close, pulling him into her lap. He was wailing loudly, painfully. She looked at Madhav, her eyes blazing. 'He's just a child,' she said. 'How is he to know what death is?' She stroked the little boy's hair out of his eyes, patted his back. 'Just a child,' she repeated.

'And so is this one.' Balram reached out and caught Madhav's arm. Pulled him back, tugged him so that Madhav was plastered to Balram's bony side. Elbow digging into ribs, the rank smell of the man's unwashed clothes seeping into his nostrils. 'He is a child, too,' the old man repeated, his hand on Madhav's shoulder.

It took a while for the toddler to stop his whining. Someone grudgingly offered him a tiny lump of jaggery. Not that the morsel would do much to assuage his hunger, but its sweetness would pacify him. Madhav watched, envious.

'Do you have nothing to eat?' Balram asked.

Madhav shook his head.

'Perhaps we shall find something when we stop,' the old man said. 'We will have to forage.' He looked up and about, at the trees under which they passed, at the land surrounding them. One good eye, sharp and clear, taking in everything. 'Not that there seems much here that we might be able to eat.' He shrugged, resigned. 'We shall see.'

The cart went on, the bullocks' flanks heaving and sweaty, ropes of saliva hanging from their mouths. The man who was driving the cart began to suggest they should stop, only to be shouted down. How could they even think of stopping, when every step could mean the difference between life and death? When one of the bullocks stumbled and fell, making the cart tilt dangerously and spill a couple of its passengers, they picked themselves up and dusted themselves off. The collapsed bullock and its companion were given water from a muddy stream nearby, and then they set off again, moving at a snail's pace.

'How did you end up here, child?' Balram asked. 'Is there no one else in your family?'

Madhav did not know what to say. Had anyone survived, he wondered. His father and brothers had not; but his mother? His sisters? Surely if they had been alive, he would have known. He would have seen them, heard them.

If he had not been cowering in that ditch.

In the beginning, he had struggled to get out, scrabbling uselessly for a handhold in the damp, crumbly mud walls of the ditch. Finally, when he had heard the noise of an army of hooves and shod feet approaching, he had given up his attempts to get out. It was, he had realized, far safer to be in the ditch than out. He had crawled further into it, to where the undergrowth hiding it was thicker, where there was less chance of somebody spotting him. Huddled, knees drawn up against his skinny chest, arms clasped around his legs, he had tried to still the chattering of his teeth. Tears had welled up, spilling down his cheeks.

Eventually, when the noise had died down and he thought the coast was clear, he renewed his attempts to get out of the ditch: by now he was realizing that if he stayed there much longer, he might end up surrounded by enemy troops.

He recalled it now, recounting to Balram that eternity of pain and loneliness. 'I went home,' he mumbled. 'Just to see if there was anybody.' He did not finish that thought; his throat closed up with tears before he could say what he had found there.

Madhav felt a touch on his shoulder. 'As long as there is life,' said the old man, 'there is hope. And when there is hope, one can do anything.'

'Even bring back people one loved?' asked Madhav, resentful. 'Go to Yama and ask him to return all those he stole?'

Balram's good eye regarded him with interest. With respect, even. 'No,' he said, after a moment. 'Of course not. Can Death ever return any prize he has won? But if you make something of your life, perhaps those who loved you and now watch over you will have something to be proud about.'

4

One of the bullocks died the next day. They abandoned it and created a makeshift contraption to move the remaining bullock into the centre so that it could pull the cart on its own. Soon enough, they realized that it was too heavy a load for one animal to pull. All those who could, took it in turns to get off and walk for as long as they could. But they were tired, too, and hungry.

A little before sunset that day, when the bullock was so close to collapsing that they had been forced to make frequent stops to allow it to rest, the man driving the cart finally said, 'We should stop. We've been moving continuously since the day before yesterday. If we don't stop—' His voice was drowned out in the clamour that arose, the shouts of anger and fear. After all, someone pointed out, they had seen other carts, people on foot, the odd individual now and then on horseback, all of them fleeing, and all with hair-raising tales to tell of invading troops just hours behind. The same invaders who had torched their villages, had raped and pillaged and killed without a thought.

'If we stop, that is what will happen to us too!' A woman moaned.

'To go on is our only hope for survival,' someone else said.

The argument threatened to end in blows, but came to an abrupt halt—when the bullock went down on its knees.

And did not get up again.

'These can be eaten,' said Balram, tilting his chin towards his turban. It lay on the ground, curled into a cloth nest filled with red berries. They looked translucent, soft. Like little jewels, bright and juicy. 'It's makoi,' the old man added, helping himself to one. 'Don't eat too much of it, though. It can bring on stomach aches and vomiting if you have too much of it.'

Madhav, huddled beside the old man on the ground under the mango tree where they had spent the night, did not comment. He was too busy eating, too busy sifting through the few other things they had found in their brief foraging.

'Be careful what you choose,' the old man had cautioned Madhav when they had gone hunting for things to eat. 'If you do not recognize something, it is better to avoid it.'

'But what if I cannot find anything I recognize?' Madhav had asked.

'Look, then,' said the old man, 'for birds. See what they eat. If you see a bird eating a fruit, you can be sure that the fruit is fit for us to eat, too. Even if it is something you would not normally eat. But if you see a snake eating a fruit—and no birds eating that same fruit—stay away from it. It is likely to be inedible.'

Madhav had seen no snakes, and all he had seen by way of birds were a few sparrows pecking in the dirt, and a crow perched on a high branch. He had seen no fruit, either, but he had come across a small copse of young kanju trees. And, recognizing them for what they were, had felt the first brief surge of hope since his family had been killed. He had gathered a large number of the papery brown discs that were the seedpods of the kanjus; he had also found some figs, small and overripe, but edible.

When he had emerged from the kanju trees, Madhav had seen that Balram had already returned to the spot they had chosen as their camping ground. The old man had brought some makoi, and what he appeared most proud of: a pigeon. Balram had dug a hole in the ground, and having plucked the pigeon and wrapped it in green leaves, had placed it in the hole, atop a pile of dry twigs.

Madhav ate the last of the makoi while Balram tried to

light a fire, striking stone against stone, angling it towards the heap of kindling to encourage a spark that would ignite it. Madhav, meanwhile, wiped his hands on his dhoti and began opening the kanju pods. They were the size of coins, and within the thin, brittle sheath of each was a small, edible seed. Peeling them and putting the seeds aside was monotonous work, but he had nothing better to do until Balram's pigeon was cooked and ready to eat.

'It will not take long,' Balram said; he was observant enough to have noticed Madhav's fidgetiness, his wordless fretting. 'Less than an hour.'

'What if the enemy arrives while we're here?' Madhav asked. 'We won't even be able to fight them off on our own, you and I.'

Balram had finally got a tiny fire going; he fed it with more twigs, more dried grass. Then, scraping loose leaves and dirt over the fire to trap it in, he sat back, watching as stray tendrils of smoke began to drift up from the firepit he had constructed. 'Even with the others beside us, we would not have escaped,' he said. 'What were we? Unarmed men, wounded, crippled. Women and children.

'If it is any consolation,' he added, swiping at the smoke with one hand, 'I doubt if anybody will pay much attention to us. You and I pose no threat to anyone. What would they get out of attacking us?'

'They could kill us for the sake of it,' Madhav said. 'Just because we are the enemy.'

The old man shrugged. 'It could be. Here, let me help you with that kanju. It will get done faster.'

'How did you kill the bird?' Madhav asked, after a while. 'You could not have climbed the tree.'

In answer, Balram reached into the wide cloth belt at his waist and drew out a catapult. 'This.' He fiddled around further in his belt, and pulled out a hammer and a chisel. Heavy, the wooden handles of both tools well used and worn. 'And with some help from these once it fell to the ground,' he added.

Madhav grimaced, but his curiosity was piqued. 'Are you a hunter?'

'Not usually, no. But a childhood friend had taught me. This was his catapult, he made it for me. I have never lost the knack.'

'But the hammer? The chisel?'

'The tools of my trade. I am a stone carver.'

Madhav looked at the old man with renewed interest. 'What do you carve?'

Balram chuckled, the few remaining teeth in his mouth showing in a flash of brownish-yellow. 'Anything that comes my way. Flowers. Gods. Dancers. Animals. It does not matter. It is my task to give shape to the stone.'

'But where?'

'Wherever needed. Temples. The homes of wealthy men.'

'Palaces?' Madhav's eyes gleamed. The kanju seed he had been peeling lay forgotten in his hand.

A sudden sparkle came into the old man's eyes. 'When Prithviraj Chauhan claimed the throne at Dilli, I was among those who worked at his fort.'

'Qila Rai Pithora?' the boy's voice emerged as an awed whisper. 'Did you see him? The king?'

Balram laughed. 'Of course not. Stone carvers don't go about banging away at their work while the king is around. He's the king; he doesn't supervise the building of his fort. He rules from it.'

Madhav looked down at the half-peeled kanju seed in his hand, and returned to work.

'But he's not the king any longer,' he said, after a while. A bird called somewhere in the undergrowth. There was a sudden shuffling, the rustle of dry leaves, a thud, a hoarse cry as something was taken prey by something else. Silence fell once again.

'What will happen now?' Madhav asked.

Balram prodded the steaming mound under which the pigeon cooked. 'I don't know,' he said.

Nobody in Dilli seemed to know either. The city was in ferment, rumours flying thicker than arrows in its bazaars. Although Muhammad of Ghur had defeated Prithviraj Chauhan at Taraori, nobody was quite sure what would happen next. The more optimistic thought that the Chauhan's allies might come to the rescue and send Ghuri back, tail between his legs. That would bring Dilli back under the control of Prithviraj Chauhan, of the Rajputs who had ruled the city for so many centuries.

The more realistic admitted that there was little hope. Whether Prithviraj Chauhan had been killed on the battlefield or taken away as captive to Ghur, it did not really matter; the undeniable fact was that Muhammad of Ghur had defeated him, and now Ghuri, or whoever he designated, would rule Dilli. For now, Govindraj, who had administered Dilli on behalf of his father Prithviraj Chauhan, continued to oversee the city.

Nobody knew what would happen next, but most of them agreed that there was no going back. What was coming was inevitable.

Balram's hand felt heavy on Madhav's thin shoulder. It had grown heavier over these past two days, ever since they had first seen the faraway walls of Qila Rai Pithora loom on the horizon. The old man had held his head high and refused assistance all the long week they had been together on foot, but even Madhav could see that the long trek was taking its toll. Along with the lack of proper food, the infrequent and inadequate rest. And, hovering like the shadow of death over it all, the fear.

Balram had finally unbent enough to use Madhav as a support on one side. A mere support, something to stop him stumbling over a tussock or a rabbit hole hidden in the grass. Then, as they had walked on and the weariness had grown ever more burdensome, he had begun to depend more and more on the boy.

A passing cart-driver, his vehicle loaded with onions, had

taken pity on the old man and the child. He had given them a ride just short of Yoginipur; he himself had to travel on towards the Yamuna.

'There are no fires,' Madhav had murmured, as they drew nearer to the city. 'And it seems quiet, does it not?' Surely, he had thought, the soldiers who had ravaged the villages near the battlefield would not have spared the city of the man they had defeated. He had expected to find Dilli—a city, something he could not even begin to imagine—smouldering, its many palaces and temples ablaze or already in blackened ruins.

But the truth bore no resemblance to his imagination. The fine palaces were nowhere to be seen, though that was possibly because they were shielded by the massive stone walls of the fort. The temples and houses were less grand than he had thought they would be. The cattle and horses and goats and hens and stray dogs were as smelly as their cousins in the villages. There was garbage, there were sewers. There were pickpockets and beggars. Cripples. People very like those he had known in the village. Thin, poor. Living in shabby huts, with their roofs thatched and dried cow dung cakes heaped against the outer walls. There were fewer fields here, fewer cattle, and the air in his lungs felt somehow less fresh, but otherwise—otherwise it was something one could get used to.

It took Madhav a few hours to overcome his initial awe. By the time he had stopped gaping at the fort walls, the sun had set. Balram and he sank down on a packed earth platform surrounding an old banyan tree, and Madhav looked at the old man. Balram was gazing into the distance.

'What will we do now? Now that we have come to Dilli? Why did we come to Dilli?'

Balram turned, a slight smile on his lips.

'Which question would you want me to answer first?'

Madhav shrugged.

'We came to Dilli because this is as good a place as

any to be in. And there is safety in numbers. You can get mercifully lost in a crowd, lost enough to disappear.' His good eye dimmed, and for a brief spell he seemed to lapse into a reverie. Then he looked back at Madhav. 'And as to what we will do here: we will make a living.'

'How?'

Balram had stretched out his withered leg and was massaging it, his hand moving in sure, firm strokes. 'What trade were you born into? Your father was a farmer, is that right?'

Madhav nodded.

'But you cannot do any of that here.'

'Why not?' Madhav burst out. 'There are fields here, even in Dilli. I have seen people growing vegetables and wheat and barley—'

'And you must carry on the family tradition?' Balram said. The words may have sounded brutally honest, but the compassion in his tone took away any sting in them. 'How much had you learnt? Can you nurture a crop from ploughing to reaping? Do you know what to do if weeds refuse to vanish? Or if fungus attacks? Insects?'

Madhav shook his head, tears filling his eyes. They had never been far below the surface these past few days, but now they came, spilling over.

The hand that had been massaging the leg reached up to rest on the boy's tousled hair. 'Would you like to learn how to carve stone, instead? I cannot teach you farming, but carving is something I know. If nothing else, it will help you to earn enough to keep body and soul together.'

Madhav gazed out, past the barley field that lay beyond. To the ragged huts, the smell of burning cow dung, the less easily discernible aroma of cooking food. In this city, there were reminders of the village he had known, of home and family.

'I must farm,' he said quietly. 'We have always done that, all our family.' He rubbed vigorously at his cheeks, scrubbing off the tears. 'I must.'

'Then you will, someday. When you have the fields, the plough, the bullocks to pull it. The seed. You need all of that, Madhav.'

'And someone to teach me.'

Balram had gone back to rubbing his leg. He winced as his fingers found a sore spot, a knot in the muscle. 'You will learn,' he said.

'There is nobody to teach me.' Having first protested against leaving the fold and abandoning the work of his ancestors, Madhav chastised himself for doing so. Tried, stubbornly, to point out all that stood in the way.

'Then you will teach yourself,' Balram said, heaving a sigh. 'Those are the lessons that you will never forget. They are also the hardest.' He reached for the worn stick which he used as a crutch. 'But for now, let us get something to eat.'

✿

They had little to buy anything with. Madhav had not a coin, not even of the smallest value, and Balram too was pitifully poor. 'And who knows when I will get work?' he had muttered, sacrificing a coin for a thin pile of chapatis with a small helping of lentils piled on top.

'You said stone carvers did well,' Madhav said, his tone accusatory, his words muffled by the mouthful of food. They had seated themselves under the banyan tree. It was pleasant there, quiet and peaceful. Balram had divided the food into two portions, keeping the smaller one for himself. Some figs, gathered on the journey and allowed to dry in the sun, had also been taken out.

'We do, when times are good. But in times like this?' Balram shook his head. 'When there is no knowing whether the king is dead or alive, who will be fool enough to spend money on something like stone carving? Beauty requires time and effort and money. When one fears for one's life and wealth, why invest in beauty?'

Madhav had not understood much of that, but he had

gathered this much: that stone carving was not a profitable trade to be in. 'People always need food,' he said, cautiously.

Balram merely nodded; he did not repeat his arguments. But the next morning, Madhav saw that he took special care while tying his turban. He tweaked his proud grey moustache so that its tips curled up. And he chewed, for what seemed to Madhav like an hour, on a fresh twig from a neem tree.

'Are you going somewhere?' Madhav finally asked.

'We are going. To see the temples.'

And what temples they were, not too far from Qila Rai Pithora, and mirroring what Madhav supposed was the grandeur of the fortress. Twenty-seven temples, Jain and Hindu, standing cheek by jowl, a panoply of carved pillars. There were, Balram pointed out among the carvings, urns overflowing with foliage and flowers. Kalashes, the traditional brass pots kept at doorsteps, each with an auspicious coconut nestled in mango leaves. Rows of temple bells. Niches with idols of the deities. Dancing figures. Warriors. Lotuses. All rendered in stone.

'Did—did you carve all of this?' Madhav asked, awestruck.

Balram laughed. 'This was carved well before my time, child. It is beautiful, is it not?'

Madhav nodded, his eyes alight. 'I have never seen anything like it. It—it's like heaven.'

'And you can get a chance to create heaven on earth.'

Madhav was not listening; he was moving on, threading his way between the pillars, his fingers roaming over the carved stone. Balram watched the boy. His good eye twinkled, indulgent and hopeful.

'Come, Madhav,' he called, after a while. 'Let me show you something.' He took Madhav's hand and led the boy forward. They walked into the courtyard beyond the pillars, to a tall black column which stood there, majestic and solid and seemingly timeless.

Madhav squinted up at the carved pinnacle, curled like a lotus bud, curved like a water pot, with ring upon ring of dark metal. 'It's just a pillar,' he said, the disappointment obvious in his voice. He glanced up at Balram, his latent perceptiveness telling him that there had been pride in the old man's face when he had brought Madhav up to this pillar, so there must be a reason for that pride. And that by his offhand dismissal of the pillar Balram's pride had been wounded.

'Not that we have anything as grand as this in our village,' he added. 'Or anywhere nearby. I have never seen anything like this.'

Balram burst out laughing. 'And you never will,' he replied. 'Put your hand to it. Well?'

'Well, what?' Madhav looked up, puzzled. 'It's hot, from the sun. It is metal, after all.'

'And iron, too. Does that not surprise you? It has stood here, out in the rain and the sun, for who knows how many centuries now, and there is not a sign of decay on it. No rust, not a single patch.'

Madhav trailed his fingertips over the curved surface with greater respect. 'Our plough and sickles would turn rusty within days if we didn't oil them,' he murmured. 'How does this stay clean? Who cleans it? It isn't greasy.'

'Nobody cleans it. It just is.' The old man's hand trailed its way up the side of the pillar. 'Does it feel solid?' he whispered. 'Does it feel as if it's loose?' There was a twinkle in his eye.

Madhav frowned, puzzled. He shook his head. 'Why, should it be?'

'Have you heard of Vasuki?'

Again, the shake of the head.

'Vasuki is a naaga, the snake that curves around the neck of Shivji. He is the King of the Snakes, he is worshipped. He was used by the gods to churn the ocean of milk, the kshir sagar—' Balram broke off, seeing, no doubt, the look of utter bewilderment on Madhav's face. 'But that does not matter. They say that a sage once came to King Anangpal Tomar—you have heard of him, yes? Good. The sage told Anangpal that the base of this pillar is embedded in the hood of Vasuki.' Madhav snatched his hand hurriedly back from the pillar. Balram gave him a fleeting smile. 'The entire earth rests on Vasuki's hood,' he added.

'Anyhow, the sage also told Anangpal Tomar that as long as this pillar stood, he would be king here.'

Madhav scowled. 'But the pillar stands. And Anangpal Tomar is not the king. Even Prithviraj Chauhan is not king any more,' he added.

'Listen to the rest of the story,' Balram said, his hand resting on Madhav's shoulder. 'Anangpal Tomar decided he had to test that story; perhaps he did not fully believe the sage. So he got together his men and his horses and many bullocks, and he tried to pull the pillar out. They struggled and strained, and all that happened was that they loosened the pillar. They could not pull it out.

'But it was enough to rouse Vasuki's anger, and he caused Anangpal to lose his kingdom. The pillar, they say, may seem well-rooted, but deep down, it is loose. The "dheeli keeli", they call it—the loose nail. And that is where Dilli derives its name from. A loose nail.'

Madhav reached out a tentative hand to touch the surface of the pillar. With reverence, with the awe due to something that had actually made a kingdom collapse, that had reduced a powerful king to a mere name. 'And Prithviraj Chauhan?' he whispered. 'What did he do? Did he push the pillar in, when he became king?'

Balram began to shake his head, then stopped in mid-action, his eyes narrowing as a sound—till now nothing more than a murmur, the buzzing of distant bees—began to take shape. Madhav had heard it too, and had recognized it for something to be taken note of. Without a word being said by either of them, they came together, Madhav hurrying to Balram's side.

'Quick, find a hiding place. There. That little shrine, near the peepal tree.' Balram was already moving towards it, limping as fast as he could.

By the time the first riders had appeared beyond the temples, the two of them were safely hidden behind the shrine, wedged into the massive crack rent in the trunk of the peepal by some long-ago bolt of lightning. They peered out, watching with wary eyes.

The group of horsemen who had appeared between the trees, heading for the temples, proved to have been the vanguard for a larger contingent. There were ranks of foot soldiers, and many bullocks, the animals yoked to carts on which were piled rolls of thick rope, each the thickness of a man's arm. There were mules and donkeys, and elephants, dragging tree trunks that had been stripped of bark and branches, but otherwise left intact. Intact, solid, and frightening.

'What are they going to do?' Madhav whispered. He saw the group of men and horses come to a stop in front of the temples. The horsemen leading it dismounted, and grouped themselves behind the man Madhav supposed was their leader. That bearded, moustached face was weather-beaten, angular and alien, unlike any other people Madhav had seen so far. His clothes, too, were different: strange and dark and heavy, the legs wrapped in clinging material very unlike the billowing dhotis Madhav or Balram wore.

The arrival of the group had been too visible, too audible, to have gone unnoticed. Even as the men dismounted, a youth, shaven-headed and with his robes flapping about agitatedly, appeared at the doorway to the nearest temple. One horrified glance at the newcomers, and he had whipped around and run back inside. Within a matter of moments, more priests came rushing out, along with the few devotees who happened to be there at the moment.

Meanwhile, orders rang out, in a language that sounded guttural and crude to Madhav's ears. Even before their leader had finished speaking, the foot soldiers had gone to work. The rope was pulled off the carts and uncoiled, and a team of men carried one end of it to the nearest temple. While one team unharnessed the bullocks from the cart and knotted the end of the rope to the yoke, the men at the other end coiled the rope around a pillar. Round and round, from just below the intricately shaped capital at the top to the kalash carved at the base.

'No,' Balram whispered. 'No!'

There was a flurry of fear, of consternation. The acolytes and junior priests hovered at the fringes while the head priest hurried forward, pot-bellied and stooped, towards the soldiers. He wavered for a moment in front of them, before veering towards the man Madhav had mentally slotted as their leader. Perhaps there was an air about him that made the priest, too, recognize him as more than just another soldier.

On the air drifted the sound of the priest's voice, his pleas and his wails. What were they going to do, why would they harm these temples? The gods lived here. They had been revered for centuries.

The warrior watched dispassionately. He may not have understood the words, but surely he understood the emotion. There was no mistaking the entreaty, the fear that trembled in every breath of the old priest's voice.

Behind them, the men finished their work with the rope. An order was called out. The bullocks were prodded, making them turn and begin to move off. The rope, its middle coiled on the ground between pillar and yoke, uncoiled.

'No!' Balram shouted, and before Madhav could stop him, he went hobbling out of their hiding place, towards the temples.

He was being as foolish as the old man. And, perhaps like the old man, he would get killed for his efforts; but there seemed little point in just sitting around, waiting to see what would happen. After all, if Balram were to be killed, he would be left without even that meagre support, that one friend and mentor and somewhat-parent he had acquired since that terrible day of the battle. Madhav squared his thin shoulders and followed Balram.

The priest was down on his knees in the dust, the tears flowing down his withered cheeks. Behind him, the other priests and devotees echoed his wails. Two acolytes, bolder than the others, were tugging frantically at the rope tied around the pillar, but even as Madhav watched, soldiers moved forward and pulled them away. No blood was spilled; the men seemed more amused than annoyed at this attempt to thwart their work.

Balram did not appear to notice what was happening behind him. All his attention was concentrated on the man who led the soldiers. 'Do you understand Hindi?' he asked, and then, noting the incomprehension on the man's face, he nodded. Even as the bullocks reached the farthest end of the rope, pulling it taut, Balram reached into the pouch he always carried with him, and pulled out the tools of his trade. He held the chisels and the hammer out in his palms, exhibiting them to the man in front of him. The soldier's eyes narrowed, still unable to understand.

Balram mimed carving, the chisel in one hand, the hammer hitting it, the chisel moving gently as it chipped away pieces from an imaginary block of stone. Behind him, there was a sharp snap, followed by a low shuddering rumble. The bullocks were pulling with all their might, but the pillar still stood sturdy and unshaken. Someone from amongst the onlookers started sobbing.

Balram pointed at the temples, indicating the carvings. He held up his chisel and hammer, pointing them towards the stonework too.

Finally, the general seemed to understand. He turned to one of his men and said something. They turned, both of them, to look narrowly at Balram, and beyond him to the temples. Balram had finally got their attention; he used it, gesturing to them to stop the bullocks. Holding up that chisel and hammer.

'What does he expect them to understand?' Madhav murmured to himself.

Whatever it was, it seemed to have made some impression on the man. His expression had changed from one of mild interest to one of perplexity. Perhaps he was intrigued by the fact that unlike the priests and the worshippers, Balram was not weeping or pleading for the demolition of the temple to be stopped. His was, apparently, a different reason. A reason that had something to do with his being a stone carver.

Another pair of bullocks had been added to the team pulling at the roped pillar. Together, at a command from their driver, the quartet moved forward again. For a few moments, it seemed as if the pillar would not be toppled; but then it began to tremble. A shower of debris, bits of dried mortar and old moss, dust and dry grass fluttered down from the space that suddenly emerged between the pillar and the roof it had been supporting.

For a moment, the pillar teetered, and then it crashed to the ground, raising up a cloud of dust that enveloped them all.

When it cleared, Balram was still standing in front of the general, his chisel and hammer in his hands.

The general turned to the man beside him and said something. The other soldier nodded, and mounting his horse, rode off in the direction from which they had come. The general turned back, and lifted a hand, summoning another who was overseeing the work being carried out by the bullocks and their handlers. A word, and the work stopped there too. The bullocks were unyoked, the rope went slack.

The dust settled. Balram stood, hands limp by his sides,

his withered leg bent awkwardly. The general nodded to him, then indicated the ground, gesturing to Balram to sit.

They were to wait. For what, Madhav could not guess.

A quarter of an hour went past. Balram had seated himself on the ground, and sat there as if rooted. Still, patient, timeless. Madhav paced. The priests and worshippers hovered about, a couple of them weeping over the pillar that had been toppled. The soldiers and their animals waited, both fidgeting, both restless. The general, hands clasped behind his back, walked slowly, purposefully, around the periphery of the temples, gazing at the carvings. His expression remained unreadable.

The sound of hooves jolted everybody, man and animal, out of their reverie. The soldier the general had dispatched on his mission was back, and with him had come a surprising figure. Seated on a small and timid pony—no warhorse, this—was a middle-aged man clad in a fine dhoti and kurta, with a string of pearls around his neck. His turban was of fine silk edged with gold, and his shoes were embroidered with gold. A man of consequence. He dismounted, a watchful expression on his face as he took in the sight around him. Madhav helped Balram to his feet.

The general moved forward and said something to the newcomer, and to Madhav's surprise, the newcomer replied in that same alien tongue. A brief conversation ensued, no more than a couple of sentences on either side, before the newcomer turned to Balram and asked, in Hindi, 'What is it? What have you been trying to tell them?'

If Balram was taken aback, he did not show it. He looked the man straight in the eye and said, 'Why are they pulling down the temples?'

The man had obviously not been expecting such a blunt question. He blinked, briefly thrown off guard. Then he said, 'They need to clear this space.'

An evasive reply, and one that did not satisfy Balram.

'Clear this space? For what? They will build something else here, then?'

The man heaved a sigh, as if exasperated. 'You should know,' he said in an irritated tone. 'You seem old enough to know. It is the way of the conqueror. The signs and symbols of the defeated give way to those of the victorious.'

Balram nodded. 'True. What do they intend, then, to build in the space that will be cleared when the temples are removed?'

'A mosque. That is what they call their place of worship.'

A hiss of resentment ran through the group of devotees that had pushed closer and was now huddled within earshot, listening to every word of the conversation.

'Our temples are being broken so that the invaders can build a house to worship their gods?' asked one of the priests in a high-pitched voice brimming with indignation. 'Why? There is so much space! Why destroy our temples?' His voice cracked.

The general, who was now standing beside the newcomer, put a question to him. An answer was provided, and a remark returned.

'That is the way it is,' the newcomer said, speaking to the assemblage. 'There is no point arguing about it.'

A buzz of anger surged up from the devout little group, but a word from the general, and his soldiers moved forward, hands on the hilts of their swords. The anger stayed, but its expression was suppressed, the voices stilled.

'Who will build the mosque?' Balram asked.

Stone workers, of course. Masons and builders, working to the designs provided by the conquerors.

'You will not bring your own craftsmen, your own workers from your land?'

'Of course not. That would be impractical, to bring so many men so far.'

By now, the dhoti-clad newcomer was only acting as interpreter, not offering his own opinions. The general was the one talking, pausing only long enough between phrases or sentences to allow his words to be translated.

And—the warrior's gaze wandered across the temples, at the richly carved pillars—it seemed there was no dearth of skill here. It would be cheaper and much faster to employ local workers. They could not wait ten years for the mosque to be built.

'If you employ local workers, it would take them many years too to carve something as exquisite as this,' Balram said. 'You are warriors, so perhaps you do not know how long it takes to quarry stone, to dress, carve and assemble it. How long will you wait? Or perhaps your mosques are plain? Mud, piled up and baked under the sun?'

The interpreter obviously chose not to interpret that insult.

When Balram's point had been translated for him, the general had just one query. 'Then what?'

'Then it is logical to make use of these,' Balram said, indicating the temples. 'Such beautiful carving, so well placed together. Why not dismantle the temples and reuse the pillars?'

The general was taken aback and his interpreter looked shaken, but the reaction from the small crowd around them was unanimous. A wave of anger rippled through it; murmurs, hisses of indignation, gasps. The Hindus, almost to a man, were outraged. Madhav himself stared at Balram, wondering how the old man could have uttered such blasphemy. Dismantle a temple? Surely that would condemn him forever. The gods would never forgive him.

'How would that be possible?' asked the general, ignoring the fury of the hoi polloi, as if it made no difference to him. 'Our religion does not permit the depiction of animals or people in decoration, and your temples are full of those.'

'They are full of depictions of flowers and trees and geometric patterns too,' Balram said. 'Are those forbidden as well?'

The general considered, chewing meditatively on his moustache as he did so. 'No,' he conceded. 'They are not.'

'And what motifs will you expect our stone carvers to depict when they decorate this mosque of yours?'

The general thought, probably trying to recall the patterns he had seen on the mosques of his native Ghur. 'Stars,' he said, after a moment. 'Geometric shapes, yes. Flowers too. But,' he glanced beyond Balram, looking at the bands of carving, the lotus buds and garlands, the kalashes with mango leaves and coconuts, 'but not like this. They look different.'

'Of course they do,' Balram said. 'I am a stone carver; that was what I was trying to convey to you earlier. I know stone, and I know my fellow carvers. All of us grew up learning our craft almost from the time we learnt to walk. Unless you take young boys back to your land and have them become apprentices to your stone carvers, they will not learn the exact way in which your people carve flowers or stars or whatever.' He paused, waiting for his words to be interpreted.

'If you want our carvers to work on your mosque,' Balram said when the dhoti-clad man had finally fallen silent, 'you will have to accept the motifs we make, our flowers and garlands and bells. And those,' he said, indicating the carving on the pillar which lay on its side next to them, 'are already carved. Why destroy something only to have it made all over again? It would be a waste of time and effort and material.'

He fell silent and waited patiently for the man to translate for the benefit of the general. They had a brief conversation, the foreign soldier and the Indian, and then the Indian turned back to Balram. 'You do realize,' he said in a guarded way, as if not yet conceding anything, 'that some of the carving will be completely unacceptable? They will destroy the figures of the deities, the animals.'

Balram inclined his head. 'It is better than having the entire temple crushed.'

The man turned back to the warrior beside him. There was a discussion again, a more prolonged one than before. Behind Balram, the knot of Hindus shifted restlessly, resentfully. Someone murmured something about a traitor, about someone conniving with the invader. Madhav, standing off to one side, neither with Balram nor with the others, wondered whom they referred to. The dhoti-clad man or Balram?

The animals and the other soldiers were getting restive. An elephant snuffled, shifting about so that its chains jangled, loud and sharp in the still air. The elephant's mahout caressed its neck, murmuring to it.

Finally, the man in the dhoti turned to Balram. 'The commander here,' he said, 'says he has come with instructions from Qutbuddin Aibak himself, to take whatever decision he sees will suit the interests of Aibak best. There is no reason to antagonize the local populace'—there was no sign of his appreciating the irony of his words, given that he was himself a member of this local populace—'and the commander sees the logic of the argument you put forth.' He inclined his head briefly towards Balram, acknowledging him. 'He agrees that dismantling the temples will be the wisest course of action, since it will save time and money in building a mosque.'

The commander chewed on his moustache. He looked around at the elephants, at the bullocks that were standing gazing into the far distance. He said something, gesturing towards the animals. Madhav could guess what he was saying, even before the interpreter translated his words.

They had brought these animals, and the heavy ropes, the battering rams, everything to pull down the temples. To take them back now would be a waste of time and precious resources. It would draw the ire of Aibak. They could not go back without doing some of their work.

Balram looked around. At the temples, at the animals waiting beyond, and then back at the commander and the interpreter.

'I know something of how these stones are fitted together,' he said. 'If it be your wish, I can help dismantle the temples.'

ଓ

'How could you do that?' Madhav blurted out. They were sitting under the tree that had become home for them. It had been a long day, long and exhausting. Physically so for Balram, who had eventually had to sit down on a fallen pillar and direct the soldiers and their animals; emotionally for Madhav, who could not fathom why Balram had acted thus.

'You betrayed us, you betrayed your own gods!' he cried out now. 'You helped them pull down the temples so that they could build their mosque there!' He could hear the childish sob in his voice, but he did not care. He was too angry to worry about anything else.

'What would you have had me do?' Balram asked, his expression as mild as his voice. He was massaging his lame leg, working the knots out of it. 'You realize what would have happened, don't you? They would have razed the temples to the ground. This, I thought, was better.'

'How is it better? The temples are destroyed. Our gods are gone.'

One grey eyebrow tilted up. '"Our gods are gone?"' Balram echoed. 'Our gods dwell only in idols? Not in our hearts?'

'That was not what I meant! I—I mean, the temples are as good as destroyed anyway, aren't they? It will be so humiliating to see them changed into something that is used to worship their gods.'

'Their God,' Balram corrected absently. 'They believe in one God.'

But Madhav was not listening any more. He turned away from Balram in disgust, and made his way towards the little pond nearby. He sat on its bank, looking at the waterbirds that waded along its fringes. The sun gilded the water, then painted it orange and red, and still Madhav sat there, staring into space.

After nightfall, one of the men from the huts beside the pond came by. He was headed for the banyan tree, where he liked to sit after the evening meal, making rope: something to bring in a little extra money, he said. With his sack of dry grass slung over one shoulder, he stopped by the pond long enough to wonder why Madhav was sitting there all by himself; and Madhav, awkward about admitting the truth and not willing to betray Balram's betrayal, made an excuse about having lost himself in play.

He did not need to capitulate when he accompanied the man to the banyan tree, where Balram was still sitting. Balram glanced at Madhav and wordlessly pushed forward a handful of roasted chickpeas wrapped in a piece of cloth.

'Qutbuddin Aibak,' said the man, as he put down his sack and seated himself beside them. 'That is his name, the general whom Muhammad of Ghur has sent to hold Dilli. They say he was once a slave, but that he impressed Ghuri so much, Ghuri made him one of his generals.' He began to draw handfuls of dry grass out of his sack as he spoke. 'Imagine, Dilli to be under the control of a former slave. How humiliating!' He shook his head, disgusted.

But Balram merely shrugged. 'A slave may be a king if he is worthy,' he murmured. 'Do you not think that should give us hope? Who knows, perhaps one day, this child here,'—he tilted his chin in the direction of Madhav, who sat sullenly by, eating—'this child may be a minister, or a courtier?'

The rope-maker laughed at that, at what he presumed was a facetious joke. But Madhav, darting a quick glance at Balram, was surprised to see no trace of sarcasm in the old man's expression.

***

An hour after dawn the next morning, an odd thrumming made itself heard. Growing louder with every passing moment, resolving itself into individual sounds. Hoofbeats, the thudding of shod feet marching in step, the trundling of carts. And war drums, beaten long and strong.

It was them, the warriors whom they had seen the previous evening at the temples. People came out of their houses, abandoned their fields, to stand by the wayside and gape. Balram and Madhav and the farmer who made rope joined the others to watch.

Madhav, setting aside the rancour he felt at what he deemed Balram's betrayal, slipped his hand into Balram's calloused but strong one. 'I'm scared,' he mumbled. 'They will kill us all, won't they?'

Balram shook his head. 'They are now the rulers,' he muttered. 'Why would they needlessly kill their own subjects? We are the ones who will now have to pay taxes, who will toil for them and serve them. If we do not show open signs of rebellion, there is no need for them to kill us. That is how it always is when a land is conquered.'

Madhav wondered if Balram had ever been through this before. Had he been among the conquered before? Had he seen his home destroyed, his family killed? Had he been left bereft of everything simply because on some faraway battlefield one army had defeated another?

Balram squinted at him when Madhav asked the question. 'Yes,' he said after a moment. 'But never like this. Never by people so different from us.'

'What will they do now?' Madhav asked, but Balram remained silent. Perhaps he had no answer to give.

It did not take long for the city to discover, for men were sent out later that day from the fort. A group of men, consisting of a drummer, ten soldiers armed with lances and swords, and one man who carried a long scroll with strange markings on it. Madhav could not read; neither, he learnt, could Balram. But there was no need for anybody to read the scroll; this was an official proclamation. It was read out by the scroll-bearer in a loud, ringing voice. Muizuddin

Muhammad—what a tongue-twister of a name, thought Madhav—had defeated the armies of the craven Prithviraj Chauhan. Dilli, a satrapy of Ajaymeru's, was now to pay tribute to Muhammad. Govindraj would continue to sit on the throne of Dilli, but the tribute that earlier went to Ajaymeru would now go to Ghur.

It was amply clear what that meant. Govindraj would be a puppet, no more than that. And hovering nearby, always watchful for any rebelliousness on the part of Govindraj, would be Qutbuddin Aibak.

'I do not understand,' Madhav said, when the scroll-bearer and his little entourage had moved on to another neighbourhood. 'Who is the king, now? Govindraj ji is not king, is he? He never was; he merely ruled as governor for his father. So who is king, now that Prithviraj Chauhan'—he swallowed—'is gone?

A hoot of laughter made him, and Balram, turn around. There was a woman behind them, broad-hipped, thick-waisted and with a massive bosom that heaved under her yellow sari when she laughed. 'Child,' she said, clapping a huge rough hand onto Madhav's shoulder, 'what should it matter to you who is king?' Her hand moved to his head, resting there as if in benediction for a moment before she drew it away.

'To us, it hardly matters,' she said, her voice softer now, as if she did not think it a laughing matter any more. 'They will collect taxes, whoever they are. They will bully us and their soldiers will press us for free food. We will be expected to provide free labour.' She sighed and turned away. 'Things will be no better.'

'Who is she?' Balram whispered to the man standing beside them, when the woman was out of earshot.

'Yogi Maiyya. She has a food stall outside the Yogmaya Temple. Prithviraj Chauhan's soldiers were constantly forcing her to give them meals without them having to pay a single jital.'

Balram grinned. 'Yogi Maiyya? The goddess herself?' He had snapped off a juicy stem of grass growing out of the bulging bole of the fig tree under which they stood. Chewing at it, he added, 'Or her parents thought she was. She does not strike me as divine.'

The other man chuckled. 'She's a formidable woman. I sometimes think she knows everything about everybody in Yoginipur. She certainly knows many of the people worth knowing. Not to visit their homes, but she knows their connections, their relationships, what dirty secrets they harbour. She's a woman worth knowing.'

'And you know her?'

The man's grin turned wry. 'I know her, but she doesn't know me. I am too minor a man for Yogi Maiyya to know me.' He reached up to adjust his turban. 'Such are the ways of the gods,' he said with a laugh. 'We hope and pray that they will pay attention to us, but they are looking elsewhere.'

He had already turned his back and moved away when Balram murmured, 'Perhaps one never made enough of an effort to draw the attention of the gods.' The man did not hear. Madhav heard, but did not understand fully.

'Come, Madhav,' said Balram. 'We shall have a good meal today, shall we? Let us go to the Yogmaya Temple.'

5

A Year Later

Vikram Samwat 1249 (1193 CE)

Yogi Maiyya sat cross-legged on a worn reed mat, chopping vegetables into a large and battered copper platter. Behind her, over a stove consisting of a crisscross of soot-stained bricks with a fire of cow dung cakes, sat a large iron pot in which lentils had been simmering for the past half hour.

In the year since they had first made her acquaintance, Balram and Madhav had come to appreciate just how remarkable a woman Yogi Maiyya was. Solid, dependable, immensely self-confident, and yet with a core of kindness and generosity that nothing could shake. She had taken them into her heart. In the week it had taken Balram and Madhav to make a hut of their own, put together with reeds and mud and other bits of debris, she had come every afternoon and every night, bringing them food and giving suggestions. How to keep the rain out, what to do to deter snakes, how to strengthen the roof of the hut. She was a woman of astonishing abilities, her mind formidable, the depth and scope of her knowledge impressive.

'It astonishes me,' she said, 'how quickly things change. Here we had been, consoling ourselves with the thought that even if Govindraj ruled as a vassal of Ghur, at least it was still a son of Prithviraj Chauhan who was our king. Even if only in name. Now even that consolation is gone.'

For Aibak, or his master Ghuri, had finally tired of letting Govindraj rule Dilli. Govindraj had been assigned the fiefdom of Ranasthambhapura, far to the west of Dilli. He had left Dilli, and now Dilli was to be ruled directly by Aibak himself.

Madhav listened to the conversation with only half an ear. All his attention was concentrated on the block of sandstone before him. When Balram worked on pieces as small as this—something the size of a mere coconut—he positioned the stone in his lap. Cradled it while sitting cross-legged, chipping easily at the stone, the chisel coming down just a whisker away from his legs. He did not let Madhav do that, though. Too early, he said. Get to know the stone first, let it speak to you. Let it reveal its secrets and become your friend. Only when you know it shall nestle safely in your lap must you grant it a place there.

So Madhav worked, somewhat awkwardly, with this lump of red stone wedged between two miniature pillars of hard grey stone that had been buried partly in the soil. It was a new piece of stone, brought by Balram this morning. 'You have seen enough to begin practising on your own,' the old man had said. 'Start with these.' He had presented to Madhav four lumps of stone. One was pale grey, knobby: Madhav had recognized it instantly as quartzite, the hard rock typical of Dilli, so hard that it was foolish even to think of carving anything beautiful out of it. Another stone was slate-like, glinting in the sun, while the third was a piece of buff stone, with veins of red running through it. Last, but the one which caught his eye immediately, was the sandstone.

'Remember what I told you,' Balram had said, settling down in his usual place, opposite Yogi Maiyya's makeshift kitchen. 'The rules of classifying stone. Is the stone purush, masculine? Or stree, feminine? Or neuter?' Madhav's mind had raced, swiftly turning over all the lessons Balram had imparted. Lessons, he said, which had been written in the many sutras of the *Shilp Shastra*, the ancient text which governed the art of stone carving. Masculine or feminine stone was best carved for decoration. Neuter stone, durable and prosaic, could be used for floors, for slabs.

Madhav had examined the lumps of stone Balram had put before him. He had begun by testing them for durability, cutting them to see how they would behave. The shimmering stone, too friable and fragile, had disintegrated in his hands, as he had suspected it would. The sandstone and quartzite had been true to their type: the quartzite stubbornly hard and the sandstone easy, soft, a delight. He had lifted it with triumph in his smile. 'This,' he had said. 'This is what I will use.'

Madhav now sat before the sandstone he had chosen. He straightened it, positioning it so that the cut surface lay horizontal. He could sense, on the periphery of his vision, that Balram was no longer watching him. The old man relaxed now, secure in his teaching, assured that the next few steps Madhav could complete on his own, without supervision.

'It was a consolation, yes, to be ruled by someone who continued the lineage we knew,' Balram said to Yogi Maiyya. 'But Govindraj never really had a say after the battle. Since then, he was just a puppet.' He paused, reaching out to rub his crippled leg. It was a habit, Madhav had noticed, that came on when Balram was disturbed about something.

'I wonder how they mean to go on.' The fingers rubbed more deeply now, digging into the useless muscles.

Madhav went to the earthen water pot beside Yogi Maiyya and bent to pour out a finger's length of water into the little red earthen cup that stood, upside down, over the mouth of the water pot.

He returned to his place, sat down, and tipped the cup over his fingertips. Waited, then carefully poised the tip of his forefinger above the stone. A single drop of water hung briefly there, twinkling in the sunshine, before it fell to the stone below.

A moment passed, and another.

'Well?' Balram said. He had fallen silent. The soft swish of Yogi Maiyya's knife as she peeled onions was the only sound in the immediate vicinity.

Madhav grinned. 'It's intact. The stone has not absorbed it.'

Balram returned the grin. 'The quality of the stone is good, then?'

'Hmm.' Madhav wiped the water off the stone with his palm, eager to get down to work.

'What will you carve?'

Madhav shook his head. He said nothing, and Balram did not press him for an answer. Instead, he turned back to Yogi Maiyya. 'Can you find no way to dilute the pungency of those onions?' he complained, shifting away from her a little. 'Soon I will be sitting across the lane, but crying nevertheless.'

'Perhaps we will all be crying very soon,' Yogi Maiyya said with a bitter smile. 'Who knows what the invader will do to this city. I fear Dilli will fall apart.'

Despite Yogi Maiyya's gloomy predictions, Dilli had not fallen apart. Govindraj had gone and now Qutbuddin Aibak, the general who had once been commander of the Dilli garrison of Muhammad of Ghur, sat on the throne. Not that Aibak was Sultan; no. As Govindraj had first ruled Dilli in the name of his father Prithviraj and then as a tributary of Ghuri's, so Aibak too, ruled in the name of Ghuri. Muhammad of Ghur was the true lord of Dilli; Aibak was his vassal, no more.

'If Aibak was a slave, perhaps he will understand the plight of the poor,' Balram said to Madhav. 'Let us hope he does. I am sick of waiting for Dilli to get back on its feet. If things don't return to normal soon, it will get difficult to survive.'

Madhav knew what he meant. In all the months they had been here, they had made ends meet by doing odd jobs, whatever would bring in even the smallest coin. Occasionally, Balram had been lucky and found an opportunity to work stone. Not the delicate carving that he had shown Madhav, worked painstakingly over many months, but more plebian, practical things. Helping to carve a waterspout for a merchant's home. Putting to rights a broken pilaster at the temple of Yogmaya—a temple which, despite its imposing size, had escaped the wrath of the invaders, as had the Dadabari Temple of the Jains. Perhaps even Aibak realized that these two temples were far too important to the local populace for him to take on the wrath of the people by demolishing them: who knew what would prove the last straw on the camel's back?

But in the midst of the uncertainty and anxiety, there were moments of joy, of simple pleasure. As Madhav was learning, while acquiring a new skill.

'I will carve a lotus from the sandstone you brought me,' he said. 'That lump of stone is the right size. And the right shape.'

Balram nodded his approval. 'Do you have all your tools ready?'

'I have sharpened the chisels. And wound new rope around the handle of the hammer.' Madhav looked up at Balram. 'Yogi Maiyya said,' he added in a small, hesitant voice, 'that there might be a lot of work coming our—your—way.'

'If the rumours are correct, it will be our way, Madhav,' Balram said. 'They will need every man they can get, even apprentices.'

Madhav's forehead crinkled. 'What is it? What for?'

'The Turk, Aibak, intends to build a place of worship. A large one.'

'A mosque? That is what they call their temple, is it not? What does a mosque look like?'

But Balram would not hazard a guess.

A week passed, then ten days. Yogi Maiyya had shown Madhav how to make a paste out of the henna leaves he had picked from the bushes near the temple, and he used this paste to draw a rough outline of the lotus he hoped to coax out of the stone. When the blackish-green paste had dried, Madhav rubbed it off to reveal a deep orange-red hue beneath.

He was now working on the stone, excited but also nervous, fearful that Balram would see it before it was done. Would notice flaws, would tell him how wrong he was going—and would shake to bits whatever little confidence he had. So Madhav worked on his own, carefully chipping away at the stone, hidden behind a makeshift screen he had erected from a torn reed mat stretched between two sturdy twigs. Balram did not comment.

Two weeks later, when Madhav had progressed far enough to begin to see the flower taking shape in the stone, Balram said, 'I will go tomorrow to where the temples stood.' He saw the puzzlement in Madhav's eyes, and explained. 'The twenty-seven temples.'

Madhav felt a pang at the memory of that day, when Balram had helped Aibak's men begin the demolition of the temples. The resentment he had felt then at what he regarded as a betrayal of his religion had gone now, softened by his own growing appreciation of the skill that had gone into making those temples. He had gone back there a couple of times with Balram, and walked slowly round the dismantled remains of the temples, admiring their beauty, marvelling over the skill of the men who had created it.

Then, he had realized what had compelled Balram to stand up against their destruction. Obliterating such beauty would have been a sin.

'That is where Qutbuddin Aibak is building his new temple,' Balram said. 'And when something is being built, men are needed to build it. Masons and bricklayers. Stone carvers.' He paused. 'Will you come with me?'

Madhav did not go. 'I want to finish this lotus,' he told Balram, when the old man got up that morning. 'If I begin work elsewhere, it might put me off my stride. Let me finish first, then I'll think about it.' Balram nodded, concentrating on tightening his turban, making sure it sat properly, looked neat. A man hoping to get employment with the government should be presentable.

Madhav watched him limp down the narrow lane, and then he went back to carving the lotus, but his heart was not in it. He was thinking of the temples, and of how those pillars and pilasters and lintels would be incorporated into the mosque. How did a mosque look different from a temple? And since this religion prohibited idols, what would there be to distinguish the mosque from another building?

When Balram returned several hours later, dust-stained but looking contented, Madhav followed him into the hut. 'So?' he asked. 'Did you find work, then, at the mosque?'

'Not yet. Yogi Maiyya had given me the name of a man I should approach, but he wasn't there today.'

'Yogi Maiyya knows the invaders?' Madhav gaped.

'Of course not.' Balram wound up the turban and set it aside, before helping himself to a long drink of water. 'But it is not as if Aibak himself is going to be supervising the building of the mosque. He is the governor, after all; he will depute his own men to do the work, and they will need men from Dilli to help them.' He wiped his mouth. 'Not just builders and carvers, but also administrators, men to hire the workers, to pay them, to oversee the work. It was one of these men that Yogi Maiyya referred me to.'

They had wandered outside the hut as Balram spoke. Madhav settled himself down to work but did not yet pick up his chisel. He could sense there was more Balram had to say, and he did not want to get started on his work until he could devote his entire attention to it.

He was right. Balram sat down beside Madhav, and after a few moments of silence, in which he absently caressed the emerging lotus in the stone, Balram spoke. 'We have to get used to this, child,' he said. 'What we knew, what we were familiar with, is gone. Prithviraj Chauhan is dead. We are now the subjects of Muhammad of Ghur, through Qutbuddin Aibak.

'We have to get used to the new order of things,' he continued. 'We have to accept that Aibak is now our lord, whether we want him to be or not. The sooner we adjust to this new life, the better it will be for us.'

Perhaps, had he still been a sheltered farm boy who knew nothing of how the world functioned outside his own village and its fields, he might have remained silent. But in the year and more that he had been obliged to stand on his own two feet, Madhav had grown bold enough to ask questions, bold enough to speak up when he did not agree.

'Surely there can be no pressing reason to work on Aibak's mosque,' he said quietly. This, after all, was what this conversation was about: Balram trying to justify his seeking work at the place where Aibak would have his mosque constructed. 'There must be others who have work for stone carvers and builders and so on.'

Balram nodded. 'Eventually there will be. Perhaps it will happen only when the mosque has been built. I think that is why Aibak wants to build it. Not so much as a house of worship, but as a symbol of his power here. When people see it, they will see not just the strength and the beauty of the building, but the might of the man who conquered Dilli.' He patted Madhav on the shoulder. 'Someday we will work for the merchants and the nobility and others. For now, to keep body and soul together, I must not turn away from the opportunity I may find with Aibak.'

That evening, after sunset, they made their way as usual to Yogi Maiyya's for their meal. 'Did you meet Sridhar Sahu?' Yogi Maiyya asked Balram.

Balram shook his head. 'He was not there. There were other men, though. The man who will be supervising the construction.'

Yogi Maiyya huffed. 'That won't do. You should go to the man I told you about. Go and find Sridhar Sahu. He is an astute man. Did I tell you? He has even learnt their language. They trust him; he is one of us. Tell him I sent you. His wife knows me.'

Balram nodded. 'I will.'

The next day again, Balram went to see if he could meet Sridhar Sahu, the man Yogi Maiyya had referred him to. Madhav stayed home and spent much of the day helping out in the fields nearby, earning part of a yam here, a handful of rice there. Some spinach, a cupful of milk. By the time Balram returned in the late afternoon, Madhav was back home, sitting cross-legged and busy at work. The outlines of the lotus, petal unfurling beyond petal, could now be clearly seen in what had earlier been only a lump of stone.

Balram was so excited, he did not even bother to go inside and take off his turban before he spilled out his news. 'Do you know who Sridhar Sahu turned out to be?' he said. 'The man who acted as interpreter that day at the temples.' He sat down next to Madhav. 'He recognized me, so I did not even need to mention Yogi Maiyya's name. I was taken on and given a job, as soon as I asked for it.'

'They are different from us,' Balram said later, as they lay under the banyan tree that night after their meal. 'But not utterly unreasonable.' He waved a hand vigorously at a persistent mosquito, shooing it away. 'Soldiers, of course, not architects or builders, so it is difficult for them to convey all that they have in mind. The men who will be doing the actual building—the masons, the bricklayers—are quite lost.' He laughed. 'Qutbuddin Aibak's man, the one who is responsible for building the mosque, has shown them drawings of what it should look like.'

'Did you see the drawings?' Madhav asked. 'What do they look like?'

'I caught a mere glimpse. They are very different. Tall walls. No spires, no sacred sanctums. A vast courtyard.'

He sat up suddenly, too excited to keep lying inert for

long. The assurance that work, good long work and well paying, was coming his way, had done Balram a world of good.

'They want strange new things. The pillars, yes. They will retain them, though not all the carvings. But also strange curving structures. Instead of laying a beam flat across the top of two pillars to make the top of a doorway, they want a—a'—he groped for a way to describe it, this peculiar architectural element he had encountered for the first time today, and that too, only in a drawing made by someone who probably did not know anything about construction. 'It looks like this,' he said, finally, placing his hands so that the fingers of one curved towards those of the other, the tips touching at the top. 'Like a hemisphere. Half a melon.'

Madhav made a face. 'How strange that would look. How can you have a building that looks like that? All curved?'

Balram shrugged. 'We will see. The masons and builders have only so far seen what the soldiers have drawn for them, what they have described. The soldiers have not the faintest idea of how it is to be built. Our builders will have to solve that problem for themselves.'

'So when will you go there to work?' asked Madhav when Balram had lain down again. 'Until they have solved that problem, what will there be for you to do?'

Balram grinned. 'There is a lot to be done. The mosque—they call it a masjid, you know—they want the masjid built without any delay. There are fresh pieces of carving to be done, massive stone screens that will form one end of the masjid. The stone for that has already been quarried and brought to the site. We will begin work on that. Drawing, carving, smoothening. There will be a lot of work.'

Madhav lay back and stared into the sky above, at the sprinkling of stars, so many and so beautiful. As if a giant spider had spun many webs across the black velvet of the sky, and the dew had already laid drops of glitter across each string.

The night sky looked exactly as it had two, three or even four years ago. For as long as he had looked up at it. It would go on looking the same, he realized, for long after he and the memories of him were ground into dust. The heavens were eternal. The gods were eternal. The petty feuds and battles, the shifting power, the struggles and strife that raged on this land below were inconsequential to them. They did not care that Qutbuddin Aibak had taken his place on the throne of Dilli and was replacing their temples with a mosque that honoured what he called God.

And Balram, seemingly without a qualm, was working on that mosque. A Hindu, employed by another Hindu, on behalf of a Muslim regime. To make a house of worship to honour an alien god.

As Balram had said, he would have to get used to it. He would have to adapt, as Balram was adapting.

6

Madhav carved his lotus. Slowly, over the days, it took shape, the petals spreading out from the circular pad in the middle. The faint lines along the petals, the little bumps on the centre that hid what would ripen into lotus seeds.

Initially, he spent only half the day carving; the rest of the day he spent in small tasks, errands and so on for those who lived around. Anything that would earn him something to keep him from thinking that he was sponging on Balram. When Balram would return from work, Madhav would be waiting for him, eager to hear everything that had taken place. There was so much to hear, so much to devour. It sounded fascinating, and within a few days, Madhav had realized that he could no longer be happy just hearing about it.

So, on the sixth day of Balram's beginning work, Madhav changed his daily routine. Now, as soon as Balram had left, he would start work on the lotus. Hammer and chisel in hand, he would sit hunched over the stone till it was time for lunch. After a hurried meal at Yogi Maiyya's, he would return to work. It was tiring; his back ached, and his hands, still the soft hands of a child, were bruised and blistered. But he persevered.

One day, finally, he looked down at his handiwork. The sun was setting, and its dying rays fell full on the lotus he had carved. The sandstone was already red, but the orange-pink of dusk set it aflame until the flower blushed a deep alluring red. Madhav bent and blew at it, removing the last grains of dust.

It was done. His first independent piece of carving, and he was proud of it. Now he could go out and tell the world that he was ready to be a stone carver.

That evening, when Balram came home, Madhav asked him if he could come to the construction site of the mosque the next day.

Balram nodded. 'Of course. I have already asked for you. You will be welcome there.'

That night, before sleeping, Balram placed the stone lotus in the tiny household shrine with its collection of little clay idols. He folded his hands briefly before it and closed his eyes, asking for the gods' blessings on the child who was now going to follow in his footsteps.

Balram had told Madhav that the pillars, the lintels, the beams—in fact, much of what had comprised the temples—were still there. Taken apart, of course, but not destroyed. 'We are doing the work of filling in what is missing,' Balram said, as they walked towards the site, 'of bridging the gap between temple and mosque.'

Madhav looked sceptical. To him, it seemed impossible that what he saw as components of a temple could ever appear as anything else. Surely it would take much imagination and skill to put all these odds and ends together and conjure up a mosque.

'Go,' Balram said, 'look around if you wish. I will be there,' he inclined his head slightly, off to the left. 'Come when you have finished.' He had moved away a few steps when he turned to look over his shoulder. 'Don't wander far. And if anyone should ask, give them my name. Say I work for Sridhar Sahu.'

Madhav nodded. The name of Sridhar Sahu was distasteful to him: he still thought the man a traitor for having learnt the invaders' language, and for having been in their employ when they came to destroy the temples. But he had realized too, that if it had not been Sridhar Sahu, it would have been another, perhaps another who would not have listened to Balram and would have allowed the temples to be demolished rather than merely dismantled. And Sridhar Sahu, after all, had given Balram this work, enabled him and Madhav to have a more stable livelihood.

Madhav wandered through what remained of the temples. The pillars, carefully taken apart and placed in great stacks that stood taller than him. He made his way through the stacks, and puzzled at the odd way in which some of the carvings had been vandalized. A statue of a Natraj, Shiva caught in his cosmic dance of destruction. A dancing girl, all sensuous curves. A Ganpati, his trunk resting on a prosperous belly. Elephants and tigers and caparisoned horses. All seemingly attacked with clubs, hammers, swords, he knew not what. Faces obliterated, bodies smashed. There was the occasional—very occasional—one here or there that had escaped, but it was the exception. The purely geometric patterns, the representations of flowers and temple bells, the auspicious water pots, the coconuts carved in stone: they were untouched.

The iron pillar was untouched, and it stood where Madhav had seen it last. Perhaps Qutbuddin Aibak, whatever his religious beliefs, was sufficiently in awe of Vasuki, the Serpent King, to let him slumber in peace. Or perhaps he did not wish to risk losing this newly-won city for the sake of curiosity.

'They have told us what we may carve and what we may not,' Balram said when Madhav joined him half an hour later in the open ground where the stone carvers were at work. A few more had arrived, men old and young. None as old as Balram and none as young as Madhav, but men whose scarred hands and sinewy forearms spoke of their skill with stone. They were still settling into their work, chatting lazily as they went about setting up their workplaces, getting out their tools, positioning the stone.

'Do you remember what they'd said when they came to destroy the temples?' Balram asked. 'That their religion does not allow the depiction of living beings; for them it is blasphemous.' Madhav nodded, a twinge of hurt rising up at the memory of those defaced idols he had seen in his tour of the temples.

'So we may not carve horses or lions or dancing girls,' Balram said with a twinkle in his eye as he set up his tools. 'Much as we may want to. But flowers, bells, coconuts: those are all permitted.'

Madhav sat down on his haunches next to Balram and looked at the masses of newly quarried stone around them, some already worked into smooth panels, ready to be carved. He had seen gold, buff and red sandstone, but some of the other colours here were so unusual, he could not take his eyes off them. 'This is so beautiful,' he breathed, reaching out a tentative hand to point towards a greyish-green block of stone. 'What will you carve from that?'

Balram smiled. 'It may not come to me, Madhav,' he said, undoing the strings around a piece of sacking wrapped around a yard-long panel of stone.

It was a beautiful piece, the colour of honey, gleaming like gold in the morning sunlight. A pattern had been traced on it in henna: a series of curves between two broad straight lines. Stylized waves. 'The Ganga and the Yamuna,' Madhav whispered, bewildered. 'Do they worship our goddesses, too?'

A brief smile played on Balram's thin lips. 'Of course not. Do you not remember? They worship only one God.' He had begun working now, the chisel gently chipping away at the stone, following the lines the artist had drawn onto the surface. 'But to their alien eyes, this is just a pattern, and we may carve it.' He grinned at the irony of it. 'Ganga and Yamuna, immortalized in a mosque, and Aibak not even aware of it! We could worship here, Madhav. See?'—he gestured to the side, where another stone carver was at work. 'There is a kalash, too, just as in our temples. Coconut, mango leaves and all. When this is finished, we could enter and forget this was supposed to be a mosque. It could remind us of our own faith, you know.'

Madhav did not say anything immediately. Balram kept working, his hands moving surely. Madhav watched him, and after a while, he said quietly, 'Does it not offend you to create something beautiful for their mosque? After all, these used to be our temples. Yes, you stopped them from destroying them, but all said and done, the temples are gone. The way they were taken apart and are now being put back together to worship another god—don't you think this, what you're doing, is a betrayal of your gods?'

It was a genuine question, the anxiety and confusion of a child speaking. Balram listened, and his hands stilled long enough for him to answer.

'For me, my god always dwells within me,' he replied. 'An idol in a temple is not a god. It is only the creation of a man like you or I. It is there only to remind you of god. Its desecration does not destroy your god; it merely destroys the work of the man who made it.' He rubbed gently at a narrow groove he had carved in the stone. 'See. Some weeks from now, you will be able to see the Yamuna in it. Perhaps Aibak and his men will see nothing but a row of connected circles, which they might view as shells or flowers. I don't know. But it's only my work. It's not a god.'

He shook his head. 'I cannot let religious sentiment get in my way of earning a living. Will sitting back and refusing to work for Aibak do anything for me? Perhaps those who are well-off can afford to take a stand like that, but I cannot.' He resumed his work, his hammer and chisel moving along the groove, smoothing it out.

'I have heard it said,' said Madhav after a moment, 'that Aibak will impose his religion on us. He will pull down the rest of our temples too and make us worship in his mosque.'

'Aibak's men are a few thousand,' Balram said, without looking up from his work. 'We are more than ten times that number. Perhaps a hundred times; I do not know. If they try forcibly to convert us, will it not antagonize far more people than they can hope to ever control? A man cannot be forced to worship a god. He may be forced to show respect, but that force will only make him hate the man who forces him.

'No, Madhav,' he said. 'I do not think you need worry about that.'

ꕥ

On that first day, Madhav hovered close to Balram. He did not even attempt to lift chisel and hammer; he was still too much in awe. Instead, he ran errands, he fetched water for Balram, helped shift the stone, sharpened Balram's spare chisels, and built a small shelter out of broken branches to ward off the noon sun.

Balram had already spoken to the man in charge, and had been allowed to retain Madhav as an informal apprentice. 'You will not be paid anything yet,' he explained to Madhav as they walked home that evening. 'Until you can carve independently, you will remain an apprentice. But this will be good practice for you. I cannot think of another place where you will get better practice.'

The next day, as they got ready to leave their hut, Balram lifted the small sack in which Madhav had kept the hammer and chisel that were now his. 'Here,' he said. 'Take this along. Let us see if you can start doing some carving today.'

The first half of the morning passed in Madhav helping Balram. When they took a break to have a sip of water and some of the food they had brought along, Balram took advantage of the free time to introduce Madhav to the other stone carvers. Most of them had already seen and taken note of Madhav the previous day; to introduce Madhav to them as Balram's apprentice was but a formality now. They were accepting, some of them a little surprised perhaps that a boy already on the brink of adolescence could be taken on as an apprentice. But these were turbulent times, and they had learned to take many odd happenings in their stride.

The stone carvers were all men, but there was one boy among them. Nandu, the son of the carver Keshav. Nandu, already showing a certain skill in his work, proud of his talent and not inclined to be modest about it, either.

Madhav, never one to make friends easily, had tried to stay by Balram's side, but amidst the men pressing about, Balram had drifted away. Madhav sat down by himself and took out a handful of roasted chickpeas from a fold of cloth around his waist. He had just begun eating when a shadow fell across the stone block in front of him, and there was Nandu. A plump boy, with the sleek and well-fed look of one who had never known hunger. His voice, when he spoke, was supercilious and his tone sarcastic, as if he knew full well that Madhav was barely even an apprentice yet. Madhav felt the first stirrings of hatred in him. He disliked this boy, disliked him intensely.

'I am helping my father carve the pilasters,' Nandu said, his voice full of self-importance. 'Baba is carving the kalashes at the base of each pilaster. I have been given the task of carving the column. Have you seen the pattern? Like the backbone of a fish, fine lines, all at a diagonal.' He went on to explain, drawing a pattern in the dust with the end of a twig. Explaining the intricacies of how he was making sure each line was perfectly parallel to the others. Madhav wanted to listen, wanted to learn. But to pay attention to this pompous boy was to feed his pomposity. Madhav looked away, trying to appear indifferent. Nandu continued to chatter.

There was a sudden rustling, a buzz, a murmur. The men, many of them already back at work, looked up. Some were rising, straightening dhotis, hastily retying turbans that had been set aside. There was a chorus of namaskars, of Ram-Rams. Madhav turned to look.

'Oh,' said Nandu beside him, looking up as well. Madhav could have sworn the boy had been curious when he looked up, but his tone was flat, his expression one of boredom. 'It's Sridhar Sahuji.'

Madhav recognized him, of course. That smooth face,

that silk dhoti, the turban, with its edging of red and gold.

When he began to speak, it was in a voice reverberating with self-assurance, with the knowledge that when he spoke people would listen to him. Madhav remembered that day more than a year back, when Aibak's warriors too had paid heed to this man. That memory reminded him that Sridhar Sahu was a powerful man, even in the court of Aibak.

Half of what he said Madhav could not understand, though he did grasp this much: Sridhar Sahu had come to tell the stone carvers about the money they were due for their work. When they would be paid, and how much for what work. How much would be deducted if they had not turned up on a particular day, or if their work had not been acceptable. There were other announcements he made, things that were boring, too full of numbers and odd words that were dull and senseless to Madhav.

Finally, however, the man had finished speaking, and the workers clustered around him had exhausted their seemingly endless stock of anxious questions. The stone carvers saluted Sridhar Sahu and returned to their work. It was then that Sridhar Sahu, about to turn away, noticed the two boys. Or rather, he noticed the boy who wanted to be noticed.

'Ah, Nandu,' he said. 'How have you been, son?'

Madhav watched, bewildered, as Nandu went scampering up to Sridhar Sahu. 'I am well,' that high-pitched voice was saying. 'Baba has put me to work carving the columns of the pilasters. Have you seen them, babuji? Come,'—and he was sliding a hand familiarly into Sridhar Sahu's, as if they were the best of friends—'come, I will show you.'

Interlude

'What are you trying to say?'

Just one sentence, and whispered so softly that she barely heard it. But even so, she could hear the sarcasm—or was it humour?—in the words. As if he were smiling. Shagufta looked at the man's face. It was impossible for a man to recover from such grievous wounds in a matter of mere hours, and he had not, of that she was certain. But he looked less haggard, less as if he could drift off into death at any moment.

'You asked for a story,' she said.

'And you are giving me a tale of what it is like to be invaded.'

She had not thought of it that way. She said so.

'But that is what it is.' He sighed. 'Water.' It was a murmur, barely audible.

She reached for the little earthen cup, and putting an arm beneath his shoulders, lifted his head enough to give him a few sips. When he sank back against the pillow, she drank too. Her throat was parched, even though she had drunk from the cup every now and then. So much, she realized, that her bladder felt uncomfortably full. She muttered an excuse and left the room to go out into the lane. When she returned, he was lying with his eyes closed. His forehead was beaded with sweat.

'You did not answer my question,' he said. 'Not really.'

Shagufta got out a clean cloth and pressed it to his face, wiping in gentle strokes across his forehead, down his cheekbones and his jaw, to his neck. 'It is a story,' she said. 'You asked for a story. I am telling you one.'

'It is odd,' he said, after a moment. 'But it seems to me more than a mere tale. Are you a professional storyteller? I have never seen—heard—a woman storyteller.'

She poured some of the water onto the cloth and wrung it out before wiping his face and neck again. 'No,' she replied. 'No, I am not.'

'Yet you tell it with such feeling.'

She looked up at that, wondering if she should tell him the truth. But no; he was, after all, a stranger. A stranger she had sheltered, true. A stranger she had, possibly against her better judgement, cared for. Still, a stranger.

'Do you want me to continue?' she asked. 'Or shall I stop?'

He shook his head. 'No. Don't stop. It helps pass the time, this tale of yours.'

7

Five Years Later

Vikram Samwat 1254 (1198 CE)

'Who would have imagined, then?' said the young man who stood at the entrance to the Jami Masjid. He was a tall man, though not yet out of his teens—perhaps seventeen, perhaps even a year younger. He was not fat, but he lacked the almost skeletal thinness of the old man beside him, who leaned on the younger one's arm more than on the stout stick he used for support.

The old man nodded and craned his neck, squinting up at the neat arch-shaped doorway above them. 'And to think the masons did not even know how to build that. They haven't done a bad job of it.'

Madhav chuckled. 'According to that man who claimed to have been a tile maker in—where was it? Isfahan?—they have the shape right, but the mechanics wrong. He says that is not how an arch is made. Not stones cleverly cut and positioned one on top of the other, but one beside the other, standing almost vertical to the ground.'

'I heard. They will fall. And they will bring the rest of the ceiling down with them,' Balram grunted, dismissive.

'Not according to him. He said that true arches have a central stone which keeps the arch in place. All the arch's strength is concentrated there at the top, in that one stone.' Madhav indicated the highest point of the false arch above them. 'Not here, of course. He thought this would collapse within a few years.'

'Ah, well. What's done is done. Perhaps for the next building project Qutbuddin Aibak embarks upon, he had better send for masons from his homeland.' The old man tapped Madhav's arm. 'Come on, lead me in. Is there a step here?'

Slowly, carefully, they moved inside. It was odd, this building, its look alternating between Hindu temple and Islamic mosque. The entrance with its strange lettering—carved with such frustration, with no understanding of what was being inscribed—curving and swirling above. Verses, they had been told, from the holy book of the Muslims. Nobody had bothered to say what they meant, whether they were in praise of the Muslims' God, whether they said what rewards awaited those who prayed or what punishments awaited those who did not.

Beyond that lay a tiny domed room, its dome too, having been dismissed as a fraudulent pretender by Nooruddin, the Persian tile maker who had visited Dilli last year as they had been putting the finishing touches to the Jami Masjid. 'That is no dome,' had been his scornful verdict when he had seen it. 'Just as that arch outside is no arch. A dome is an extension of the arch. Just as the keystone is the strongest part of an arch, so the central stone, at the top of a dome, is its strongest. It holds the dome together.' He had tut-tutted, and had said how even tile makers and stone carvers in Persia, men who were not even builders or stone masons, knew the principle of creating an arch.

'But he could not find fault with the carving,' Balram said with pride.

'How could he? It is beautiful.'

They were walking through the small copse of stone pillars, remnants of the temples that had birthed part of this mosque. Over the years, Madhav had seen places where the soldiers had been careless in obliterating signs of the animals and humans their religion forbade in its art. Here, hidden away near the base of a pillar, was a seated figure, sitting cross-legged on a lotus. There, in a dark corner, was a small dancing figure. A woman, voluptuous and wanton. And here, in full view was a kirtimukh, a monstrous face engaged in the act of swallowing its own body. A Turkic soldier, in a hurry and unfamiliar with the iconography of Hinduism, might have glanced only cursorily at this and dismissed it as a harmless lotus. Without noticing the bulging eyes, the fanged mouth.

They stepped out into the courtyard. The sehan, they had been told it was called. This was where the Muslims came to say their prayers, to kneel in orderly rows, all facing west, where the holy city of their religion was located, many thousands of yojanas away across the seas.

'Let us go closer,' Balram urged Madhav. 'I can barely see.'

When they arrived at the tall screens of stone soaring up into the sky, the old man let his fingertips wander over the carving. Lacelike, the buff and red and grey-green of the stones fitted together to create startlingly beautiful designs: lotuses, lotus buds, little geometric patterns, wide bands of calligraphy. The waves of the Ganga and the Yamuna.

'Four years it was in the making,' Balram said. 'Four years. So much we did in so little time.'

'You can be proud of what you have done,' Madhav replied.

'And you can be proud, too. You went from being a farmer's orphaned son to one of the best young stone carvers in Dilli. I dared not hope, then, that you would show such a talent for the craft. But you made good progress, and you made swift progress.' He patted Madhav's shoulder, that shoulder which was now higher than his own stooped one.

Madhav grinned, a dimple flashing briefly in his cheek. 'I was taught by the best,' he said. 'And perhaps Nandu helped, what with that sneering self-importance of his. From the very first day, he tried to make me feel inferior, and it made me resolve to be better than him.'

They had reached the iron pillar that stood in the vast courtyard of the mosque. Balram squinted up at it, at this potent symbol of a Hindu belief in a divine serpent. 'What do you think, Madhav?' he said softly. 'Do you still think they will force their religion upon us?'

Madhav gave an embarrassed shrug. 'You are reminding me of my childish fears.'

'At that time they were the fears of most people,' Balram said, his tone neutral. 'But they are too few and we are too many, and all said and done, they need us. They need the taxes they get from us. The labour and skill we provide.' He rubbed his good eye—it was watering, no longer as good as it had been five years earlier—and blinked. 'We will live on, I suppose. Invaders and invaded, side by side. Never quite trusting each other, but forced by circumstances to dwell on the same piece of land.'

'Rather like Nandu and me,' Madhav remarked.

ɞ

'Why can you not send one of the servants?' Gayatri demanded petulantly, flinging her plait back over her shoulder. The glossy black braid, half as thick as her arm, swung down to her hip. 'It isn't as if I have nothing to do, Ma.'

'And what are you doing, pray?' Ratna asked, pressing a folded square of red cloth into the top of the small wooden box she held. She had already packed it with her husband's lunch: chapatis and dry lentils, and carrots cooked with spiced peas. 'Gadding about, as always? Sitting on the swing under the mango tree?'

She was interrupted by approaching footsteps, and there, standing in the doorway, was Yogi Maiyya. Older, greyer, her face beginning to show wrinkles, but as self-assured and sharp-eyed as ever. And as dear a friend to Ratna as she had proved to be in the very first year they had spent in Yoginipur.

Ratna rose to her feet, closing the lid of the box, a smile of greeting warming her face. She gestured to her friend to sit, before turning back to Gayatri and holding out the box. 'Take this to your father,' she said. 'I cannot send any of the servants because none of them are free. Go. Pull your odhni over your head and no one will know who you are.' She saw the hesitation, the resurging defiance in Gayatri's face, and added testily: 'Don't dawdle! Would you have your father wait for his lunch?'

Gayatri gave her mother the briefest of glances. It was not quite as defiant as earlier, considering the visitor in their midst, but it was still far from compliant. She pulled her odhni over her head, picked up the wooden box and left the room. The two women heard her call to the lone maidservant still in the house: 'Lakshmi! Close the door after me. I'm going out.'

When they had heard the door shut, Yogi Maiyya seated herself on the wooden stool by the window. It was her usual place: from here she could see the corner of the Yogmaya Temple, and her food stall. She had an assistant now, a thin, knobby-kneed girl called Subhadra. Nobody, not even Subhadra herself, knew who she was, or who had abandoned her on the threshold of the temple. But Yogi Maiyya had found her one day, begging in the lane outside, and had taken pity on her. Subhadra was sitting at the stall now. There were no customers yet; it was too early for lunch, but there was work to be done, and Subhadra was diligent enough to do it even without Yogi Maiyya needing to keep an eye on her. But old habits were hard to break, and Yogi Maiyya found it hard to be anywhere in the vicinity of her food stall without needing to look at it, to reassure herself that all was well.

'What was that about?' she asked, turning away from the window and looking at Ratna. 'Why did you send her to her father? One of the maids could have gone; you have taken over their chores before. There is more to this.'

Ratna sighed. 'It is her father.' She bent to lift the small silver box in which she kept the ingredients—the shaved areca nut, the lime, the catechu and the betel leaves—for the paan. As she worked, making a paan for each of them, she shook her head. 'Gayatri and her father are cut from the same cloth. Both stubborn, both very certain of what they want. And both devoid of any understanding of what society deems proper.

'You will never believe what this is about,' she continued, lowering her voice. 'He tells me he has found a groom for Gayatri, a young man he has known for several years now.' She reached for a little silver tray of shaved coconut and sprinkled some on the betel leaf. 'The man will be there today. That is why her father wants Gayatri to come there, so that this man may see her.' Even to her own ears that sounded shockingly unorthodox. 'Perhaps he does not want to make it too formal yet,' she added lamely.

Yogi Maiyya did not seem to notice. 'Who is this man?' she asked. 'A trader? That, I suppose, is the only sort of man your husband would consider as a son-in-law.'

Ratna shook her head. She handed one of the two paans she had made to Yogi Maiyya. She closed the paandaan, setting it aside. 'No. A stone carver.'

Yogi Maiyya's eyebrows arched.

Ratna nodded. 'I find it hard to believe too. But he has something else in mind. He says the boy is very capable, and very ambitious.' She picked up the paan she had made for herself but did not yet put it in her mouth. 'My husband says that since we have no sons, and only daughters, we must remember that his business will have to be handled eventually by the sons-in-law.'

'And this man will make a worthy inheritor?'

'My husband thinks so.'

'A stone carver?' Yogi Maiyya murmured. 'How did your husband happen to meet a stone carver?'

'When the Jami Masjid was being built. When my husband was handling the hiring and deployment of the workers on behalf of Qutbuddin Aibak'—even after the passage of five years that name still felt so foreign, so odd on her tongue—'and one of his duties was to visit the site. He used to meet the workers there, every time he went. He got to know some of them. This boy was there too, barely even an adolescent when he began work on the mosque.'

The curiosity in Yogi Maiyya's eyes had grown into something more: a gleam of anticipation, of simmering excitement. Ratna wondered why Yogi Maiyya should be so eager to know about a man whom she had only just been told about. 'Is that so,' Yogi Maiyya said. 'I wonder ... what is his name? Do you know?'

'Nandu,' Ratna said, puzzled. 'Why?'

But Yogi Maiyya shook her head and said that it was nothing.

ଓ

When the Jami Masjid was built and ready, Balram had put down his tools—literally, one evening, after he had finished carving the last swirl of river water on a panel—and heaved a sigh. 'That is it,' he had told Madhav. 'My life's work is done.'

He had looked around, his eyes misting over. Taking in the grandeur of the nearly complete mosque, the knots of people around, both workers and curious passersby. Imprinting it all on his mind's eye. 'I cannot carve any more, Madhav,' he had said, handing over his sack of tools to the boy. 'I cannot see well enough. Soon my hands will begin to shake, and I will create a crow where I had set out to create a swan.' He had laughed, and Madhav had recognized, even in the seeming mirth of that chuckle, the underlying sorrow.

But he, like Balram, had seen the truth. He had realized that Balram was bowing out gracefully while he was still capable, still respected for his skill. It was the dignified way to retire.

So Madhav had taken the old man's bag of tools. He had taken his blessings and his recommendations, and in turn had assumed the responsibility of looking after Balram. No words were said about it. None were needed. Balram had looked after the boy when he was young; Madhav would return the favour, even though neither of them thought of it as a favour.

'Go to Sridhar Sahuji,' Balram told him that evening when they had returned from their visit to the Jami Masjid. 'I have heard he is looking for men to do some work at Aibak's palace. It won't be as lucrative as the Jami Masjid, and he will not need half as many men, but still.'

Just five years he had been carving stone, and he had had by no means an early start. But Madhav had a natural talent for stone carving, and even now that the work on the mosque was long over, he did not have to fret about where he would get work. As he made his way through the bustling market of Yoginipur and towards the fort where Qutbuddin Aibak had installed himself, Madhav marvelled at how life had changed for him. He had been a farmer's son, far removed from cities and city life, and here he was. Helping build a capital for a regime.

Between the clutter of stalls, shops and huts that crowded the dirt road and the wide road leading to the fort was the small, neat one-storeyed building that Sridhar Sahu had made his office. He had positioned himself here for the past five years, within easy reach of both master and men. Outside the door, a stout stick clutched in a burly fist, was a man who looked like a wrestler. Inside, in the two tiny rooms, would be sitting Sridhar Sahu's small battalion of workers: his clerks, messengers and servants. In the inner room, the largest room of the building, would be Sridhar Sahu himself. Sitting cross-legged and upright on a mattress, his slope-topped desk in front of him, surrounded by all that made him the powerful and influential man he was: ream upon ream of paper, scrolls, slips of parchment and birch bark. Promissory notes and memorandums, ledgers of accounts and correspondence. Sridhar Sahu was a businessman, inside and out, and he had made it his business to make sure he was indispensable to Qutbuddin Aibak.

Madhav squared his shoulders. He had never been inside

this daunting edifice on his own. In his mind he went over what he intended to say, and how he intended to say it. Quietly confident, Balram had said. Respectful but not obsequious, self-assured but not conceited. Sridhar Sahu valued men who showed that they valued themselves, yet could not bear anyone who was too full of himself.

He took a deep breath and stepped forward.

Out of the blue, rushing out of the narrow alley off to the left, came a slim figure that collided with him. A whirl of deep blue ghagra, the fragrance of jasmine. There was a cry of pain, a sharp and sudden ache in his shin as the girl's foot—slipping out from under her—banged into his leg. Madhav instinctively put out an arm to stop her from falling. His hand closed about a slim wrist crowded with glass bangles.

'What do you think you're doing?'

Two huge eyes, dark brown and fringed with long eyelashes, were glaring into his face. She tugged her wrist free, and in the same movement, swung her arm back and slapped him. With a hissed 'How dare you!' she turned to go.

'I save you,' snapped Madhav, 'and this is the gratitude I get? If it hadn't been for me, you'd have been sprawled in the dirt now.' He was aware that other passersby were stopping, looking curiously on. There would be gossip, but there was no reason for him to fear gossip. Right now, all his attention was focused on this girl, this feisty beauty who had come tumbling out of nowhere and shaken him up. He stared unabashedly at her, unable to take his eyes off that lovely face. Vaguely, he noticed that she was carrying a wooden box, wrapped in rough but clean cotton, under one arm.

'If you'd been looking where you were going, I would never have fallen in the first place!' she retorted.

'You should have been looking where you were going,' Madhav shot back. He noticed that the girl's gaze had darted towards the doorway of Sridhar Sahu's establishment, and instinctively, he glanced in the same direction. The doorkeeper, who had seated himself on the small platform beside the door, was looking on with amusement.

'I was looking where I was going,' the girl said and moved forward, trying to make her way past Madhav. 'Get out of my way!'

Madhav blinked, suddenly realizing. 'To—to Sridhar Sahuji's? Why?'

She looked daggers at him and spat out a curse. Her voice was low, the word muffled enough to have been heard only by Madhav.

He felt a thrill deep down in his loins. Oh, she was wonderful, whoever she was. He had no experience whatsoever of girls, but Madhav knew the type he found intriguing. Not the quiet, demure type. Not the sort of girl who shrank if anyone so much as looked at her. No. This was the type of woman, bold and bright-eyed and strong-minded, that attracted him. He wanted to know more about her. He wanted to reach out and stop her from going.

'I told you to move,' said the girl, through gritted teeth.

Madhav did not obey. 'Who are you?' he asked. And then, realizing that that sounded almost predatory, he added in a softer tone, 'At least tell me your name.'

'Why don't you tell me yours,' she said with exaggerated sweetness, 'so that I can let my father know?'

With that, she brushed past him, the wooden box banging against his ribs, and went up the steps leading to Sridhar Sahu's office. She paused at the door to say something to the doorkeeper, who flinched. Then, without waiting for him to show her in, she pushed against the wooden leaves of the door and let herself through.

The doorkeeper hurried down the steps, but Madhav had already taken himself off. He ran as he had run only once before, from that long-ago battlefield. And only when he was far, far away from the area did he stop to look back over his shoulder and make sure he was no longer pursued. Then, with a dazed look, he slowed down and stopped. Looked up at the clear blue sky above, and at the distant bulk of the Jami Masjid, its stone screens soaring to touch that sky.

Madhav smiled.

'I thought,' said Subhadra, 'that Balram Dada had recommended you for work.' She was sitting on her haunches, her worn green sari tucked up around her knees, its end wrapped around a waist so thin that her ribs showed, clear and distinct as fingers. A pile of dirty pots and pans was beside her. On the other side were two water pots that she had filled from the baoli, the stepwell that spread behind and below her. Subhadra dipped the rough skeleton of a dried gourd in the pile of ash that served as detergent, and continued to scrub a pot so wide-mouthed she could have easily sat in it.

Madhav sat opposite her, watching with unseeing eyes as Subhadra worked and talked.

'Balram Dada came to the stall this afternoon for lunch,' she said, 'and told Yogi Maiyya that you had gone to find work with Sridhar Sahuji. Yogi Maiyya said'—she paused, a little unsure, before taking the plunge—'she said she would put in a word if you needed it. She knows Sahuji's wife.'

Madhav scowled. 'I know that,' he muttered. 'She told us years ago. We hadn't needed a recommendation then, and I don't need one now.'

Subhadra shrugged. 'Of course not. All you have to do is go to Aibak and tell him you'd like to do this, this and this, and he will snap his fingers and give the necessary orders.' She shook her head, chuckling wryly.

Madhav glowered. 'Don't be ridiculous.'

'Then why?' A thought struck her. 'But I suppose you don't even need a recommendation to Sridhar Sahuji, do you? He must have seen you often enough in all those years you worked with Balram Dada at the mosque. Balram Dada always says how skilled you are, surely Sridhar Sahuji will happily take you on without a recommendation from anyone?'

'I don't want to work on Aibak's palace, that's all. There will be other work. There always is.'

That could not be argued with, and Subhadra did not refute it. 'Pour some water over my hands, will you?'

Madhav complied, standing up to lift one of the pots and pour the water in a slow, steady stream. When Subhadra's hands were clean, she took the water pot from him and began rinsing the pots and pans she had scrubbed.

'What will you do then?' she asked when she was finished, and had begun to stack the clean vessels up, readying them to take back to the food stall.

'I'll find something.' Madhav bent and picked up the now empty water pots, tucking one beneath each arm. 'I'll fill these and bring them,' he told Subhadra. 'You go along, don't wait for me.'

Subhadra looked narrowly at him, her eyes searching his face for some clue. 'There's something you're not telling me, isn't it?' she asked. 'Something has happened. You're tense about something, worried—'

Madhav did not wait to hear the rest. He put the water pots down so suddenly and with such force, they may well have cracked. 'Stop it!' he snarled at her. 'Stop pestering me, damn you! Why must you go on and on and on?' He stood a moment, his chest heaving and his eyes blazing, and then he turned and ran out of the baoli. Subhadra gazed after him, a confused expression on her face, until he had vanished from sight.

Yogi Maiyya was busy at the food stall when Subhadra returned from the baoli. The old woman looked up from the mound of dough from which she was breaking off lumps to roll into chapatis. 'What happened to you? I was getting worried, you were so late.'

Subhadra bent, sliding the bulky bundle off her back and lowering the two water pots she had brought back from the baoli; she had left the other two there and would return to fetch them later. 'Madhav had come to the baoli,' she replied. 'I was talking to him.'

'Here, I've kept some jaggery for you. And some puffed rice,' Yogi Maiyya said. 'Eat up and then help me with these chapatis.'

It was only when Subhadra, her snack eaten, had joined Yogi Maiyya at the stall and was busy rolling out chapatis, that Yogi Maiyya spoke. 'What did Madhav say?' she asked.

But even Yogi Maiyya, on being told of Madhav's puzzling behaviour, was not able to decipher its meaning. Something must have happened, she agreed; but what, she could no more hazard a guess than could Subhadra.

Their curiosity was satisfied much later, when Balram came to eat his dinner. Madhav, who usually helped him to the food stall, was not there today, and a neighbour had assisted Balram there. All of Yogi Maiyya's other patrons had already eaten and gone; she and Subhadra, therefore, also served themselves and ate with Balram.

Balram heaved a deep sigh in response to Yogi Maiyya's gentle enquiry about Madhav. 'He does not want favours from Sridhar Sahu,' he said. 'He says he will go to Sridhar Sahu now only when he can stand straight and tall and show him he's worthy.'

'Worthy of what?' Yogi Maiyya asked, mystified. 'I am sure Sridhar Sahuji is already convinced of Madhav's skill.'

'Not worthy of work,' Balram said. 'Worthy of his daughter.' He squeezed his eyes shut, pinching the bridge of his nose as he did so. 'That boy.' He shook his head in a gesture of exasperation, and when he opened his eyes, they were brimming with despair. 'He met Sridhar Sahu's daughter outside her father's office today.'

'What! Gayatri?' There was astonishment in Yogi Maiyya's voice, and the next moment, recollection. 'Ah, yes. I remember; her mother did send her off before my very eyes. So Madhav saw her.'

'And fell in love with her.'

Yogi Maiyya snorted. 'Fell in love with her? At one glance? I would have credited Madhav with more sense. Not that she's a bad girl, but'—she shook her head, helplessly. 'Who would have imagined it? Madhav? So sensible, so level-headed? And to fall in love at first sight with a girl he can never have?'

Neither of them noticed that Subhadra, who had finished eating and had gone off to do her work, was staring, eyes wide and blank, as she set things straight in the little kitchen. In silence, she picked up the platters and bowls, taking them to the large cane basket behind the stall. In silence, she stacked them in the basket. In silence, too, she began scraping off the dried food, scrubbing the dishes with ash, rinsing.

She was silent, but the tears flowed unhindered down her cheeks.

8

Madhav lay on a thin reed mat under the banyan tree. His head rested on his crossed hands, and he stared up with unseeing eyes into the vast green of the canopy above. There were birds there, and squirrels, nibbling at the ripe fruit. Occasionally an overripe fruit, red and soft, fell to the ground. One had fallen onto the white muslin of his dhoti, but he had not even noticed it.

'It has been four days now,' said a quiet voice. 'And you have brooded all this while.' Balram, leaning heavily on his stick, lowered himself to the ground.

'I have worked too,' Madhav said, immediately defensive.

'I am not accusing you of being lazy.' Balram reached into a fold around the waist of his dhoti and drew forth a tiny drawstring pouch, from which he extracted a few slivers of areca and a generous pinch of lime. Pulling the drawstring shut, he began to use the pad of his thumb to vigorously rub the lime in the cupped palm of his hand. 'I merely wonder how long this is to continue.'

'I do not bother you.'

'You do not try to. But I am bothered. I cannot help but be bothered.'

Madhav turned his head away.

'You know she is not for you, Madhav. She is a rich man's daughter. Sridhar Sahu is as high above the likes of you and me as—as Aibak is above Sridhar Sahu. It is folly to imagine she could ever be yours.'

Up above, in the leaves of the tree, a couple of pigeons began to coo with a maddening intensity that made the air hum.

'Six years ago I could not imagine I would be working in Dilli,' Madhav pointed out. 'Things change, and in ways most people would imagine impossible.'

Balram tipped the slivered areca nut into his palm. A few brisk rubs from his thumb, and the areca nut was mixed into the lime. He gathered it all up into a ball and tossed it into his mouth. 'And so you think you will march up to Sridhar Sahu and demand his daughter's hand in marriage? And Sridhar Sahu will welcome you with open arms?'

Madhav frowned. 'You make fun of me? You think I aim too high, and so you mock me?' He sat up. 'You will see. And so will Sridhar Sahu. You will all see.'

'I do not mock you, Madhav.' Balram put a hand on the young man's arm. 'All I am trying to point out is that Gayatri is not a prize easily won. If she were my daughter, I would happily marry her off to you. But I am not Sridhar Sahu. He does not know you as I do.'

Madhav's anger had dissipated; so had the confidence, the self-assurance. In the space of the few moments it took Balram to speak, the younger man's shoulders had slumped, all the fight gone out of him.

Balram watched him and continued to chew, slowly, rhythmically. 'Do you know,' he said, after he had swallowed, 'why Gayatri went to her father's workplace that day?'

It had not occurred to Madhav to ponder over that, though now that he thought about it, it was certainly odd, for a wealthy girl, the daughter of so well-respected a man, to be out alone, even if she was going to her father's office. At the very least, she should have been accompanied by a maid, perhaps even sitting in a palanquin. 'No,' he admitted. 'How would I?'

'Let me tell you then,' Balram said, 'what Yogi Maiyya told me.'

By the time Balram finished—and the telling of it was quick—Madhav was sitting bolt upright, eyes wide with amazement. 'Nandu?' he burst out when Balram fell silent. 'Sridhar Sahu wants to marry her to Nandu? Why? Marrying her to that worthless creature would be like placing a priceless pearl necklace around the neck of a flea-riddled monkey!'

'Sridhar Sahu does not think so, obviously.' Balram leaned back against the bole of the tree. 'Whatever you may say, Nandu knows his work. And he knows how to kowtow to people like Sridhar Sahu.'

'He's an insufferable, conceited little bastard.'

'To us, yes. To Sridhar Sahu, no. What difference does it make to Sahuji how Nandu treats us? As long as he accords Sahuji the respect due to him?'

'But don't you see? If he marries Gayatri, he—he will not love her.'

'With Sahuji hanging over his head, seeing he behaves?'

Madhav shook his head, unconvinced. 'You don't see. I have spent years working alongside Nandu. He has only one love in his life, and that is money. It is all he wants. He has been flattering Sahuji and fawning over him for that reason and no other. Perhaps he merely wants Sahuji to further his career, to get him lucrative assignments. But will he say no to a marital alliance too? No. And I don't mean that he will ill-treat Gayatri. Just that he will not love her. There is a difference.'

'And it is important that she be loved?'

Madhav gave the old man a long, level look. Then, getting to his feet, he said, 'If Sridhar Sahu will not consider me as a son-in-law, then maybe I should approach Gayatri directly. She appears to me a girl who may be good at getting her own way.'

Lunch was over, and there were a few hours to go before customers would start turning up, demanding dinner. Yogi Maiyya had retired to her hut nearby for a siesta, leaving Subhadra to complete the chores. Subhadra did not mind; she had a teenager's energy, after all, and cleaning, washing, cutting and kneading were, to her mind, good ways to occupy herself. Besides, she liked the time that she could spend alone with herself.

She was not alone today. Madhav, putting aside the huffiness of the previous evening, had come to the stall and was talking to her as she prepared the vegetables for dinner.

'If I even try to go to her home and ask for her, I will be turned out,' he said. 'It's stupid to even think of doing that.'

'Then why not accost her in the street? That was how you first met her, was it not?'

Madhav shook his head. 'I cannot keep sitting outside her house in the hope that she will come out alone.'

'Then find some reason to have her come out.' Madhav, had he been not quite so wrapped up in his own troubles, would have heard the annoyance in her voice. 'You're clever enough. I'm sure you will think of something.' She attacked a heap of peeled onions with her knife, slicing them so briskly that even Madhav was taken aback and cautioned her to slow down.

The next moment, he was back to his own woes, his problems with his endeavours to woo the girl he had so precipitately fallen in love with.

'No. Even if I pretend to bear a message from someone—her father, perhaps—her mother won't let her go with me, alone.' He paused. 'Help me, Subhadra! Please. I can't do this without you.'

Subhadra did not look up. She continued to slash furiously at an onion, ignoring Madhav as if he had not spoken.

'What is the matter?' Madhav burst out. 'Is this how much our friendship means to you?' He was annoyed now, and his frustration made him insensitive as he blundered on. 'Remember when Yogi Maiyya first brought you here, how much you cried? How alone you were? If I hadn't played with you then, if I hadn't befriended you, you'd still be crying.'

Subhadra laughed and reached up to swipe at her streaming eyes with the back of her hand. Madhav heard neither the bitterness in the laugh nor saw the tears. He was on his feet now, pacing about, agitated.

'And it's not even as if I'm asking for very much, you know. All you need to do is take her a message. I think'—he stopped, chewing his lip—'I think—'

Subhadra cut him off. 'No,' she said, abruptly. 'I will not do it. I don't care what you think or say. I won't do it.'

When Yogi Maiyya emerged from her siesta a few minutes later, Madhav was gone. Subhadra was sitting by herself, still cutting onions.

'They are very pungent today, are they?' said Yogi Maiyya, when she saw the tears streaming down Subhadra's cheeks. Subhadra nodded. Yogi Maiyya patted her shoulder gently, and went about her own work.

ॐ

Eventually, Madhav resorted to subterfuge. He had toyed with the idea of confiding in Yogi Maiyya and asking for her help, but Yogi Maiyya, like Subhadra, seemed suddenly inimical to him. She did not push him away as Subhadra did, but when Madhav had accompanied Balram to the food stall that night for their evening meal, there had been something harsh and wary in her eyes. Madhav had guessed, astutely enough, that even if he asked Yogi Maiyya for help, she would not give it. He would have to manage a meeting with Sridhar Sahu's daughter on his own.

Having bathed and donned a new dhoti, Madhav examined his reflection in a metal plate and, deciding this was the best he could do, headed for Sridhar Sahu's house.

At the door, he told the maidservant who came to the threshold that he bore a message from Yogi Maiyya. 'For Gayatri Devi,' he added.

He had been worried the woman would turn him away. But she nodded in a bored way, and muttered, 'Wait,' and went inside, leaving him standing at the threshold.

He glanced around, taking in the view of the courtyard with its little tulsi plant growing in the centre. The windows looking onto the courtyard were quiet, the walls freshly whitewashed, the air fragrant with sandalwood. The house breathed wealth.

Jingling ankle bells broke his reverie. 'Yogi Maiyya sent someone for me? But I hardly know her,' he heard a musical voice saying. And there, stepping through a doorway and into the courtyard, was Gayatri. She was alone; the maid had probably gone off to attend to some other chore after informing Gayatri.

Her eyes widened when she saw him, and immediately hardened too. 'Why have you come here?'

She had recognized him, thought Madhav with a surge of joy. It would have been humiliating if he had had to remind her of their encounter the other day.

'I came to see you,' he said.

Her eyes narrowed. Madhav could not guess at the emotion. Fear? Surprise? Consternation? Embarrassment? Annoyance? A little bit of everything, he thought. He opened his mouth to soothe the fear, which he imagined would be the foremost. 'I am not a bad man,' he began to say.

She made a sound of disgust and turned to go, and in that moment, Madhav realized that he would never have another opportunity, that his only hope of ever getting her to understand him was slipping away. Suddenly desperate, he lunged forward, reaching for her wrist. He caught it, but she had already moved forward, hurrying away from him. His hand on her wrist pulled her up, snatching her back and, though he had not intended it, straight into his arms. Her back hit his chest with such force and such unexpected suddenness that they both fell.

The stones of the courtyard were hard. She was light, deliciously light, but the breath had been knocked out of him and his head had taken a hard knock. She was screaming as she scrambled to her feet. Kicking him in the shins and the knees, crying. From somewhere deep within the house came the thud of running feet. Then someone was shouting in a voice bordering on panic, 'What happened? Gayatri! What happened?'

Without waiting to attempt a defence, Madhav got to his feet and ran.

He ran all the way from Sridhar Sahu's house to the little baoli—the quietest, most secluded, most forgotten place he could think of—and took shelter there.

There was a painful lump on his head, and when he reached up to feel it, his fingertips came away red with blood. Madhav descended the steps of the baoli and scooped up water to bathe the wound. When he had attended to the wound, he curled up under the tree at one end of the baoli enclosure. There, with his head in his hands, he wept for the humiliation that had been his.

This was not what he had thought would happen. He had accepted that there was a possibility of Gayatri refusing him, but in his mind's eye, his reaction in that situation would have been one of dignity, of honour intact even in the face of rejection. He would have been the gentleman, not the overwrought, love-crazed adolescent he had proved himself to be. If he had not lunged at her, if he had not tried to stop her… so many ifs. He gritted his teeth and tried to swallow the pain.

Other than a couple of fidgety lapwings which circled above the baoli, their black-and-white wings stark against the blue of the sky, there was nobody to witness his shame.

He was more composed when Subhadra arrived a little later, bringing a bundle of clothes to be washed. She did not see him at first; she looked preoccupied. Besides, he had made sure he was hidden behind the massive bole of the tree. He did not want to be an easy target if Sridhar Sahu's men came by, searching for him.

He heard the rhythmic wet squishing as Subhadra pummelled her laundry, and peered out. When he saw she was alone, he emerged.

'What are you doing here?' Subhadra asked, in an awed whisper. 'I thought you would have gone.'

Madhav sat down on his haunches. 'You know about it?'

'Of course I know about it. Two servants of Sridhar Sahuji's came to our stall, wanting to know if Yogi Maiyya had sent a message for Gayatri.'

Madhav winced.

'Yes,' Subhadra continued. 'Yogi Maiyya didn't know, of course, and I don't think she guessed. She was as mystified as anyone else would have been. The two men couldn't do anything about it, so they left.' She gathered up the pile of clothes she had been scrubbing, and carried them across to a drain at the other end of the baoli. Madhav picked up her water pots and poured water into the small stone trough into which Subhadra had put the clothes. While she rinsed the clothes, he went down to the water's edge and filled her water pots for her. When he rejoined Subhadra at the trough, she glanced up at him and said, 'This Gayatri, she does not know your name, does she? Only your face?'

Madhav nodded miserably.

'If she cannot provide a name, her father will not be able to find you,' Subhadra said. 'Unless Gayatri or the maid see you and identify you, there is nothing to fear.' She had finished rinsing the clothes, and now, one by one, squeezed out the clothes and flung them over her shoulder, readying to take them back home.

'I have to go,' she said to Madhav. 'Do you need something? Are you hungry?'

Madhav shook his head. 'I'm not hungry. But I need to talk to Balram Dadu. Can you tell him to come here?'

'You know he won't be able to get here on his own. I'll bring him myself, but only late at night. After dinner is over.' He helped lift one full water pot onto her head, and the other into the crook of her free arm. 'Be careful, Madhav,' she said, and then she was gone, leaving behind only a row of wet footprints that evaporated even as he watched.

'Here,' Subhadra said, pushing a small package, an envelope of banana leaves, into Madhav's hand. He felt the warmth of fresh-cooked food through the leaves, smelt the earthiness of lentils. A lump rose to his throat at the unexpected thoughtfulness. And at the irony of it all.

'Eat,' Balram said in a soft voice, while Subhadra led him to the tree. Madhav took over from her, slipping one hand under the old man's elbow. 'Eat,' Balram repeated, when they sat down. 'You must be starving.'

'I have to tell you—'

'You can say what you must once you have eaten. Where you have waited these many hours, you can wait a quarter of an hour longer.'

'I will have to leave Dilli, it's too dangerous for me to stay in Yoginipur,' Madhav mumbled in a strained voice after he had gobbled down the food. Subhadra, it appeared, had been discreet enough to not have said anything to Balram, but the old man was wise enough to put two and two together. He had realized that Madhav's self-confessed fascination for Sridhar Sahu's daughter, coupled with Madhav's subsequent disappearance, must be linked to Sridhar Sahu's servants looking for a young man purporting to bear a message from Yogi Maiyya. Madhav did not need to say much; only the confession of his foolishness and the sheer bad luck that had hit him.

'Where will you go?'

Above them, the sky was clear, studded with thousands of stars. So vast, thought Madhav in a surge of misery. Such a very vast land, such a very big world, and he was all alone. After his family had died, Balram had taken their place, and then Yogi Maiyya, though she was rather more distant. And Subhadra. Skinny little Subhadra, with her sharp eyes and that temper that could flare up in an instant and die down just as quickly.

He did not know how he could possibly live without them.

Somewhere outside, not too far away, a fight broke out between the mongrels that lurked about. Yapping and snarling ripped through the night.

'I don't know,' Madhav said.

'Why should you go?' Subhadra spoke up. She had been sitting quietly all this while, wrapped in the shadows, a dark little figure huddled by Balram's side. Madhav had half forgotten that she was there. She turned to Balram and repeated to him all that she had said to Madhav earlier that day, and when she was done, Balram looked at Madhav.

'Subhadra is right,' he said. 'It is not as if you really harmed the girl. Anyway, Sridhar Sahu has more important things to do than to chase all over the city in search of a stranger who inadvertently bumped into his daughter.'

'And what if I bump into her again, accidentally?' Madhav shook his head. 'No, I cannot stay in Dilli any more.'

'A girl like her probably does not go out too often on her own,' Balram pointed out. 'And in any case, Yogi Maiyya has told me Gayatri is to be married soon. Once she is married, she will not even accidentally come in contact with any man other than her husband.'

'Married to Nandu,' Madhav said, through gritted teeth. 'To that fool.'

Balram shrugged. 'That is none of our business, Madhav.'

The three of them sat in silence, Madhav mulling over his choices and regretting all that had happened, the other two waiting for him to say something. Finally, it was Balram who spoke. 'Don't do anything foolish, Madhav,' he said. 'All you need do is keep low. It is not impossible in a city as large as this, with hundreds coming and going. There is no need to run, but there is no need to take risks either.'

Madhav looked up. The moonlight was bright, silvery in its intensity, and it lit up his face. 'I will not do anything foolish,' he said. 'But how can I stay on and watch Nandu strut about? How can I look on while he marries Gayatri?'

After Balram and Subhadra had gone, leaving him alone at the baoli, Madhav had time to sit back and ponder over all that happened. He had to acknowledge that Balram was right: it would be pointless to run away. Where would he go, after all? This city was the only home he had known for six years now. He had been gone so long from his own village that he now did not even know where it was, or whether it still existed. No; his only hope was to stay on in Dilli, somehow.

He could disguise himself, move to another part of town, perhaps closer to the Yamuna. He could find employment that would keep him well out of the orbit of Sridhar Sahu and his kin. It was not impossible.

In the cool of the night, with only the moon and the stars as witness, the idea began to seem a good one, the plan downright easy. He fell asleep, curled up under the tree, with a smile on his lips.

In the harsh glare of the sun, the dream withered and doubts crept in. The only work he was good at was stone carving, and the world of stone carvers was a small one. Sooner or later Nandu would hear of him, and between him and Sridhar Sahu—no, that was not a thought he wanted to consider.

When the sun had risen high enough for Balram to be awake, Madhav surreptitiously made his way to the hut which had been his home these past few years. Having made sure there was nobody around, he slipped into the hut, startling Balram. 'It's only me,' he said, sitting down. 'I had to come and meet you, Dadu.'

'You have decided to stay?'

Madhav shook his head. 'I don't think so.' He told Balram what conclusion he had reached, and Balram reluctantly nodded.

'You are right,' he said. 'I think I was being optimistic. Perhaps a little selfish too; I was thinking only of how lonely I would be without you, how much I would miss you. I think

I convinced myself that you would be safe enough in Dilli.' He glanced towards the door. 'Hmm. I think—Madhav, will you pass me my stick and help me up? Thank you. Now wait here. Stay inside, make sure nobody sees you, yes? I will be back.'

He did come back, but by then Madhav had fretted himself into a bundle of nerves. And by the time Balram had taken off his turban, sat down and drunk some water and massaged his leg, Madhav was close to tears. Finally though, Balram heaved a long sigh of relief and stretched out. 'Yogi Maiyya has promised to help,' he said. 'She knows a lot of people who matter. She will be able to find someone who can tell you where to go, whom to ask for work.'

'Outside Dilli?'

Balram nodded. 'She has said she will try.'

Madhav chewed at his lower lip. 'But I don't have time. What if Sridhar Sahu's men are already on their way here?'

'They are not. I have been outside these past few hours, boy. I have not seen Sridhar Sahu or any of his men on the rampage.' He sat up and placed a gnarled old hand on Madhav's shoulder. 'Don't worry, Madhav. Yogi Maiyya has promised to come here this evening, and I trust her; she is a resourceful woman. I think she will be able to do something for you.'

Balram had to go out again; a friend, as old as him, had come by to chat. He had brought along a chaupar board, the thick cloth worn and faded but still usable. He had been keen to sit outside the hut and play, but Balram had persuaded him otherwise. The nearby banyan tree, just round the corner, would be equally suitable. So they had gone, leaving Madhav, unnoticed by the visitor, all alone by himself in the hut.

The rest of the day passed, for Madhav, agonizingly slow. He pottered about the hut, occupying himself with small chores, and when he could not think of anything else to do, he lay down and tried to sleep.

Sleep did not come. His mind refused to rest, wandering tirelessly over all that had happened, worrying over what might or might not happen. He was swamped by humiliation and regret, by anger at Nandu and by the unfairness of it all. And there was the impending loneliness, the fear that he would once again be all alone. Six years ago, when Muhammad of Ghur's invasion had turned his life upside down, Madhav had found himself flung into the world alone and friendless. Would that happen again?

He must have drifted off to sleep sometime in the late afternoon, because when he next knew, someone was shaking his shoulder. Madhav came awake with a start, scrambling up. 'It's only me,' Balram whispered. 'Yogi Maiyya's here. Come outside; nobody will see you. It's all quiet.'

'You could go to one of the other big towns,' Yogi Maiyya said, chewing on a mouthful of paan. 'Agroha, for example. My friend gave me the names of a few people who might be able to give you work there.'

'Your friend?' Madhav asked, wary. 'Who?'

Yogi Maiyya looked uncomfortable. 'Ratna,' she said. 'Sridhar Sahu's wife. But I have not told her whom I need help for. And in any case, she does not know you. Or that you were the one who went to her house.'

'At least hear her out, Madhav,' Balram said.

But Agroha did not seem a good idea, after all. Yogi Maiyya conceded that Sridhar Sahu, having originally been from Agroha, still had connections in that town. Though he had not been there since he had moved to Dilli, there were still people in Agroha who would wish him well. And they were the very people to whom Ratna could refer a young man she had never met, but whom Yogi Maiyya vouched for.

'It's too risky,' Madhav said. 'No, not Agroha.'

Yogi Maiyya nodded. 'Ratna also suggested Suryapur. That was where they were initially bound, she and Sridhar Sahu, before he decided to stop at Dilli. Suryapur is a big city, and busy. There is trade, and many wealthy people. Where there is wealth to spare, there will be buildings. Work.'

Ratna had supplied a name. She did not know where exactly in Suryapur the man lived, but she was certain people would know him. A merchant named Shantinath, a good man, with a good head for business. He had once been a partner of Sridhar Sahu's, when they were together in Agroha. Ratna had not heard of Shantinath ever since he had left Agroha for Suryapur many years ago. But he must still be in Suryapur, she thought; after all, if he had returned to Agroha, he would surely have stopped by in Dilli to visit Sridhar Sahu. Perhaps Sridhar Sahu had received news from him over the years. Letters, possibly. She did not know.

'She speaks highly of him and of his kindness,' Yogi Maiyya said. 'She is certain that if you go to him, even if you do not carry a letter of recommendation, he will do what he can to help you.'

'In any case,' added Balram, 'there is this to be said for Suryapur: it is very far from Dilli. If Sridhar Sahu ever came to know it was you, I doubt if he would think it worth his while to pursue you all the way to Suryapur.'

'It is so large and busy,' added Yogi Maiyya, 'that even if Shantinath cannot give you work, there will be others. You may have to work your way up, starting at the very bottom, but you have age on your side. And talent, and a desire to succeed.'

'And desperation,' agreed Madhav, with a sigh. 'Thank you, Yogi Maiyya. I will leave for Suryapur tomorrow.'

9

Six Years Later

Vikram Samwat 1260 (1204 CE)

The morning's worship at the Yogmaya Temple had just got over. Dozens of devotees emerged from the temple, holding brass or copper platters, their foreheads dabbed with sandalwood paste, their faces still aglow with the smug righteousness of the devout. At the end of the lane, the stream of dispersing worshippers divided into two. The majority of these took the path to the cluster of houses nearby. A few went the other way, towards the fort. The last man out of the temple, a thin, middle-aged one with a potbelly, was stopped as he set off towards the settlement.

'Babuji,' said the man who had accosted him. 'Can you tell me where Yogi Maiyya is? She used to have a food stall next to the temple, but I cannot see it any more.'

He was a young man, perhaps just a year or two above twenty. Lean, but not skinny, and with a pleasant face, even if it could not be called classically handsome. The older man regarded him with interest. 'Have you been away long?' he asked.

The other blinked, puzzled. 'Yes. I have returned to Yoginipur after six years. Why?'

'I thought as much.' The other man shook his head in regret. 'If Yogi Maiyya was a friend of yours, then I am sorry to have to break the news to you. She died two years ago.'

The young man's eyes widened, as if in dismay. Then: 'Would you happen to know if the girl who used to help her is still around? In Yoginipur?'

The man's face creased into a smile of affection. 'Subhadra? Yes, she is still there. She now runs the stall, though she's shifted it into one of the little lanes. On the other side of the temple.' He waved a hand to his left, gesturing towards a cluster of thatch-roofed huts flanking a narrow alley. 'She will not be there right now, though. She usually arrives about three hours before noon.'

The young man murmured his thanks. The other, obviously a householder eager to get back home, went his way. The man he left behind stood by himself for a few moments, wondering what to do. Then, since it would be stupid to return to the distant travellers' inn where he was lodged, only in order to return to this part of Yoginipur two hours later, he made his way towards the lane the man had pointed out.

He came awake, bleary-eyed and stiff-necked, briefly disoriented. The previous night had been a restless one and he had had to set off early to get to the temple in the morning. Sitting down to wait in the cool shade of a mango tree to while away the time had put him to sleep even before he had realized he was feeling drowsy. Now he sat up, rubbing the back of his neck, and looked about to see what had woken him. A sound, but what, he did not know.

Ankle bells, jingling as their wearer, hidden right now by the surrounding huts, came along the lane. The young man squinted up, looking at the sun, wondering what time it was.

Round the corner of a hut, its mud wall painted with two terracotta-red birds and a border of white triangles, came a woman. A young woman of about eighteen, dressed in a yellow sari. A glossy black plait swung about her hips, and her silver anklets jingled as she walked. A pail of water swung from one hand; the other clasped a couple of pots by their necks, and a bulky bundle hung from one shoulder.

The young man, who had risen to his feet, stared. The woman directed a fleeting glance at him as she walked on—the sort of glance one might give a passing dog, or a crow perched on a fence, devoid of anything approaching interest. And then suddenly, she stopped. Huge kohl-lined eyes stared at him. Her jaw dropped. 'Madhav?' she whispered, as if half scared that he was an apparition.

Madhav stared back. 'Subhadra?' he said. 'Subhadra.'

He had helped her carry her load and had gone to the nearby well to fetch more water before sitting down beside her at her stall. 'We can talk while you're preparing lunch,' he had said, when she threw a thousand questions at him, one after the other. 'We will have plenty of time to talk then. But if you don't get started now, you will have nothing to serve your customers.' He looked around. 'Can I do anything else to help?'

'Nothing. Sit beside me and tell me everything.'

She had changed, Madhav thought, even as he spoke. There were the physical changes, of course, which one would expect: when he had last seen her, she had been a girl, only just stepping into womanhood. Now she was a woman. And while not a beautiful one like the almost-forgotten Gayatri had been, a striking one nevertheless. Her mouth mobile, her eyes flashing, her form filled out, not angular and coltish. Her voice mellow.

But more than that, what had changed was her demeanour. If somebody had asked him what sort of woman he thought Subhadra would grow into, he would have described someone very different. Someone submissive, self-effacing, hard-working, quiet.

Of those qualities, the only one this woman possessed seemed to be the ability to work hard. Her hands flew as she chopped and sliced, stirred and kneaded and performed dozens of other tasks—all while listening to him. Interrupting him now and then with sharp questions. Why had he finally returned to Dilli? Where had he found employment all these years, and lucrative employment too, from the look of his clothes? And if he had done so well for himself, why had he not found the time to come even once to Dilli to see how they were?

'Surely there must have been one letter-writer, one courier

in Suryapur,' she remarked cuttingly when he told her of arriving in that city five months after he had left Dilli. 'One man who would have written two sentences on your behalf to say you had arrived safe and sound?'

'Who had the money to pay a letter-writer or a courier?' Madhav said with a sigh. 'I barely made it to Suryapur, as it was.' It had been a hard, arduous journey, one performed on foot for much of the way. Except when a passing bullock cart had stopped, the driver taking pity on the exhausted youth, enough to offer to take him the next yojana or so.

That had been all too rare an occasion. And since the handful of coins Balram and Yogi Maiyya had pressed on him when he was leaving had given out within the month, he had had to stop every time he came to a settlement where there was a chance of getting some work. Lifting and carrying loads, digging wells, weeding fields, harvesting crops. 'I did everything except carve stone,' Madhav remembered with a rueful smile.

Eventually, he had arrived in Suryapur, only to discover after a week's enquiries that though some merchants were acquainted with Shantinath of Agroha, they had no knowledge of where the man could be found. He was certainly not in Suryapur.

'Not in Suryapur?' Subhadra's eyebrows drew together in a frown. 'But Yogi Maiyya said Gayatri's mother had been quite certain. She would not have lied; I have met her several times and she is a good woman, not like that daughter—' she broke off in sudden consternation, and became very busy in picking through spinach she had just cleaned. Madhav watched her with a twinkle in his eyes, but he did not comment upon her mortification or press her to complete the sentence. Instead, he carried on speaking.

'Oh, he had lived in Suryapur for several months,' he agreed. 'That much was correct. But they told me it had never been his intention to settle in the city for good.'

It had taken much asking around to discover the truth.

Shantinath had gone back to Agroha. If Madhav wanted to meet him, he would have to go all the way to Agroha, ninety yojanas.

It made no sense to attempt the journey. Even with his still superficial knowledge of Suryapur, Madhav could tell that this was where he would get work. Even a stroll down a street was enough for him to see the many buildings being constructed, the palatial homes, the temples, the merchants' establishments. There was plenty of work here for a stone carver. Besides, it was not as if he had known Shantinath; it made no sense to go all the way to distant Agroha in his wake.

So Madhav had stayed on in Suryapur and gone looking for work. It took him some time to find work that suited him, but he was patient, and he was willing to do other jobs in the meantime, even tasks that required nothing more than willing hands and a strong back. Within a month, though, he had found work, at a mansion being built for the scion of a wealthy family.

'There was a lot of work,' Madhav said. 'A lot of carving.'

It had paid well, and it had brought him recognition, leading to more work. He did not say so, but Subhadra, looking at the unadorned but obviously fine clothes he wore, could tell that Madhav had done well for himself.

'And how have things been here?' he asked. Subhadra was making chapatis now, tossing each fresh chapati into a basket she had lined with cloth. Many chapatis, thought Madhav; more than he remembered Yogi Maiyya making. She must be doing brisk business.

Subhadra shrugged. 'You can see for yourself.' She worked on in silence for a while before adding, 'Balram Dada kept saying he would wait until you returned, but even he knew, I think, that he wouldn't last. The gods were merciful, at least he did not linger on and on. He died in his sleep one night. Slipped away quietly.' She flipped a chapati on the griddle, and went back to rolling out another on the round wooden board in front of her. 'With Yogi Maiyya, it was terrible. She slipped and fell during the rains, and broke a leg. The bone would not knit, and she took to her bed.' Her mouth twisted with remembered anguish. 'She never got up again, and by the end I was praying every day that the gods would put her out of her misery.'

Madhav murmured a few words of solace, and then, by way of consolation, added, 'You are carrying on her legacy. Doing well, too. You feed more people than Yogi Maiyya did, don't you?'

Subhadra flushed and shook her head, but she was smiling as she did so. 'They come here because it is convenient.'

'And they'll be coming soon,' Madhav murmured. 'Is that right? Around noon?'

Subhadra nodded. 'Yes. Why don't you sit here awhile? Eat something. Make friends. I will introduce you to people.'

Madhav shook his head. 'Not now,' he said as he rose to his feet. 'There is someone I need to meet.'

She glanced up at him, dismay written all over her face. 'Gayatri? You've returned to Dilli to meet her? She's married, Madhav. She's been married all these years.'

'To Nandu?' Madhav smiled briefly. Subhadra nodded, her eyes dull. 'I know, and do you know, I stopped caring a long time back.' He heaved a sigh. 'It was just the mindless infatuation of a boy, not real love. For all I know, she might not be a nice woman at all. If I had had my way, I might have ended up being utterly unhappy.'

Subhadra scowled. 'You do care. You're just trying to justify it to yourself.'

He laughed at that. 'No, Subhadra. Believe me, I do not love Gayatri any more. And she is not the person I've come to Dilli to meet.' He glanced down, past her. 'That chapati is burning.'

The man he went to meet was a moneylender, his place of business beside a cowshed. The smell of dung hung heavy on the air. Madhav ignored it and presented the letter he bore. He had already shown the letter to the clerk who sat just inside the doorway and following a whispered consultation between the clerk and the moneylender, had been allowed to present it to the moneylender. The moneylender had merely given him the benefit of a somewhat supercilious glance before extending a hand for the letter.

'Hmm,' he said, putting the letter on the sloping top of the low desk before him. He did not smile, but the bored contempt was gone from his face. 'Shantinath writes highly of you.'

Madhav inclined his head in acknowledgment of the compliment. 'He is kind.' If this man knew Shantinath, as Madhav was aware he did, he would know too that Shantinath was not an overly generous man. Upright and honest, yes, but not a believer in charity. He gave freely neither of his considerable wealth nor of his equally considerable influence. If he had written of Madhav in glowing terms, it was because he genuinely appreciated Madhav.

'I doubt it,' the moneylender said drily. 'He writes that I should give you as much money as you ask for. How much do you want?'

Madhav named a sum, and was privately amused to see the effect on the man. He looked perplexed. 'That is all? When did you arrive in Dilli? Are you staying with relatives, or friends?'

'I arrived last evening.' Madhav mentioned the location of the inn where he was staying. He admitted that he had nobody to call his own in Dilli; and, on the heels of that thought, came another: there was Subhadra, who had greeted him with all the warmth and familiarity of an old friend. But he had not asked her about herself. She must be married by now, she must be a wife and a mother.

He could not fathom why the thought should be so unappealing. A friend, after all; that was all she was, and why should he feel as if Subhadra's being married meant that he would, therefore, be deprived of her friendship? Surely Subhadra was large-hearted enough to give to all who had some right to her love and loyalty, whether they were husband or child or childhood friend.

The moneylender was saying something. Madhav turned back to him, blinking. 'What?'

'I said I will write a note for you. Give it to the clerk outside and take the money from him. When will Shantinath come to Dilli?'

'Perhaps in a week's time.'

The man nodded. 'What will you do in the meantime?' he asked, scribbling on a slip of paper. He tucked the note under the desk and opened one of the fat ledgers bound in red cloth that sat beside him on the mattress.

'I don't know,' Madhav said. 'Perhaps I shall go and have another look at the masjid. It had not been long ready when I was last in Dilli.'

The man closed the ledger and nodded approvingly. 'There is not only the mosque now, of course,' he said. 'With that stumpy tower now part of the scenery—that will interest you, I think, all that stone carving.'

Madhav had not the faintest idea what the man was talking of. He nodded, accepted the note with a murmur of thanks and went out to the clerk.

The small pouch of coins tucked into his waist, Madhav set off towards the mosque he had helped build. A tower, he wondered as he walked along. What for? Was it supposed to be an annexe to the mosque itself?

It was only when he drew closer, when the land fell away and the trees thinned, that he saw it. It was not tall; only about the same height as those grand sandstone screens they had carved for the mosque, but it was beautiful. The sandstone cladding was similar to that of the mosque in that it was a mosaic of colours, but this was more uniform. A paler shade of red here, a deeper one there. Almost terracotta dark in this one strip, a faded pink there. And here and there interspersed with cream or buff. But only sparsely.

Madhav walked slowly around it, looking up. Circumnavigated it in clockwise fashion, almost as if he were a devotee in a temple, careful to follow the prescribed path to complete the circuit. He smiled at the thought. This, next to the mosque, was almost certainly a religious structure of some sort. It would be unthinkable for a Hindu to think such things.

But it was lovely, from the alternating curved and angular contours of it to the bands of carving. The rows of flowers, the curving vines, the neat little garlands with their temple bells. He grinned this time, not even bothering to suppress the smile as he squinted up into the sunshine. It was ironic that he had been thinking of temples while walking round the base of the tower, and here it was, festooned in carved temple bells. He wondered if Aibak had even realized that they were supposed to be temple bells. Or had he known but not cared? Had he recognized their beauty for what it was and not bothered about any other meaning that could be ascribed to the design?

'Do you like it?'

Madhav turned. There was a man there, a worker by the looks of him, wiry, dark-skinned from years in the sun. Perhaps forty years old.

Madhav nodded. 'It is beautiful.' He reached out a hand, placing it on the warm stone that curved upward into a band of calligraphy in the strange letters of the invaders. Hardly invaders now, whispered a voice in his head. Aibak is well established in Dilli; he will not leave in a hurry. And these buildings are further proof of that.

'Did you work here?' he asked the man.

'I did. And I still do. This is not complete yet,' the man said. He pointed up. 'Look.'

Yes, he was right. Madhav had been too busy admiring the carving to notice that the crenellated upper edge of the tower was still incomplete. The rough masonry beneath the outer shell of carved stone was visible here, looking rather like lumps of stone embedded in a dried riverbed. That had to be finished, the outer layer of stone added, a roof put on top.

'You are not from hereabouts,' the man observed. 'I doubt if there is anybody in Yoginipur who has not seen this tower being built.'

Madhav inclined his head, agreeing that he was not from Dilli. He had been away long enough for it to seem very new to him, in any case. 'What is it supposed to be?' he asked. 'A tower for the mosque?'

The man shrugged. 'Who knows? They have not told us. We are here to mix the mortar, to bind stone with stone.' He scratched his armpit. 'If you ask me, I think it is Aibak's way of saying he is here to stay. After all, the mosque has managed well without a tower so far. The muezzin has called his people to prayer all these years without a tower to shout from.' He yawned. 'Why bother now?'

'A victory tower?' Madhav ventured. 'Though it's short for one.'

'Oh, he intends to raise it higher, I'm sure. We will have to wait and see.' The man stretched and changed the topic. 'Is this your first time in our city?'

'No; I lived here till some years back,' Madhav replied. 'But I was beginning to miss Dilli.' And how true that was. How much he had missed the handful of people he had grown to love, how much he had missed the city itself. He rested his palm on the warm stone, letting his fingertips wander gently over the fine carving.

The man was watching him narrowly. 'Are you a stone carver?' he asked suddenly.

'Why do you ask?'

The man shook his head. 'There is something in the way you touch the stone. I have seen that look only in the eyes of men who love the stone as only a carver can.' He paused. 'And those hands. Slips of the chisel and accidental hits from a hammer leave scars on hands that one rarely sees otherwise.' He grinned. 'And I have worked in close proximity to carvers for many years. Well? Are you one?'

Madhav dipped his head in silent acknowledgement. 'What of it?'

'You are very well-dressed for a stone carver,' the man observed. 'Which means you must have done well for yourself. Which means you are exceptionally talented. Of course,' he conceded, with a twinkle in his eye, 'it could also mean you are a thief by night and a stone carver by day, or that you married well. But I consider myself a good judge of character, and you do not look a thief. And which wealthy man would marry his daughter to a stone carver?'

Madhav bit back a smile. Yes, indeed. Which wealthy man would marry his daughter to a stone carver? It had been a futile dream and he, Madhav, had been young and foolish to let himself be deluded by the glamour of that dream. Of course, Nandu too, had been a stone carver, he reminded himself. And Nandu had married Gayatri. But that had been because Nandu was a very different man; Madhav could never be like him.

But he had been lucky too, more lucky than he could have imagined.

'Are you looking for work?' the man said. 'If you need it, you should go there,'—he pointed off to his left, beyond the arches of the mosque. 'The stone carvers do their work there. Their chief is Nandu. He will recognize a good man, I am sure.'

This time Madhav burst out laughing. He could not help it.

10

Subhadra turned to look over her shoulder when she heard footsteps. For a moment her eyes lit up, her face turning so radiant that it stopped Madhav in his tracks for a moment. 'Have you eaten?' she asked.

'Not yet. Is there any food left?'

'There is. I will set out a platter for you.'

The platter, a shallow copper one that she put down in front of him, came as a pleasant surprise. There, neatly arranged in little bowls, were all the foods he especially liked. The spinach cooked with ginger and peppercorns. Spiced chickpeas, yoghurt, sliced cucumbers. A heap of rice. A chapati, hot and fresh, gleaming with ghee.

'Eat,' Subhadra said. 'I'll make more chapatis.'

It was delicious, much better than anything Yogi Maiyya had ever cooked. The sweet, made from chickpea flour and sugar, was ghee-laden and fragrant with cardamom. Madhav finished it all, barely stopping to draw breath. When it was over and he had rinsed his hands, he sat back with a deep, happy sigh of satiation. 'Thank you, Subhadra,' he said. 'That is by far the best meal I have ever eaten in my life.' She looked embarrassed by his praise, so he went back to being the teasing friend of old. 'You must have a wealthy clientele indeed,' he said. 'And I can wager they have made you the wealthiest woman in Dilli. How much do you charge for that?'

Subhadra laughed. 'You think that is what I sell?' She was clearing up, scraping out leftovers from the pots and pans and putting them away into smaller dishes. 'Chickpeas and rice. That was what I made today. Plus chapatis for those who can afford it. The rest was for you.'

Subhadra stacked the empty pots and pans on one side, to be cleaned later. Rag in hand, she set about cleaning the wooden plank which acted as counter and table, as workbench and shelf.

Madhav reached out to take the rag from her. 'Give that to me, I can do it.'

She looked up into his face. 'You needn't feel obliged. I wanted to feed you; I wasn't hoping to be paid, in kind or otherwise. It just felt so good to be able to talk to a friend after so long.' There was a catch in her throat, and she turned away, scrubbing vigorously at the wooden plank.

'But surely—your husband?' Madhav blurted out.

The words had barely left his mouth when she turned on him, her eyes blazing. 'You think if I had a husband I would be sitting here cooking food for others? And cooking fancy food for another man? What—while my husband gallivants about, or lies on his back, snoring? Oh, you—what a fool you are!' She threw the rag at him, and with a sob of frustration, sprang to her feet and grabbed the battered old basket which served as dustbin.

Before Madhav could say anything, she was walking away, carrying the basket, heading for the nearest rubbish dump where she could empty it. Madhav had to run to catch up with her, and even then, by the time he reached her, she had already emptied the basket. She was wiping it out angrily with a couple of leaves torn from a nearby peepal tree. Madhav tried to take the basket from her, but Subhadra moved away, not willing to forgive him yet for his obtuseness. 'You don't need to help me,' she said curtly. 'I have managed on my own so far, I can manage now. I don't need you.'

Madhav stood, arms folded across his chest, and waited until she had finished. When she began walking back to her food stall, he asked, 'Why are you angry with me? Do you hold it against me that I went away? That I wasn't there when you were left alone, after Balram Dada and Yogi Maiyya died?'

Subhadra had reached her little kitchen. She put down

the basket and turned to him. 'I would be very childish to blame them for dying. And as for you—well, you had got yourself into a lot of trouble. There was no alternative, was there?'

'Then why are you angry?'

The end of her sari had been tucked in at her waist while she worked. Subhadra now freed it, and shook it out. Then, after she had used it to wipe her face, she straightened up and looked him in the eye. 'If you cannot fathom even that much, Madhav,' she said, 'you are as foolish and as blind as you were when you were sixteen years old.'

With that, she returned to her work, dismissing him without another look or a word. Madhav stood there for a moment before walking away. There was a ghost of a smile on his face as he went down the lane and past the Yogmaya Temple.

Madhav did not return to Subhadra's food stall the rest of the week. Instead, he went about Yoginipur, meeting this man and that. He carried letters of introduction to men as diverse as merchants, shopkeepers, masons, suppliers of building materials, and—on the last day—a government official. For this man, a foreigner like Qutbuddin Aibak, Madhav did not have a letter. Instead, one of the more influential merchants he had met accompanied him to the officer's quarters at the fort.

The conversation was brief but convoluted, since the officer spoke only very perfunctory Hindi. But the objective was met: the officer promised that on the next day that Qutbuddin Aibak set apart for a public audience, Madhav and another man would be allowed to present their petition.

'You're fortunate that Aibak is currently in Dilli,' the merchant said, when they had ended their conversation with the officer and were headed out. 'He rules, not from Dilli, but from Lahore. He just happens to be in Dilli these days.'

'We knew he would be here,' Madhav replied. 'Shantinathji has connections at the court in Lahore. He is kept informed.'

The merchant lifted an eyebrow. 'Why does Shantinath not then seek an audience in Lahore itself? Surely Shantinath can afford to go there, if it is so important? Since Aibak spends most of his time in Lahore, it would be so much simpler to present a petition there.'

Madhav grinned. 'There are reasons,' he said. 'Shantinathji will be here, in Dilli, and he would be grateful to be allowed to plead his case before the Sultan.'

When he had parted ways with the man, he sank into a reverie. Heading for the old baoli, he sat under the tree and stared out over the surface of the water. Over the six months since the monsoon, so much of the stepwell's water had either evaporated or been used up that only the lowest six steps were still submerged. The rest of the water was all gone, vanished.

It was something like that with him, he realized. When he had left Dilli, anger and resentment had festered in him, but it had evaporated, gone. He still wanted to help get justice done, but he did not seek anything else. After all, what did it matter if Sridhar Sahu had chosen Nandu to be his son-in-law? And what did it matter if Gayatri had panicked that day and caused such a furore that he had ended up fleeing the city? None of it mattered any more.

Much had changed in these last few years. He had grown up, not just physically, but emotionally too. He was less mercurial, more contemplative, he liked to think. A better judge of character. Or so he hoped.

If all went well, the following day would see the close of one chapter in his life and the start of another.

If all went well.

ꕥ

Aibak was not a large man, but he had considerable presence. Beneath the turban, hooded eyes looked watchfully out at the crowd gathered for the audience. The moustache, heavy and drooping, hid a firm mouth that spoke only occasionally, and then to ask a brief question or to pass an order. This was not a man given overly to talking; this was a man who kept his ears and eyes open, and noted all that went on around him. A dangerous man, thought Madhav.

Equally formidable seemed the officer who stood by Aibak's throne—or large chair, whatever one preferred to call it. His name, Madhav had heard, was Altamash. Like Aibak, he, too, had been sold into slavery and eventually bought by Muhammad of Ghur. And like Aibak, he had impressed the Ghurid ruler enough for him to elevate Altamash to a rank beyond any a slave would have dreamed of. Muhammad of Ghur had made Altamash his personal attendant, and had later sold him to Aibak. Aibak, who now depended upon Altamash to look after the Ghurid Empire's interests here in Dilli.

'A favourite,' murmured Shantinath, standing so close to Madhav that their shoulders brushed. 'A confidant and a trusted officer, and almost certain to be successor to Aibak as well.'

Before Madhav could say anything, he was interrupted. The courtier was announcing them, summoning them to come forth before the throne. Shantinath was bending, prostrating himself before the man seated just above them. Madhav followed suit and listened as the moneylender began to say how indebted he was to His Lordship for having condescended to—

Aibak growled something at a clerk standing beside him. A Hindu clerk, acting as interpreter, who had bent to whisper in the ruler's ear even as Shantinath began speaking.

'His Lordship would like you to get to the point,' the clerk said. His face, smooth and expressionless, was inscrutable. 'Please do not waste words.'

Shantinath flushed, taken aback. 'I—I see. It is,'—the unexpected admonition appeared to have flummoxed him, but he squared his shoulders and went on, now no longer prostrate, but kneeling.

'I have come with a complaint for which I beg redressal. Sixteen years ago, the man I was in partnership with stole all my money. While I was out of town, he embezzled the wealth I had entrusted to his care—' he was going deliberately slowly, pausing every now and then to allow the clerk to translate for the benefit of Aibak. Now, as the clerk fell silent and Aibak raised a hand, Shantinath looked up in apprehension.

'Sixteen years ago, His Lordship did not rule Dilli,' the clerk translated Aibak's brusque words.

Shantinath bent his head. 'True. But the man who wronged me is today answerable to His Lordship. I accuse Sridhar Sahu of having stolen from me. I have the evidence, too.'

ଓ

There were four men and a young boy sitting at Subhadra's food stall when Madhav arrived. The boy and two men were finishing their meals, but the other two appeared to have just begun. Subhadra was handing them fresh chapatis even as Madhav came into sight, but as soon as she saw him she abandoned her customers and came rushing out.

'Is it true? Is it really true, what they say? That Sridhar Sahuji had stolen money? Tell me, tell me!'

Madhav looked over her shoulder at the men, who were looking on with curiosity. 'Your customers look as if they would like to hear the story too,' he said with a grin.

'They can hear it tomorrow,' she snapped. 'When the entire town knows every detail.' She bit her lip. 'I suppose I had better go and attend to them. It won't take long. Shall I get you something to eat? Yes? Sit, then.'

When he had finished eating, and when the last of the other patrons had gone—having waited with ill-disguised impatience to eavesdrop on whatever Madhav might have to say—he told her the entire story. Of how Shantinath, about sixteen years earlier, had returned to Agroha after four months in Suryapur, only to find that in the time he had been away, Sridhar Sahu had shifted to Suryapur—or that was what everybody had been told. And not Sridhar Sahu alone; he had, to everybody's surprise, taken his family and all his worldly belongings. Those belongings, as Shantinath soon discovered, included the shared profits of the two partners.

'Shantinath wrote to his friends in Suryapur, asking about Sridhar Sahu,' Madhav said. 'But of course, nobody knew of him there, and Shantinath soon realized that he had no way of knowing where Sridhar Sahu had gone.'

Shantinath had made good money during his brief tenure in Suryapur, but it would not last forever; he had to get back to his family and home in Agroha, and build up again the business his partner had ruined. So, cursing and vowing vengeance, Shantinath set about trying to recoup his losses.

'A year ago, however, he came to Suryapur on work,' Madhav said. 'And since I had made the acquaintance of several merchants and moneylenders who knew him too, I was soon informed that the man I had asked for six years ago on my arrival in Suryapur was back, visiting the city.'

So even though Madhav no longer needed Shantinath's help or his recommendations, out of simple courtesy—and a shrewd realization that it was useful to form connections with influential people—he had gone to meet Shantinath. By way of an introduction, he had mentioned how he had come to learn of Shantinath. And thus, through an odd twist of fate, a coincidence no one would have imagined, the truth emerged.

Shantinath had set about immediately planning his exposure of the man's misdeeds. 'He went to the keepers of the law in Suryapur,' Madhav explained. 'He had, after all, complained all those years back about Sridhar Sahu. He had even written a letter to the chief officer of the law. He got that out, with the officer's own seal and signature on it as proof of receipt. And he got letters as proof from all his friends and associates in Suryapur, testifying to his quest for Sridhar Sahu. These past two months he has been in Agroha, gathering more evidence to prove his accusation.'

'Which he has achieved?'

Madhav nodded. 'Aibak initially refused to believe it, but his man, Altamash, intervened. He was the one who advised Aibak, I think, to at least examine the evidence Shantinath offered.'

So Aibak had called for the sheaf of letters and scrolls that Shantinath had brought with him. There and then, with a soldier sent in the meantime to fetch Sridhar Sahu, Aibak got his clerk to interpret each document and read it out aloud. By the time an unsuspecting Sridhar Sahu came striding into a now-crowded court, Aibak knew it all.

The proof was damning, and the very sight of Shantinath came as such a bolt out of the blue for Sridhar Sahu that he was unnerved to begin with. He attempted to deny it all, but there was little conviction in his words. And those papers pointed to Shantinath's long and arduous quest to find the man who had run off with his hard-earned money. Sridhar Sahu tried to say he was not the same man and that he did not recognize Shantinath; his face said otherwise. He denied having appropriated the money; the letters proved him wrong.

And there was too, the fact that pretty much everybody in Dilli knew of Sridhar Sahu's power and wealth. There was no denying this man's prosperity; Aibak himself could have borne testimony to it. Where that wealth came from, and why it had always been, in Dilli, so much more than Sridhar Sahu had possessed in Agroha: these were questions it was not difficult to answer once the damning evidence had been presented.

'So there it was,' Madhav said. 'Aibak could not but believe it. Sridhar Sahu has been imprisoned and will be further—um—questioned, I suppose.'

'Tortured, you mean.'

Madhav shrugged expressively.

'What of Shantinath?'

'Aibak has promised him compensation if his accusations are proved correct.'

'And what will that compensation be?'

'How can I say? That is for Aibak to decide.'

Subhadra said nothing. For once, she was not working; Madhav's news was momentous enough for her to have set aside her work for later. She had sat through his narration of all that had happened, listening with undivided attention. Even now, with his tale over, she sat still, her hands in her lap.

'Aibak will be a fool if he keeps on as servant someone who is a proven thief,' she said after a moment.

'Not necessarily a fool. He is certain to realize that if he pardons Sridhar Sahu—and that for a wrong done to another man, not to Aibak himself—Sridhar Sahu will be indebted to him for life. He would then do anything for Aibak or his kin.' He noticed a fly hovering near Subhadra's hair, and reached across to shoo it away. 'And as long as Shantinath gets his compensation, I don't suppose he will care much whether Sridhar Sahu is driven out of Dilli, made to beg in the city's streets, or retains his post under Aibak.'

'Does Shantinath not intend to stay on in Dilli then?'

Madhav shook his head. 'He is happy in Agroha. That is where his family is, that is where his business is.'

'And you, Madhav?' The fly was back, and Madhav again lifted his hand to swipe at it. To his surprise, Subhadra lifted her own hand and caught his, lowering it so that she could enfold his hand between both of her own. She looked up into his face, her eyes large and expressive. There was a lurking apprehension in them, a shyness—and paradoxically, a boldness too. 'What about you, Madhav?' she said softly. 'Where are you happy? Where is your home?'

For a long moment, Madhav said nothing. Her hands

were warm. Not the soft hands of a pampered beauty like Gayatri, but the calloused, strong hands of a hard-working, independent woman with a mind of her own. These were hands that could hold a man, uphold him and be by his side. The hands of a companion, a friend.

'Not in the village where I was born,' Madhav said. 'Not in Suryapur, which I never really loved.'

She waited.

'What do you think, Subhadra?' he asked. 'Do you think Dilli would be a good place for me to spend the rest of my life? Would I find friends here, do you think? A wife?'

Subhadra laughed, the sound so joyous and light-hearted that it made him thrill just to hear her.

'What do you think?' she said.

Interlude

'Trust a woman to introduce a romance into the story.'

Shagufta, her throat aching and dry, frowned at the man. He was grinning, his lips curving up attractively at the corners, his eyes crinkling. If he had not been so badly injured, if he had not been an enemy soldier ... she shook her head, shaking off the thought. Instead, she reached for the cup of water and sipped from it, sighing with relief at the soothing coolness of it.

'You are derisive of love?' she asked, when she put the cup down. Her throat was feeling better, but she was irritable. Tired, sleepy, hungry, and painfully aware that there was very little to eat at home. If she had to cook, she would first have to go out and find fuel. Wood or cow dung. And then the lighting of the fire—she could not do it inside here; that would be suicidal. But outside? Outside, where anybody could see the smoke, smell it, see that here was a survivor? She abandoned the idea. The parched gram was still there. And if she slunk out, she might find some more peelu.

She wondered if she dared enter one of the homes, their front doors burst open, that she had seen. Surely the raiders could not have carried away every single thing that was edible? Somewhere, she might find foodstuffs left behind. A handful of jaggery, perhaps. Some nuts, or dried fruit.

The man was saying something. She looked at him, and her abstraction must have been mirrored in her face, because with a sigh of disgust he said, 'You ask a question, and then you do not even bother to listen to the answer.' He looked away.

It was not as if he was her lover, or a husband. Or a son, a brother, a father, any man she may feel obliged to coax and wheedle, even if only a little. Just a stranger she had brought in. Why, even she did not know. Perhaps because she had seen him lying in the street, clasping his bleeding waist—where the arrow had entered—and still mouthing curses at whichever companion had left him there. Or whoever had shot that arrow into him, or slashed at his legs with a sword. She had not understood his words, but his determination had reminded her of Ibrahim. There had also been something about his face that had brought to mind the thought of Ibrahim.

Perhaps that was why she had stopped in her mad run homewards to approach him. To bend and peer cautiously at him. To wonder if this man, now hovering on the brink of consciousness, would kill her as soon as he was fully awake. She had straightened up, looked around, her gaze sweeping the street. Nobody was in sight—or nobody alive, at any rate. Nobody would see her if she helped this man. Nobody would brand her a traitor. Nobody would know what Shagufta had done.

And the realization that there was nobody, probably not even hiding in any of the nearby houses, had helped her decide. She was being foolish, she had thought, even as she dragged the man to her home.

'You're an odd woman,' he said. The half-scornful grin of a minute earlier had gone, replaced by puzzlement. 'You suddenly shrink into yourself, as if you're going away somewhere, within yourself. What is the matter?'

Shagufta rose to her feet, her knees stiff. 'I'm going out to see if I can find something to eat,' she said. 'Do you want anything before I go? I don't know how long I will be gone. I could be back in a few minutes, or'—she swallowed—'or, who knows? Maybe I will never return.'

'You had those fruit earlier. Those pungent things. Do you not have more of them? Or anything else?'

She shook her head. 'A little parched gram. It would not be enough for both of us. And whatever else there is, would need cooking, but I dare not light a fire.'

The man shifted, grimacing as he did so. 'My things,' he said, looking about him. 'My weapons? Did you find anything with me? My coat? There was a pocket, with some odds and ends in it. Food.' He lay back, the brief spell of talking eroding his strength. 'See if you can find it.'

Odds and ends, she thought as she rummaged with some impatience through the bundle of bloodstained clothing she had dumped in the corner. The coat stank of sweat and was splotched with old blood. But yes, there was the pocket. Quickly, Shagufta turned it out into her lap.

They had come prepared for a long and arduous campaign; the amount of food this man had carried on him made her stomach growl and her eyes widen. Almonds, walnuts, raisins, dried figs. Dates. Dried apricots. Some roasted grain she did not recognize.

'Why did you not tell me?' she snapped at him, turning back, showing him handfuls of what she had found. 'Why? Why did you let me go out? If you had told me—'and then, before he could answer, she sank onto her knees and began stuffing raisins into her mouth, gobbling them as if terrified that he would take them away. And, when her mouth was full, her cheeks ballooned up, she suddenly burst out crying.

'My mind had stopped working,' he said, in a soft voice, when she had straightened up and gathered the sticky remains of the raisins that had spilled from her mouth onto her clothing. Shagufta hurriedly pushed the bits and pieces into her mouth, not bothering what he thought. He was looking on, his eyes surprisingly gentle. Pity, she thought. He pities me, this woman so poor she scrabbles like a starving animal at anything that comes her way.

She turned away, her cheeks flushed.

'Will you not give me some? I am hungry as well.'

'It was not a romance,' she said defensively, when she had sat down and placed the food in front of him. She had brought out a wooden platter, somewhat scratched and worn, but whole. On it, carefully rationed, she laid out the nuts and the dried fruit. The rest of the food she kept safely away. 'It was a story of how someone went from being a poor farmer's son in an unknown village to one of Dilli's most respected stone carvers.'

The man looked amused. 'Just because he inadvertently met up with that wronged merchant in that city—that city with that convoluted name?'

'Suryapur. And Shantinath.' She shook her head. 'No. That was coincidence. Pure luck. But then some might say that it was the working of God. That God wanted it so.'

'Allah wanted,' the man said, his voice hard.

'I am talking of people who are Hindus.'

'But you are no Hindu. Why must you talk as if you acknowledge the presence of a Hindu god? They are infidels. All that is there in their destiny is hell.'

'So you say,' Shagufta snapped back. She was about to tell him the truth, but she bit back the words. There was no need for it, and he would not understand. She wondered if he understood even what she had said thus far. 'Let it be,' she said, quietly. 'Eat.'

He ate in silence, his head and shoulders propped up on a rolled-up sack that she had shoved under him. His fingers dipped into the nuts and fruit on the plate, slowly but surely diminishing the paltry heaps. Shagufta watched with resentment, and then felt guilty for that resentment. It was, after all, his food. And if she had not dragged him in and sheltered him in her house, this would not have come her way. She would be out there, amidst the corpses and the debris of three days of pillaging, looking for things to eat.

'Water,' said the man. 'This makes me thirsty.'

She gave him water, and when he had settled down again he said, 'So what happened then? Finish your story.'

She was still annoyed at him. 'What else is there? I have told you what I know.' She took back the cup from him and wiped it. He remained silent, watching her as she leaned across to place the cup upside down on the mouth of the earthen water pot. When she had finished, she wrapped her shawl more closely about her. It was cold, so cold. And all her blankets she had sacrificed for him. But surely there was a quilt around here somewhere? Shagufta frowned, trying to remember if she had thrown it out, that quilt which Ibrahim had been using ... she got up briskly and went to the far end of the room to look in the things piled up there.

'Just like that?' he asked. 'Just like that, you say your story is over? In the middle of something?'

The gumption. It was her story; she could decree it over when she wished. But Shagufta, despite her annoyance, said, 'In the middle? Of course not. Sridhar Sahu got his just deserts. Shantinath, though he did not stay on in Dilli, was able to recommend Madhav highly enough for him to get immediate employment at the site where Aibak was building his palace, the Kasr Safed. Madhav and Subhadra got married and had six children.'

She had found the quilt. It smelt old and musty, of things she would rather not remember. A good bit of its stuffing had leaked out from a huge rent in it, and what remained was all in lumps scattered across the two layers of cloth that made up the quilt. But, hefting it in her arms, she could tell that it would still warm her far better than her shawl could.

'That is it,' she added. 'The story is over.' She suppressed a little yelp of triumph as she unearthed an old scrap of thick cloth: it was smelly and dusty, but it would do to mend the hole in the quilt.

'Well, tell me another then,' he said. He sounded peevish, and Shagufta smiled to herself. And peevish he should be, she thought. It served him right. She had taken care of him these past few days, giving up her own sleep, her own comfort, even the safety of her own home to venture out, all for him. Her sore throat, her aching back and stiff legs—all the result of sitting still all this while, droning on and on—and had he been grateful? No.

She should mend the quilt. But a perverse urge to irritate

him, to make him realize that he should be grateful for all that she had given up for him, made her decide to do that later. She folded the ragged quilt in half so that its hole was hidden inside, and then lay down with it over her. 'I have been talking all day. And I did not sleep last night either,' she said. 'I'm going to sleep.' And with that, without saying goodnight, without asking him if he needed anything, she blew out the flickering wick of the little earthen bowl of oil in the corner.

In the dark she heard him say, 'You are being petty. And I am wide awake.'

Shagufta made a face and turned over on to her side.

☙

She came awake to odd sounds: a thudding and then a sizzling. Her eyelids felt so heavy, her body so weighed down and tired, she did not stir, did not even open her eyes.

Her senses sharpened as she slowly woke. She could hear heavy breathing, punctuated by an odd rattling, rasping noise. The sound of a man in pain. Past the mustiness came another smell—the smell of burning oil.

With a muffled curse, she threw off the quilt and peered out.

The man was sitting up, his back against the wall. One leg was stretched out, hairy and bare up to mid-thigh. She could see the worst of his wounds just above his knee, the size of her palm, the flesh cut so badly that she had had to pack it with whatever herbs and ashes she could find before bandaging it and muttering a prayer. A prayer that she herself had only half-believed; the wound looked very bad even to her unknowing eyes.

Beside him burned the lamp she had put out the previous night. He had relit it and was holding the blade of his dagger over it. Moving it back and forth, holding it so that the flame licked at the steel.

She guessed what he had been doing, but she could not

stop herself from exclaiming, 'What are you doing!' as she scrambled up.

'Cauterizing the wound,' the man said, without looking at her. All his attention was focused on the blade in his hand, heating up slowly in the inadequate flame. 'A wound that deep should have been cauterized hours before. I was too weak to even realize'—he lifted the blade, peered at it, and lowered it again to the flame—'that it was so bad.'

She felt a little guilty. She should have known enough to cauterize the wound. She even remembered peering anxiously at it, looking for signs of festering, for oozing pus and dead flesh, while he had lain unconscious. But she could not summon up the courage to do what she hoped would not need doing. She had tried to reassure herself that the herbs and the hot water with which she soaked the cloth to dab at the wound would do their work.

'Hot enough, I think,' said the man, as he lifted the blade from the flame. A ghost of a smile hovered about his lips, but she could see the strain in his face. The next moment, even as she watched with horrified eyes, he pressed the flat side of the blade down on the wound. The smile changed to a grimace, his teeth showing, his eyes squeezed shut in agony. A moment, or an eternity—and then he dropped the blade. The smell rose in the air, acrid and nauseating.

How terrible, thought Shagufta, that the smell of charred meat could be so appetizing if one knew that it was an animal, a goat perhaps, that was being prepared for food. Now that she knew that a man's flesh, cauterized, smelt the same, the very memory of cooked meat made her stomach churn. She would turn vegetarian perhaps, and never eat flesh again.

He collapsed against the wall, his face streaming sweat despite the chill. Shagufta hurried to him, to draw away the lamp and extinguish it, to move the dagger away and to cover his leg. As she rolled a fresh length of clean cloth around his thigh, he moaned.

'You bore so much,' she said quietly, 'and yet you flinch at my bandaging of your wound? And I know I cannot possibly be any gentler.'

She did not look up, concentrating instead on her task. But she heard the grating laugh, combined with an underlying hiss of pain. 'Another's fingers cause more pain, do you not know?' he grunted. 'With yourself, you know how much you can bear, and where the pain is worst.' A low chuckle followed. 'Rather like the heart itself, is it not? Others can inflict far greater pain than one can on oneself.'

She had finished. She drew away, sat back on her haunches and looked into the pale, drawn face of the man. This was the longest she had heard him speak. It seemed hard indeed, to remember that till the night before last he had not said anything. That he had been unconscious before then.

'What is your name?' she asked.

He blinked, surprised at the suddenness of the question. 'Why do you ask?'

'Who are you?' she repeated. 'A soldier? A philosopher? Or a little bit of both? You reveal so much of yourself with just a few words, yet you wonder why I should want to know your name?'

His expression changed from one of faint suspicion to one of amusement. 'Why should you need to know my name? So that if I die here today you will know what to write on my gravestone?' He saw the fleeting look of hurt in her eyes and softened his tone. 'I did not mean to offend you. Nasiruddin. That is my name.'

Shagufta could not prevent the laugh that burst from her.

'What amuses you so? Is it a name that means something vile in the local tongue?'

She shook her head. 'Not if you consider the Sultan to be vile.' She grinned. 'And many do. Sultan Nasiruddin Mahmood Shah Tughlaq is a weakling, they say.'

The man guffawed. 'That is ironic indeed. So your Sultan bears my name? Who would have thought.' He shook his head, his mood changing to one of bitterness, regret. 'They told us nothing, you know. Just what was absolutely necessary. Our generals, our commanders, our captains, they knew. We only knew we were headed for Dilli. Not who ruled the city, nor what the city was like.'

You are as changeable as a day in the monsoon, Shagufta thought. Sunny one moment, grey the next. But she did not say anything. She was like that too, she knew. Temperamental. Emotional. She had no right to accuse the man of those shortcomings, if shortcomings they were. She had never thought of them as such.

'And I still do not know,' he said. 'We saw some buildings, but it is all a blur now.' He stretched out his leg, wincing as he did so. 'But now that you tell me this story about the mosque that Sultan—Aibak?—commissioned. Yes. I remember seeing that. It was impressive. I remember the tower too.' His eyes narrowed. 'In your story you said it was stumpy, only a storey high.'

Shagufta had been searching through a tattered wicker basket she kept in a small niche at the back of the room. She had found a needle, somewhat rusted but still sharp, and some thread. This would do to mend the quilt. She fetched the cloth she had found the previous night to mend the hole, and sat down with it and the quilt. Having threaded the needle, she began work. One short straight stitch after another, binding the cloth to the edges of the hole.

'Did it not occur to you,' she said, 'that storeys may have been added to the tower? Aibak ruled two hundred years ago.'

'So Aibak added to his tower,' he said after a while. 'The tower is a good testament to his victory.'

Shagufta shook her head. 'No. Aibak died before he could add even one more storey to the original one he had built.'

'Then?' he asked. 'His son? His successor?'

'His successor, yes. His son, no. Altamash.'

'Ah. The man who was in attendance when that moneylender's thievery was exposed?'

Shagufta nodded. 'Two years after Shantinath accused Sridhar Sahu, Muhammad of Ghur was killed. Qutbuddin Aibak had been his slave, of course, and the death of Muhammad meant that Aibak was quickly able to attain his freedom. He became the first Sultan of Dilli. In name, not merely in fact.'

'You seem to know your history well,' the man commented. His tone was neutral; she could not tell whether he said it in praise or in derision.

'It is the history of my city,' she replied. 'And my family has lived in this city for the past two hundred years. We are tied to Dilli.'

There was silence for a while, broken only by the persistent whining of a dog somewhere outside. Perhaps it was hurt. Or hungry. But no, she thought, with all those corpses lying about, why would a dog go hungry? Shagufta felt a rush of bile to her throat and straightened up suddenly, her work forgotten.

'What is it? Do you not feel well?'

She did not answer him immediately. She had flung aside the needle and was too busy drawing in deep breaths, pressing her fingertips to her temples, trying to push away what lay outside these four walls.

'Allah! What is the matter with you?'

'Nothing, nothing.' She squeezed her eyes shut, gulped. 'Something came into my mind. Made me feel sick.' She swallowed, opened her eyes. 'It is all right.'

He was staring at her, his gaze disconcertingly penetrating. 'This must frighten you,' he said, his voice a mere murmur. 'This invasion. The loneliness. At least people with families have each other. You are all alone.'

Shagufta had picked up her needle again. 'Perhaps there is an advantage in being alone,' she remarked. 'One is spared the worry. I need worry only about myself.' She shook her head. 'And I have learnt not to worry overly about myself. What is the worst that can happen, after all?' She looked up. 'Shall I tell you a story? A different one?' She shook her head in the very next moment. 'Or not completely.'

'Not completely a story? Or not completely different?'

'Not completely different. But that you shall see for yourself.' She held up the needle, tugging at a snarl in the thread, pulling at it with growing impatience until it finally snapped. With a sigh, she removed the useless thread and found more to push through the eye of the needle. 'This is the story of Jayshree and her best friend,' she said.

11

Twenty-one Years Later
Vikram Samwat 1281 (1225 CE)

Jayshree's father brought home the third matchmaker on the day Jayshree turned fourteen.

The first matchmaker had been ushered in with much joy and anticipation after a twelve-year-old Jayshree, having bled embarrassingly and alone for a miserable four days in a tiny room away from the main body of the house, had been declared a woman. A woman, ready to be married. A woman, as her father realized to his consternation after she had fled into the mango orchard behind the house, who refused to be married.

'Let her be,' Jayshree's mother said, preferring the path of patience and cajoling to coercion. 'It will take time for her to get used to the idea. Some girls are like that.' She was comfortably secure in the belief that it was just a matter of time, and so, with some grumbling, her husband gave in. In any case, short of tying his daughter down and forcing her into the marriage, there was little he could do. Jayshree, even at twelve, was not a girl you could push into something she did not wish to do.

A year later, on her thirteenth birthday, another matchmaker, a pandit, was brought home. This time, Jayshree's mother advised her husband to use cunning. Have the horoscopes matched, settle on the dowry, and then, only when there was no going back, tell Jayshree. Headstrong as she was, even Jayshree would know better than to do something that would utterly destroy her family's honour.

They had not imagined that Jayshree would overhear her mother and their old cook discussing what would appeal to the palate of a pandit. She heard them weighing the merits and demerits of kheer and laddoos, fruit and savouries, wondering what would appeal to Panditji. And since there were no festivals, no funerals, and no religious ceremonies planned for any reason she could think of, Jayshree came to the conclusion that Panditji was coming for some reason that was being hidden from her. She guessed what it was, and so on the auspicious day, when the pandit arrived, she burst into the room just as her father was beginning to press laddoos on the man. 'I do not wish to marry,' she said, standing on the threshold, clutching the carved wooden doorpost. 'Not right now. Please.'

Her father threw her out, but the damage was done. The pandit thought the girl shrewish and obstreperous. Who would marry one such as this? He did not wish to go about recommending a girl such as this, no matter how beautiful she was. A woman should be like a pomegranate, he said, waxing eloquent. Even if she was beautiful on the outside, what really mattered was what lay inside, beneath the shell.

He had gone, but Jayshree asked her mother that day, 'Ma, must you be in such a hurry to marry me off? I do not wish to go away so soon.'

'You are our only child,' her mother said. 'Your father fears for you. What if something should happen to him, and you are left all alone? We will not live forever, Jayshree, your father and I.'

'Not forever, Ma,' Jayshree said in that blunt way of hers that had stopped shocking her mother a long time ago. 'Just another three years? Four?' She looked up at the sky, at the vastness of it, stretching to the far horizons. 'There is so much to be seen, so much to be experienced, Ma,' she added in a dreamy voice. 'If I get married now, I will end up like you. Tied to home and hearth, with only my husband and my children for company. That may suit you, but I do not want it, not now.'

Her mother tried to reason with her—this was too shocking a statement, even for Jayshree—but to no avail. Jayshree had shaken her head, stubborn till the end. 'No,

Ma,' she said with an air of finality. 'Not now. And I warn you, if Baba tries to force me into getting married, I will say no. I will run away, I will not care about his honour or anything.'

Which was why that day, when her father brought the third matchmaker home, Jayshree's mother drew her husband aside and told him what their daughter had said. When he scoffed, she heaved a deep sigh and said, 'If I were you, I would not go against her wishes. She will do just as she pleases, no matter what. And surely we can wait another three years? It will not be much.' She knew, as did her husband, that people would laugh at their having a seventeen-year-old daughter still unmarried. But who did not already laugh? Jayshree, hot-headed and impetuous, had long been sniggered at or scolded.

And Jayshree celebrated her fourteenth birthday by climbing the tallest tree in the mango orchard. She picked six of the ripest, most fragrant mangoes she could find, bundled them up in her odhni and walked off alone to her favourite place in Yoginipur.

Qutbuddin Aibak had died fifteen years before, following an accident on the polo field. He had been buried not in Dilli, but in faraway Lahore—Jayshree had only heard of it; she could not imagine what it was like. She had no interest in it, either. Not in Lahore, not in Aibak, not even in Altamash, who had, after a gap of a few months, been crowned the Sultan of Dilli.

When her parents talked of the days of their youth, they often said how strange that word, Sultan, had sounded in the beginning. So foreign, so unfamiliar. Like the men themselves, who had swept into Dilli and taken over the city. How difficult it had been to adjust to these new rulers, these outsiders with their alien ways and alien religion. Jayshree knew that her parents, like many others of their generation, had still not adjusted.

But Jayshree had grown up with this, and she accepted

it. Besides, the world of politics and state and rulers was not her world. Hers was a world of stolen mangoes, of solitary walks under the trees. Of defying her parents' attempts to get her married. Of sneering at the neighbourhood girls who, with bovine docility, did exactly as society had trained them to do.

Jayshree smiled as she looked up, beyond the trees, at the carved stone screens of the Jami Masjid. Such a beautiful building, she had thought after her very first glimpse of it. Her father had brought her here, he said, when she was two years old. Her words had only just begun to make sense, but her happy laughter and the way she had raced to the carvings, touching them, clapping her little hands—'You liked them, I could see that,' he said.

And she liked them still. Loved them. She came here every few days, drawn to the beauty of the place. It did not matter that her mother disapproved. It did not matter that people thought her half mad to spend hours wandering around, touching the carved stone with something close to veneration, trailing her fingers along the smooth curves and sharp angles of the Qutb Minar.

She sat under a fig tree and began to unwrap the mangoes. The old fig tree was a giant, its bole huge and gnarled, its leaves a thick, glossy green. Somewhere far above, a woodpecker pecked industriously at the tree trunk, its staccato pounding the only sound in the still air.

Jayshree chose with special care the plumpest of the mangoes, its thin skin a uniform yellow. Rolling it between her palms, she softened it further. Lifted it to her nose and inhaled the fragrance of it. The smell of summer, the luscious richness of the best fruit in the world.

Jayshree lifted the mango to her mouth, bit off the little stump of stalk that remained and spat it out. She pressed, squeezing the mango, sucking.

The calm was shattered by a sudden flurry of shouts right behind her. And about her, around and above and behind, and seemingly below. A body slammed into her, throwing her off her perch on one of the thick above-ground roots of the tree. The mango went flying, Jayshree fell against the tree trunk and for the next few moments, there was utter pandemonium. There was dust, loud screaming, the banging of a stout stick against the ground.

Jayshree looked up, dazed and livid, into the face of a slim young man who stood beside the tree, holding a sturdy stick as tall as himself. His turban was half unravelled, and he was heaving deep breaths.

Jayshree scrambled to her feet, dusty and with her odhni torn. Her back hurt and one elbow was bleeding, but she was too angry to care. 'How dare you!' she began, but before she could proceed any further, the youth lifted a hand in a gesture of silence. At the same time, the stick in his hand swept down, sideways and up. From the end of it dangled a snake: sinuous, lethal-looking, and dead, its head bashed to a bloody pulp.

'A simple word of thanks will do,' said the young man in a dry voice. An oddly high voice. Jayshree shifted her gaze from the dead snake to her rescuer's face. Her eyes widened.

'You're a woman.'

'And you're observant.' The woman flung the snake aside and, bending to gather some fallen leaves, used them to wipe off her bloodied stick. A lithe woman, slim-hipped and none too buxom. But a woman nevertheless, if one looked closely. It was there in her features, too feminine to be a man's. And it had been there in the brief glimpse that Jayshree had seen of a tunic stretched taut beneath a cloak swinging open as the woman had lifted the stick with its serpentine trophy held aloft.

Jayshree watched, fascinated, pressing her odhni to her bleeding arm.

'Have you nothing better to do than stare?'

Jayshree flushed and took refuge in attack. 'And who would not stare, pray, at a woman dressed as a man?'

'What is wrong with how I am dressed? These skirts and veils and whatnot'—a tilt of her chin indicated Jayshree's attire—'they come in the way. Just look at you. Falling all over the place, tripping over your clothes. If I hadn't happened to come by, you'd have been lying here, turning blue and foaming at the mouth.' She had finished wiping her stick and leaned the weapon against the tree before dusting her hands on her baggy trousers and asking, 'What were you doing? Just sitting and sucking on mangoes?'

'It's as good a way of passing the time as going about dressed in outlandish clothes and beating the bushes for wildlife,' Jayshree retorted. For a moment the woman looked as if she was going to flare up again, but then, unexpectedly, she let out a loud chuckle. 'You are more feisty than you look,' she remarked.

Jayshree was intrigued. 'Who are you?'

One eyebrow tilted up, in a gesture that indicated curiosity as well as a hint of suspicion. 'Why?'

'It is not every day that I come across a woman dressed as a man,' Jayshree replied. 'Especially not a Muslim woman.' Yes, that much she had guessed, that this woman was one of those who had come with Aibak. Or, given that she was perhaps only a few years older than Jayshree, one whose parents had made their way to Dilli with Aibak. The skin, so much fairer than Jayshree's own. The eyes, brown. The hair, not the deep rich black Jayshree was familiar with, but a lighter, browner hue. Most of all, the features, the set of which was different from her own.

And her clothes, from the tunic to the loose trousers, to the boots: all so different from the combination of dhoti, shawl and sandals favoured by the Hindus. Even the way the turban was tied was different.

The woman smiled, her eyes twinkling in appreciation. 'You are not as stupid as you first appeared,' she murmured.

Jayshree frowned at the insult, but persisted. 'Well then? Who are you?'

'In what way? Who are my parents? Where do I live? What do I like to do when I'm not saving fools?'

She was incorrigible. Jayshree whirled around and walked away, calling over her shoulder as she went, 'It wasn't even a dangerous snake!'

She walked on, towards the Jami Masjid, aching with curiosity all the while.

'Jalaluddin,' called out a voice behind her. 'Jalal.'

Jayshree stopped and turned. The woman, her stick now clutched loosely in one hand, was walking towards her.

'Jalal?' Jayshree asked, when the woman came up to her. She frowned, bewildered. 'I do not know much,' she confessed, 'but I always thought Jalaluddin was a man's name.'

'Do you not think it suitable for a woman who dresses as a man?' The woman grinned, but this time her smile was free of sarcasm. 'It means "glory of the faith". Jalal means "glory",' she added.

'And you,' said Jayshree after a moment, looking the woman up and down, 'are the supposed glory of the faith? Your parents must have had high expectations of you.'

The woman's gaze shifted to the tall carved screens of the Jami Masjid beyond them. Jayshree, watching her intently, wondered what the woman was thinking. That gaze was difficult to interpret. Was there yearning in it? Fear? Or was she simply daydreaming?

'I suppose so,' Jalal said. Then, with what Jayshree would come to recognize as her way of getting out of conversations she did not enjoy, her new friend dismissed the topic by peremptorily introducing one of her own. 'What did you do with the rest of your mangoes? Left them scattered in the dust under the tree, didn't you? For the birds and the squirrels to feast on?' She glanced back at the tree, then grinned at Jayshree. 'Shall we go find the rest? I could do with a mango or two. I deserve it, do I not? Even if the snake wasn't dangerous.'

And so they got to know each other, Jayshree and this strange woman named Jalal.

She was twenty years old. A good six years older than Jayshree, though she did not look it. She looked perhaps sixteen, at the most seventeen. But that, thought Jayshree, was possibly an illusion created by the clothes she wore. The masculine garments did not merely serve to cloak Jalal's gender, they blurred her age as well. If she were dressed in the garments of a Muslim woman, thought Jayshree, she might look her real age.

'Do you never dress as a woman?' Jayshree asked Jalal the next time they met. They had arranged—when they parted that day, both of them dusty and sticky with mango juice—to meet again. At that same tree near the Jami Masjid; it was far enough from the mosque to shield them from curious eyes. And who would not be curious—and outraged—to see a Hindu girl and a Muslim lad chatting together?

Jalal shook her head. 'Don't ask silly questions. Just because you're young, it doesn't mean you should leave your brains in the ditch.' She had brought along a double handful of jamuns, their skin black-purple and glossy, their flesh so astringent that Jayshree refused to eat any after the first bite. Jalal cheerfully put the rest of the fruit into her lap and devoured them, heedless of the way their juice stained her mouth and clothes. 'I have parents, you know.' She swallowed. 'And other people in the household. Servants. If I dressed like this all the time, they would think me mad.'

'So you do wear skirts and veils and all?'

'Of course.' Jalal nibbled at a jamun. 'Almost all the time when I am at home.'

'Then why not when you go out?'

Jalal made a face. 'How many Muslim women have you seen trotting about in the streets of Dilli?'

'Not many,' Jayshree conceded.

'The ones you do see,' added Jalal, 'are so heavily veiled, they must be suffocating inside all those draperies. What's more, they'd be inside an airless, stuffy palanquin.' She sighed. 'I used to be subjected to all of that when I was a little girl. It was enough to put me off being protected all my life. It's stifling.' She gritted her teeth. 'Pushing you down into the earth, that's what this is all about. Devised by men to keep women under their thumbs. And women give in to it, because they know no better. Stupid fools.'

Jayshree blinked, a little out of her depth. She could not think of anything to say, though, so she kept silent. And Jalal, interpreting her silence as a sign of being affronted, said, 'What is it, Jayshree? Did you think I meant you when I spoke of women being fools?' She looked sincerely contrite, and touched Jayshree's hand gently. 'If you thought so, I apologize. I meant most women.'

Jayshree nodded, a little surprised. They went on to talk of other things, but that day, as she walked back home from the Jami Masjid, Jayshree wondered about Jalal. She did not merely dress differently, she thought differently too. Not an ordinary woman, this, and she intrigued Jayshree.

Jayshree had never known any Muslims. To her, they were an exotic race, never mind if it was nearly fifty years—or was it more?—since they had first entered Dilli and established their control over the city. Never mind that she had been born in a city ruled by Muslims. For all practical purposes, the Hindus and the Muslims lived in two separate worlds. Their religion was a mystery; their food, their clothing, their language, their way of life—nothing did they share with the Hindus and the Jains.

Her father and the other men who had worked for Aibak and now for Altamash, had slowly begun to understand the men who now ruled the city. Understanding did not necessarily breed harmony or sympathy; at best, it lessened the enigma that was the Muslim. Now and then, very occasionally, she heard her father say something. A passing remark about the beliefs or ways of the Muslims. A startling revelation about how they worshipped only one God—one! And that too, with no face to identify him by, no idols, no statues to hang garlands on or perform rituals before.

This woman, Jalal, was part of that enigma, and yet she was not.

She spoke Jayshree's language. She loved mangoes with as abiding a passion as Jayshree's. Not surprisingly, she was also as adept at climbing trees as Jayshree was. She let drop the occasional word of appreciation for Jayshree's attire, once going so far as to borrow a particularly pretty blue odhni and draping it across her own head and shoulders. And looking suddenly strikingly beautiful.

Jayshree had taken back her odhni with a look of envy in her eyes, mixed with puzzlement. 'You look beautiful in women's clothing,' she had said. 'You should wear it more often.'

'I do. I told you, I don't wear this,'—Jalal indicated her tunic and trousers—'at home.'

'You should wear women's clothing all the time. It suits you.'

Jalal shook her head. 'Too tiresome. I told you.' She grinned. 'And think! What if a man should see me looking so ravishing and carry me off?'

A thought struck Jayshree. 'But why aren't you married yet? You are twenty years old! How is it that your parents have not made you marry so far?'

Above them, in the branches of the tree a squabble broke out between a pair of squirrels. With much angry chittering they ran along the branches, their little black-and-grey striped bodies racing about, tails following like tiny plumes of smoke.

Jalal looked uncomfortable. She pretended to be too

engrossed in the activities of the squirrels to have heard Jayshree's question. When Jayshree repeated herself, this time with more vehemence, Jalal looked at her with something akin to awkwardness.

'In our family we are not so particular.' Her voice faltered. Her eyes darted away, looking at the mosque and the tower beside it.

'Not particular? How can that be? I thought all girls were married off as soon as they were old enough.' Jayshree frowned. 'I don't know any other Muslims,' she admitted, 'but from all I've heard, your people are no different from mine when it comes to marrying off their daughters.'

'Perhaps others do,' Jalal conceded. 'But in our family, we are not forced.' She watched as one of the squirrels darted into a hole in the tree and then turned around to bare its teeth at its opponent. Jalal looked back down and sighed. 'And I cannot marry just anyone.'

There was silence. Jayshree digested this piece of information.

'Your father must be extremely wealthy,' she ventured.

Jalal shrugged in response, a non-committal shrug that Jayshree took to mean affirmation. 'Only a very able man can be married to me. Not just anyone.' She fiddled with the end of her turban, which hung down past her shoulder almost to her waist. 'And my father,' she admitted, 'has enough troubles of his own trying to keep my brother in check. My eldest brother is good and capable, but the other—' she shook her head.

Jayshree was curious and saw no reason to hide it. 'What of him?'

'He is unruly,' Jalal murmured, her voice just above a whisper. 'He is too fond of things he should stay away from. Wine and women and song. That is all he devotes himself to.'

'How does property pass amongst your people?' Jayshree asked. 'Is it divided amongst the sons? Or will your eldest brother get it all and give to your other brother what he pleases?' This was intriguing, she thought. And it made her feel very grown up. Not a mere child gossiping about dolls and clothes and other girlish things, but a woman. A woman discussing important business. About families, and inheritance, relationships, people.

Jalal said nothing for a while, gazing unseeing into the distance. 'Let it be,' she said finally. 'It is complicated. And who has the time for things like that? Come, let's go down to that gully over there. I think I saw a ber tree last time when I was coming up. Perhaps there will be fruit on it.'

12

She was a strange woman, strange and mysterious. Perhaps that mystery was because she was a Muslim, a foreigner, a woman born and bred into a culture, a language, a religion and a way of life that bore little resemblance to Jayshree's own. Even if she had been born in Dilli, Jalal had nothing in common with the younger girl.

But no, that was not it. For if they had nothing in common, they would not have so easily become friends. But were they really friends, Jayshree wondered. Did one keep secrets from one's friends? Did friends not share every intimate detail of their lives with each other?

This friendship was not like that. Jalal said little about her family or her home. What little Jayshree knew she had gleaned from either a stray comment or as reluctant, inadequate answers to persistent questions. A wealthy father and—from what Jayshree could guess—influential. Jalal did not say what he did for a living; perhaps, thought Jayshree, he was a nobleman. A warrior? A merchant? She did not know. There were the two brothers, of whom there had been that fleeting mention.

'Instead of always asking about me, why do you not tell me something about yourself?' Jalal asked one day. 'And not just about yourself, but about your people. Your family, your neighbours.' She was not satisfied with mere gossip about who was buying what for an upcoming festival, who had borne a child, or who was getting married. That did not appeal to Jalal; she brushed it off with an abruptness that wounded Jayshree. 'I am not interested in such petty things,' Jalal would say, waving a hand in dismissal of the very idea. 'Tell me things that matter.'

The things Jalal considered of importance were the oddest, the most outlandish matters: things that Jayshree did not even notice. Jalal wanted to know where they got water from, and whether it was clean or not. Why there were always beggars sitting in the lanes surrounding the Yogmaya Temple. Whether the watchmen patrolled the lanes and bylanes of the city at night, and took prompt action if there were crimes. Why Jayshree's father and others of his stature and prosperity—which, Jayshree had shyly assured her friend, were not to be scoffed at, 'Even if we aren't of the elite'—kept so much of their money stored at home instead of investing it in schemes that would aid the public.

Jayshree frowned. 'Why should Baba do that? What will he get out of it?' She was not an especially devoted daughter, but this sounded illogical enough to make even her hackles rise. 'Whatever Baba has today, he has earned by his own hard work. Nobody helped him out. Why should he help others?'

Jalal's mouth twisted in a wry smile. 'Let it be,' she said with a sigh. 'You will not understand.'

'Why? Because I'm too young?' Jayshree snapped back, now thoroughly incensed. 'Or because I'm stupid?'

'Because you are too young, I suppose. And naïve. Sheltered. You cannot be blamed, of course; it's common enough. If I were in your place, I suppose I would be much like you, though possibly without the guts to run away every time my parents tried to get me married off.'

The compliment mollified Jayshree somewhat, but not enough to make her abandon the topic. 'Tell me,' she persisted. 'If nobody ever tells me anything, how am I supposed to know?'

Jalal turned to look at Jayshree, her gaze speculative, as if she was trying to decide whether or not to say anything.

'It is not as if your father would simply give away his wealth,' she said finally. 'It would be like an investment. There are many such methods, you know.' She tugged at a fresh green blade of grass and pulled it up to expose the slender green stem which she twirled about absently as she spoke, her eyes riveted on the thin blade swaying and forming circles in the air. 'Let us say, for example, that a rich man gets an inn made along a highway. The poor people who pass by could stay for free—they will be grateful for the shelter, no matter how rudimentary—and those who can afford it could be charged a fee. It could still be profitable, and yet it could benefit the poor.'

'But why would my father do that? That is the Sultan's job! He has the power, but he also has the responsibility. After all, we pay taxes—and isn't that what taxes are meant for, to help the poor? If the Sultan and his officials use all that money to feather their own nests—'

'Have you ever wondered who pays for roads to be made and maintained?' Jalal cut in. 'Why your houses aren't broken into? Who appoints and pays the watchmen who patrol the streets at night? Who makes sure that even when there is drought, you still get food to eat? Who creates work for thousands of workmen by building palaces and mosques and whatnot, even when he doesn't need them?' She was talking so fast and in such a heated voice that she was almost panting. 'You have the gall to complain about being expected to do your bit, even when you can afford it!' Her chest heaving, she turned aside with a gesture of disgust. 'Oh, go away! I expected better of you, but you're just like all of them. You can't see beyond your own petty affairs.' With a grunt of anger, Jalal rose to her feet and strode off.

Jayshree sat still for a moment, staring indignantly at the other woman's retreating back. A moment only, of indecision and of anger so blinding that she wanted to hit Jalal—and then she sprang forward, running the few steps that separated them to grab Jalal's elbow and swing her about with such an unexpected show of strength that it caught Jalal by surprise. She stumbled and fell, and Jayshree nearly fell as well.

'What the—how dare you!'

'I did not mean to throw you to the ground. It was

an accident,' Jayshree muttered, extending a hand to help Jalal up. The older woman was already picking herself up and ignored the proffered hand, even batting it away when Jayshree tried to touch her. Jayshree withdrew a little, stepping back and looking Jalal in the eye. 'Your people invaded our land,' she said, in as controlled a voice as she could muster. 'You took over everything, our land, our resources, all that we have. And you claim to be taking care of us?'

'Rulers change.' Jalal bent to brush her baggy trousers. She rubbed ruefully at the newly scuffed toe of one boot. 'Your people only complain. I would wager they complained when the ruler before Aibak sat on the throne. If one of his descendants ruled today, you'd be spouting the same nonsense.' She straightened, heaving a sigh of what sounded very much like resignation. 'Let it be.' Her voice was soft now, not gentle, but despairing, disillusioned. 'Goodbye.'

'No. Wait.' Jayshree put out a hand, and this time, instead of grasping Jalal's arm, merely touched it. It took effort to restrain herself, to not lash out. 'You think I'm being selfish? That we are too self-centred? I don't know about the others, but I do know about myself and my family. If Prithviraj Chauhan still ruled Dilli, yes—perhaps things would be much the same for the city. But for my family, there is a reason we can never warm to the Sultan. This Sultan.'

Jalal's eyes, so far expressionless, narrowed. 'What do you mean?'

'Come with me. I will show you.'

ꟹ

'Come,' Jayshree said, as they stepped out of the little copse of trees that marked the end of the path. 'To the Qutb Minar.'

She led the way to the tower, which was not much of a tower: too stumpy, too unimpressive, despite the exquisite beauty of the carving that covered its facade. Jalal trailed behind, looking about suspiciously. 'What is it?' she whispered when Jayshree finally came to a stop in front of the Qutb Minar. From somewhere not too far away came the sounds of conversation, but there was nobody in sight.

'Hurry up,' Jalal urged. 'Hurry up and say what you have to. Don't waste time. There are people around, even if we can't see them right now.'

Jayshree had put out a hand to touch the curving wall of the tower. She glanced over her shoulder with hard, steely eyes. 'Look at this,' she said.

Jalal stepped forward, her impatience and unease overtaken by her curiosity. She stared at the wall, looking at the curlicues, the fine calligraphy carved into the stone. 'So? You brought me here so I could read this out to you?'

Jayshree's eyes widened. 'You can actually read this?'

Jalal gritted her teeth. 'Hurry up, Jayshree! Can't you see, we could be caught any moment! They will think me a man, and then both of us will be in trouble.'

'All right, all right. No, not those inscriptions, whatever they may be. Look at this.' Jayshree pointed to something etched into the stone, in the corner. Not a random scratch or a slip of the chisel, but a mark as deliberate as the carving across the rest of the stone.

Jalal peered closely, before drawing away with shrug. 'I cannot read your script. What is written?'

'Nandu,' Jayshree replied, her voice quiet and full of pride. 'It is the name of my father. He carved this. He carved part of that mosque too'—she tilted her chin, indicating the massive screens of the Jami Masjid less than a hundred yards away—'and he left his mark here.'

'You brought me here to show me this?' Jalal added something under her breath.

Jayshree pretended not to notice. 'You don't think it anything important,' she said. 'I suppose not. But if you think about it, this was one of the first buildings to be constructed by your people when they came to Dilli. And these are important buildings. The men who were commissioned to work on them were the very best that could be found. My father was one of them.'

'Yes, I can see that. Now let us go, please.' Jalal was so restless, she was almost hopping about now. But Jayshree dug her heels in.

'No. You do not see,' she retorted. 'I am not bragging or trying to boast about my father; I am trying to show you what this place means to me. This was where my father established himself. This was where he first met my grandfather, my mother's father.'

'Can we not discuss this elsewhere?' Jalal hissed. 'It's almost time for the afternoon prayer; any moment now, and people will come flooding in. We will be seen. They will think I am a man. We will be—'

They both heard the sound of approaching hoofbeats, of tramping feet and voices. Jalal, without wasting a moment, grabbed Jayshree's arm and whisked her away behind the bulk of the tower, away from the path. They stood there, backs pressed to the stone, Jayshree with her odhni pulled across her face and her voluminous ghagra drawn close to her legs. 'Who is it?' she whispered. 'The muezzin hasn't even called out yet; who can have come?'

'We aren't the only ones who can roam about here whenever we wish,' Jalal murmured, a frown between her eyebrows. 'Wait here. Stay out of sight. Let me see.'

She moved away, walking swiftly out of the shadow of the tower. A few steps, and her speed slowed to a saunter. A young man swaggering about, enjoying the view of the tower and the mosque. Jayshree risked a glance outwards. She could see the dust rising beyond the thorn bushes and tussocks that flanked the path leading from the city. Whoever it was, came in a considerable entourage. Nobility, she guessed. Those were shod feet she heard, and horses—who had horses in such numbers, except the nobility?

She frowned. A courtier?

They came into sight, an imposing cavalcade with, at its centre, a gilded palanquin with brocaded curtains. Clustered round the palanquin were maids, veiled but on horseback, and ahead of them rode horsemen with lances in their hands and swords at their belts. More men, wearing the leather tunics of soldiers, walked in two short but daunting columns that stretched on either side of the palanquin, in front and beyond.

A royal lady, Jayshree realized, for the soldiers were the Sultan's men, and they would not be guarding a lady who was merely an aristocrat, not royalty. It had to be Altamash's queen, the Sultana Shah Turkan. Or could it be the Princess Razia? That would be interesting, she thought; bazaar gossip had it that the princess was an unusual woman, not one given to conforming. But then, maybe she would not be moving about in such a conventional manner, either. It must be the queen, after all.

The palanquin and its escort were nearing Jalal, she noticed, and her friend had correctly stepped out of the path of the approaching procession. No; she had not just drawn away, she looked as if she was trying to burrow her way through the bushes.

Jayshree scowled. There was no need for Jalal to vanish; it was not as if a royal entourage would, without rhyme or reason, assault a passerby. All Jalal had to do was bow and stand aside, and that was it. Surely Jalal knew it.

But even as Jayshree watched with growing bewilderment, Jalal struggled, trying to free herself from thorn bushes that had caught on her clothes. There was a brief flurry, a struggle; then Jalal freed herself and raced for a tree that marked a break in the thorn.

Her behaviour was suspicious, and the soldiers obviously thought so too. Jayshree watched with a sinking heart as an order rang out—the leader was calling to Jalal to stop—and two foot soldiers hurried forward. Jalal was moving fast, not stopping to look back, not even when the soldier called out to her to stop.

The soldiers plunged into the undergrowth and were hidden by the dense screen of acacia and thorn bushes. An angry scream rang out a few moments later, and by the time the rest of the cavalcade had come abreast of the tree, the soldiers emerged from the bushes with Jalal, her arms pinned to her sides.

The leader of the group had already dismounted: his voice snapped out a question. Jalal did not answer. The question was repeated, and again greeted with an insolent silence.

At that, the man's arm whipped out, slapping her across the face—and Jalal flew into one of her rages. Jayshree winced and squeezed her eyes shut. Stupid, stupid Jalal. She had made things bad enough by fleeing when all that was needed was to stay put. Now, when she might have kneeled and begged for mercy on the pretext of having panicked in the presence of royalty, she had made matters worse. She seemed to have even forgotten that, as the daughter of a nobleman, she could expect leniency.

But Jalal was not thinking. She had erupted into a blind fury and lashed back at the commander, screaming at him.

For a few moments, Jayshree could see little through the shifting dust and the movement as the soldiers milled about Jalal and the commander, while the maids huddled around the palanquin, which its bearers had pulled back out of possible harm's way. There was yelling, the frightened neighing of a horse, and Jalal's voice. Her indignation had got the better of her; she had forgotten, perhaps in the heat of the moment, that she was supposed to be a man, and that men did not have voices so shrill, so obviously feminine.

Jalal was still shouting when the brocade curtain of the palanquin was pulled back. A head—veiled, capped by a headdress that glinted with gold and jewels in the sunlight—poked out. Jayshree, watching surreptitiously, noted the unmistakable imperiousness of the woman, the way the maids bowed as one, the soldiers froze. This was the Sultana. There was no doubt about it.

Shah Turkan was summoning the commander of the guard, demanding the captive be brought to her. Jalal, suddenly silent, was straining back, trying to escape. But the men who held her were stronger, and she was dragged forward.

Far away as she was, Jayshree noticed the sudden stiffening of the Sultana's shoulders. Though Shah Turkan did not raise her voice, the silence around her was suddenly so profound that Jayshree could hear every word of the incredulous question that she put to Jalal.

'Razia, what are you doing here dressed like that?'

Jayshree stared, rooted to the spot, her mind grappling uselessly with what she had heard. She watched as the soldiers, as of one accord and without any express command, moved swiftly back, leaving Jalal—no, Razia, the Princess Razia, that was who she was—to stand alone, facing the Sultana.

She was too far to hear what the Sultana said, but she saw Shah Turkan draw back the brocade curtain and beckon her stepdaughter in. The palanquin had already been lowered to the ground. The princess got in, the Sultana leaned out to give a command, and the entire entourage having wheeled about, went back the way they had come.

Jayshree watched them go, wondering in an abstracted way why the Sultana had come here anyway. Had she been on her way to the mosque, or was this just a brief excursion to escape the stuffiness of the palace?

It did not matter, it did not concern her.

As she made her way home, she was surrounded by the sounds she loved. The chittering of squirrels and the chirruping of birds, the gurgling of a stream nearby. Beyond, the sounds that were so much a part of life in a big, bustling settlement: the voices, the trundling of wheels, the hoof beats, the feet. People, working, arguing, loving, hating.

She heard it all with unhearing ears. She saw it all, from the grandeur of the mosque and the tower with the dusty wildness of the low hills beyond, to the busy marketplace of Yoginipur. Yet she saw nothing. Had a man been murdered in front of her very eyes, she would not have noticed.

'So madam deigns to come home,' her mother remarked caustically, glancing up from the row of heavy ceramic jars in the courtyard. Quartered limes with ginger. Raw mangoes with mustard oil and turmeric and a dozen other spices. They had been sitting in the sunshine every day for the past three days, and Jayshree had promised Jalal that when they were ready, she would bring some pickles for her friend.

Jayshree walked past her mother without a word and went into her room, pulling the door shut. Her mother, puzzled and perhaps a little worried too, called out, wanting to know what was wrong. But Jayshree, deaf and blind to everything except the pounding in her head, saw nothing and heard nothing.

By the time Jayshree's mother began banging on the door and shouting—her voice rising higher and higher into near-panic with every passing moment of silence—Jayshree had slumped to the floor, tears coursing down her cheeks.

Interlude

'You said,' remarked Nasiruddin, 'that this was the story of the girl and her best friend. But it sounds to me more like she wasn't merely good friends with Jalal, but in love.' His lips curved in a twisted parody of a smile. 'Such devastation, and all because she discovered that her best friend had been fooling her all the time. No, such a reaction can stem only from an emotion far deeper than friendship.'

Shagufta had finished her sewing a long while back. She had put away her needle and thread, shaken out the quilt and admired her handiwork, even as she continued to tell her story. Now she was huddled into the warmth of it, her back resting against the wall. She revelled in the comfort of it, so warm that it even softened the sting in Nasiruddin's words.

And perhaps what he said was not completely bereft of all logic. What logic, after all, was there in emotion?

'I do not know,' Shagufta admitted. 'Who is to know the thoughts of those who lived long ago?'

'We can guess, I suppose,' said Nasiruddin.

'But does it matter? Does one need to pinpoint what emotion Jayshree felt for Razia in order to appreciate that she felt betrayed?'

The man raised his eyebrows, as if questioning her statement. But he said nothing to refute her, and Shagufta, settling deeper into the quilt, wondered fleetingly what was happening in other parts of the city. Did Dilli survive? Did its forts still stand, its markets still flourish? Or was the devastation she had recoiled from in the neighbourhood a reflection of the rest of the city?

She did not want to think. 'Let me get back to my story,' she said.

13

Eleven Years Later

Vikram Samwat 1292 (1236 CE)

It was sweltering, such a hot day that Jayshree, nursing her youngest, could not resist the temptation to open the window. She had pulled her odhni over her breast, of course, and she let the thin woven-reed curtain at the window remain in place: she was not that brazen.

The baby, nearly seven months old, was the youngest of Jayshree's four children and the second son. Her second child, born three years after her marriage, was also a son. More than a decade it had been, she thought, since that momentous day. More than a decade since she had first met the princess.

That was how she always thought of her, not as Jalal, not as Razia, but as the distant and aloof princess. A princess who had come out of her palace to explore the world, to play, to have a secret laugh at the poor girl she had so effortlessly fooled. A bitter taste rose in Jayshree's throat at the memory.

Now, a wife and mother of four, Jayshree thought of herself as mature; then, as a fourteen-year-old, her emotions unchecked and her heart liable to shatter at the merest slight, she had fallen apart. She had refused to tell anybody what had happened; not her father, not her mother. An old maid, who had been Jayshree's nanny when she was a child, was the only one to whom Jayshree had once confided about her friendship with a Muslim girl who called herself Jalal. Even to that maid, though, Jayshree did not speak of what had happened that day near the Qutb Minar. It was too mortifying a truth to be told. And who would believe it?

From that day on, too, Jayshree had never returned to the Qutb Minar or the area around it. Just once, out of curiosity, she had gone to the nearby hermitage of the mystic Qutbuddin Bakhtiar Kaki, but that was all. Qutb Sahib, for whom it was said the Qutb Minar had been named. Qutb Sahib, who preached universal brotherhood and charity, who did not discriminate against anyone, be they poor or rich, powerful or helpless, Hindu or Muslim. Jayshree had been moved by the peace and tranquillity that pervaded the space. She was awed, too, by the devotion of those who gathered round the sage, listening to his discourses, singing and playing music in praise of a divinity whose identity, perhaps, was different for different members of the gathering.

Just last winter, in the wake of such a gathering, Qutb Sahib had collapsed. Four days later, he was dead. A man so revered that the Sultan, weeping all the time, had led the funeral prayers for the saint.

And now the Sultan was dead too. There were hundreds—possibly thousands—in the empire who would mourn him, remembering him for the reforms he had instituted, the robust administrative system he had set up. Jayshree did not mourn him. To her, he was the man who had been the ruin of her grandfather. When Qutbuddin Aibak had been inclined to dismiss Shantinath's accusation against Jayshree's grandfather Sridhar Sahu all those years ago, Altamash had intervened, and because of that intervention Sridhar Sahu had lost everything: reputation, honour, much of his wealth. Jayshree had not been born then, and had seen none of it. But her mother Gayatri, embittered and furious, had told her all about it, and it had fostered in her a deep hatred for the man who had caused her grandfather's downfall.

It had also been the reason for Jayshree's recoiling from the woman whose identity she had so unexpectedly stumbled on. That Jalal was not a mere commoner but a princess had been a shock in itself; that she was the daughter of the very man Jayshree had despised all her short life had been the biggest blow of all. The days following the incident at the

Qutb Minar had been filled with loathing. Loathing, of course, for the devious princess, but loathing too, for herself. How could she have been so blind as to not realize whom she was befriending?

It had taken Jayshree a long time to forgive herself for having, even if only briefly, been friends with the enemy. She had to come to terms with the realization that all said and done, she had been little more than a child, and could therefore not be blamed. And that the princess, had never shown any signs of being evil. She had even, when Jayshree thought back to their first meeting, saved her from a poisonous snake and possible death.

As she placed her baby on her shoulder and patted his back, Jayshree felt a pang of sorrow for the daughter thus left bereaved. Her own father's death two years earlier had been hard to get over, even though he had never been an overly affectionate man. And people said that Altamash had doted on his daughter. He had been so fond of her, so sure of her ability, that he had allowed her her own way in a lot of things, much to the annoyance of his chief wife, the Sultana Shah Turkan.

'You will never believe what has happened,' Jayshree's husband had said when he had come home last evening. The city had been abuzz all through the day; even Jayshree, confined to the house as she was, tied down by baby and domesticity, had learnt that the Sultan had died. 'One would have thought that he would have nominated one of his sons his heir. But do you know what the Sultan did?' Her husband had said, unwrapping his turban, 'He proclaimed his daughter the next Sultan. His daughter! How can a woman rule?'

Jayshree had been tempted to tell her husband that a woman could probably rule as well as any man, if not better. Especially a woman like Jalal.

'Are any of the sons suited for the throne?' Jayshree had asked, her voice carefully tempered to sound mild. 'Had the eldest son been alive today, he may have made a fine Sultan. But one is too young and the other too profligate—how can either be considered a good candidate as Sultan? I think Altamash did well,' she had said, even though it had galled her to say something in praise of Altamash.

'Anything would be better than a woman,' her husband had said stubbornly. 'You wait and see, the nobility will not stand for it.'

☙

'Didi?'

It was Jayshree's old maid, who had been her nanny as a child, and who, when Jayshree was married, had accompanied the girl into her new home. She was a thin woman, her grey hair now mere wisps around an almost-bald skull. Jayshree was perhaps a quarter of her age, and yet she called Jayshree 'Didi', elder sister.

'Yes? What is it?'

'Is he sleeping?' the woman whispered, looking towards the cradle in which Jayshree had just put her baby down. 'Leave him to me,' the old woman added. 'I'll fan him while he sleeps. Go to the kitchen; I made the cook squeeze some sugarcane juice for you. Drink it while it's fresh.'

Jayshree obeyed, relieved at the brief respite from her duties as a mother. But she could sense that something was in the offing; a favour, even so small a one, would not be granted by the old woman without the expectation of something in return.

She was right. Later that evening, as Jayshree sat in the courtyard rolling laddoos, the old woman came and seated herself on the ground beside the rope bed on which Jayshree was sitting. She was carrying a handheld bamboo fan, and this she began swinging, slowly and rhythmically. Jayshree drew in a breath of the welcome little breeze stirred up by the fan, and waited for what would come.

'Your friend is going to be the ruler,' the maid said.

Her face was impassive, a fine thread of silver hair falling across one wrinkled cheek.

'What do you mean? My friend?'

'The princess. She is your friend, isn't she?'

Jayshree, suddenly wary, stilled the rolling of the laddoo in her hands. She had been right, the maid was going to ask for something. But that it would be connected to the princess: that Jayshree had not envisaged. She waited, her heart weighed down by dread, for whatever was coming.

'You told me about her, don't you remember?' said the maid.

'I didn't tell you who she was. I didn't know myself then.'

'Yes, but I was intrigued. From what you told me, it seemed obvious that this was a rich woman, one from a family of considerable status. A nobleman's daughter—you thought so too, didn't you? I was curious. I wanted to know who she was.' She shifted the fan to her other hand. 'And then that day, when you came home so shaken, looking as if the earth had opened up—you refused to say what had happened, and you never went back to meet your friend. Do you remember, I even asked you if your friend had left the city?'

Jayshree nodded grudgingly.

'And you gave me no explanation. You just said you didn't want to go back.' She paused. 'So I went instead. A few days later I went to the mosque to see if I could find anyone there.'

Jayshree stared, dumbstruck.

'Yes. I had to see for myself. She wasn't there the first few days, but I didn't give up. I kept going there, and one day, there she was, a young woman dressed as a man.' She laughed in remembered triumph, her voice raucous and jarring.

'She did not see me, but I watched her,' the maid went on. 'She waited a long time, I think about an hour. When she left, I followed her back to the city. She went into the palace, creeping in stealthily through an obscure little door, not the main gate. I could not follow her in, but I saw a passing maid bend to greet her. That was when I realized who she was.'

The maid's hand slowed, and finally, she put the fan down, fidgeting with the woven bamboo strips as she got around to what she really wanted to say. 'Your friend is going to be the ruler,' she said, in a low voice. 'She will be powerful. She will be able to do anything.'

Jayshree was gripped by a sense of foreboding. 'So?'

'If you were to ask her for a post for my nephew, she might agree. A palace guard, perhaps? Or a groom in the stables, a servant. Anything. If only he can get into service at the palace, it will change his life.' She sighed. 'You know how it is, Didi. He has been the bane of my existence all these years. Perhaps I indulged him too much after his parents died. Perhaps he was just too headstrong to start with.'

'What makes you think getting into service at the palace will make a difference?' Jayshree snapped. 'What if he proves as useless there as he has at every other occupation he has tried? Will I not be blamed?'

'There is discipline in the palace,' the maid replied quietly. 'There is the fear of consequences. What is the worst that will happen if he's working for a shopkeeper in the city, or for any other petty businessman? He will get scolded and thrown out. Or if the master has a vicious temper, he will be beaten. In the palace he could be executed if he didn't do his work well.'

'I doubt it,' Jayshree said.

'Please.' The maid looked up, her rheumy eyes brimming with tears. 'Please help me, Didi. At my age, I should be able to sit back and rest, not be working and worrying for a grown-up man. I am so tired.' The tears spilled out, slowly making their way down into the furrows that bracketed her mouth. Once they had been laugh lines, but no more; now they were just a sad reminder of the days when there had been laughter in this woman's life.

Jayshree wiped her hands and sat back, looking at the pile of laddoos she had made. They were perfect, uniformly spherical and flawless. Who would have imagined that a mind deep in turmoil could have wrought something like this, she thought.

She sighed. Either she simply refused to do what the maid asked, or she did what would no doubt prove to be an embarrassment for her. Her conscience would not allow the former; she had no choice, really, but to steel herself to beg for an audience with Razia.

The Turkic aristocrats who comprised the elite of Dilli shared with Jayshree's husband their disdain for a woman as ruler. They would not bow to a woman, no matter how courageous, how skilled at both statecraft and warfare, no matter how much she felt for her would-be subjects. No matter, even, that she was the designated heir.

They would not accept her. She was a woman.

It was the old maid who brought the news as soon as Jayshree was up and about in the morning: the princess, it seemed, was not going to be allowed to rule Dilli, after all.

'Hey Bhagwaan, even this hope has been snatched away!' the maid wailed, collapsing on to her haunches, her head in her hands.

But all Jayshree could feel was a deep sense of relief. Relief that she would be spared the acute embarrassment of facing Jalal again, years after having broken off their friendship so summarily. Jalal, hot-tempered and unforgiving—and a Jalal, too, who had waited for her day after day—would not so easily put Jayshree's behaviour behind her.

Well, now there would be no need for Jayshree to face her after all.

14

'This is the handiwork of Shah Turkan,' Mahesh said. 'Why would anybody in their right mind want to put a dissolute creature like Ruknuddin on the throne?' He ran his fingers through the thick mop of hair on his head. Like his moustache, it already showed the odd grey strand here and there, even though he had seen only thirty-one summers. It was a trait he had inherited from his father. Madhav had begun to go grey when he was in his late twenties and by now his hair was close to unrelieved white. His face was lined and tanned, but his eyes were as bright as ever, his smile undimmed.

His smile was wry now as he nodded. 'Of course. And we know that everybody at court is in their right mind.'

Madhav was sitting cross-legged on a low, broad stool, a yard-long slab of red sandstone before him, working on a piece of carving for the mausoleum of Altamash.

Sultans, as Madhav now knew, felt a deep-seated urge to build. In Madhav's childhood and youth, there had been the mosque and the victory tower beside it. When he returned years later to Yoginipur, Aibak had commissioned his palace, the Kasr Safed. Altamash, in his reign, had added to the Qutb Minar, and had also commissioned the building of his own tomb in the shadow of that magnificent tower, just across it and beyond the Jami Masjid. The Sultan had died before the tomb that would hold his grave could be completed; and now that his dissolute son Ruknuddin was on the throne, the building of Altamash's tomb was in danger of being forgotten, of being relegated to the attic of Dilli, to gather dust. A small group of diligent, determined men still worked on it while funds and materials lasted; among them were Madhav, who headed the team of stone carvers, and Mahesh, a worker in stone like his father.

It was a square tomb, simple to the point of austerity on the outside. Inside, it was to be a different story altogether. A riot of patterns, worked in sandstone of different shades, mainly a warm red, but also pale gold. Every inch of it was to be carved into geometric patterns, arabesques, garlands, temple bells and calligraphy. On a platform in the centre was to be the Sultan's cenotaph, of white marble, as ornately carved as the mausoleum built around it

'I cannot understand it,' Mahesh said, watching as Madhav used henna to draw a pattern of diamonds on the slab before him. 'Why would a man build his own tomb? Is that not an invitation to death?' He had been saying that ever since he had heard of the commissioning of the Sultan's tomb, and he had not reconciled himself to it yet. Madhav did not say, as he had the first few times, that a man did well to prepare for his death. He bent over his work, making sure he had positioned the stone just so.

'I suppose the old Sultan did not know what would happen after his death,' Mahesh continued, his voice subdued, contemplative. 'But he was going to proclaim Razia his heir. Surely he trusted her enough to entrust the building of his tomb to her?'

Madhav dipped the end of a thin wooden rod into the pot of henna and used it, along with a long, straight rod, to draw straight lines on the stone. When he was done, he sat up and regarded his work with satisfaction. 'No,' he said. 'No, it was not that he did not trust his heir. He wanted to leave his own mark on his tomb, that was it. I think Altamash wanted his tomb to be associated with him in every way.'

Mahesh shrugged.

'And what happens now? Ruknuddin is now Sultan, and he will sanction funds for nothing that does not cater to his own enjoyment. Baba, I tell you, Shah Turkan is the one behind this. None of the nobility would have accepted Ruknuddin as the Sultan had it not been for her.' Mahesh had been working on smoothening the edges of the slab in front of him; he now set aside his chisel and bent to blow away the fine dust that had settled on the stone. 'It is common knowledge that she has bribed the noblemen, egging each of them on to reject Razia and put Ruknuddin on the throne instead.'

He sighed as he reached for the terracotta water pot beside him. 'I wonder what it would have been like,' he added, taking off the lid, 'to be ruled by a woman. Would she have been better than the men, or worse? Would there be no difference?'

☙

Ruknuddin Firuz Shah was the second of Altamash's sons. His eldest, Nasiruddin Mahmood, had had the potential to be a worthy ruler and had been gaining valuable experience as governor of Bengal when he died about eight years earlier. His body had been brought to Dilli, amidst much mourning, and a tomb built for it. Madhav and Mahesh and the other stone carvers, the masons, the bricklayers and all the other Hindu craftsmen who had built so many mosques, palaces, and other edifices for the Sultans and their noblemen, were faced with creating something they had never seen before: a mausoleum. In the few decades the Muslims had been in this land, Hindus had become familiar with gravestones, simple and unostentatious markers of the dead. A mausoleum was a novelty.

Nasiruddin's tomb had been built, not far from Qutb Sahib's hermitage, and the people called it Sultangarhi: The Sultan of the Pit. Even if he had never actually become the Sultan, Nasiruddin came to be referred to by that title, the Sultan for whose body a deep pit was dug, and an impressive mausoleum built over it. It looked like a small fort, though the gate, intricately carved in white marble, was more that of a palace.

Nasiruddin slept in his pit, and in his stead ruled Ruknuddin, lover of women and song. It was common knowledge that his mother, Shah Turkan, whose gold and connections had helped place Ruknuddin on the throne, was the de facto Sultan of Dilli.

Madhav and Mahesh plodded on, working on the tomb of Altamash. Much of the masons' work had been completed; all that remained was the decoration of the tomb, which was substantial.

'The gods alone know what will happen when we run out of marble and sandstone,' Madhav fretted. 'We do not have enough to complete the work. I shudder to think what will befall me if I go before the Sultan and beg for funds.'

'You would not have to go before the Sultan himself, would you Baba?' Mahesh asked. 'Would not the wazir be responsible? Or some other official?'

Madhav shook his head. 'Even if I went to one of them, they could not sanction funds without the Sultan's approval. Or, realistically speaking, Shah Turkan's.'

'And you do not believe she would wish her husband's tomb to be completed?'

Madhav took a deep breath. 'Does she seem a devoted wife, a grieving widow? Not once has she come to see what we are doing here.' He hunched over the pattern he was working on and went back to chiselling. 'Shah Turkan is more interested in gathering power and feathering her nest.'

'Why do the Chahalgani tolerate her?' murmured Mahesh. 'I always thought they were the men who mattered. Were they not the ones who helped put Altamash on the throne, Baba?'

Madhav nodded. Yes, Altamash had not been elevated to the post of Sultan of Dilli without help. There had been another—a man named Aram Shah—who had briefly occupied the throne after the death of Aibak. It had been thanks to the support of the influential Chahalgani, as the elite clique of forty Turkish noblemen was known, that Altamash had been invited to sit on the throne of Dilli. Altamash had defeated Aram Shah in battle, but if it had not been for the Chahalgani, Altamash might never have become Sultan.

'Perhaps the Chahalgani have even less faith in Razia than they do in Ruknuddin,' said Madhav, doubt in his voice.

'How could anyone have any faith in that debauch? It has only been six months since he was crowned and already the entire town knows that all our Sultan can think of is what lies between his legs!'

'Hush, Mahesh. The walls have ears. And the stones speak.'

'It is not only the stones that speak, Baba,' Mahesh said ominously. 'The people of Dilli may not have a say in who will rule them, but sooner or later, I think the nobility will have to admit that Ruknuddin and his mother care for none but themselves. They will ruin Dilli.'

☙

A few days later, however, they were to realize how much influence Razia wielded, at least among the populace.

It was Friday, and the stone carvers were busy in the temporary enclosure near the tomb of Altamash where they worked. The sounds of bodies moving, standing and then sitting down, rising again, the sonorous voice of the imam as he spoke in the neighbouring Jami Masjid: all of these formed a backdrop to the sounds of their chisels and their hammers. None of the men spoke, or if they did, it was in the low voice of someone in a sacred space. All Hindus, and yet all subconsciously aware that they were close to a place of worship.

And then slowly, another set of sounds began to make themselves heard. People shouting, somewhere far off. The sound of feet, perhaps hundreds of them. A clanging and a clashing.

It was one of the younger apprentices who rose to his feet and ran out to see what was happening. He was back within a few moments, his eyes wide with excitement. 'Come and see, there's a huge crowd coming,' he cried out, 'headed this way.'

'Hey Ram,' Madhav said. 'Hey Ram.' He had put down his tools as soon as he had guessed what was approaching, and now he stepped out with the rest of them to see who came, in such a loud, belligerent style. For belligerent it was, this mob that came towards them: its hundreds of tramping feet raising dust, its many voices shouting defiance, even though their words were not yet audible.

They stood, the little group of stone carvers, wondering whether to flee or to stay where they were. Some, less certain, had already slipped away towards the back, where they could easily run for safety if danger threatened. The others, including Madhav and Mahesh, continued to stand their ground, though some who had brought their chisels along clutched them rather more tightly.

As the mob neared, the shouts and the chanting of it began to coalesce into recognizable words. 'Sultan Ruknuddin! For shame, for shame!' 'Sultan Ruknuddin, make way for the rightful heir!' and so on. These were not soldiers, but they bore what weapons they had found: sticks, sickles, axes, even the rusted old sword here and there. At their head rode a horseman, a gleaming new sword held aloft like a pennant.

The crowd drew nearer still, passing the little knot of stone carvers as if they did not exist. It was as they went past that Madhav saw who the leader, with that exposed sword held high, baying for the blood of Ruknuddin, was.

'Princess Razia,' he whispered. 'Hey Bhagwaan, it is the princess.'

Thus Razia showed that she, though dismissed by the Chahalgani and supplanted by her brother, was by no means a spent force. If the Chahalgani did not support her, a substantial section of the populace did. That show of strength in front of the Jami Masjid had been proof of that. At the very place her father's mentor and predecessor had chosen to establish the proof of his power, Razia had proved that she was not to be taken lightly.

Perhaps by now the Chahalgani, too, had realized their mistake, for the next bit of news that came Jayshree's way was that Sultan Ruknuddin and his ambitious mother, Shah Turkan, had been murdered by the Chahalgani.

It was Jayshree's husband who brought the news when he came home in the evening. The old maid, offering a tumbler of water to the master, could not stop herself from asking, 'And? Who will now be Sultan, master?'

Jayshree's husband looked taken aback; the woman had caught him unawares. 'It is only rumour yet,' he said, 'but they say it will be Razia. She has won over many of the common people. And anyway, who else is there? Unless the Chahalgani decide to put an end to the dynasty once and for all.' He was carrying two cloth-bound ledgers under his arm; he hoisted them up, tucking them more securely under his armpit, and said, 'All we can do is wait and watch. In any case, for us, things are unlikely to change very much.'

Having said that, he went away into the inner rooms, calling to a servant to fetch him something to eat.

'If it is Razia,' said the maid, so quietly that the words barely carried to Jayshree's ears, 'will you go and talk to her?'

In the first few days after Razia ascended the throne it was not difficult for Jayshree to deflect her maid's repeated pleas. The new Sultan—Razia refused to let herself be addressed as Sultana, for that, she said, was a title given to the consort or the offspring of a Sultan and she was a Sultan in her own right—was far too busy. There was much to be done, to correct the many wrongs Ruknuddin and his mother had wrought in Dilli during his brief reign.

'Even if I request an audience, I will not get one,' Jayshree explained. 'She is too busy to meet nonentities like me.'

'No longer, no longer.' The old woman was persistent. 'Things have settled down. I have been to the palace gates, Didi. I have seen petitioners being allowed in. Poor people, common people. I have seen them come out, she hears them out, she listens. She will not deny you, Didi. Not you, of all people.'

Jayshree tried to put it off, making excuses. Her baby needed her, she was too busy, she did not feel well.

Until one day the maid came and fell at her feet. Tears ran down the dry, wrinkled cheeks as she sobbed. 'Help me, Didi, help me. My nephew has been arrested. They say he beat up an officer of the law in a drunken fit and that he will be imprisoned for it.' She bent, pressing her face wet with tears to the feet of a mortified Jayshree, who shrank from the gesture. 'If you do not go to your friend and plead his case, Didi, I will kill myself.'

It was not the nature of the threat that frightened Jayshree, but the tired resignation, the despair, with which it was said. It made her feel guilty for having prevaricated, that too, because of a long-festering hurt that had its roots in her own naiveté.

The next morning, with a manservant and the old woman to accompany her, Jayshree went to the palace from where Razia Sultan ruled.

She had changed. Changed not just in the physical ways that separated a woman from her younger self of a dozen years earlier—her skin not as fine, her figure fuller—but in ways that made Jayshree wonder if her long-ago friend had really been this same woman. Had she imagined Jalal? Or had Jalal been real, a young woman who had coincidentally borne a strong resemblance to this woman who now sat on the throne surrounded by deferential courtiers?

As she stood among the rabble separated from the nobility

by railings and soldiery, Jayshree raised herself on tiptoe and strained to see. Razia Sultan, it was said, had long discarded the clothing and ways of a woman and had adopted those of a man instead. Not true; Jayshree could have said that of the obstreperous Jalal, but not of the present Sultan of Dilli. True, she did not go fully veiled and she wore little of the jewellery that a woman her rank would flaunt; but in the cut of her clothes, the exceptionally wide trousers, the long flowing coat with its flared sides and its heavily embroidered hems, there was definitely a woman, not a man.

Her demeanour too was an odd yet impressive mix of the feminine and the masculine. The way she leaned forward, listening with rapt attention to the outpourings of an old man's woes, the way she winced when he lifted his tunic to show the weeping welts on his back where he had been whipped by a cruel master. The way she snapped out an order for the master to be summoned and witnesses to be brought forth. Her patience, her ability to spring on the one thing that rang false in a testimony. Her curtness and her brusqueness with the sycophantic, with those she knew as having been supporters of the late and largely unlamented Ruknuddin. Her wisdom, Jayshree realized. And her obvious suitability for the throne.

The queue of petitioners diminished, the speed varying as some took an eternity to explain their grievance, while others, perhaps more awestruck and frightened, said what they had to in the fewest of words. For some, Razia pronounced judgement there and then; for others, she gave orders to an official to attend. There were people pleading for justice, for sustenance, for favours. A mother begging for news of a soldier son who had been reported missing in a skirmish but who, she had heard rumours, was still alive. Two neighbours asking for a just settling of a disputed boundary wall over which the local village headman and his colleagues had thrown up their hands. A man, white-haired and accompanied by a younger version of himself, who stated in a soft, clear voice that he was the chief of the stone carvers working on the tomb of the late Sultan Altamash, and that they were in need of funds.

When it was finally Jayshree's turn, she stepped forward, the maid beside her. Her knees were trembling, her heart pounding. Why had she ever agreed to this?

She lifted the odhni off her face, pushing it back, and looked up into the face of the Sultan. Razia froze, but it was only for the blink of an eye, no more. 'You,' she said quietly. 'Move aside and wait here.' She indicated with an imperious sweep of her hand the space near one of the clerks of the court. 'I will attend to you later.'

'Baba? Are you all right?' Mahesh asked, as they stepped back. He laid a concerned hand on his father's arm and found that the older man was trembling.

Madhav shook his head, but said nothing. His son, however, was persistent. 'You're shaking, Baba. What happened? The Sultan has instructed her wazir to clear the funds, so what is the matter? Do you feel unwell?'

'That woman,' said Madhav, looking over his shoulder. 'That woman, in the blue ghagra, the red odhni.' Mahesh glanced at the woman, already veiled, and then back at his father. Madhav was pallid, his expression dazed.

'What about her? Do you know her?'

Madhav stood for a moment, looking uncertain. 'Let us go,' he said.

When they had made their way out of the large hall, down the corridors, and into the sunshine, he squinted up into the welcome golden warmth of the sun and shook his head. 'No,' he said. 'No—for a moment it seemed—many years ago, I knew one who was the spitting image of this woman.' He shook his head again, more vigorously this time. 'But of course it could not be her; that one must be a grandmother by now. It is a coincidence, no more.

'Come,' he said, after a moment. 'Let us go. We have work waiting for us.'

15

Once the court had been dismissed, a maid was deputed to lead Jayshree and her maid to a room where the Sultan would come when she was free. The old maid, her rheumy eyes wide with awe, was whisked away to an adjoining room by a girl, while Jayshree looked around the private chamber into which she had been shown.

A royal apartment, she had thought, would be more luxuriously decorated. This was rich, but by no means opulent. The drapes at the carved stone windows were of heavy silk, but not brocaded. The cushions and bolsters were embroidered, but there was not a single gold thread, not one sequin to be seen among the simple geometric patterns that decorated them. The salver, with its pitcher of sherbet and its goblets, was beaten silver. There was not a gemstone in sight.

Oddly enough, it reassured her. Jalal may have become Razia Sultan, but somewhere in the Sultan there still lurked the young woman who had little time for prettiness.

Voices approached, and suddenly, the curtains at the door were pulled aside. The Sultan strode in. Jayshree, standing at the window and looking out into an inner courtyard where pigeons pecked at scattered grain, turned.

Behind Razia Sultan came two female guards, scabbards at their belts. Three maids bustled in behind them, two bearing a large, empty salver, while the other carried garments which she placed on a stool near the door. She moved forward to receive the headdress—the crown, thought Jayshree, in a moment of stunned recognition; the crown of Dilli—that Razia had reached up and taken off as soon as she had set foot over the threshold.

She was already sliding her arms out of her coat. Her gaze flickered towards Jayshree and then back to her own attendant, who held out a simple light coat of pale green. Razia slipped it on and nodded to her entourage. 'Leave us.'

Jayshree watched, her sense of unease now bordering on fear as the others left the room. The curtains swung back into place and Razia turned to Jayshree, her eyes cold in a face hard as granite. 'It has been a long time since I saw you, Jayshree,' she said. 'Does my having become Sultan have something to do with it? It does, of course; you were among the petitioners.' Her lip curled in derision. 'I had not imagined you so selfish. But perhaps the years have changed you?'

The silence was profound—and filled with cynicism and contempt. Jayshree stared at the floor. 'I came because I was forced to,' she replied finally, when the silence had become too much for her to bear.

'You are easily forced.' There was a wry amusement in the Sultan's tone, no amusement at all. 'You did not want to come?'

Jayshree shook her head.

'Because you thought I had betrayed you, lied to you? You held it against me, Jayshree?'

She did not know where to look. To look up into those penetrating eyes would be impossible; she could already feel the recriminations and the accusations crowding her throat, eager to spill out. If she looked up, if she acknowledged the truth of what Razia had said, she would seal her own doom. Nobody with power would tolerate what she had to say.

'Say it, Jayshree. Say all you have bottled up within yourself all these years.' Razia sighed and sat down on a low divan beside the window. 'It is the least I owe you.'

'You owe me nothing,' Jayshree mumbled.

For a long while, Razia said nothing. Then, looking out of the window with unseeing eyes, she said, 'I thought of telling you, many a time. Each time I stopped because I could not see how to go about it. "By the way, you should know who I actually am. My father is Altamash, the Sultan. And I am Jalaluddin Razia, the princess?" I could not, Jayshree. Would you, even, have believed me? I thought there was time, that someday there would be the right opportunity, the right moment.' She turned to look at Jayshree, her eyes soft and sad now. 'I am sorry. I was being a coward.'

Said like that, it made Jayshree squirm. But she could not bring herself to say anything, and Razia continued. 'I was scared that you would desert me.' She looked down at her hands, which lay in her lap, the fingers knitted together. 'But that was inevitable, wasn't it? You deserted me anyway.'

The years rolled back as swiftly as a clap of thunder. Jayshree forgot that she was standing in the presence of the ruler of not just Dilli, but of an empire. That this woman seated beside the window could clap her in prison, put her to death, have her entire family decimated before the sun had set that day. Jayshree was no longer a petitioner before the Sultan. She was Jayshree, a young girl hitting back at the one who had betrayed her trust. 'I deserted you?' she spat back. 'As if I did not have just cause to leave! You were the one who lied to me! Was there any element of truth in all that you told me? No—all you gave me was a tissue of lies, lie piled upon lie. And I was fool enough to believe them!' The tears had welled up in her eyes and were beginning to stream down her cheeks, but she carried on regardless. 'How dare you accuse me of desertion? Only one who is trusted can be deemed to have deserted. You never trusted me. If you had, you would have told me.'

Razia said nothing, and Jayshree continued to speak, her words fuelling her bitterness, reviving that long-ago humiliation. Finally, she stopped, out of breath and with her cheeks wet with tears. Razia's face was impassive. The face of the Sultan, Jayshree thought. Removed, aloof.

'I am sorry,' Razia repeated when Jayshree had wiped her eyes. 'If it is any consolation, you should know that I tried to make amends. You had never told me where you lived, but I made enquiries. I failed. Then, since I was not able to find you, I started going to the Jami Masjid in the hope that I might find you there someday. But you never came.'

Jayshree remembered the maid telling her that she had seen Jalal there. Involuntarily, she nodded, and Razia noticed it.

'You knew? Did you come secretly, too?'

'No.'

'Hmm. Someone told you, then. When?'

Jayshree hesitated. 'Six months ago,' she admitted. 'When the late Sultan passed away.'

'And who was this? This person who knew, but held their tongue? Until it looked as if your old friend was going to be seated on the throne? It seemed a good time to speak up and ask for a favour, is that so?'

Jayshree winced.

Razia rose to her feet. 'That maid who accompanied you here? I thought so; she looked too frail to be able to provide any assistance to you here. She would then be the reason for your coming here. Why? What does she need? Is someone trying to wrench the last few coins out of her?'

'It is not a big matter,' Jayshree conceded. 'Trivial for you. But important for her.'

Razia nodded. 'Very well. Tell me.'

Jayshree had taken care to warn the maid that the Sultan had not given any definite answer. 'She has said she will send word,' Jayshree said. 'Nothing more. Do not get your hopes up.'

It was no use; the old woman was already quivering with relief, the desperation replaced by hope. 'She has not said no,' she said. 'If she meant to turn down your request she would not have made you wait for an answer, would she?'

Jayshree felt a twinge of guilt at the knowledge that she was deceiving this woman just as Razia had once deceived her. It was not the Sultan but she, Jayshree, who had not taken a decision. She who had dithered and refused to say yes or no.

Razia had not said no. But after having heard everything Jayshree had to tell her about the old woman's plea, she had said, 'A minor offence, I think, and one easily forgiven. But if I allow this, will you allow me a favour too? Will you come here? Will you serve me as companion and friend and adviser?'

A startled Jayshree had reacted with immediate refusal. She was a housewife, a mother; she knew nothing of the palace. 'And I have no interest in it. It frightens me,' she had added. 'All the palace intrigues, the plotting and conspiracies. It seems to me as if everybody is a puppeteer, pulling strings.' She had paused, struck by a thought. 'And everybody a puppet, too,' she had added in a small, awed voice.

'See?' Razia had said with a lifting of the corners of her lips. 'You are not as ignorant of the ways of the court as you imagine yourself to be.' The smile, slight as it was, was gone almost as soon as it had appeared. The Sultan had risen to her feet, her hands clasped behind her as she began pacing the floor. 'Some of the more powerful men of the Chahalgani support me. I don't know why,'—with a bitter laugh—'since I doubt they imagine a woman can rule. But they are the ones who helped put me on the throne. Perhaps they were so heartily sick of my brother's reign, they were willing to give me a chance.'

Jayshree, who also suspected that was true, had held her tongue. 'I am hemmed in,' Razia had said. 'Hemmed in and friendless. I never know where the next blow will come from, or what shape it will take. When one of these men who have sworn allegiance to me will betray me. The wazir, Nizam-ul-mulk Junaidi, is opposed to my reign. Already. It is less than a month since I came to the throne and my own wazir, the very man I should be depending upon the most, does not want me to be Sultan!'

She had stood there, her head bowed, her shoulders heaving, even though she had wept not a single tear. When she had finally turned around, her face had looked placid enough, but Jayshree, looking into her eyes, had seen the anguish there, the exhaustion and the loneliness. 'I want a friend by me,' Razia said. 'If only to keep me sane. To stand by me.'

Jayshree had still hesitated, and Razia had not tried to coerce her. 'Think over it,' she had said quietly as Jayshree had taken her leave. 'And come back to me to tell me what decision you have taken.'

'I am told you have been offered a position at court.'

Jayshree's head snapped up. She was sitting cross-legged on the floor picking fenugreek leaves. A large bundle of leaves fresh from the field lay in a cane basket beside her; in front of her was a brass platter. It was a simple, repetitive task, one that needed only her fingers to work. Her mind was free to ramble and to fret.

Her mother had come into the house and into the courtyard, soundlessly. Or perhaps she had knocked and been let in, but Jayshree had been too deep in thought to pay attention.

She was standing in front of Jayshree now, still a fine figure of a woman. Tall, her face still striking, her hair silver only in a few strands. 'Well? Is what I've been told true?'

The old maidservant had been there, hovering in the corridor when Jayshree had left Razia. Razia, as she bade Jayshree a subdued farewell, had said, 'I will be waiting for your answer. And I hope you will say yes. It shall be a relief to have you here.'

The maid must have overheard that, and she must have told Jayshree's mother. The last person Jayshree would have wanted to know about what had transpired.

She forced a smile to her lips and indicated the charpai next to her. 'Sit, Ma. Will you have some buttermilk?'

Gayatri shook her head impatiently. 'Don't try to change the subject. Answer my question. Is it true? Did the Sultan offer you employment?'

There was no help for it; thus cornered, Jayshree could do nothing but admit it.

Her mother smiled, as smugly as a cat that has feasted on cream. 'It is just what I would want,' Gayatri said. 'I hope you said yes.'

Jayshree shook her head. 'No. How can I? There is the household to be managed, the children to be looked after. And what earthly use could I be to the Sultan?' But Gayatri was shaking her head even before Jayshree had finished speaking.

'Don't make excuses! If the Sultan is so insistent that you be in her employ, she must think you worthy of it. If she wants you beside her, why should you object?' She bent and imperiously tapped Jayshree's hand, with its stalks of fenugreek. 'Stop scrabbling amidst those leaves. That can wait. Look at me.'

Jayshree obeyed.

'You are not indispensable at home, you know.' Gayatri said, brutally honest as always. 'Most of your children are old enough to look after themselves and you have plenty of competent servants. It is not even as if the Sultan will expect you to be by her side every moment, day and night.'

She must have seen the indecision still in Jayshree's demeanour, because she added, 'If it worries you so much, I shall come and live here. Will you rest easy when your mother is personally supervising your household and your family?'

Jayshree shook her head. 'No, Ma; there is no need for that.'

She chewed on her lower lip, wondering at the possible cause for her mother's eagerness. A large part of it was ambition, of course. Where most other women might draw their happiness and contentment from their possessions, the success of their husbands or the love of their children, Gayatri lived for one thing alone: fame. In a society that gave women little scope to shine, she had found herself suppressed and having to settle for second best by pinning her hopes on her husband. But Nandu had proven unequal to the task; he had not been an utter failure, but he had not soared as high as Gayatri would have wished.

And now, well into her old age, when she had given up all hope, there had come this opportunity, that her daughter should become a companion to the Sultan of Dilli itself.

It was not hard to understand why Gayatri should be willing to give up her own comfort for something like that.

But there was something, something that should have made Gayatri baulk at having anything to do with Razia Sultan. Jayshree spoke up, her voice even. 'Ma, this is the woman whose father was responsible for Grandfather's downfall. You remember that, surely. That was why I felt so guilty when I first discovered who she was.' She bit her tongue, suddenly realizing what she had said: she had admitted to having known Razia in a different avatar. But Gayatri did not bat an eyelid, and Jayshree was left to surmise that the old maid had told her what she had learnt. Gayatri knew, and had known, perhaps, for many years.

'Why did you go to her to ask for a favour, then?' her mother retorted. 'If you truly felt nothing but revulsion for her, nothing could have induced you to present yourself in court, begging her to grant your wish.'

A maid emerged from the kitchen carrying a brass tumbler brimming with spiced buttermilk. With trembling hands she placed it next to Gayatri and ran back into the safety of the kitchen.

'Well?' Gayatri waited for Jayshree to say something. When her daughter remained silent, she took a sip of the buttermilk and said, 'Your fondness for her was not killed by realizing she was your grandfather's enemy. You feel more deeply for her than you are willing to admit.'

Jayshree had gone back to cleaning the fenugreek; it gave her something to do while she tried to think her way through the haze that surrounded her. 'No, Ma,' she said.

'That is not it. I think, back then, I was overwhelmed by the conflict between my loyalty to Grandfather, and my friendship for the princess. But now, looking back, I think I was too hasty in my decision to break the bonds I had forged with her. I can't cut her out of my heart. In those few months we were friends, she dug herself in too deep for me to be able to dislodge her, no matter how hard I try.' She glanced up. Gayatri was regarding her with an expression hard to fathom: was it pitying? Sardonic? Jayshree found it hard to tell.

'I have told you my part,' Jayshree said. 'But why should you want me to accept her offer, Ma? I would think you would want me to stay well away from the family that destroyed your father.'

Gayatri took her time answering. She took a sip, then another, of the buttermilk. Finally, she smiled an enigmatic smile. 'There is a certain poetic justice in rebuilding your life on the ruins of the lives of those who ruined you. Is it not fitting that you should use Razia as a stepping stone to make your family as rich as it once was?' She saw the dazed look on her daughter's face and laughed. 'Oh, you are simple! Still as naïve as you were ten years ago, no matter that you are a mother many times over now.'

She wagged her head, that frightening smile still on her lips. 'You leave everything to me, girl. All you have to do is go and tell your friend that you will accept her offer. I will do the rest.'

The next morning, when the Sultan returned from court, she found Jayshree waiting outside her chamber. The woman on guard duty had recognized her and offered her a stool to sit on. Jayshree looked a diminutive figure as she sat there, huddled and drawn in on herself, the thick beige shawl that she had wrapped around her so voluminous that it made her look even smaller.

When she greeted Razia, though, it was with confidence in her eyes.

'I came to tell you my answer,' Jayshree said, when the two of them were alone in Razia's chamber.

The Sultan nodded. 'I can see that.'

Jayshree squared her shoulders. 'I accept your offer. But on one condition.'

'The maid's nephew? I have already said I will grant him his release if you agree. I would have done that even if you had not agreed.' Jayshree gave a silent nod of acknowledgement, as if she had known that Razia was not petty enough to keep a poor man in prison for a matter unrelated to him. 'I will even give him employment in the palace. Is that acceptable?'

Jayshree nodded again. 'It is. Not merely acceptable, but very generous. His aunt will be grateful.' She cleared her throat. 'But that was not what I wanted to say to you.'

She hesitated for so long that the Sultan had to give her a gentle nudge. 'What is it you want, Jayshree?'

Heavily shod feet tramped in a distant courtyard. Metal clanged in a loud but coordinated clash. The Sultan's troops were going through their drill, thought Jayshree. She was reminded of the disturbing murmurs that had been doing the rounds of the bazaars. The Sultan may have finally ascended the throne in keeping with the wishes of her father, but she would not last long. Perhaps she would not last even the six months her brother had. She was a woman, after all, and what could a woman do? Already there were cliques forming, ranging themselves against the Sultan. Soon they would rise up and Razia Sultan would be consigned to history.

The tension could be felt here too. Razia knew about it, Jayshree realized as she looked into her old friend's face. There was worry in her eyes, and fatigue seemed to line her face even when she was smiling. It was as if Razia Sultan was never really at rest.

'I shall be loyal to you, Your Majesty,' Jayshree said,

'but in return, I ask that you treat me as any other of your servants. Do not bestow favours on me. And if you see me taking advantage of my position, trying to feather my nest—stop me.'

Razia frowned, puzzled. 'That is an odd request,' she murmured. 'Why do you ask that?'

Jayshree shook her head. 'I cannot tell you, for it shames me. Just—please, Your Majesty—just grant me this one wish. Use my services as you will, but do not reward me for them.'

'You will be paid.' Razia's frown had been replaced by outright amazement.

'A token amount, if you will. Do not tempt me, Your Majesty. Please do not let anyone say that I rose to any height—of power, of wealth, whatever—on the strength of our friendship. Let me be Jayshree, and you be the Sultan.'

16

Madhav stepped forward, head bowed and hands folded below his waist. Beside him stood Mahesh, clutching a sheaf of papers. Around them were ranged others who were at work on the mausoleum of Altamash: masons, stone workers, the architect. The architect was an occasional visitor now that the structure of the tomb was complete; so too, was the master mason. What work remained was overseen by his assistant. The majority of the men who remained were stone carvers.

'It seems to be progressing well,' the Sultan said as she looked around, her eye travelling across the interior of the tomb. They had begun putting in place some of the carved panels, and Madhav was proud of the work. It was intricate, it was flamboyant, but it was not obscenely rich. The line between opulent and vulgar was a fine one; they had managed to stay on the right side.

'It is, Your Majesty.'

She wandered about, inside and out, trailed at a respectful distance by Madhav and his entourage. One question was asked here, another there. A suggestion was made, a nod of approval bestowed.

'Jayshree,' she said, turning to the woman beside her. 'What do you think?'

The woman who was beside the Sultan tilted her head up. It was covered with an odhni, as blue as a kingfisher's wing, dotted with tiny mirrors that glinted in the sun. Madhav glanced her way, surprised that the Sultan asked one of her attendants for an opinion.

'It is beautiful,' Jayshree said. 'Such fine carving is rare indeed.' She had lifted her odhni away from her face briefly in order to look around her. She now lowered it back into place, obscuring her face again.

The Sultan smiled. She did not cover her face; in fact, she usually went about in men's attire, even riding out on an elephant at times. Today, of course, for this unexpected visit to the site of Altamash's tomb she had come on horseback, her entourage divided among those who rode and those who came more sedately in palanquins. This woman, the one whose face brought back to Madhav his long-ago youth, had alighted from a palanquin.

Her face was Gayatri's, a Gayatri older than the one he had known. A more mature woman, her eyes quiet, her voice mellow. He realized that, on second glance, she was nothing like the woman he imagined Gayatri would have become. In face, perhaps; in demeanour, no.

The Sultan finished her inspection of the tomb and stood outside for a moment, her hands clasped behind her back, looking across the buildings around it. 'I think I shall go to the masjid for a while,' she said. 'But I want to be alone.' With a brief instruction to the captain of her guard to depute soldiers to guard the periphery of the mosque—but to allow her privacy—she walked away. The troops broke up, hurrying to their positions. The few people left, the woman named Jayshree and a couple of maids, stood outside the tomb. They looked a little lost.

Madhav stepped forward. 'Daughter,' he said gently, 'Are you Nandu's girl?'

ঙ

'How did you guess she was his daughter?' Mahesh asked, after the Sultan and her entourage had left.

'Her face is just like her mother's,' Madhav replied. 'I had seen her a couple of times, years ago.'

Mahesh worked on in silence for the next few minutes. 'You don't get along with Nandu,' he pointed out after a while. 'You have never agreed to work on any project on which he too was employed, at least not in my memory. And you knew his wife?'

Madhav let a small smile appear on his lips. 'Many years ago, before she was his wife.'

'Ah.' Mahesh chortled. 'And does Ma know about this?'

'She does. And she knows too, that I feel exactly the same about Nandu's wife as I feel about Nandu. She is a vicious woman, who cares for nobody and nothing but herself. If someone should come in the way of her ambition, she will ruin him.'

'And this woman? Do you think she is cast in the same mould as her parents?'

Madhav picked up a finer chisel than the one he had been using. He chipped away at the stone for a minute before he answered his son's question. 'I do not know, Mahesh,' he said. 'But the very fact that she is close enough to the Sultan for her opinion to be sought—that makes me think. A stone carver's daughter and the Sultan's confidante?' He shook his head. 'I wonder how she did it.'

'It could not last,' said the Sultan. She was sitting in her private chamber, her elbows on her knees, her head in her hands. Her voice was barely audible. Jayshree, standing beside her, still holding the salver with its little tray of refreshments, a goblet and pitcher of sherbet, did not know whether the muffled voice was a result of the Sultan's head being bowed and half screened by her hands, or whether it was emotion. It was emotion, she feared, and that unsettled her. Razia was the epitome of unruffled calm; in the few weeks Jayshree had been in her service, she had realized that there was little Razia seemed to fear. She was indomitable.

But not now. Razia looked up, straightened, and placed her hands very deliberately in her lap. 'Why are you still here?' she asked. 'It is past sunset. You should have gone home by now to your family.'

Jayshree brushed away the question with a shake of her head. 'That does not matter, Your Majesty. My place is with you.' She proffered the salver. Razia shook her head.

'Please have some, Your Majesty. You have not eaten since this morning. How will you cope if you do not eat?'

She seated herself on a stool only when Razia had accepted a goblet of sherbet and some fruit. 'What is the news, Your Majesty?' she asked quietly. 'Is the wazir rearing his head again?'

Razia gave a short, bitter laugh. 'Rearing his head? That is an interesting way of putting it, Jayshree. If it were only Nizam-ul-mulk Junaidi who was intent on pushing me off the throne, I might not have been so worried. But he has support now. There are others. Malik Kochi, Malik Jani, Malik Kabir Khan, Malik Izzaddin Muhammad Salari. All of them are ranging themselves on Nizam-ul-mulk's side.'

'Those names are not familiar to me,' Jayshree remarked.

'They are not all from Dilli. He has pulled them in from far and wide. And they are ready to fight beside him to remove me.

'I had never thought it would be such a nightmare,' she added after a sip of the sherbet. 'I was naïve, I suppose. When my father was the Sultan I always knew there were courtiers who did not agree with him. Some, too, who would have gladly replaced him with another if it were possible. But Abba had his men, he had enough support among the nobles to not be bothered by those who did not even pretend to owe him any loyalty.' The fingers of her free hand trailed absently along the edge of her coat where it lay draped on her thigh. 'Now I know. That was my father, and this is I.'

'There are still many who are loyal to you,' Jayshree pointed out. 'Many who know how capable you are, how suited to the title you hold. You have the mind of a Sultan, the temperament. And you are no less skilled in warfare than any warrior who has led an army.' Emotion had made her voice rise, sharp and shrill; she lowered it with a conscious effort, and ended up blurting out in a gruff little voice, 'People know that.'

'Which people? You?' A sad smile appeared briefly on

Razia's lips. 'Who will listen to you, my Jayshree? You are a woman like me. These men do not trust women.' Her despair was fast evaporating, giving way to anger. 'They would sooner have a dolt like Ruknuddin, without a lucid thought in his head or a care for his kingdom, than me! And all because I happen to be a woman!'

She rose to her feet, eyes flashing, the lassitude and fatigue gone. She raised the goblet and swallowing down the sherbet, put the empty goblet down on the salver. 'Well,' she said. 'I will show them. My father named me the Sultan of Dilli, and I have never, where it was in my power, disobeyed Abba. I will die before I will give up the responsibility he placed on my shoulders.'

☙

'I never thought I would see things like this again, not in my lifetime,' Madhav said to Mahesh. The two of them were on horseback, standing still in the shade of a small and dense copse of scrubby acacias. Far beyond them, but just within sight, was the bank of the Yamuna. Nothing could be seen of the river at this distance. Not the water, of course—they were too far for that, to see a river that flowed through a land as flat as this—but not even the reeds that lined its banks, or the waterbirds, the moorhens and herons and lapwings that nested along the water.

Matters had finally come to a head, and Razia's enemies were marching towards her capital. Word had reached her well in advance: Razia's detractors saw no reason to hide their intent, or to fool her into a sense of security. They had joined hands, they had formed alliances in full sight, and now they came to oust her from the throne.

The armies of Razia Sultan had camped here by the riverside after weeks of waiting it out within the city walls. The governor of Awadh, far away to the north-east of Dilli, had come to the aid of the Sultan, bringing with him seasoned troops. For a brief while, there had been exhilaration, hope that the armies besieging Dilli would finally be thrown back, the rebel noblemen pushed away. Not that much of Dilli's population cared one way or the other who sat on the throne. One ruler was much like the other, they had realized.

'I had thought when I first came to Dilli that it would be impossible to live under a Muslim ruler,' Madhav murmured as he slid down from his horse and stretched. 'The old man Balram tried to tell me that my fears were unfounded, and that life would go on.' He stroked his horse's neck. 'I now realize how right he was. It really does not matter whether the ruler is Hindu or Muslim, man or woman—they all have the same motivations. All they want is to rule. To show that they have power over the lives of other people.'

'That is cynical, Baba. Is Razia Sultan as mercenary? I thought she was better than most.'

'Yes, perhaps. Perhaps she and her father are—were—both more tempered, more malleable than most. They have listened to the people, they have been both fair and just at times. But ultimately, their ambition has ruled, has it not? Razia, now. She had been dispossessed while her brother became Sultan. Had she not been ambitious, she would probably have remained where she was, content to be a princess.'

'Perhaps she saw for herself what Ruknuddin and his mother had done to Dilli.'

Madhav grinned. 'You are more than halfway to being in love with the Sultan. Beware; your wife will not like it.' He shrugged, shrugging off the smile too, though the little joke had reminded him of something, of bazaar gossip doing the rounds. 'They say she is having an affair with the superintendent of the royal stables. The Amir-al-Khayi, the amir of horses.'

'Jamaluddin Yaqut,' Mahesh supplied, with a nod. 'The Abyssinian. He has probably known her all her life, I think. Was he not a slave in the court of Altamash before he rose to be a courtier?' He shook his head. 'I do not know if he is her lover or not.'

'It is said Yaqut is exceptionally loyal,' Madhav remarked. 'I wonder if he is out there.' He tilted his head towards the Yamuna, cloaked as it was in a shifting cloud of dust. Razia's ally, the governor of Awadh, had been intercepted by Razia's enemies when he had crossed the Ganga and headed towards Dilli. Taken prisoner, he had sickened and died, an ignominious end for a general. More importantly, it had been a bad blow for the Sultan. This had been one ally she would have welcomed in her fight to retain her throne. With him gone, she had been obliged to set out on her own, leading her troops into battle.

Razia's armies had pitched their tents beside the Yamuna, and at sunrise the two sides had gone into battle. The dust rose, obscuring the sight of men on foot and on horseback. Even at this distance, the air rang with the clash of metal and the screams of injured and dying men and animals.

'More than Yaqut, I would have expected Malik Altunia to be by her side,' Madhav said. 'I think this gossip about her and Yaqut is no more than a rumour set about by her enemies. They want to defeat her, never mind how underhand the method used.' He had dismounted even as he spoke, and now he loosened the girths on his horse, letting the animal relax. Mahesh followed his example.

'Malik Altunia has been by Razia's side, and deeply loyal too for longer than Yaqut, from what I have heard,' Madhav added. 'If not longer, at least in closer proximity. I remember, people said he was her childhood friend, and that when she grew up, he even asked for her hand in marriage—he loved her so much. I have heard it said that she managed to finally sit on the throne through his support.'

'And as reward she made him governor of Batrind? Not a wise decision, to send away your closest friend and confidante.'

Madhav chuckled. 'Do you know what the Turks call Batrind? Tabar-e-Hind, the Gateway to Hindustan. It is a strategic location, a town that guards the entry to this land,

and to Dilli, eventually. Perhaps Razia wanted someone she could trust to guard the frontiers of her empire.'

'Hmm. And while Altunia is guarding Batrind for her, the rebels are dragging her name—and Jamaluddin Yaqut's—through the mud. I wonder what Malik Altunia's reaction would be if any of those rumours, if rumours they be, reached his ears.'

For a long time they stood there, the two men wondering what was to become of their city, of the Sultan, of themselves. Finally, Madhav sighed and rubbed his eyes. He was looking careworn, his eyes tired and dull. 'Come,' he said, touching Mahesh's shoulder gently. 'Let us go home. We cannot tell who will win this battle, and it is pointless to stand here and run the risk of getting in the way of whoever will be rushing from here to get onto the throne.'

ᐅ

Jayshree came hurrying into the chamber, followed by a small platoon of maids, bearing between them fresh clothes, towels, hot water, ointments, and food and drink.

Razia, standing beside the bed, was having her breastplate removed by one of the female guards. The burnished metal shone, but splashes of red and brown marred it. There was a graze down the Sultan's right cheek, and the blood had dripped down her jaw and neck, pooling in her collar and drying there. Even as the woman unbuckled the straps that bound the breastplate to the Sultan's mail-clad torso, Razia rubbed at her cheek and grimaced.

'Your Majesty!' Jayshree had come to a standstill. She stared in horror at Razia, at the dishevelled, dusty and bloodied woman who stood there in men's clothing. 'They told me you were whole and unhurt. But this—this does not—.' She faltered and fell silent. Another woman might have wept; Jayshree's lower lip quivered slightly before she caught it in her teeth.

'I am unhurt. In battle, this does not count as injury.'

Razia laughed. It was a laugh of relief, of joy and triumph. 'Even if I had come back with an arm lopped off, I would still not mind it. I won, Jayshree. I won. I showed them I am the Sultan, that I am capable of defeating them—men, all of them—in battle. You should have seen their faces.' She grinned as the guard, having removed the breastplate and placed it on the floor, bent to undo the shin guards. 'Yes, I am Sultan,' she repeated with satisfaction. 'And I shall remain so.'

Later, after she had bathed and rested, and had announced her victory in court, Razia summoned Jayshree. She was quieter now, the euphoria tamped down into a more assured self-confidence. Not completely, however. In her ceaseless pacing about the chamber, from window to bed to door, Jayshree could see tension, the exhilaration that would still take some days to dissipate.

'Your Majesty,' Jayshree said, 'many have told you, and I have too, but once again, I congratulate you. You have won a signal victory.'

Razia stopped in her pacing and gave Jayshree a wry smile. 'The meekness does not suit you, Jayshree. I thought the way you scurried in earlier, scolding me for having got hurt, was rather more appropriate to the Jayshree I know.' The grin widened when she saw Jayshree's discomfiture. 'It is all right. Thank you. Why have you not gone home already? It is late.'

'I will go. I came to bid you goodnight, Your Majesty.'

'And?'

Jayshree paused, unsure. When she finally spoke, it was with lowered eyes. 'It is about the appointments. You have said you will make new appointments to the important positions at court.'

'Yes. The Nizam-ul-mulk's deputy will take his place as the new Nizam-ul-mulk. And I will put the army under the command of Malik Saifuddin Aibak Bahtu. A few others will be rewarded for their work. Why? Is there someone you wish to recommend? You, of course, will get your due reward. I mean to appoint you as—'

Before she could complete the sentence, Jayshree had cut in. 'No, Your Majesty, please. Whatever post you wish to give to me, give to another. There are others more deserving than I, others far more capable than I.'

'Others more loyal than you?'

Jayshree did not answer the question. She hung her head in silence.

'I do not understand your reason for this obstinate refusal to accept any rewards from me,' Razia said, eventually. She sounded weary and peevish. 'But have it your own way. And tell me someday, if you will, your secret. Go, now. I have work to attend to.'

17

Four Years Later
Vikram Samwat 1296 (1240 CE)

The brief spring of Dilli was nearing its end. The birds and squirrels had devoured the last of the fruit on the peepal trees. Each day was a little warmer, a little longer. The green of the leaves on the trees was beginning to darken, to take on the robustness that would have to last them through the coming summer. The water in the baolis and wells was still abundant, but people were beginning to consume it with more discretion, instinctively rationing it.

'What do you think?' Mahesh asked. The slab he had uncovered was about a yard across and a little less wide than his forearm was long. The lotuses carved on it were entwined not with the round platter-like leaves of the lotuses themselves, but with slender tendrils and tiny feathery leaves. Along the edge ran a narrow border of interlocked diamonds.

'It is beautiful,' said Madhav after a minute of running his fingers along it, admiring every curve, every little sign of the carver's skill. 'For the new mansion Bansi Lal is building?'

Mahesh nodded. 'What else is there, Baba?' His face, having lit up briefly with joy and pride at his father's praise for his work, fell. 'The Sultan is too busy putting down revolts to have time or money to build anything. When she had first been crowned and had come to see the progress on her father's tomb, I had hoped she would take an interest in construction. That we would get to work on palaces and stepwells and inns. Even mosques or tombs; I wouldn't mind that, if it allowed me to work.' He shook his head in despair. 'But she builds nothing, and half the nobility seems to follow her example.'

'Even when they do not like her,' Madhav agreed, with a small smile at the irony of it.

'Yes. She has her fair share of detractors, does she not?'

'More than her fair share, I would say.' Madhav pulled the sacking cover over the slab his son had displayed to him, and patted it absently. 'It has not been an easy time for her,' he said quietly. 'People do not let slip any opportunity to point out her shortcomings. Whether connected to governance or her private life, whether warranted or not.'

'Is a ruler's private life really his own? Her own?' Mahesh reached for the strings that had bound the sacking around the slab, and began to tie them. 'After all, a ruler should set an example. Razia Sultan shocked most people when she began to go about the city on elephant-back clad in men's clothing; but this time she has behaved in a way that's just too scandalous for words.'

'Yaqut?' asked Madhav. 'You're talking about her making him her personal attendant?'

'How can a man be personal attendant to a woman? I'm no prude, Baba, but this is outrageous! No wonder people are so incensed. I hear even Malik Altunia himself has decided to revolt against her.'

Madhav shook his head non-committally and remained silent. Mahesh mumbled on, more to himself than to his father as he busied himself in packing away his tools, but Madhav was too lost in his own thoughts to comment.

'What will happen, Baba?' Mahesh said, when they were walking home half an hour later.

'To what?'

'To us. To Dilli. They say Malik Altunia is a powerful man, and there are those who will readily ally with him against the Sultan. Will the Sultan be overthrown? And if that happens, who will become Sultan? Malik Altunia?'

Madhav placed a hand on his son's shoulder. 'When have I ever struck you as being politically minded? Do you think I know any more than what is known to every beggar in the bazaars?' He shook his head slowly. 'I wonder what the Sultan knows. And what she thinks. This Malik Altunia was her childhood friend, perhaps even the man she once intended to marry. That he should revolt against her must seem like betrayal of the very worst sort.'

They had arrived at the bazaar near the Yogmaya Temple. The stalls and shops wore a deserted look. Few people were out and about, and those who were making purchases seemed to be hurrying through the process. There was no leisurely meandering here, no stopping to chat with a passing friend.

Madhav suddenly stopped. 'Go, Mahesh,' he said. 'Go home, son. I will come on my own.'

Mahesh turned to look at his father in surprise. Madhav's gaze was fixed on something in the middle distance; his son's gaze followed his own, and Mahesh saw that a woman had just emerged from the entrance of the Yogmaya Temple. In one hand she held a silver platter on which she would have carried the flowers and the other offerings—coins, incense, fruit—to lay at the feet of the deity.

'That is Jayshree, is it not?' said Mahesh. 'Do you want to speak to her, Baba?'

Madhav nodded. 'Go, Mahesh. There is something I must ask her. Tell your mother I will be home shortly.'

Jayshree looked up at the sound of her name, and came to a halt. Thanks to the platter she held in one hand, a flame still flickering in its little bowl-shaped brass lamp, she could not offer a namaste. She contented herself by ducking her head and murmuring a word of greeting.

'Daughter,' Madhav said, 'you know who I am.'

Jayshree looked taken aback, but she nodded. 'Yes. We met some time back, I think, when I visited the tomb of Sultan Altamash with Her Majesty. You spoke to me then. How have you been, Babuji?'

Madhav did not answer her question. 'There is something I must talk to you about,' he said. 'It will take only a few minutes, no more. This,' he looked around them, at the people entering the temple, the others emerging, 'is a crowded place. Not conducive to a conversation. Can we sit there, under the peepal tree?'

'Tell me,' he said, when they had settled under the tree, 'why are you in service to the Sultan?'

Though she had acquiesced to his desire to talk to her, Jayshree had looked uncomfortable from the moment he had suggested this conversation. His words seemed to make her even more awkward. The hands clutching the silver platter, which now sat in her lap, tightened around its rim, her knuckles standing out white.

'I would have thought your mother would have forbidden it,' Madhav said, lowering his voice to a soft murmur both in an attempt to soothe her fears and to reduce the chances of anyone eavesdropping. 'Both she and your father had good reason to hate Altamash. I would have thought your mother would also hate Altamash's daughter.'

Just as Madhav was beginning to think she would not respond, Jayshree whispered, 'She does. She hates her.'

'And yet you serve her?'

Another silence, a longer one. Finally, with a suddenness that startled Madhav enough to make him blink and recoil, Jayshree banged her platter down onto the ground beside her. The little flame in the lamp jumped and flickered. 'Yes!' Jayshree said with a muffled sob. 'Yes, I do! She was my childhood friend, Babuji. I did not know who she was!'

It spilled out, in such muffled, often half-formed sentences that Madhav got only a vague idea of how Nandu and Gayatri's daughter had happened to meet and befriend the princess who was now the Sultan. He did not understand how Jayshree had come to realize the truth of her friend's identity, for Jayshree was weeping freely by the time she reached that stage of her narrative. She broke off in the middle of telling him how the maid had come asking for a favour, and how Razia had asked her to be her companion. Madhav waited patiently for her to regain her composure, and when she was calm again, he asked, 'And you could not say no? Is that what is weighing on your mind? Do you resent the fact that you have to serve she whom you and your family hate?'

'No,' said Jayshree at length. She heaved a deep sigh, and when she spoke again, though her voice was steady, Madhav could hear the tremor in it, the emotion kept in such tenuous control that it threatened to snap at any moment. 'It is not that. I do not hate her, though I thought I did. I cannot.'

'Your mother disapproves.'

Jayshree laughed, a sound devoid of amusement. 'She does not merely disapprove. Thrice now, my mother has given me sweets to be presented to Her Majesty on the anniversary of her coronation. The first time she made the mistake of telling me that I would not be a servant of the Sultan's after she had eaten the sweets.' She turned to look at Madhav. 'I fed one of those sweets to a rat my son caught. It merely nibbled at a corner, but it was dead within half an hour.'

An oath escaped Madhav. 'But—but how could Gayatri do something like that? Surely there must be some mistake.'

'What? The sweets gone stale? The milk curdled? Once, perhaps. But twice? Three times? Every time my mother has given me sweets for Her Majesty, I have tested the sweets on some creature. Every time, there has been a death. Every time, my mother has been lurking at my doorstep, waiting breathlessly to hear the outcome of my presenting of her sweets to the Sultan.'

'What have you told her?'

'That I am in no position to see what the Sultan eats or does not eat.' She lifted her head to look into his face. She looked so eerily like Gayatri, thought Madhav. A gentler, kinder version of Gayatri.

Right now, though, her face wore a look of determination, her gaze steely and her lips set in a thin line. 'Hatred is one thing, Babuji, but murder, another. Even if Her Majesty had not once been my friend, I would not want her assassinated.' Her gaze searched his face.

'You knew my mother, Babuji?' she asked, her voice earnest. 'Was my mother so maddened by her hatred even then, as a young woman? Did she always place her own interests first? Was she so ruthlessly ambitious?'

Madhav stared at her, remembering the Gayatri who had been the cause of his having to flee Dilli. A Gayatri who had screamed and flown into a panic, who had refused to listen to him.

'I did not know her well enough,' he admitted. 'I had only seen her once or twice, no more.' He shook his head, still finding it hard to believe what he had just heard. 'I would never have imagined she would do something like this. What have you done to stop her?'

A look of mortification crept into Jayshree's eyes. She looked down at the ground, a flush rising to her cheeks. 'I cannot tell the Sultan, Babuji. She may have once been my friend, but that will count for nothing if it is revealed that my mother has been trying to assassinate her. At the very least, Ma will be exiled.'

'Then talk to your mother. How can she even think she will get away with something like this? And she will drag you down too. Has she no consideration for her own daughter?'

'Her family's honour is all that matters to Ma.' The words hung, depressed and dejected, in the air.

'What if she finds some other way to get to the Sultan?' Madhav asked. 'If she sees that her attempts to harm the Sultan through you are not coming to anything, she might attempt some other means.'

Jayshree shook her head. 'No. Of that I am sure. My mother has no other access to the Sultan. Even if she realized that she might be able to bribe someone, she would not do it. She believes in poetic justice. That Razia should be killed by my hands.' She shuddered. 'Let us not talk about this, Babuji. Tell me, why did you want to talk to me? Why did you want to know my reason for serving Her Majesty?'

'Just as you have cause to hate Altamash and his family, I have cause to be grateful to him,' Madhav replied. 'My life would have turned out very differently perhaps, if it had not been for Altamash's intervention. He helped plead Shantinath's case, of course, but even beyond that: he helped me, he patronized me and helped me get work in Dilli. Later still, he appointed me the head of the stone carvers time and again. To Altamash I owe what I am today.'

He turned to look at her. 'That is why I am protective of his daughter, too. That is why I fear for Razia.'

Jayshree shook her head. 'Her Majesty has nothing to fear from me, Babuji,' she said. She sounded weary, drained of all energy. 'My mother, I know, would have me murder her. But at a time like this, when even the very man she grew up with, who helped her get to the throne and who owes his own power to her—when even he has risen up against her, to whom will she go?'

The question hung in the air. Jayshree stood up, lifting the silver platter as she did so. 'I must go now, Babuji,' she said softly. 'And if you wish well for the Sultan, pray that she may weather this storm as well.'

It was a summer of strangeness. Of unforeseen turns of fate, of friends turning foes and the bitterest of enemies coming together. Victory and defeat came one on the heels of the other. At one moment, it seemed as if Razia would continue to rule, triumphant and proud, for many years still; the very next moment, treachery and deceit swallowed up every hope and dashed every dream.

The late spring that had seen Malik Altunia, the

governor of Batrind, rise up against Razia Sultan, had also seen several of his colleagues—the rulers of neighbouring provinces, especially those near the frontier—take his side. As the spring had edged towards summer and the heat had grown, Razia had led her armies into battle against her childhood sweetheart. By her side had ridden her adviser and confidant, the Abyssinian Yaqut, whom many believed had replaced Malik Altunia in the heart of the Sultan.

If Sultans had hearts, some pointed out cynically.

At Batrind, the Sultan had come to grief.

'The news could not be worse,' said Mahesh, less than a month after they had first heard of Malik Altunia's rebellion.

Madhav had begun to refuse commissions; he said that age was catching up with him, and he needed to slow down. But even now, he had not retired: every day, for an hour or more, he worked carefully and slowly on a frieze of birds and butterflies amidst foliage. It was a labour of love, more so than any other piece of work he had ever done before. Slowly, painstakingly, an inch at a time, the stone was carefully chiselled away from the spaces the carver wanted blank, built up into curves and flourishes, feathers and curving vines and lobed leaves where he wanted life to show itself in all its splendour.

The privileged few who saw the work in progress asked Madhav whom he would present this to, for surely the final product would be a work of art, a piece worth its weight in gold. But Madhav always shook his head and said, 'We shall see. I do not think I could part with it.'

He was sitting now, resting his back against a bolster. 'What bad news do you mean?' he asked his son. 'Has the Sultan been defeated?'

Mahesh wiped the perspiration off his chest with the thin cloth that served him as turban, towel, gloves and duster at work. 'That, of course,' he said. 'Everybody knows that, I think.' He made a face. 'No; I was passing by the palace when the rider arrived with the news. She has been taken prisoner, and Yaqut is dead, killed.'

Madhav fell prey to a fever that night, and fretted his way to a protracted recovery. The rains came, cooling the heat and settling the dust, but Madhav lay weak and restless. Every few days, as soon as he believed his strength was back, he would lean on his stick and walk about a little—and then come back inside, to collapse on the bed, gasping for breath. The vaid came and examined him, and shook his head wordlessly. When he was outside with Mahesh, he spoke. 'Old age,' he said. 'He has lived far longer than most men do. And old age brings with it frailties of which we know little. He may mend on his own.'

As the weeks and months went by, the city stewed. Literally, in the humidity that hung over Dilli between one shower and the next. And metaphorically, too, for the fate of Dilli was changing, and nobody knew which direction it would take. Razia Sultan was still held captive in the fort at Batrind. It was said that her captor, Malik Altunia, was lenient, even allowing her to travel in a palanquin to the mosque for daily prayers. A prisoner allowed some privileges, but a prisoner nevertheless.

In Dilli, however, a vacant throne was an invitation for the ambitious and greedy. When it had become obvious that Razia was incarcerated, possibly for good, in Batrind, one of her stepbrothers had had himself crowned Sultan in her stead. The Chahalgani, the clique of forty noblemen who surrounded the throne, had been won over. Not perhaps because Muizuddin Bahram Shah was in any way suited for the throne, but perhaps more because a weak Sultan could be a malleable puppet for the more ambitious of the Chahalgani. Within less than a month of Razia's departure from Dilli, she had been deposed.

'Dilli is lost,' Madhav muttered in despair when Mahesh gave him the news. 'The poor girl.'

Mahesh wondered privately at his father's devotion to the former Sultan, but he held his tongue.

Madhav was recuperating, but a lassitude had set in that seemed to have more to do with his mood than the state of his health. He moved about now and then, sitting in the courtyard of his house when the weather permitted, and there was a grandchild at hand to fan him. He did not speak to visitors, he did not even look at the frieze he had been working on. Mahesh brought up the subject occasionally in an attempt to gently nudge his father back into the world, but Madhav merely shook his head and waved him to silence.

And then one day, Mahesh burst into the courtyard with astounding news. Malik Altunia, to the surprise of all of Dilli, had changed sides again. He had married the Sultan. He was no longer her captor; he was now her husband and her ally.

Madhav's first reaction was of disbelief. Whom had Mahesh heard it from? Were they to be trusted?

But no; it was official news, sent from Batrind by Razia and her new husband. A designated messenger had brought the announcement, along with the implication that Razia, her courage and her forces now bolstered by Malik Altunia's, would be coming back to reclaim her throne.

Madhav sat up, eyes gleaming and face more animated than anyone had seen it in many months. He called for a glass of buttermilk. Then he asked for some mangoes. 'And,' he said to Mahesh when he had eaten and drunk, 'bring me my frieze, my Garden of Heaven.'

Mahesh, grinning with relief, brought out the panel, wrapped in sacking and kept carefully under Madhav's bed all this while. 'The Garden of Heaven? Is that what you call it?' he asked, as he placed it in front of his father and unwrapped the stone slab.

'An old man's whim.'

'No. I did not mean to denigrate your work, Baba. It

is an apt name.' He gazed down fondly at the carving, his fingertips tracing the beauty of it. 'Finish it, Baba,' he said. 'It deserves to be completed. It would be a sin to leave something like this half done.'

ଓ

'There are those who say the Sultan realized she was left friendless when Yaqut was killed,' Mahesh remarked a few hours later when the excitement had died down. 'They think she offered herself and the throne of Dilli to Malik Altunia in exchange for her freedom.'

'Is Malik Altunia capable of occupying the throne of Dilli?' Madhav shook his head. 'If he wanted to be Sultan, he might have tried for the throne when Ruknuddin died, but he did not. No, Mahesh; I do not think Malik Altunia will try for the throne. He is a realistic man, he knows his wife's ambition. She will not give up her claim to the throne, not even to her husband.'

Mahesh's daughter had brought in a small plate of refreshments for him, along with a brass pot of water. He washed his hands and dried them, then he sat down beside his father, eating as they chatted. 'What do you think, Baba? Why had Malik Altunia revolted against Razia Sultan, if only to change sides once again? I thought he had believed the rumours of the Sultan and her relationship with Yaqut, and that had angered him. Why would he now so quickly turn around?'

'How can I say?' Madhav murmured. 'Perhaps it only took a conversation—a real conversation, not mere letters traversing such a distance—for them to realize that they did indeed love one another.' He sighed and helped himself to a sweet from the plate. 'Or perhaps it is something as simple as two people realizing they need each other in order for both of them to advance. The Sultan may have offered Malik Altunia something beyond the mere governorship of Batrind.' He swallowed, smacked his lips and muttered, 'This is good,' but it was all done absently. Mahesh, watching him, knew Madhav's mind was not on something as domestic as sweets. 'As it is, as the consort of the Sultan of Dilli he will be of far more consequence than he was before.

'Who knows,' he repeated, as he leaned back with a smile of genuine happiness on his lips. 'But I am relieved. At least this war will be over now and the Sultan can return to Dilli. She can get back to ruling her empire and we can get back to our own lives.'

Mahesh thought of pointing out that the people of Dilli had gone about with their lives while their Sultan had battled for her throne in faraway Batrind, but he held his tongue. Madhav had indeed put his life aside for this brief spell. Now perhaps he would gather up the reins and set off again.

☙

It was not to be. The monsoon began to recede, having filled to the brim the stepwells and wells of Dilli, having bestowed on the city that newly washed look that might last till winter. The rains dwindled, the humidity lifted, the air became cooler. News kept trickling into town, sometimes no more than a mere breath of information, so slight and so devoid of detail that it was dismissed as rumour even before it could spread. At other times it was so full of graphic detail, so fully recounted that it was hard to sift fact from fiction.

So when news arrived that Razia and Malik Altunia were marching towards Dilli, Madhav merely shook his head. 'So soon? I doubt it. Is she left with any troops to call her own? Her brother the Sultan now commands the armies of Dilli; they are not hers.'

Mahesh had seated himself next to his father and was watching with admiring eyes as Madhav worked on the frieze. It was nearly finished; just a few finishing touches were being chiselled in now. A tiny bee, nearly invisible, placed on a petal here. A small tendril added there, a bud on that stalk. Nothing that altered the existing design to any great extent, but something which in an undefinable way enhanced it. Without that bee, that tendril, that bud, the carving still looked complete. With them, it looked as if the artist had put not just his craft and his skill into the carving, but his soul too. 'It is beautiful, Baba,' Mahesh said, distracted from the discussion about the politics of Dilli. 'You could make a fortune out of this. Or you could wrap it up and never show it to a living soul, and know that you had created something worthy of displaying only to divine eyes.'

Madhav's attention was all on his work, so he did not look at his son, but his eyes crinkled and the corners of his mouth turned up in a brief, warm smile. It faded within moments, however, as his mind moved back to the subject he had been discussing. 'You go about more than I do, Mahesh,' he said. 'Keep your ears open and tell me what you hear.' He chipped away at the emerging shape of a fine leaf, feathery and frail, for a minute or so while Mahesh leaned back, resting after a hard day's work.

'And will you do me one more favour?' Madhav asked. 'Will you find out if that woman, Jayshree, is in Dilli, or if she is with Her Majesty. I am curious.'

'Just when everybody was certain the rains had stopped!' Gayatri grumbled. The maid who had accompanied her had been holding an umbrella made of bamboo thatch, which she had swung away as soon as her mistress stepped into the shelter of the house. 'Move away!' Gayatri snapped at her. 'You're sopping wet, you fool. Go away, make yourself useful. Jayshree, come inside with me. I want to talk to you.'

Jayshree followed her mother silently inside. A lone window looked out from the room onto a grassy field, and Jayshree had spent all her free time these past months sitting at it. In the few snatched moments from a hectic day of looking after her children and her household, she had sat at this window and seen the field come alive. From the sere brown of summer through the nourishing months of the monsoon, when she saw life spring anew. She had seen the shimmer of water in a large but shallow pond that had formed, and had watched the sandpipers and lapwings tiptoeing along the fringes of it.

But her eyes, whenever she sat at this window, were drawn inexorably to the tower that rose in the distance, beyond the field and trees, the lanes and houses half glimpsed through that screen of greenery. The Qutb Minar, today shrouded in rain.

'Your friend is coming back to Dilli, they say,' her mother said as she settled down beside the window. 'Sit down,' Gayatri added impatiently. 'I am not going to go away any sooner if you stand about like that.'

Jayshree sat down. She did not know what to say; she had not known what to say to her mother since the day she had first realized that Gayatri was trying to use her to kill the Sultan.

'They will not allow her to return,' said Gayatri, with a smugness in her tone that spoke of knowledge beyond what was freely talked of in the bazaars. Or was it merely wishful thinking? Did Gayatri believe Razia had forever been ousted from the throne of Dilli because that was what she, Gayatri, wished?

'You think I'm a fool, don't you?' Gayatri hissed. 'I can see it in your eyes. I should have seen it years ago,' she added, her tone turning bitter, 'when you were gone for hours every day, and nobody knew where. If only that idiot of a maid had told me then, I would have nipped this foolishness in the bud. Had you no shame, that you went and befriended your greatest enemy?'

'Her Majesty was never my enemy,' Jayshree said, her voice low and weary. 'I may have thought her my enemy for a while, but that was my own misplaced hatred.'

'"Her Majesty"! If she is such a friend of yours, why does she insist on such formality?'

Jayshree looked away out of the window, trying to swallow the bile that rose to her throat.

'She is not the one who insists on being addressed by her title. But because I regard her as my friend, I think it is important too that I accord her the respect due to her.'

Gayatri laughed. It would have been an unnerving sound had it been the derisive laughter Jayshree was used to hearing from her mother. But it was not; this was genuine amusement, and it made a shiver run down Jayshree's spine.

'You are a fool,' Gayatri murmured. 'What do you think will happen? That if you go about hanging by her side, constantly fawning on her and licking her boots—she wears boots, does she not, even though she is a woman—she will do something for you? For your children? She will not, I tell you she will not. These Muslims are all the same, self-serving and ruthless. They will suck the blood from your veins and feed your flesh to their dogs if it suits their purpose. Or even if it doesn't.' She sat back, suddenly looking drained.

'But they have not forced us to their ways,' Jayshree pointed out. 'We are allowed to worship our gods, we are allowed to live the way we want to. They have even given us employment; wasn't Grandfather employed by Aibak?'

'And what was the result?' Gayatri snapped. 'What did Baba get for his loyalty? Suspicion? Accusations? Summary dismissal? Nobody even bothered to listen to what he had to say—'

Jayshree rose to her feet. 'Do you think a Hindu king would have overlooked a crime like that, Ma?' She raised a hand, gesturing for silence. 'No, Ma. I think it is time you stopped trying to convince me. I am old enough to think for myself now, old enough to know right from wrong.'

'And you think that harlot is right? If you think so highly of her, what are you doing here? Why do you not go to her, eh? Go then, and see for yourself how she thanks you for your loyalty.' Gayatri stood up suddenly, her every movement stiff with anger. 'You are no daughter of mine. I will have it proclaimed far and wide,' she said dramatically. 'Your husband will leave you, your children will be taken from you. The city will spit on you.'

And with that, she turned and went out of the room, walking briskly through the courtyard, to the outer door and through it. The rain continued to fall, drenching her. Her maid, who had been sitting in the kitchen, came running out holding the umbrella, but Gayatri was already gone.

Jayshree stood in the middle of the room and wept.

'Jayshree was in Dilli till two days ago,' Mahesh said. 'But she is gone now. I spoke to her husband.' He paused and Madhav, sensing the reluctance to impart a possibly bitter truth, asked, 'And?'

'It will distress you, Baba.'

'I have lived long enough to be able to cope with bad news, Mahesh. Tell me.'

'Her mother has disowned her. Gayatri hired a drummer and a town crier to go around the main streets of the city yesterday to announce that she and her clan no longer consider Jayshree her daughter. She has no part in the family's wealth, her name has been expunged from the family tree, and they will refuse to recognize her from now onwards.' He shook his head slowly. 'What is happening, Baba? What is the world coming to?'

Madhav had been polishing the frieze. He put aside the piece of old leather he had been using and said, 'What did Jayshree's husband say?'

'He's furious. He says he'd been patient all this while because he thought she would be able to eventually secure him royal patronage. When the Sultan was imprisoned in Batrind and her brother became Sultan, Jayshree's husband thought that was the end of that relationship. He had reconciled himself to matters returning to what they had been, before his wife became companion to Razia Sultan.'

'Where has Jayshree gone now? Does he know?'

'To Her Majesty.'

Madhav frowned, puzzled. 'Why go to the Sultan, when the Sultan herself is coming to Dilli? A few days perhaps, and if Razia Sultan defeats her brother, she can sit on the throne of Dilli again.' His brow furrowed.

'Perhaps she realizes Razia has little chance of winning this battle,' Mahesh said softly. 'Perhaps she goes to bid farewell to her friend.'

Silence fell, only to be broken a few minutes later by Madhav. He had resumed his work, but his hands moved slowly, mechanically. 'Has she gone alone?'

'I did not ask. I do not think there was anybody from the household she could have taken with her. Perhaps someone at the palace? After all, she served at the palace several years; she would know people there.'

Madhav looked troubled. 'Who in the palace would have the courage to defy Sultan Bahram Shah and go to his sister's aid? Even if only as the escort for Jayshree?' He shook his head. 'I hope she is not alone in her endeavour, but I fear she is.'

'There is nothing we can do except wait,' Mahesh said. 'And hope that all is well.'

Their hopes were to be raised soon after with the news that two of the prominent courtiers at Bahram Shah's court in Dilli had defected and joined Razia and Malik Altunia. Defected with their retinues, which could only mean those many more men to fight on Razia's side. Madhav gave a small, pleased smile when Mahesh brought him the news. 'It is good,' he said simply.

With Diwali only a few weeks away and the Hindu households of the city beginning to clean their houses, to paint and polish and decorate, further news arrived. One piece of news today, another on its heels a day later, until it was well-nigh impossible to tell what was true and what was not. All knew that the Sultan had led his armies into battle against his sister. Now rumours filled the market: he had lost. No, he had won. How could he not win? No, they had come to terms, they would rule jointly, brother and sister.

Until the day Sultan Muizuddin Bahram Shah returned to Dilli at the head of his armies, his banner flying high. He and his men were dusty, scarred and blood-spattered, but there was a fierce joy, a triumph in their tired faces and injured bodies that was all the evidence needed of the outcome of the battle. Later that evening, the Sultan's official proclamation was read out in all the squares and the main gathering places in Dilli.

Razia, the usurper, had been routed. Along with her supporters, she had fled the battlefield in ignominy, never to show her face again. Sultan Muizuddin Bahram Shah was, by the grace of Allah, still Sultan, still the defender of his city and his people, still the man to whom Dilli owed its everything.

That was the extent of the official announcement. From returned soldiers and gossipy courtiers, other news trickled out into the marketplaces the following day. Razia Sultan, Malik Altunia and those with them had fled to the town of Kapisthal. Perhaps they had intended to merely stop there for a few days to recoup their forces before making their way north-west to Batrind.

But the people of Kapisthal were not friendly, and attacked the ex-Sultan and her entourage. Razia and her soldiers, their wounds and their humiliation still fresh, put up what resistance they could. But it was futile; when the dust had cleared and the attackers began to gather the spoils of their victory, Razia, her husband Malik Altunia, and most of their men were dead.

'Who would have thought,' Mahesh said, as he walked along the path beside his father, 'that a woman so mild and meek should turn out to have been such a tigress? So fearless?'

'Razia was never mild. Do you not remember her brandishing a sword and leading the rioters at the mosque, demanding the throne for herself? Do you not remember her going into battle against those who questioned her right to the throne?'

Mahesh smiled. 'I was not talking of Razia, Baba. Jayshree. She was a mild woman, was she not? She had been brought up to be a housewife, not a soldier. Yet, see how she acted. See how she died.'

'Not with a sword in her hand, from what little I could gather.'

'No, but in a way befitting a soldier. Fearlessly. She could have stayed on in Dilli through it all. She could even have returned to Dilli on her own after Razia was forced to flee. But she did not.'

Madhav walked on, his steps slow. They were nearing their home now, after the walk from the main bazaar of Yoginipur. At the bazaar that morning, they had found a man with a bullock cart who had agreed to take them all the way north beyond the city, to where Razia had been interred. The man and his bullocks had waited while Madhav and Mahesh had gone on foot, searching for the tomb of the woman who had once sat on the throne of Dilli.

This area had been the abode of the hermit Hazrat Shah Turkman Bayabani, the Saint of the Wilderness. A man who eschewed the city and preferred to dwell in the wild. A man who had died in the wild, surrounded by the trees, the birds and the animals amongst which he had lived.

Razia had died in the same year as Shah Turkman Bayabani, yet her life had been nothing like the mystic's. A Sultan, a woman who had spent her tumultuous life trying to hold on to what was hers by right, and who had failed. And a man who had wanted nothing from life but peace and solitude.

'Her tomb is a travesty,' Madhav had murmured sadly as he had stood there, looking down at the grave. 'A few bits of rock, bound together with mortar. Is that a tomb worthy of an emperor?' He had not seemed to notice that he had referred to the dead woman in the masculine. 'And look at her father's tomb. Or even that useless Ruknuddin's. Razia deserved better.

'Let us go,' he had said after a moment. 'This place distresses me more than I had thought it would.' As they had walked back to the bullock cart, he had remarked, 'Poor Jayshree. Who gathered up her ashes, I wonder? Did anyone immerse them in the Yamuna? Is her spirit safe now?' As they had climbed into the cart, he had said, 'I think she would have been happiest next to her friend. Even if she was a devout Hindu till her last breath, she would have been happy to have her body interred there.'

'Someday perhaps we can build her a little memorial,' Mahesh had said by way of offering comfort. 'Not a tomb, but a shell of a tomb.'

Now, as they stepped over the threshold into their own home, Madhav said, 'Do you remember that frieze I was carving? The Garden of Heaven, I called it.'

'Yes. Have you found a buyer for it, Baba?'

Madhav shook his head. 'No. I never intended to sell it. You do not sell a portion of your own heart. I had thought,' he swallowed, and Mahesh saw tears gather in his eyes—'I had thought I would offer it to Razia Sultan when she reclaimed her throne.'

'It might please her spirit if you were to affix it to her tomb,' Mahesh suggested. 'It would make her tomb look more like the tomb of a ruler, too.'

'No.' Madhav slid his feet out of his sandals. 'No. The way she was treated by fate, perhaps that bare tomb is the most suited for Razia. At least it tells the true story.'

Interlude

Shagufta fell silent. Moments passed, the only sound in the room that of her breathing, deep and agitated. Opposite her, Nasiruddin watched with curious eyes. 'It is a mere tale,' he said in an oddly consolatory voice; odd, because he had not struck her as a sensitive man. 'It is a story, no more. And the best thing about stories is that if you do not like the way they end, you can change them.'

Before she could interrupt him, correct him, there came to her ears a distant sound. A growing hum, resolving itself with every passing moment into distinct, recognizable components. Shouting, the clash of steel on steel, on iron and on brick. A crash as wood splintered, a dull whump as a fragile wall collapsed.

She was scrambling to her feet even before she had begun to fully comprehend what was happening. Day after day when all the sounds had been those of the crows and vultures, the dogs and the occasional jackals, she had not let go of the thought that she could not possibly be the only human being left alive in this city. There had to be others. Dilli was too large to be left so completely desolate that the invaders could sow salt on its ruins and move on.

Shagufta stood, ear pressed to the door, straining to recognize who approached, whether friend or foe.

'Who is it?' He must have risen to his feet as noiselessly as a cat; she had not even realized that he was now standing beside her, his face gaunt and his eyes huge with weakness and the fever that perhaps still lingered.

Shagufta shook her head as she drew away from the door, forcing down the terror that was threatening to overwhelm her. This was too much like that day when they had invaded Dilli. She could again feel the panic beginning to set in. Would she be able to hide in time?

But did she even need to hide? What if they were her

townsmen? And anyway, in times like this, could she even trust a man of Dilli? In days of turbulence, a woman was not seen as a fellow human being or a fellow inhabitant, a perhaps-neighbour. With no man to stand beside her and claim her as mother, wife, sister or daughter, she was easy prey. Those she thought friends would take their pleasure of her with no more thought than a raider would.

'Who is it?' he repeated, his whisper now more insistent, the fear beginning to creep into his voice.

It occurred to her that he had been a raider, too, this man whom she had pulled into her home and looked after, sheltered. He did not frighten her, did not make her fear for her life or her virtue—or whatever was left of it, by society's standards, she thought with a private and bitter smile. It was ironic, perhaps, that her friends would be his foes, and his friends her foes.

'I do not know,' she admitted.

'Then perhaps it is best we leave as quickly as we can,' he said. He was already moving across the room, pulling on his boots and picking up his sword, the blankets he had been wrapped in. Folding them, tucking them into the sack she had pushed, as a makeshift pillow, under his head. 'Get together whatever you need. Leave nothing you can carry and cannot do without.'

She obeyed, but not without a sarcastic remark. 'You behave as if you are the victim. I have seen this before, when your lot decimated this city.'

He had the grace to look sheepish at that.

Less than a minute later, she was pulling the door shut behind her. Somewhere far to the right, where the lane joined the main street, she could hear the approaching mob. Panic washed over her; for a moment she could not decide whether to go back into her home, or run, or hide herself in the shadow of the trees behind the lane. She turned, this way and that, heart pounding and a sob rising to her lips.

He tugged at her elbow, pulling her along with him. 'We

will circle around,' he whispered. 'They seem to be searching each house. If we get behind them, we will be safe.'

There is no safety here, she wanted to say, but she followed him, balancing her pitiful little bundle of belongings on her hip. She wondered now why she had bothered to pack the things she had: her few clothes, the necklace of cheap beads Ibrahim had once given her. They were so paltry that they would have probably remained safe, unstolen, if she had left them behind.

He took a long and circuitous route, leading them deeper into the maze of lanes that surrounded her home. He seemed to be relying on instinct to take them as far as he could from the crowd.

'I think they've gone to the left,' Shagufta whispered. Her wrist, where he grasped it, was aching, and she had a stitch in her side. Despite his limp, he moved fast.

'Yes. Just a few yards more—we can turn in there, that looks as if it will lead to that little mosque. It is a mosque, is it not?'

It was a mosque, but deserted. Dead leaves and twigs littered the courtyard, and the water in the hauz, used for ablutions, was green and rank. Nasiruddin looked about swiftly, taking in the surroundings—the trees that surrounded the mosque on two sides, the wall on the other—and nodded in satisfaction. 'This will do,' he said. 'We can shelter in the mosque, and if we hear anybody approaching, it will be easy to slip into the trees.'

'What about the mob?' Shagufta whispered. 'What if they should come here?'

'Look at that dust, those leaves: they have been disturbed very recently, no earlier than this morning. They have been and gone.'

She was still nervous, but she followed him in, through the central of the three arches of the mosque. He looked around, searching for the most appropriate place to sit, and she stood for a moment before the little mihrab, the closed arch that marked the direction of prayer. It had been years since she had been in a mosque. Longer than she could remember.

'If you must pray, go down on your knees.'

Surprised out of her reverie, she turned to look at Nasiruddin. At the far end of the mosque, just a few yards from the nearby trees, he had laid down their things. It was a spot well chosen, sheltered but well situated for a quick escape into the trees.

'I was not praying,' she said quietly as she settled down with her back against the wall and drew a blanket about her. 'I have not prayed for many years now.'

'Not even when your city was attacked and you cowered inside your home? Did you never pray that you would be spared?'

'Those were not prayers,' she said stubbornly. 'That was desperation, and loneliness. Had I truly believed, I would have been at peace. I would have known that I would be saved. It is when one doubts that one babbles and begs for salvation.'

He gave her an odd look, as if he did not understand what she was saying. Or as if he did not believe her.

They heard, in the distance, the muted roar of the mob as it went its way. A few pigeons came flying and alighted in the courtyard, pecking at the seams of mortar between the flagstones. A parakeet called, its ringing call echoing. Another answered. All was silence.

'How long before sunset?' the man asked. His mouth twisted in a half-humorous smile. 'Do you know, I have seen only one sunset in this city of yours, and that I barely saw, because of the battle. I remember the redness, but now I wonder if it was the setting sun I saw, or just the blood all around. I thought night fell, but perhaps the blackness was just me losing consciousness.'

'I think the sun will set in about two hours,' she replied. 'When should we go back?'

'To your home? Not before nightfall, I think. It may be still too early for safety.'

'There may be jackals at night.'

He patted the sword, which lay atop the sack beside him. 'Armed men may get the better of me right now, but jackals? No, there you may rest assured.'

She nodded, but he must have noticed the distant look that had come into her eyes. 'What is it?' he asked. 'What are you thinking of?'

A more composed Shagufta, not tired and scared, might have shrugged off the question or changed the topic. But this Shagufta who had been abandoned by everyone, even the god she had once believed in, was too bitter to prevaricate or be diplomatic. 'We are so fond of building mosques and temples,' she said, 'And setting up for ourselves divinities to worship, but to what purpose? Does any of it make a difference? Who is to know whether there really is a heaven or a hell? What if there is nothing, after all? What if when we die, it is really the end?'

Nasiruddin looked mildly shocked at this blasphemy, but he smiled, too, a small smile of satisfaction. 'You are confiding in me,' he murmured. 'Thank you.' Then, because she looked uncomfortable, he added, 'But I have one thing to say to your questioning of religion: it is their faith that helps many people get through their lives. Misery, poverty, disease and death are inevitable. But if you believe that there is one, all-powerful and kind, it helps you survive. Just the hope that there is a heaven after death is enough. There may not be,' he conceded, 'but the hope keeps us going.'

'But what if your faith deserts you?' Shagufta burst out. 'What if you have done everything your faith requires of you, and it still lets you down? What if you have been brought up in a household whose every breath was a prayer, but you discovered one day that it was all a sham?'

The silence that followed her outburst was palpable. Just a moment earlier, the air had been filled with sounds: the chirping of birds, the faraway howling of a dog, the rustle of her clothing, the scrape of Nasiruddin's boot as he shifted his stiff leg, trying to make himself comfortable on the broken flagstones of the mosque.

All of it stopped. There was utter silence, as if the world had shut itself up, animate and inanimate alike. When the tears began flowing down her cheeks, she thought she could almost hear the flow of the water, the drops sliding down her cheeks and falling with a soft splash onto her hands.

'Was that how it was with you?' Nasiruddin asked gently. 'Did you discover religion was a sham?'

She wondered if she should tell him or not. Who was he, after all? What debt he had incurred by her care of him, he had repaid. He had fed her from the store he had brought along, and now he had brought her to safety. Most important for a storyteller, he had listened to her. They had shared food, they had shared fear. He was no stranger any more. Perhaps not yet a friend, but more than an acquaintance.

'Not really,' she admitted. 'Yes, religion was strange for me, confusing. But not a sham, I don't think so. I don't know.'

'What happened? Do you care to tell?'

She shook her head. 'No.'

He looked taken aback, as if he had been expecting a confidence and was startled at its being withheld. Then, realizing she had noticed his reaction, he chuckled. 'And here I was, hoping for another story—a good long one—to pass the time until we could go home.'

Home, she thought. Home? she wanted to ask him. Is not your home far away, far to the west? Since when have you begun to regard my home as yours? Who gave you the right?

But she merely inclined her head, accepting the comment for what it was. Probably no more than a manner of speaking. 'I can tell you a story still,' she said, her voice soft. 'About a man who found himself in much the same predicament.'

'Stuck in the wilderness while trying to escape a mob?'

'Stuck between the religion he had been brought up to think was right and proper, and a way of life that was utterly alien to all of that. Would you like to listen?'

18

Eighty-one Years Later

AH 721 (1321 CE)

'This accursed city cannot make up its mind,' Badrinath said, wiping the perspiration from his face and bare chest. 'The flowers of spring have still not wilted, but the sun is so hot, you would think it is the height of summer. Who would believe we were shivering just two months back, too?' He spat into the dust and went back to his work. Beside him, his son Girdhar worked on, chipping quietly away at the stone. Eighteen years old and an exemplary son: diligent, hard-working, obedient.

'He is a son to be proud of,' Badrinath said now and then, though never in Girdhar's presence. 'When I die, I will die a contented man, because I will leave the family's name and fortunes in good hands.' He was not the only one who saw and recognized Girdhar's worth; there were others too, among them the fathers of daughters of marriageable age. Proposals had come their way and Badrinath, having examined them, had turned each down, because no match was good enough for Girdhar.

'Other men are fathers well before they reach twenty,' Badrinath's wife Kalyani had protested the last time a match had been refused. 'If you keep turning away every proposal, what will happen? Who knows when the gods will snatch us away, and then? What of Girdhar, then?'

Badrinath had shaken his head smugly, self-confidently. 'The gods watch over us, Kalyani. Do we not pray to them every day? Do we not offer them the first morsel of everything cooked in this house? Do you not bathe their idols and light lamps before them? Then? Then how can they be anything but pleased? You mark my words, Kalyani—our devotion will stand us in good stead. The gods will watch over us. When the right girl is found, there will be a sign. We will know who she is, even if she comes to us clad in rags.'

Kalyani had looked sceptical, but she had held her tongue. Twenty years of married life with this man, who was more a proselytizing priest than a stone worker, had taught her not to oppose her husband when it came to matters of religion. Fourteen years old when she was married to Badrinath, Kalyani had been religious enough in the way a Hindu woman was expected to be religious. She had been taught the rituals, she had memorized each legend, each story. She knew which deities were worshipped when and how; she knew that Kali Mata liked red hibiscus to be offered to her, and that Shivji's pooja would be incomplete without an offering of the white and mauve flowers of the apple of Sodom.

And yet she had not been prepared for life with Badrinath. For Badrinath took religion more seriously than life itself. For him, nothing may be done without the express approval of the gods. His gods were his life, and—by extension—the lives of his wife and his children. Kalyani had learnt soon enough that her husband was capable of blinding rages if he suspected her of not honouring the gods.

Once, when Girdhar was a small boy, he had fallen and skinned his knees. Kalyani had tried to staunch the blood, but the rags she had pressed to his knees were soaked with blood within moments. A panic-stricken Kalyani had scooped up her child and run with him to the vaid.

That evening, when Badrinath had come home, he had seen the bandages on Girdhar's knees. Even before he could hear the entire story, Badrinath had reached for the hefty stick that he kept beside the door to chase away stray dogs. Kalyani had been thrashed in full sight of her children as they cowered in a corner. Badrinath had wielded the stick harder and harder with every blow, whipping himself into a frenzy of fanatical rage.

'Had you no faith in the gods?' he had snarled. 'Is this

what you have learnt in all these years? To turn to man when the gods are here?' Why had she not taken Girdhar to the little household shrine? Why had she not brought down the jar of precious Ganga jal, replenished every few months with water from the sacred Ganges, which Badrinath insisted on getting himself by walking all the way to the river, far away in the foothills at Mayapuri? One drop on the boy's tongue, a drop on each knee, and he would have been healed. But no. She had shown a lack of faith, and for that, who knew what punishment the gods would mete out?

Badrinath had stormed out, still shaking with rage, and Kalyani had waited until she could no longer hear his footsteps. Only then had she, slowly and painfully, hauled herself up. Girdhar had helped press a wet cloth to her back to wipe away the blood, and then had slipped away to the vaid's to fetch some dried herbs that would help her heal. Thirteen years had gone by, but the scars still remained on her back and legs, though they were faint now.

It had taught her and Girdhar that it was futile to imagine that Badrinath would put anyone, even his own flesh and blood, before his gods. He would sooner lose a child than displease a god.

ଓ

'Two days more and this work will be done,' Badrinath said. He and Girdhar were carving rows of lotus buds on strips of red sandstone that would decorate the house of a merchant. It was undemanding work, so mechanical that it required little concentration. Badrinath chipped briskly at a curling petal as he spoke. 'Will you go to Bhushan, then? Is that his name, your friend?'

Girdhar nodded. 'Bhushan, yes, but he's hardly a friend, just an acquaintance. He saw my work and said I had talent.'

'And that he would be able to find work for you? Good. Go to him today itself. Who knows how long it will take for him to find suitable work for you? I already have that idol of Shivji to be made; it will see me through the next few months, I should think. But if you sit around idle for too long, it will do no one any good.'

'Yes, Baba,' Girdhar murmured obediently.

The exact nature of Bhushan's work was not known to any of his acquaintances. Those who outright asked him how he earned a living were answered with a shrug and joke about how the times made it impossible for a man to survive by doing everyday tasks. Bhushan appeared to know everybody that mattered: merchants, priests, shopkeepers, officers, even the nobility of Dilli. Today, Bhushan would be overseeing the digging of a well behind this nobleman's house; tomorrow he would be approaching a matchmaker, asking discreet questions about so-and-so's son ...

'Ah, yes,' he said, when Girdhar showed up at the sweet shop outside which Bhushan was to be found when not busy with other work. 'You are the stone carver, are you not?' He was sitting cross-legged, a dried leaf-bowl full of laddoos cradled in one palm. 'I remember you, you're good.'

Girdhar dipped his head in acknowledgment of the compliment. 'You had said you might be able to find some work for me,' he said.

Bhushan was chewing a laddoo, the crumbs falling into his dhoti-clad lap. 'Yes,' he said, when he had finished. 'And a fine place it is, too. Mind you, it won't be for long—the task is a small one, but it will boost your worth, that is for certain.' He broke off, extending the laddoos to Girdhar. 'Here, have one.'

Girdhar stared at the lime-sized balls, golden brown and redolent of roasted gram flour and ghee. His first instinct was to accept one. His second, following instantly, was to recoil. The training of years made his brain race, searching for signs. Did Bhushan wear the sacred thread that marked him as a Brahmin? Would accepting food from him be in keeping with the demands of his caste? The halwai who ran the sweet shop was a Brahmin, everybody knew that; but Bhushan?

'Go on,' said Bhushan, seemingly oblivious to his young acquaintance's dilemma. 'There are plenty.'

It was embarrassing to stand there, just looking on. Surely Bhushan must know? There was nobody in Dilli, nobody in the length and breadth of this land who did not know and did not acknowledge the importance of one's caste. Caste was what defined you, and it was horribly fragile. You could lose caste by what might seem the most insignificant of actions. By walking on the same side of the road as an untouchable, by breathing the same air. Or, of course, by accepting food from someone of a caste lower than your own.

Bhushan was no fool. He would know. If he offered Girdhar a laddoo, it would be because he knew that it was permissible for him to do so.

'Thank you,' Girdhar said, taking a laddoo. It was warm and delicious, down to the last crumb.

'Do you want some buttermilk? No? Very well, then. Let us be going.'

'Where are we going?' Girdhar asked, when they had walked for nearly a quarter of an hour. All the places Girdhar had thought would provide avenues for work for a stone carver had been left behind: the houses of the merchants, the temples.

'To Qutb Sahib's tomb. It's not much further, that turn there—what happened? Why have you stopped?'

Girdhar stared, wide eyes full of dread.

Bhushan's eyes narrowed. 'Don't tell me you are one of those who refuse to work on anything to do with Muslims.'

Girdhar shook his head.

'It promises to be good work. If you do it well, and I know you can, it can pave the way for more work, better work.' He must have seen the obstinate refusal in Girdhar's expression, because he added, 'And you will be paid well for it. I can guarantee that.'

Girdhar remained silent.

Bhushan was regarding him with a shrewd, calculating eye. 'You are Badrinath's son, aren't you? I should have known. But I had thought you more intelligent.' It was a slight, and yet it was a compliment too. Girdhar did not know how to respond, so he maintained a studious silence and hoped Bhushan would let him go. They stood by the side of the road while a bullock cart trundled by, the driver turning to look at them with curious eyes. A pair of lapwings rose, calling loudly, from the bushes beside the road.

'The Muslims are here to stay,' Bhushan said. 'There are hundreds, perhaps thousands, who have been born and bred here. Dilli is now as much their home as it is ours.'

His throat dry and constricted, Girdhar blurted out, 'Then do you not spurn them? Do you—do you talk with them, meet them? Does that not make you lose your caste?'

'My god resides in me,' Bhushan answered. An amused smile played about his lips. 'What is the worth of caste? Drape a sacred thread on a donkey and he will become a Brahmin? Throw a dead cow in front of a Brahmin's house and he will turn untouchable?' The smile turned to an outright laugh. 'When we die and our ashes are immersed in the Yamuna, do the ashes of the Brahmins keep to their own waves, their own currents? Do the waters not mingle?'

By the side of the road, the two lapwings had alighted and were stepping cautiously through the reeds fringing a shallow pond.

'When it is a matter of your livelihood,' Bhushan concluded, 'one should leave aside petty considerations like that. If somebody accuses me of losing my caste because I helped a skilled man in need of a job, so be it.' There was a flash of defiance in his eyes, but when he spoke, there was sympathy in his words and in his tone. 'I understand how you feel, though. It is hard to shake off what you have been taught from your infancy.'

He squinted down the road, into the distance. The bullock cart could still be seen, a smudge enveloped in dust, moving slowly towards the horizon. Another few minutes and it would disappear behind the trees, the little cluster of domes and minarets and flat-roofed buildings that signalled the end of the road. 'I must be going, they will be waiting for me. Do you want to come and see the place? Even if you will not work there?'

Girdhar shook his head. The abhorrence of the alien religion was so deeply rooted, so intrinsic a part of him, that he did not have to stop to think. There was only one answer. 'No.'

Bhushan nodded. 'Very well. If you change your mind, come and see me. Or go to Qutb Sahib's shrine, if I am not at the sweet-seller's. I am usually at the dargah these days.' Then he was gone, walking swiftly down the road, his pace measured and purposeful.

Girdhar's gaze followed Bhushan for a while before he turned to go back the way he had come. Twice he stopped, and once he turned back to look down the road Bhushan had taken. But then he went on towards the town, back home.

'So did Bhushan get you some work?' Badrinath asked that evening, as father and son sat cross-legged on low wooden stools. Kalyani and her younger daughter had set before them large brass platters with their dinner, having first offered each dish at the household shrine. Girdhar had waited, listening to his father pray in a loud and sonorous voice, thanking the gods, promising them the fidelity of the household. Badrinath had tipped water into his cupped palm and sprinkled it around his platter, murmuring more prayers, while Girdhar followed suit.

Now, at Badrinath's question, Girdhar paused long enough to steady himself, to make sure the half-truth sounded like the complete truth. 'He took me to see the place. I did not care for it.'

Badrinath looked up, curiosity in his eyes. 'What was it?'

Girdhar realized with a sinking heart that he had not thought this through. He should have realized that his father would wonder why Girdhar would turn down an opportunity for employment. What could he say? That he had been called upon to carve lewd friezes for the local brothel? To decorate a chest in which a bandit could store his plunder?

He shook his head. 'It was nothing much. Nothing'—he had been going to say 'worthy of me', but changed it to 'that appealed to me.' It still sounded pompous, so he added, 'It was uninspiring, Baba.' Even to his own ears, his voice sounded nervous.

Badrinath frowned. 'As your father, I am proud of your skill,' he said, his voice cold. 'But vanity has been the downfall of many a man more talented than you.' He continued to eat. 'When I was your age I did not scoff at work, never. No matter if it paid next to nothing, or if the few jitals it earned me did not arrive till months later. I did not complain about work being uninspiring.' The fury was controlled, but it was there, unmistakable.

Beside him, Kalyani sat down, placing a bowl of millet kheer next to his platter. She took down the little bamboo fan from its nail on the wall, and began to fan her husband and her son. Silent as ever, listening.

And silence had fallen too, over the room. Badrinath said no more until he had finished his meal. Then, as he rose, he said, 'Go back to Bhushan. If the work is still available, accept it. Even if it is uninspiring.'

Later, lying in his bed, Girdhar wondered why he had not told his father the truth. Badrinath would have approved of—no, that was a mild word; not approved, but heartily endorsed, applauded—his turning down work at a Muslim shrine.

He did not know why he had hidden that, even at the cost of being scolded.

The next two days passed in a strange whirl of indecision and mental turmoil for Girdhar. It was nothing immediately visible to those around. His mother remarked that he looked listless; his father scolded him for looking lost, or not paying attention. But that was all.

Girdhar went about his work, ate his meals, and participated in the many small but essential daily rituals Badrinath expected of his family. When Badrinath reminded him to go to Bhushan, he nodded obediently. 'Today,' Badrinath said. 'Go today. Work disappears as quickly as it emerges. If you do not take up a task, someone else will take it.'

Girdhar was too confused to go to Bhushan. What would he tell Bhushan? That he had reconsidered? Or would he ask if there was other work, not for a Muslim master? He did not know. There was the indecision, but there was also the shame: the humiliation of going back to Bhushan, his tail between his legs.

He wandered about, flitting aimlessly between market and well and mango orchard, and back again. He finally washed up at a quiet little temple beside a pond. Girdhar went in, sat down cross-legged in front of the doe-eyed idol of Shri Ram, and bowed his head. The prayers rose to his lips without active thought from him; he murmured the deity's praises, he made an offering, he came out with the handful of puffed rice the priest had pressed into his hand.

He had hoped, when entering the temple, that he would emerge with his path clearly marked out for him. But nothing had changed; he was still as lost, still as undecided.

Girdhar spent the rest of the afternoon under the peepal tree beside the temple. The puffed rice he strewed about him and watched as the birds and squirrels feasted off it.

Finally, when the sun was halfway down to the horizon, he rose to his feet and set off. This time, though, he did not go back towards the town; instead, he made his way towards the tomb of Qutbuddin Bakhtiar Kaki.

It was nothing like a temple, he thought as he stood outside, not daring to venture in. Through the doorway he could see no signs of a bell, nothing to announce the arrival of a devotee, nothing to act as a salutation to divine powers. But that was perhaps because this was a tomb, not a mosque. And there was no equivalent to a tomb in the religion he knew and followed. You lived a Hindu, you died a Hindu, you were cremated a Hindu. Nothing was left of you except a small heap of ashes, which were tipped into the waters of a sacred river and allowed to whirl away. Nothing on which to build a shrine, no matter how virtuous and untainted a life you may have led.

This Qutb Sahib, he thought, was no god, was he? He had heard that the Muslims believed in only one God. One. The thought was laughable. What could one God do all by himself? Would he watch over every living creature, judge the good and the evil, command the weather and the winds, fight injustice, pour blessings on the worthy and punish the wicked and attend to the millions of prayers, uttered and unspoken, all on his own?

An old woman and a boy went by him, stepping carefully over the threshold and into the courtyard beyond. As he watched the two figures move away, Girdhar sobered. No, the thought of a single God was not laughable; it was frightening. One God, one omnipotent deity. It was not as if you could get away with angering one God, and there would be another to take his place, another to whom you could direct your prayers. If not Durga Mata, Vishnuji. If not Vishnuji, Shivji. Ganeshji, if not his fearsome father. Or millions of others. There was more than one God for each Hindu in this land.

And one God for all the Muslims. Every single Muslim in the world.

He did not know what to make of it.

There was a gnarled khirni tree nearby, and because he did not want to stand here, looking so conspicuous, Girdhar went to the tree. It was only when he reached it did he realize that he would not be alone here. Death and life were already there, together. Beyond the tree was a shallow bowl-like dip in the ground, and in its centre was a grave. A simple grave, made of mud bricks covered over with plaster, with a small space—perhaps the length of a forearm and half as wide—left unbuilt on top, bare earth. Beside the grave, cross-legged on the grass, sat an old man, his head bobbing rhythmically as he sang. It was a quiet song, like a lullaby. Even though he could barely hear the words, let alone understand them, Girdhar instinctively knew that this was a prayer, a hymn. A song perhaps, for the peace of whoever lay interred in that piece of ground.

Girdhar's shadow fell across the grave and its attendant, and the old man broke off in the middle of his devotions. Before Girdhar could step back, the old man had turned to look up at him.

His face was lined, the skin thin to the point of translucence. The beard and the moustache, though thinning, were white and well-trimmed. The eyes, a vivid brownish-green, a colour Girdhar had never imagined eyes could be, were startlingly bright. But what made Girdhar stand there stock-still, gaping at the old man, was the look on his face. He had never seen anyone look so serene, as if nothing could shake his calm. As if he wanted nothing, could want nothing.

A smile, as unsettlingly tranquil as the look in those eyes, appeared on his face. 'Yes, child?'

Girdhar stared, unsure, embarrassed. He did not know the protocol at Muslim shrines. Should he apologize for having interrupted this man's prayers? Or should he simply turn around and walk away?

'I was looking around,' he said, in an awkward voice. 'Searching for someone. Someone called me here.'

The old man's eyes were soft as he gazed at Girdhar. 'Yes,' he murmured. 'We are all called. Some of us heed the call, and some are too busy to pay attention. It is not always loud, not always easily heard. You are young, to have heard.'

Girdhar flushed, embarrassed. 'No, no,' he blurted out. 'You misunderstand me. I mean I was called—by a man, a man named Bhushan. He said there would be work here for me. I am a stone carver.'

The old man rose to his feet with the aid of a sturdy and beautiful stick, its knob inlaid with mother-of-pearl, its tapering length finely carved. He was a fine-looking gentleman, thought Girdhar, his clothing elegant and obviously expensive, his turban a dazzling white, and the ring on his finger studded with a deep red stone that looked as if it held all the fire, all the blood, all the vermilion in the world.

A low dip of his head, a salutation—or was it a seeking of blessing? Girdhar could not tell—in the direction of the grave, and he turned away, making his way along a thin, barely perceptible path that took the gentlest route out of that little hollow and up to where Girdhar was standing.

'I know of no such man,' the old man admitted when he had reached Girdhar's side. 'But come inside, into the dargah. Perhaps your friend—Bhushan, did you say?—is inside. Even if he is not, there may be someone who might know.'

Bhushan had not been there, but a busy-looking man, a twig broom in his hand and a bulging water-skin slung over his shoulder, nodded when asked. Yes, Bhushan had been here the previous day, and would perhaps come again the next day. He returned to his work and Girdhar, standing by himself in the courtyard, looked apprehensively around.

He was so out of place here, he thought. The only one in a dhoti, the only one with a caste mark on his forehead and a sacred thread hanging across his torso. Despite Baba's assertions, he had never been able to summon up any pride in the symbols of his faith or his caste. Now they were even more embarrassing, shouting to the world around him that he was an outsider here.

'Did you find your friend?'

It was the old man. When they had entered through the gateway and into the enclosure, he had taken temporary leave of Girdhar—'I must pay my respects to Qutb Sahib; I will be back soon'—and now he was back. A whiff of incense hung about his person.

Girdhar shook his head. 'I was told he might be here tomorrow.'

'Good. Then I will have the pleasure of seeing you again tomorrow?' The look of tranquil sweetness on the old face widened into a smile.

Girdhar stared, so surprised that he was startled into saying, 'Does it not bother you, that I am a Hindu? Or—or these other people?' His gaze sped about the courtyard and the people who were scattered across it. The families sitting in front of the saint's tomb. The women in the covered verandah ringing the shrine, their heads and faces covered. The sweeper, now approaching the far end of the courtyard.

'Not here, not at Qutb Sahib's dargah,' said the old man gently. 'Qutb Sahib was a Sufi, he believed in the equality of all men, in universal love. If anyone here were to hold your religion against you, they would be disrespecting the memory of Qutb Sahib.'

That sounded sanctimonious, thought Girdhar. Religion, he had realized, had a way of creating anger where one would expect empathy, of setting aflame wet wood. No matter how saintly this Qutb Sahib had been, there was no surety that his devotees would be as forbearing as him. The most pious of people, from what he had seen, were not necessarily welcoming of those different from themselves. Or even, he thought, remembering the harsh orthodoxy of his father, even welcoming of those like themselves. Baba was, if anything, as unforgiving and intolerant of his own kin as he was of Muslims.

But Girdhar said nothing to refute the old man. He had not the courage, and there was something about the calm sweetness of the old man that made Girdhar only nod in a non-committal way.

It did not occur to him till long after he had left Qutb Sahib's dargah that he had not even bothered to ask the old man his name.

'Well? Did you go and meet Bhushan?'

Girdhar scrubbed vigorously at his feet, intent on avoiding his father's eyes. One stern glance from Badrinath, he knew, and he would end up spilling it all out, every last detail, down to his visit to the shrine. Beside him, Badrinath straightened, returned the little brass water pot to its place beside the bucket of water, and began to wipe his hands and feet with the thin cotton towel slung over his shoulder.

'I looked for him. He wasn't at the sweet shop.' Which was true, of course.

'Did you leave a message for him there, then?'

'Umm.'

Badrinath, who could never have imagined prevarication from his son, interpreted the neutral sound as assent. 'Go back tomorrow,' he said, nodding. 'See if he's there. I know his like; he will give the work to another, and refuse to even look at you after that.'

Perhaps, thought Girdhar that night as he lay on the thin reed mat that served as a bed, Bhushan's forgetting him might be all for the best. That way, he too, might forget the strange sensation of having visited a place unlike any he had ever seen before, of glimpsing a way of life and of worship that was unsettlingly foreign and strange. Perhaps, if he never met Bhushan again, the experiences of the day would slowly slip out of his memory.

But he could not forget. He tossed and turned and again and again there hummed in his ears the sonorous crooning of that old man as he knelt beside that secluded grave outside the dargah. There appeared, behind his closed eyelids, the old face, its eyes tranquil and its smile gentle.

Girdhar finally fell into an exhausted sleep shortly before dawn.

ᘛ

Girdhar awoke to unfamiliar sounds: the laughter of his mother, the bright chatter and giggling of little children. A young woman's voice, loud and uninhibited.

It was Yamini, the elder of his two sisters. A year younger than Girdhar, she had been married four years now and was mother to boisterous twin boys, who had accompanied her this morning on a visit to her paternal home. Baba was out, Girdhar guessed as he rose and went out; if he were around, Ma would not be laughing, Yamini would have been more subdued.

'Your Baba has gone to the temple to help the priest with a ceremony,' Kalyani said when her son, sitting down to eat breakfast, asked about Badrinath.

'And he didn't insist you go along with him, Ma?' Yamini asked, a mischievous twinkle in her eye.

'Even your father realizes there is too much to be done at home in the mornings to allow that.' There was a hint of wry amusement in Kalyani's voice. Girdhar, picking at the roasted chickpeas in his palm, marvelled at the way his mother changed, chameleon-like, depending on whether his father was present or not. Submissive, silent, almost cowering when he was there. Cheerful and relaxed when he was not.

Yamini's children, having explored their grandparents' home, and checked on the parakeets they knew nested in the neem tree beside the wall, came running back to Yamini. There was a flurry of conversation between the mother and her children—Girdhar did not pay attention, but there were questions being asked, pleas, entreaties for permission. Could they go next door? They had seen an interesting-looking goat tied up there. Could they try climbing the little phalsa tree outside?

By the time Girdhar had finished eating and had drunk down a tumblerful of buttermilk, Yamini had attended to her sons. They were gone, well away from the adults but near enough for safety. All that could be heard was the occasional burst of childish laughter from somewhere in the vicinity.

Yamini was helping Kalyani and her sister prepare the vegetables for lunch when she suddenly said, 'Oh! I nearly forgot. Something interesting happened on Basant Panchami; I had meant to tell you.'

'Basant Panchami was a month ago,' Yamini's sister observed, her tone accusatory. 'You came in between, Didi.'

'Yes, yes. But Baba was at home both times, and I couldn't have said this in front of him. Do you think I'm stupid?' Yamini reached out to take a basketful of pea pods from her mother. 'Give that to me, Ma,' she said, 'I'll shell those. You do something else.' She turned back to her sister. 'Baba would kill me if he heard I spoke to a Muslim,' she said, by way of explanation.

Girdhar stiffened. 'A Muslim?'

It was as if those two words were a cloak, falling dark and angry across the happiness that had surrounded them just a moment ago. Yamini looked up, suddenly wary. 'I didn't mean'—she began to say, then stopped. 'It wasn't as if'—Again, she broke off; this time because Girdhar had placed a hand on hers.

'I am not judging you,' he said softly. 'I was just startled, that was all.'

She still looked wary, and the two other women had gone silent, tense. Girdhar could think of only one way to make them understand. 'Tell me. I met a Muslim too, the other day. An old man, at the dargah of Qutb Sahib.'

He could see the consternation in her eyes, the bewilderment. He could almost see the questions rising to her lips. What had he been doing at a Muslim mystic's tomb? And why did he honour Qutbuddin Bakhtiar Kaki with that respectful 'Sahib'? Who was the Muslim he had spoken to?

Did Baba suspect the quiet revolt against his many strict rules?

'Who?' Yamini's voice was a hoarse whisper. Her eyes were wide, so wide that he could see the whites around her eyeballs.

'I'll tell you, but later. Tell us what happened at Basant Panchami.'

The story was quickly told. On Basant Panchami, the day the Hindus celebrated the coming of spring, Yamini had gone to the temple. It was late morning, and the women of the neighbourhood had gone together, clad in their bright new clothes, carrying platters with the usual complement of coconuts, little lamps, a handful of rice—but with more than the usual number of flowers. Jasmine, oleander, hibiscus, lotus. Pink, red, yellow, white. Petals heaped on their platters, garlands hanging around their necks and slung from arms.

'And just as we reached the well—you know, the one between our house and the temple—we saw an old man sitting there. A Muslim. He looked so dejected. Drooping shoulders, sad eyes.' She broke off to clutch her mother's arm. 'Ma, you should have seen his eyes. Such beautiful eyes, for a man. White hair and frail, thin skin, but such beautiful greenish-brown eyes—'

It could not be him, thought Girdhar. No, there must be dozens of old Muslim men in Dilli with beautiful greenish-brown eyes.

'He saw us and the next moment—oh, how he surprised us!—he came rushing forward, asking us what we were up to, where we were going. He seemed fascinated by our clothes and all our flowers. So we told him about Basant Panchami, about spring.' She paused to draw breath and have a sip of water before she continued. 'Then he told us that his very best friend, the man he regarded as teacher and mentor, was sunk deep into gloom. This friend's nephew had died, and the uncle was mourning him so deeply it seemed as if he would soon follow his young relative into the grave.'

There came to Girdhar's mind the memory of that grave, half hidden in that shallow bowl of earth near the dargah of Qutb Sahib.

'Then?'

'He stopped only long enough to ask Lakshmi from where she had got the mustard flowers on her platter, and then he was gone.' She stopped, seeing the disappointment in her family's faces and giggled. 'Hah! I knew you would want to know more!' One of the little boys had come wanting something to eat, so she gave him a handful of fresh green peas and sent him on his way before turning back to the adults.

'Two days later I was going to the temple with Lakshmi when we saw him again. He was by the well, and he greeted us when he saw us. Can you imagine, he had been waiting for us, to say thank you! He told us that seeing us on Basant Panchami had given him an idea of how to cheer up his friend. He had dressed in bright yellow clothes and gathered bunches of mustard flowers. And then he had gone, singing and dancing and celebrating spring, to his friend's house. And the friend had smiled! Smiled and become himself again, after so many weeks of mourning.' She sat back, a smile of satisfaction on her face.

'That was it?' Yamini's sister was incredulous, even scornful. 'This was what you were scared to mention in front of Baba?

Kalyani intervened before Yamini could respond. 'You acted wisely,' she said to Yamini. 'Your Baba would have been furious if he had known you spoke to a Muslim.' Her mouth curved into a smile. 'But you helped a man, and that is what matters.'

'Do you know what the man's name was?' Girdhar asked later, as he walked Yamini back to her house. Both toddlers, worn out from hours of unfettered enjoyment, were fast asleep, one in his mother's arms, the other on his uncle's shoulder.

'Amir Khusro,' Yamini said. 'One of the men watering his cattle near the well told us. He's quite a personage, it seems. In court and otherwise.'

19

'No,' said Girdhar, in a voice barely audible to Bhushan. There were other people at the sweet shop: various customers; the owner; his assistant who was frying something in hot oil. All seemed engrossed in whatever they were doing, but there was no telling who might be listening.

'Not everybody is eager to overhear what you have to say,' Bhushan said with an exasperated sigh as he heaved his bulk off the worn bench and followed Girdhar to a little domed pavilion that stood nearby. 'And so what if they overhear? It's not as if I am another man's wife and you're arranging an assignation with me.' He grinned, showing paan-stained teeth.

'I cannot have my father come to know of this. I have been looking for you these past few days. I even went to the dargah—'

'Yes, I was told. So, have you decided to take up that work after all?'

Girdhar shook his head. 'No, not at the dargah, Baba would kill me.' Pushing away the fear, he added, 'Is there something else you can think of?'

Bhushan shook his head. 'You know how it is. With the city having just changed hands, there will be turbulence for a while.' From the sweet shop, he had brought along two small pedas wrapped in a leaf bowl. He took a bite of one, and held the other out to Girdhar, who shook his head. 'But wait and see. Once Ghiyasuddin Tughlaq has consolidated his reign, he is certain to get down to constructing something. A palace, a fort, who knows? All these kings do that.' He had finished one peda and began on the second one. 'It's a matter of time. Sooner or later the Tughlaq will decide to build his palace, and then there will be plenty of work for stone workers. Maybe he will commission other works too. A mosque? A tomb, in preparation for his death?' He shrugged.

'No, no!' Girdhar sat down somewhat violently on the floor of the pavilion. 'Baba would never allow me to work for the Sultan.'

'Why? It's got nothing to do with religion. I mean,' Bhushan conceded, 'though the Sultan is a Muslim, a palace wouldn't be of a religious nature. There's nothing remotely religious about stables or granaries or gateways or chambers. Why should your Baba have any objection to that?'

'It's a long story,' Girdhar said. 'There was some ancestor who was treated unfairly by a Sultan. I don't know; Baba doesn't talk about it. But it embittered his entire family. Baba and Baba's father, they were brought up to despise the aristocracy, the Sultan. Their religion.'

'Sultans change. None last longer than their own lifetimes.'

'Baba says their poison remains. He says it does not matter who is Sultan. As long as a Muslim sits on the throne of Dilli there is no hope for the Hindus of the city.'

'Rubbish.' Bhushan, his sweets eaten, wiped his hands on the end of his dhoti. 'I am curious, though,' he said. 'You don't sound as if you are convinced. Scared maybe, of displeasing your father, but you don't seem to share his views.'

Girdhar squirmed. Even as Bhushan spoke, it had dawned on Girdhar that agreeing with Bhushan would be tantamount to betraying his father—but it would be the truth. The truth might seem to smack of disloyalty, but it was the truth.

'No,' he admitted. 'No, I do not think the way Baba does.' He paused, then, flushed and uncomfortable, added on a qualifier. 'Not any longer.'

'Of course. You are a grown man, you have eyes and ears, and you see that the world is not the black and white of fairy tales. Not all Muslims are vicious and evil, not all Sultans are—'

Girdhar cut him off. 'But you do see why Baba would never agree to my working on anything for the Sultan either.'

A silence fell, awkward and desperate on Girdhar's part, thoughtful on Bhushan's. 'What if your father were not to know where you were working?' Bhushan asked after a while.

'How would that be possible? Baba would ask, and he would come and see, too.'

'Would he come all the way to the riverbank, do you think?'

That startled Girdhar. 'The riverbank? The Yamuna? Why—'

'There is some work in the offing near there,' Bhushan admitted. 'A baoli has to be excavated and the stonework done for it. There will probably be more buildings around too, perhaps later.'

'I mean,' said Girdhar, 'that if you think he wouldn't go all the way there, that means there's something not quite right about that, either. It's another commission Baba would not approve of, is that it?' He saw the truth in Bhushan's eyes, and asked, 'Who is having this baoli dug?'

A small smile appeared on Bhushan's face. 'Nizamuddin Auliya,' he replied. 'You do not know who he is, I suppose.' He stretched, looking up at the sky, noting the position of the sun. 'I should be getting along.'

'But who—who is Nizamuddin Auliya?'

'Come and see,' Bhushan invited.

The journey by bullock cart was a long one. By the time they arrived, the sun was at its zenith, burning down mercilessly on the river. The Yamuna was a thread of gleaming silver: not yet as thin as it would become before the monsoon arrived to replenish it, but certainly not the full, foaming waters Girdhar had seen a few months earlier when they had come here to immerse the idol of the goddess Durga.

They stopped short of the river. 'This is where he lives,' Bhushan explained, as he led Girdhar down a wisp of a path that snaked its way between trees and bushes. It was not silent, but the sound was the voice of peace, of birds chirping in the trees, of squirrels and the distant gurgle of the river.

'This is his hermitage,' Bhushan said as they emerged from the trees, pausing at a low wall enclosing a small set of houses. 'Nizamuddin Auliya is not merely a holy man for the Muslims, he is revered by many Hindus as well. They talk of the many miracles he has performed.'

'A holy man?' Light dawned. 'Like Qutb Sahib?'

If Bhushan noticed the use of the honorific for Qutbuddin Bakhtiar Kaki, he did not show it. 'Yes,' he said. 'Like Qutb Sahib. Not surprising, considering the connection between them.' He did not bother to wait for Girdhar's next question. 'Qutb Sahib's disciple, Sheikh Fariduddin Ganjshakar, was master to Sheikh Nizamuddin Auliya. They are all of the same silsila, the same order. The Chishtiya Order, that is what they call themselves. They believe that all men are equal, that none is created above another. They believe—'

'In universal love? Yes, I know.' Girdhar allowed himself a small smile of satisfaction at the astonishment in Bhushan's expression. 'I had gone to Qutb Sahib's dargah, you know. I wanted to see for myself, wanted to understand what the place was like. It was very different from what I thought it would be.' He fell silent, remembering what he had imagined and what it had turned out to be.

'You had thought they would throw you out? Because you are a Hindu?'

Girdhar was surprised that Bhushan had guessed what had been going through his mind, but Girdhar was beginning to realize just how astute Bhushan was. He nodded. 'Nobody seemed to mind that I was there, nobody told me to go or even questioned me.' He amended his words. 'Except for the one man, and he was kindness itself. I saw him at a grave outside the dargah, and there was such serenity in his face, it—it was unsettling. It turned my mind upside down.'

'Was he the one who told you about Sufi belief?'

'Yes.' Girdhar thought of recounting what Yamini had told him. That his acquaintance from the dargah may be a prominent courtier named Amir Khusro. He stopped himself; he was not sure of the old man's identity, and in any case, he did not want to sound boastful.

'Here we are,' Bhushan said, stepping off the path and through the little wooden gate that led into a courtyard. The murmur of conversation drifted through from the courtyard.

A little group sat there, most of them seated on rugs spread on the flagstones. The exception was an old, bent figure on a rope bed, neatly but austerely dressed. Those who sat before him ranged in age from perhaps ten years to about fifty, a very motley group indeed. They were so engrossed in what the old man was saying that they did not even notice the arrival of the two newcomers.

But another did. From a doorway off to the right came a figure that was familiar to Girdhar.

'You are here, my young friend,' the old man said, a twinkle in the greenish-brown eyes, a gentle smile on his lips. 'And is this Bhushan? Yes? Have you found him, then?' There was perhaps a deeper, mystical meaning to his question; Girdhar did not know, and felt too shy to ask. The old man turned to Bhushan. 'I have been told about you; I suppose you have come about the baoli? My friend will finish his discourse shortly, then he will talk to you.' His arm extended, gesturing in invitation to them. 'Come inside and wait, have something to eat if you will.'

'Khusro Sahib,' Bhushan said as he bowed, hands folded together, 'pray do not worry yourself on our behalf. We shall wait. You must not inconvenience yourself.'

The twinkle in Amir Khusro's eye turned faintly mischievous. 'I am not going to be churning the buttermilk and bringing it to you,' he murmured. 'In any case, I must go now. I cannot keep up with all the changes at court any more, but I am expected to be in attendance.' He shook his head in a resigned sort of way and was gone, only the faint scent of sandalwood lingering in the air to remind them of his recent presence.

ଓ

'I did not think it possible there could be a grown man in Dilli, unless he were blind and deaf, who did not know about Amir Khusro,' said Bhushan, shaking his head in disbelief. 'Nizamuddin Auliya—well, I suppose if one was brought up by a father like yours, there may be a chance one would be oblivious. But Amir Khusro? He is Dilli personified.'

Girdhar was irritated at the slight to his own knowledge, but he had to concede, even if only privately, that there might be truth in what Bhushan said.

Yes, Baba had made very sure that Girdhar was brought up in a house that denied, as far as it was possible, even the very existence in Dilli of the 'invaders', as Badrinath insisted on calling all Muslims. Since Girdhar was a toddler, his friends had been carefully chosen, the places he was allowed to visit spelled out to prevent even accidental proximity to Muslims. Girdhar was allowed to go to the temple, the neighbourhood bazaar, and the few homes around theirs; the neighbourhood of course was staunchly Hindu. By the time he was old enough to work, Girdhar knew without being told what work he could accept and what he must refuse.

No matter how much he wanted it though, Badrinath could not completely cocoon his son. There was always someone around who knew nothing of Badrinath's bigotry, or who, if he knew, could not care less. Girdhar heard fellow stone carvers boasting of the fine carving they had done at this mosque or that tomb. He heard snatches of conversation in the bazaars. Genuine news, and gossip: what the Sultan had decreed, which battle he had gone to fight. Who was raising the flag of rebellion, who was certain to be crushed.

But he had not heard of Amir Khusro.

'No,' Girdhar admitted. 'I do not know who Amir Khusro is. A courtier, yes, I did hear of that, and he seems to me a mystic. What else?'

'What else, he asks.' Bhushan, a look of amused disbelief in his eyes, shook his head. 'He is a courtier, yes. But not just any old courtier; he has served under I don't know how many Sultans; I have heard my father speak of him from when he was a child. And he's served them in important capacities: he has been sent as emissary to far-flung courts, he has gone on expeditions, he was once even taken prisoner. I believe there was quite a daring escape involved there, I don't know the details.' He glanced at Girdhar, who was looking suitably impressed. 'He has written biographies of Sultans, he has written histories. He is a poet, a singer, a musician. When Nizamuddin Sahib's disciples gather here after discourses, especially in the evenings, they sing Khusro Sahib's songs.'

Yes, thought Girdhar. The first time he had encountered Khusro, the old man had been singing. At that lonely grave near Qutb Sahib's dargah.

'Ah.' Bhushan scrambled to his feet. 'The Hazrat Sahib is getting up. His discourse must be over. Let us meet him before he goes off to pray by himself.'

Girdhar held back. 'You go,' he murmured. 'I—I will go and sit by the riverside and wait for you there.'

'Are you certain? Didn't you want to know more about this baoli that's planned? You could get work here, you know, and your father would be none the wiser.'

Girdhar was adamant, if politely so. 'I need time to think. You go on; I will wait by the river for you.'

☙

The river was beautiful. Girdhar had seen it before, of course; they came here at least a few times a year, to worship the Yamuna, to offer it flowers and fruit and sweets, to let its sacred waters wash away their sins. But those visits were all early in the day, with the sun glittering on the waves, the air clear till the far bank.

Not today, not now. The sun was sinking, the water turning from blue-grey to gold, to orange, to pink and red, its tones shifting as rapidly as the currents themselves. Above, a noisy flock of geese flew, their wings flapping and their honking carrying on the breeze. Something moved among the reeds nearby, picking its way gingerly through the soft mud. A purple moorhen, its bright red bill and blueish plumage drab against the more gaudy colours of the sunset.

Girdhar watched the land, the sky and the river grow more colourful, the hues deepening and intensifying until they reminded him of a woman's cosmetic box with its vermilion and turmeric, its sandalwood. A scattering of light clouds, golden below and pink above, hung over a red-tinted horizon. High over his head the sky turned suddenly mauve, then an otherworldly shade of deep indigo.

And all the colours mirrored, refracted and crystallized in the river below. Split into a hundred other shades, given a thousand other tones.

Then suddenly, as if in a huff at the lack of applause, the sunset withdrew its colours. One moment, he was looking at a panorama of incomparable beauty. The next, it was gone, a curtain of deep grey thrown over it all.

'It is exquisite, is it not?'

Girdhar turned to look over his shoulder, and made to get up.

'No,' Amir Khusro said, placing a hand on Girdhar's shoulder. 'Don't rise. I will sit beside you, if I may.'

Amir Khusro, thought Girdhar, looking at his companion with awe. Till a couple of days ago he had only heard of this man through Yamini, and while it had seemed an interesting coincidence, he had not grasped the significance of it, of the man who had crossed the path of both him and his sister. But now he knew, and he was awestruck.

He wished he could think of something to say, something intelligent or profound: but what burst from his lips was the most mundane of questions.

'Whose grave was that, Khusro Sahib?' He asked. 'At Qutb Sahib's dargah the other day,' he added. 'When I first saw you, you were sitting beside a grave and singing.'

For a few moments, Amir Khusro did not answer. He stared out over the river, its water now dark enough to be black. Somewhere far away on the opposite bank, a jackal howled. It was joined by another, and then another, until the air was filled with their humourless and maniacal laughter.

'I hope my singing sounded better than that,' Khusro said with a small, self-deprecating smile. 'I do not know whose grave that was. Someone unloved and unmourned, I fear. A few years ago I was visiting Qutb Sahib's dargah when I saw that grave for the first time. It was new then, the earth fresh on it. But you know how it is with new graves?' His eyes flickered for a moment, taking in the caste mark on the young man's forehead, the sacred thread about his chest, and perhaps remembering, even if he did not comment on it, that this man was a Hindu and possibly did not know.

'There are invariably flowers, or some incense sticks. Something to show that those who interred the dead still remember them.' His eyes wandered to the rosary wound around his wrist. 'There was nothing there. Not one wilted petal, nothing to show that anybody cared.

'In those days, I used to go to Qutb Sahib's frequently,' he continued as he unwound the beads from about his wrist. 'Sometimes with my friend, sometimes alone. Each time, I would go to that grave, just to see. I was hoping, I think, that my first impression would prove to be mistaken.' He took the first bead of the rosary between forefinger and thumb and caressed it, not yet telling beads, but preparing to.

'Nature took over that grave,' he said. 'No flowers were ever put on it but those that blossomed on the weeds that grew. Nobody came to pull away the weeds or to remove the twigs. It was a picture of neglect, of forgottenness. As if, with that man's passing, he had passed out of the lives of those he had known in life.'

He looked at Girdhar. 'At least one prayer must be said for a soul, no matter how inconsequential, no matter how evil.' His eyes twinkled. 'Perhaps more than one if the soul in question has not been especially virtuous,' he added.

No, Girdhar thought; prayers made little difference, because a man's deeds decided his fate. The sum of his deeds would grant him escape from the cycle of birth and rebirth, or send him back to live and die and live again, in some form or another, until his soul finally found nirvana.

But that was what his religion taught him. Perhaps the Muslims, with their single God and their foreign beliefs, thought differently.

'Who knows whether it will matter or not,' Khusro murmured, almost as if he had heard Girdhar's unspoken words. 'But it saddened me to think that that man lay in his grave without a single soul to remember him, let alone grieve for him. That was why I prayed beside his grave.'

Girdhar gazed at the old man with new respect. Respect not for his age or for his stature, or even for the achievements Bhushan had mentioned, but respect for who he was. Girdhar could think of no one who would take the time and effort to pray by the grave of a stranger whom even the world had forgotten. Or who would act the buffoon in the hope of making his friend smile.

Or who would take the time to sit beside a strange young man and confide in him.

'Girdhar! Girdhar, where are you?'

It was Bhushan. Girdhar scrambled to his feet. 'I beg your pardon, Khusro Sahib,' he said, his head dipping in a quick, imprecise salute. 'I must go. May the gods keep you.'

Later he was to wonder if that had not been a horribly gauche thing to say to a man who believed not in many gods, but in only one.

Night had fallen with such frightening rapidity that Bhushan said, 'It is pointless to try going back to Yoginipur today. No one will be ready to take us all the way, anyway.' Girdhar, anticipating his father's reaction were he to stay out all night, did everything he could to change Bhushan's mind, but to no avail.

'What will you do?' Bhushan said, resignedly. 'Walk?' As if to underline his words, a sudden chorus of howls broke out from the jackals further downriver. They were close, too close. And with little habitation between the river and Yoginipur, with nothing but the occasional oil lamp flickering outside the stray hut, it could be dangerous.

Girdhar insisted on trying to find a bullock cart driver who might consent, and Bhushan, with a good-humoured smile, consented to wait while Girdhar searched—fruitlessly. Of the two drivers he found, both with their cattle already unyoked, one had looked incredulous and the other, with a derisive guffaw, asked Girdhar why he was so eager to die an early death.

Bhushan, with a knowing look on his face, nodded and suggested they go back to the hermitage of Nizamuddin Auliya. 'We'll get shelter there for the night,' he said. 'That's where I always stay, when it gets too late for me to go back to Yoginipur.'

That, realized Girdhar, might entail accepting food from the hands of Muslims, or at least sleeping in close proximity to them. Neither was any longer unpalatable to him, but the thought of what Badrinath's reaction would be if he should discover the truth, made him baulk. 'You go,' he told Bhushan. 'I saw a little temple near where I met the bullock cart drivers. I'll rest there.' He paused, unwilling to admit to what was weighing on his mind. He took the plunge, nevertheless: in any case, Bhushan already knew something of Badrinath. 'Can we leave before dawn, please? My family will be worried.'

'Where have you been? Where have you been, you bastard!' Badrinath shouted as he clouted Girdhar. Hard, so hard that his ears rang and his head spun. Then again, this time with the other hand, on the other side of Girdhar's face. Girdhar went reeling and Badrinath stood over him, panting, as he picked himself up. His face was red, his eyes bulging. 'Where did you go, you scoundrel?' he snarled. 'Were you in the fields with some village girl? All night long, you bastard? All night long?'

Behind them they heard a gasp of mortification and dismay from Kalyani. His younger sister was clinging to the doorpost, her eyes huge.

'No, Baba,' Girdhar said. 'I went with Bhushan. To the Yamuna.'

Suspicion flashed in Badrinath's eyes. 'With Bhushan? Why? Is he getting you work near the river?'

During the long ride from the riverbank to Yoginipur, Girdhar had thought long and hard over what he would say when this question was asked, as it inevitably would be. There was only one thing to do to be at peace with himself, and to ensure that Badrinath did not kill him in the process.

He swallowed. 'Yes.'

'What is there?'

He could feel the flutter of fear in his throat, like a butterfly trapped there, choking off his breath, flapping its wings frantically. 'A temple,' he murmured.

'Don't mumble, speak up!' Badrinath's hand swung out, his knuckles catching Girdhar hard on the edge of the jaw. Girdhar stumbled but kept his balance. In a slightly louder voice, he replied, 'A temple, beside one of the ghats.'

Badrinath glared at him. 'Which temple? One of those we visit every time we go to worship the Yamuna?' His voice was accusing, his suspicions not yet allayed.

'It's a small temple, north of where we go.'

Girdhar had seen it last evening as he had walked towards the riverbank. It had been dark, inadequately illuminated by a little bowl of baked clay filled with a palmful of oil. There had been light enough only to see that the temple was small and plain. Very early this morning, before Bhushan had come to fetch him, before even a temple priest had come to the temple to perform the morning's devotions, Girdhar had gone to the temple again. Not with devotion in his heart, but deception.

The shrine was no taller than his shoulder and made of the local grey stone, so hard that it could barely be carved. The little idol was so crudely chiselled, so misshapen and disproportionate, that it had taken some effort to recognize the deity as Krishna. An idol that could do with some replacing, Girdhar had thought as he had peered in, his fingers brushing the threshold of the shrine and rising to his forehead of their own volition.

There had been no feeling of piety, no surge of emotion. The idol had been just a chunk of shaped stone, the river beyond just a river, not a goddess.

'The idol is in need of replacement,' he said now.

Badrinath's eyes narrowed. 'How much are they paying you for this work?'

'It hasn't been decided yet,' Girdhar lied. Not glibly, for he was new to this. 'Perhaps—perhaps they will decide when the time comes.'

For a moment, Badrinath looked as if he was going to say something about Girdhar's lack of enterprise. But there was another consideration, and one Badrinath would himself have applauded, as Girdhar well knew: the work was being done to honour a deity. Badrinath could not, without being disloyal to his long-held beliefs, protest against anything this work entailed.

He nodded, somewhat mollified. 'It is for the glory of the gods. And the good thing is,' he brightened up, 'that you can bring the stone and do your carving right here. It will bestow blessings even as Krishnaji emerges from it.' A rare smile shone on his face. 'It is fitting, too, that you should carve it. Girdhar, carving Girdhar. Will you depict the Lord with the mountain resting on his finger?'

20

Bhushan looked sceptical. 'I will admit I had not thought you would accept it. I simply took you there so that you could see another side of the world.' He rubbed thoughtfully at the stubble on his jaw. 'What are you going to tell your father?'

Girdhar told him the story he had woven for Badrinath's benefit. 'I had thought, if I could get away every day, or a few days at a time, to the riverbank, I could spend most of the day working at the baoli, and then maybe an hour or so creating the idol. It needn't be anything intricate; it can get done easily enough. I know I can do it.'

'And gift it to the priest? That might certainly earn you many blessings.' Bhushan grinned.

Girdhar shrugged. 'It does not matter either way. For me, it is just an excuse. I could think of no other.' He hesitated. 'But there is a problem. My father insists I work on the statue at home.'

There was silence as Bhushan mulled over this fresh obstacle. 'Help me,' Girdhar said. 'Tell me what to do.'

'You could tell your father that the priest has asked if you can do the work sitting right there in front of the temple. I once knew a priest in Mathura who did that—and not just for the idol, but every bit of the temple. All the stone carvers had to work in the temple yard. The priest said it would bestow sanctity on the carvings if they were done within sight of the shrine.'

Girdhar looked doubtful. 'I don't know if Baba will accept that.'

It was Bhushan's turn to shrug. 'I cannot think of anything else. You could start off by bringing the stone home and working on it for a few days. Then tell your father that you cannot find inspiration and that you need to go to the river. Tell him,' his face creased into a wicked grin, 'tell him Krishnaji beckons you to the Yamuna.'

'But the work on the baoli will be half done by then!'

'Not so soon,' Bhushan said comfortably. 'There is the excavation to be completed, the foundations to be laid. Only then will the stone workers begin their work. There are still a couple of weeks to go.'

ᘓ

Girdhar, working on the statue of Krishna he had taken upon himself to create, had been trying to gather up the courage to tell Badrinath that he would have to go to the Yamuna. When Bhushan had suggested it as a way of getting around Badrinath's opposition, it had seemed possible. Now, with the days going by, Girdhar's courage had started to wane. Badrinath watched him at work, criticized, commented, and gave him advice. If Girdhar deliberately pretended a lack of inspiration, Badrinath's sharp gaze would see the truth behind the lie.

The days went by. Bhushan had promised to let Girdhar know when work would begin and he would be required at the baoli. Girdhar waited, worked, and fretted.

And then came a bolt out of the blue, a piece of news so odd it seemed almost ludicrous.

Girdhar had gone to the bazaar to buy some groceries, and as he was walking home, he overheard a conversation between two passersby. 'What happens to Hazrat Nizamuddin's baoli, then?' a man asked another. 'If there is nobody to work on it, will it remain half dug until the Sultan completes his fort?'

The other man laughed. 'By then the Sultan will think up some other project. He will not let the Hazrat finish this project.'

'Not that Nizamuddin Sahib has much respect for the Sultan, from what I've heard. Let us see what happens. I hope Nizamuddin Sahib does not put a curse on this city for the sins of its Sultan.'

It took careful, discreet enquiries to unravel this intriguing conversation. Girdhar was cautious; he dare not have his father discover that he had been curious about something he was not supposed to even know of.

Ghiyasuddin Tughlaq, newly come to the throne of Dilli, had decided to build a citadel for himself. It was not unexpected; every new Sultan did it.

Except that Ghiyasuddin Tughlaq was in a hurry to have his fort built, and he cared not for the reverence accorded to the city's resident saint. If Nizamuddin Auliya was building his baoli, it was none of the Sultan's business. All he cared for was to have his fort built, and without any delay. Perhaps, too, he wanted to prove to the people of Dilli that his power surpassed that of a mere hermit. And so Sultan Ghiyasuddin Tughlaq passed a decree: none of the workers of the city were to be employed at any construction site other than that of Tughlaqabad, the fort that was being built. No mansions, no temples, no wells, no houses, no inns and shops. Nothing was to be built but the fort.

Girdhar mulled over the news, wondering what would happen now. Would his subterfuge have been all for nothing? Was there a chance that, once Tughlaqabad was made, work at the baoli would begin again? Should he wait?

There was only one person he could ask.

It took time and effort, as well as swiftly decreasing patience, to find Bhushan. Finally, Girdhar ran him to earth at Qutb Sahib's dargah.

'What? Haven't you heard?' Bhushan said, with a grin. 'The men have already worked out a way around it. Work won't stop at the baoli.'

He explained. A loophole had been found in Ghiyasuddin Tughlaq's edict, which impelled all workers to be at the construction site of the fort while work was ongoing there. But the fort was being constructed, as was natural, only during the day; nobody worked at night. At night, therefore, the workers were free to work elsewhere. At Nizamuddin's baoli, for instance.

'They're working at night?' Girdhar gaped.

'Why not? It's not as if they are defying the edict. If work at the fort finishes by sunset, and the workers have to leave the site, why not go to the baoli?'

'Why go? I mean, all that way, and at night. And they must be tired, from having worked all day.' Girdhar shook his head, unable to understand. 'It cannot be that the Sultan pays them so poorly that they must work at the baoli too, to make ends meet.'

Bhushan looked as if he was going to say something, but he shook his head. 'I don't know,' he admitted. 'Why don't you go and see for yourself?'

☙

If he had to go to the baoli, he would be gone for at least a day. Possibly for longer. Girdhar, walking home, realized that he would have to resort to some more deception.

'I will have to spend a few days at the temple, Baba,' he said, when he was sitting beside Badrinath next morning. 'The idol is—I do not know; I cannot see my way ahead. I need inspiration.'

Badrinath, who was eating his breakfast, looked up. There was curiosity in his eyes, but no more. 'There is inspiration aplenty in Yoginipur. Why go all the way to the Yamuna?'

Girdhar took the plunge. 'I feel it in my bones, Krishnaji calls to me.' His heart was pounding, his mouth dry with apprehension. 'I feel stifled here, Baba, my hands falter. It seems to me as if I will be able to see Him emerge only if I am there, beside his river.' It sounded so hollow, he thought, so trite.

Badrinath said nothing until he had finished eating and washed his hands. 'When will you be back?'

Girdhar had come prepared for flat denial, or, at the least, questions. And conditions to his going.

He reminded himself that the conditions could still come;

the conversation was not over. 'As soon as I know the way forward,' he said. That, at least, was the truth, if nothing else was. He did not know which way to turn yet; he could only hope that his working at Nizamuddin's baoli would show him the way he had to go. 'Once I know, I will be back.' That was not quite the truth, he knew, because he might never be back.

He had once overheard an old man say, 'When I cannot decide what to do, whether to choose this path or that, do you know what I do? I toss a coin high up in the air. Even as it comes down, I find my answer. It is what my heart wishes, and it has nothing to do with whether the coin comes up heads or tails.'

Girdhar had tossed up an invisible coin, and his heart knew the answer. And, paradoxically, his heart dreaded the answer, too.

'Very well,' Badrinath said. 'Go, then. Ask your mother to make you food to last you for a while. And if you are not finished at the end of the week, send word, so we know you are well.'

By the time he arrived at the hermitage of Nizamuddin Auliya, having begged a ride from a passing bullock cart, it was nearing sunset. Girdhar hoisted his sack on to his back and set off.

Bhushan had told him where the baoli was being dug, so he made his way there. This area, Bhushan said, was named Ghiyaspur. Girdhar wondered at the irony of the name; surely it could not be named for the autocratic Sultan who had so peremptorily imposed his will on the people of Dilli, even daring to oppose the much-revered Hazrat Nizamuddin Auliya. Perhaps, he thought, there was some other Ghiyas, a mystic like Nizamuddin, someone Girdhar knew nothing about.

He arrived at the baoli and stood at its lip, staring. There was a great gaping hole in the ground, but not a single man. Nobody going down into that bowl of earth to add to the foundations he could see, nobody hovering about near the stone slabs piled in rows at the far end.

But there was a boy there, about twelve years old, attending to a row of lamps lined up in front of him. He was cleaning them, polishing them, and filling them with oil. He looked up, startled, when Girdhar's shadow fell across the ground before him.

'Is this where the baoli is being dug?' Girdhar asked, solely because it seemed like a valid opening for a conversation.

The boy shook his head. 'No,' he said solemnly. 'Didn't you know, they've found diamonds and emeralds here? Everybody is very excited. We're going to dig up the treasure and bury the Sultan here instead.' He had gone back to his work midway through that sarcastic put-down, so he did not see Girdhar's face flame with anger. Girdhar stared at the thin back clad in a long white shirt, the skinny legs likewise encased in white cotton. A neat boy, from the skullcap on his head down to the leather toes of his shoes.

Girdhar's anger melted into puzzlement. This was no urchin, no mere labourer. He may not be richly clad, but the mere fact that he wore shoes and that his clothing looked far from threadbare, was enough to mark him as the scion of a wealthy household. What then was he doing, performing such a menial task?

'Who are you?' he asked, his curiosity overcoming his resentment at the insolence of this stripling.

'Why?'

'Why what?'

'Why do you want to know?'

He was incorrigible. Girdhar made a sound of disgust and waved a hand at the boy who was, in any case, not even looking at him, he was so absorbed in his work.

Girdhar wandered around. Ramps of wooden planks, weighted down with stones, led from the lip of the excavation into its belly. He peered down. It was already dark as a moonless night down there, even if the last blush of the sunset still lingered up here. The lamps the boy was preparing would be needed, every last one of them.

Girdhar had helped in the repair of their neighbourhood baoli back in Yoginipur a few years earlier. Along with his father, he had carved new brackets for the gateposts. Back then, he had been too young to even wonder how the baoli was constructed; and anyway, that had consisted only of repairs, not fresh construction.

Now he was old enough and curious enough to want to know more. How did the workmen strike the balance between digging deep enough for water to fill the conventional well that was dug beside the baoli, and not digging so deep that the groundwater welled up and filled the baoli itself? For the baoli was not supposed to be a deep well; it was a shallow well. A well that filled with rainwater in the monsoon and, if the gods were kind, kept the community supplied with water for the next few months.

He turned away, looking towards the entrance, hoping to see workers approaching. He was eager to start working, eager to find out more.

'When will the men arrive?' he called to the boy. He would much rather have avoided the impudent brat, but it could not be helped.

'In half an hour or so, I should think,' replied a deep voice that sparkled with amusement. Girdhar whirled around.

It was Amir Khusro.

'You must not blame him,' Khusro Sahib said. 'Surely you remember being twelve? Did you never jump at the opportunity to show off your wit, especially to an adult?'

Girdhar tried unsuccessfully to suppress a scowl. The boy had nearly finished his work; two lamps, and he would be done. He flashed a quick grin at Khusro Sahib before returning to his work, and Khusro Sahib, seating himself on a pile of slabs, informed Girdhar that this precocious child was Mushtaq. He lived in Ghiyaspur, where his father was a trader.

'I did nothing to invite his rudeness,' Girdhar said peevishly.

Khusro Sahib smiled. 'Perhaps he feels a certain sense of superiority, since he is familiar with this place and you are not.' He patted Girdhar's shoulder. 'Forgive him. He is only a child and you are already a man. Men do not hold grudges against children.'

That made Girdhar feel ashamed of himself. He mumbled something to the effect that he would teach Mushtaq a lesson, before asking whom he should apply to if he wanted to work at the baoli.

'I will make you known to the man.' Khusro Sahib paused. 'I have met Bhushan since you were last here. He said your father may not approve of your working here.' He looked out over the dark cavern of the future baoli. 'I am glad you have been able to come.'

There was a question there, even if it had not been expressed in so many words. Girdhar found himself blurting out the truth, telling it all. His deception of his father, the lie, the concocted assignment, the excuse made to enable this sojourn by the river.

'But you have done some work on this statue at your home, yes? Then it is not really deception, I think. You are working, Girdhar, on a statue that will glorify God.'

Girdhar mulled over that for a few moments. 'Whose God, Khusro Sahib?' he asked finally. 'The work I have told my father I am doing is for the god I was brought up with, one of millions of gods. Yes, I am carving an idol of Shri Krishna, but that is only an excuse, because I have not been commissioned for it. When it is done I will go and present it to the priest at the temple, and he can do with it as he wishes.'

He noticed that the boy, Mushtaq, was carrying the lamps, one in each hand, two at a time, to the edge of the cavern. He may be impudent, he may have an inflated sense of his own worth, but he was a good worker, reliable and diligent.

'But my real work is for your God,' Girdhar finished.

'Is it? A baoli does not serve God,' Khusro pointed out. His eyes twinkled.

'Nizamuddin Sahib is having it dug. He is a holy man.' Girdhar stopped. He guessed that Khusro knew what he meant, and perhaps knew too that Girdhar would find it difficult to articulate his meaning. 'Any work done for a Muslim,' he said, his voice low and strangled, 'is work my father would disapprove of.'

Some of his desperation, his fear of being found out, must have leaked through into his voice, because the hand that had moved away from his shoulder returned to rest on it.

They sat in silence. Mushtaq had gone away, and gone with him were the last colours of the sunset, melting away into near-darkness. A single lamp that Mushtaq had left burning beside the gate spilled a pool of yellow light around itself, but the rest was all deep, dark shadows.

'Many of the men who work at the baoli are Hindus,' Khusro Sahib said. 'I do not think they come here because they feel any compulsion to do so. Or because of the wages they receive; most of them will make as much if they chose to work at night somewhere in Yoginipur itself. Why come all this way?'

It was a question that Girdhar had pondered over long and hard too, without arriving at an answer.

'Perhaps more men see goodness in doing good than in praying ceaselessly,' Girdhar ventured, when it seemed as if Khusro Sahib was not going to answer his own question.

'Perhaps. They will come soon; you can see for yourself.' Khusro smiled. 'Where will you stay while you work here?

I do not suppose you intend to follow the example of the other men and go to and fro every sunset and every sunrise?'

Girdhar shook his head. 'I won't go back for the next few days. I—I don't know where I'll stay. I do not need much; I have brought some food with me and I can always sleep under a tree.'

Khusro Sahib nodded. 'If you should be in need of shelter, come to my friend's hermitage. You will get a roof over your head.' He straightened, eyes suddenly alert. 'The men are arriving,' he added. 'Can you hear them?'

And yes, drifting on the air came the creak and squeak of cart wheels, the hoofbeats of the odd horse—or was it a donkey?—and the blurred murmur of men talking, of feet, of rustling clothing and of the occasional laugh. The night's work at the baoli was about to begin.

21

'How does your idol progress?' asked one of the men, as the little group of stone workers gathered around their work area, drawing their tools from the makeshift satchels—mostly a piece of old cloth with its ends knotted together, though one or two of the men had proper sacks. There were fewer than a dozen of them, because the work here right now was more for the masons, not the stone workers. The stone workers were not expected to display their artistry, their ability to summon flowers and intricate patterns out of rock. No, this was simple, clean, plain. The baoli was for the use of the people, not the glorification of the man who had commissioned it.

Girdhar grinned. 'It is progressing. I went to the larger temple, south along the bank. There's a statue of Krishnaji there which is a fine template.'

The other man grinned in response and someone laughed. 'Pray that your father does not see the original. He will have your hide for it, will he not?'

A week, no more, and he had already settled in so well that all the stone workers knew what he was up to and why he, unlike the rest of them, did not travel all the way back to Ghiyasuddin Tughlaq's fort to work every morning. Perhaps not all of them approved of his hoodwinking his father, but they did not deride him for it. They, too, were guilty of subterfuge. Ghiyasuddin Tughlaq had not expected that these men would find a loophole to wriggle out of his decree binding them to his fort.

Girdhar spent his days by the riverside under a shady tree. Through the day, with occasional breaks to rest or to daydream, he worked on the foot-tall Krishna he was carving. It was a good statue, well-proportioned and representative of the deity. The peacock feather dancing at his forehead, the bent arms that held a flute to his lips. The eyes, full of both mischief and wisdom. The clothes that hung in graceful folds, the dhoti clinging to slim but sturdy calves, the stole hanging from broad shoulders. A Krishna that would be the pride of the temple.

It did nothing to him. It evoked nothing except the pride of a worker for his creation. Girdhar wondered if that was true of other artists who painted, or carved, or otherwise created images of the divine. Like him, did they feel no reverence for what they had made, simply because they knew this was mere stone, or clay, or parchment that had been shaped into a likeness of a god by the skill of a man? Did they see the workmanship and not the spirituality that the layman assigned to the work?

No, Baba was not like that. Baba would have said that it was the deity who had emerged from the stone or the clay. To Badrinath, the worker was a vehicle, no more. No wonder he had so readily believed that Krishna would reveal himself to Girdhar beside the Yamuna. As far as Badrinath was concerned, there was nothing ridiculous about it.

Girdhar wondered, as he went about his work, what excuse he could make to prolong his stay here. Could he say his hand had slipped and the chisel had gouged out a piece where there was no hope of correction? That he would have to start all over again? Even as he bent to his work of chiselling away the edges of a stone slab that was to be fitted into one wall of the baoli, Girdhar shook his head silently. Badrinath would not accept that excuse; he would say Girdhar had been at the Yamuna long enough to have gathered all the inspiration he needed.

He was so deep in thought that he did not notice the sound of approaching hooves and the clang of steel until a voice rang out: 'Who is in charge here?'

☙

The masons, stone workers and unskilled workers huddled around the bull-shouldered officer who headed the contingent. There were not many soldiers: two, besides the officer, were on horseback, and six others were on foot. They were not out, after all, to take up arms, but merely to deliver a message. An imperial edict, it had already been announced in both Yoginipur and Ghiyaspur, said the officer; now it was being read out at the exact place for which it had been formulated.

Given that most of these men who worked at the baoli lived in Yoginipur and worked at the fort during the day, it was hardly surprising that news of where they worked at night was no secret. Their families and friends knew it; perhaps several of the men boasted of it, of how they had found a way to get around the Sultan's petty vindictiveness. A harmless conversation might have been the start, but it had become common knowledge in Yoginipur soon enough. And what was known in the bazaars of the city in the morning invariably reached the Sultan's ears before noon.

Ghiyasuddin Tughlaq, furious at the way his orders had been flouted, had retaliated by slapping a ban on the sale of oil.

Less than twelve hours from now, when the sun rose and the bazaars opened, there would be no oil, no ghee, no fuel for their lamps. Households would probably survive: dried cow dung was their fuel, the moon their source of light. Those who could not bear the thought of eating boiled food would perhaps make ghee, by boiling down milk. It would be inconvenient, but not unbearably so. The wealthier households would grumble about it, and would probably have their servants cook milk until it had turned to a rich, fragrant dark brown mass, the fat leached out into pure clear ghee. Ghee in the lamps, ghee in the food, ghee to light up the house. The poor, with limited resources, would manage as best as they could until the ban was revoked.

It was obvious to all: this ban was aimed to inconvenience one person, one project. Nizamuddin Auliya's baoli was being constructed at night, and the workmen would not be able to work without oil for their lamps.

They stood around dejected, after the soldiers had left. Mushtaq, the cocky child whom Girdhar had so despised when he first came to the baoli but who had turned out to be an amusing and witty character, hopped about impatiently. 'But we are close to finishing, aren't we, Chacha?' he asked, tugging at the foreman's elbow. Almost as if he himself were among the workers, not just a child who helped their work by keeping their lamps well-trimmed and clean.

Mushtaq's refusal to be considered an outsider, and his persistence, perhaps, made the foreman deign to explain. 'We are not close to finishing. Yes, we have reached the water, but there is still much to be done. The sides have to be shored up, the slabs have to be finished and bound with mortar—it requires many weeks' work still.'

'What if we gathered firewood?' asked one of the men. 'We could use that to light up the area.'

The foreman was shaking his head, as were some of the others around, even before the man had finished. 'We would need a lot of firewood. Who would gather it? Mushtaq and Girdhar? The rest of us come here from Yoginipur only to work; for us to spend time gathering so much firewood would be a waste of precious time.'

'I could get others,' Mushtaq piped up.

'No. In any case, firewood takes time and effort to ignite and it burns up too fast. The light is inconsistent, and it can be dangerous. Sparks fly, burning wood disintegrates. It would be more hindrance than help for most of us.' He saw the defiance in Mushtaq's eager young face and added, 'There would be smoke wafting into a worker's face if the wind blew his way. Sparks would fly, and what if a man, intent on his work, stepped too close to the fire, or a burning ember rolled towards him?' He shook his head again. 'No, it will not do.'

'Then? What will we do?' Mushtaq was not to be silenced so easily. 'Will we sit around and wait until the Sultan's fort is built?'

'A fort will not be built so soon,' said one man glumly. 'It will take many months, perhaps years.'

'It is not a question of the fort.' They turned, to a man, towards the gateway—only two rough-hewn gateposts right now, no more. There stood Amir Khusro.

'If he was in such a hurry to have his fort built,' Khusro Sahib said as he approached the group, 'His Majesty would not have relied only on the workmen of Dilli. He would have brought in labourers from all corners of the empire.' He had reached the little crowd now, and a path opened for him, letting him pass without pausing to the centre. 'Also, if he needed it to be done quickly, would there not be more teams of men, working through the night as well?' He shook his head. 'The truth is, our Sultan has little love for my friend.'

A despondent silence followed Khusro Sahib's words. If Amir Khusro, high-ranking nobleman that he was, should sound so despairing, what hope could there be for the rest of them? If he did not say that he would plead with the Sultan, what could they do but put down their tools and say goodbye to the half-constructed baoli?

'Then?' Mushtaq asked, speaking for all of them, his voice high and urgent. 'What then, Khusro Sahib? There is no hope, then?'

Khusro Sahib looked down at the boy. A twinkle appeared in his eyes and a smile made the corners of his lips curl upward. 'Did I say that, Mushtaq? No. My friend is coming; he will soon be here. If he says we must despair, then we will do so. We will rend our clothes and tear our hair out and rub dust into our scalps and weep so loud that Heaven itself will quiver…' Khusro Sahib's eyes suddenly narrowed into thoughtfulness.

For a long moment he stared unseeing into Mushtaq's bewildered face. Then he cleared his throat and said, 'Listen carefully, my child. *Ik thaal moti se bharaa, sab ke sir pe aundhaa dharaa. Chaaron ore woh thaali phire, moti usse ek na gire.*'

Mushtaq stared into the old man's face, puzzled. The men standing around were frowning, some as bemused as the boy, some, by the doubtful looks on their faces, perhaps beginning to wonder if Khusro Sahib was in his right senses.

'I don't understand,' Mushtaq mumbled. 'What do you mean?'

'You tell me,' Khusro Sahib said, his smile widening into a mischievous grin. 'You tell me what I mean. Do you want to hear it again?' His gaze moved around the men pressing in around them. He saw the curiosity in some faces, the scepticism in others. When he continued, it was in a voice raised high enough to carry even to the fringes of the crowd.

'A platter full of pearls?' Mushtaq muttered, when Khusro Sahib had finished. 'And wandering all around, but without a single pearl dropping from it?' His eyebrows drew together. 'Is it a riddle, Khusro Sahib?'

'Of course it is a riddle. What is the answer?'

Some of the men were smiling now. But they kept quiet, waiting for the child to find the answer for himself.

'Think, Mushtaq.' Khusro Sahib murmured the words of the riddle again, this time saying it slower, his deep, rich voice lingering lovingly over each syllable.

'The sky! The stars are the pearls!' Mushtaq said excitedly. 'Is that right, Khusro Sahib? It is, isn't it? Am I right?'

Khusro Sahib smiled and put his hand into the deep pocket of the long, wide-sleeved coat he wore. He drew from it a lump of deep amber jaggery wrapped in a bit of fine new muslin. 'And here is your reward for it.'

'Thank you,' Mushtaq said absently, accepting the treat, 'but why, Khusro Sahib? Why did you ask that riddle? Do you mean we should work by starlight?'

Khusro Sahib's smile turned to a laugh. 'No, Mushtaq,' he said. 'No. How could we? Even the moon does not give out enough light for us to be able to work by it.' His gaze travelled over the company, looking into the faces around.

'No. But there is a sky, and there is He who made the sky and the stars. He who could create something so wonderful—He will not desert us, I think.

'I will go and tell my friend of this latest development,' he said, giving Mushtaq's shoulder one last pat. 'Let us see what he advises. After all, this is his baoli.'

The news ran, swift as a river in spate, through Yoginipur. Before dawn, people knew that the Sultan had banned the sale of oil—and the more canny among them guessed the real reason for the ban. Bhushan, having mulled over it, went hurrying to a nearby muleteer whom he knew, and hired a mule to take him to Ghiyaspur.

When he returned late the next afternoon, Girdhar rode behind him. They had taken it in turns to ride the mule from Ghiyaspur to Yoginipur; it had made the trip a longer and more tiring one, but they were in Yoginipur at last.

Bhushan's good-natured face was clouded with worry when they reached the main bazaar of the settlement. 'Are you certain?' he asked Girdhar, as the younger man dismounted.

Girdhar nodded.

'Do you want me to come with you?'

Girdhar could not help but grin at that. 'You look even more terrified than I feel. One bellow from Baba and you'd run away!' He patted the mule's neck and looked up at Bhushan. 'No, I will go alone. This is my business, my decision. It is best I be the one to tell Baba.' The smile, already belied by the barely controlled fear in his eyes, wavered. 'Besides, if Baba whips the hide off me or makes me soil my dhoti, at least there will be no one but my mother and my sister to witness my disgrace. And they've seen it often enough.'

'Go, then. I will be at the sweet shop.'

Girdhar first made his way to Yamini's house. It seemed

important to him that she, since she had met Khusro Sahib, be told. There was also a niggling fear that if their father were to react the way Girdhar expected him to, Girdhar may not live to see his favourite sister again.

'Are you mad?' Yamini whispered when she had heard him out. A whisper, because the toddler in her arms was in a half-doze, and she did not want him to come awake. Girdhar knew that even if the child was fast asleep in his bed, Yamini would still have spoken in a whisper. Her eyes were huge, her lips dry. 'No, you are joking, aren't you?'

Girdhar shook his head.

Yamini stared down into her child's face, his cheek now fallen against her shoulder, his mouth drooping open on one side. 'I'll put him down,' she murmured. 'Wait for me.'

When she returned, the infant deposited without mishap in his bed, it was to stare into her brother's face with a mixture of bewilderment and apprehension. 'You must be mad,' she said in an awed whisper. 'How can you? How can you even think—hey Ram, Baba will kill you.' She caught Girdhar's arm, clutching it with sudden strength. 'Are you certain? Are you absolutely certain? Because if you're going to go to Baba and say something like that, you had better be certain.'

'I am certain,' Girdhar said after a moment. 'I have made no promises yet, but I am certain.'

She bit her lip. The hand grasping his wrist loosened its grip and fell away. Yamini looked away and Girdhar, watching her, wondered what she was thinking. That he was a fool? A traitor? He did not think so: Yamini was not like that. None of them were. Only Baba.

When she turned to look at him again her eyes were full of tears. 'You will always be my brother,' she said, her voice choked. 'Won't you?'

'Blood does not turn to water over something like this,' Girdhar assured her.

But as he walked away from her hut a few minutes

later, it was with the sickening fear that those words would probably not be echoed by their father. Badrinath would not accept that his blood could be guilty of treachery of this magnitude.

ᛋ

Badrinath was surprised to see Girdhar, but not unduly so. 'You should have come home sooner,' he said by way of admonishment. 'Or at least sent word. Is your work done? Is Krishnaji carved?'

'I did not come because of that, Baba.' His heart was hammering so hard against the wall of his chest that he feared his father would hear it. 'I came to talk to you about something else.'

Badrinath squinted, suddenly suspicious. 'What? Did you make a mistake? Do you have to start all over again?'

The distrust in his father's eyes, though it had nothing to do with what Girdhar was going to confess, made the knot of fear in his stomach change to nausea. It made him wish he had never met Bhushan, never set foot in Qutb Sahib's dargah, never met Amir Khusro, never gone to the baoli being built in Ghiyaspur.

The realization that he would regret all of that gave him strength. 'No, Baba,' he said, willing his voice to remain firm. 'No, I did not do any of that. The idol is complete. I finished it four days back.'

'Four days back? Then why have you come home only now?'

Girdhar steeled himself and drew in a deep breath. He had to say this all at once because if he paused, he would be lost. 'I did not come earlier because my work was not finished, Baba. I had completed the idol, but that work I did only in the daytime. Not at night. At night'—his heart had, inexplicably, climbed up into his throat now, and was making it difficult for him to speak—'at night I work at the baoli that Nizamuddin Auliya Sahib is building. The Sultan—'

He was interrupted by a cry of rage. Badrinath had scrambled to his feet and was lunging towards him. Girdhar, his body trained by a short lifetime of experience, moved of its own accord, his legs folding under so that he curled up, foetus-like, with his arms wrapped around his knees. The blows began to rain down on him and from somewhere beyond the din and the dust, he heard panicked screaming. His father's shouting, the thudding of his fists and his kicking feet, his own stifled moans, those screams.

And then, there was a sudden silence: Girdhar, through the blur, thought it was the eye of the storm, his father gathering strength for a renewed assault. Or perhaps his mother—she had been the one screaming—had stopped him. When moments passed and it was only Kalyani's screams, now ragged with fear, that rent the air, Girdhar looked up.

It was not his wife who had stopped Badrinath; it was Badrinath himself. He had fallen to the ground and lay there, his face contorted, his body twitching in some sort of seizure. Girdhar stared, shocked at his own sense of relief, the sudden euphoria. The next moment, he got over it and bent to reassure his mother.

'I'll go and get the physician,' he said, and had to repeat it, because she was shrieking loud enough to drown out every other sound. Neighbours were coming, hurrying to see what had happened. Girdhar saw a friendly face, a woman who lived two houses away, and rushed to her.

'Look after Ma. I'm going to fetch a vaid.'

It was not fatal. It was not even as crippling as Girdhar had feared it would be. 'A seizure, yes,' said the vaid, when Girdhar accompanied him back to his home to collect the medicine the vaid had prescribed. 'But not a severe one. He will be all right, given time to rest. Are you home for good now? Badrinath had told me you had gone to a temple beside the Yamuna.'

Girdhar nodded. 'I have to go back there,' he replied. 'But not for a while yet.'

When he came home carrying the little bundle of dried herbs and minerals the vaid had given, it was to find Badrinath asleep. Girdhar handed his mother the medicine, and told her what the vaid had said. 'I'll give it to him when he wakes,' Kalyani said. Her face looked ravaged, every line a furrow, every spot a pit. 'He will be all right, won't he?' she asked. She had already asked the vaid that several times while he had been attending to Badrinath, and she had put the same question to Girdhar as soon as he had appeared at the door.

'Yes. He needs rest.'

Kalyani leaned against the doorpost and closed her eyes. Tears trickled from under her eyelids and down her cheeks; she swiped at them ineffectually. Girdhar put an arm around her shoulders. 'Come, sit down,' he murmured. His younger sister, who had been sitting at Badrinath's bedside keeping an eye on him, peeked out of the room. Girdhar beckoned to her. 'Come and look after Ma. I'll sit with Baba.'

Kalyani caught him by the arm. 'What are you going to do? What had you said that made him so angry?'

Girdhar looked down into his mother's face and wondered. Was his mother being loyal because she loved her husband despite his tyranny, his bigotry, his lack of mercy? Or was it a question of mere practicality? Her husband was the one whose earnings kept her clothed and fed; if he were to die or end up crippled, what would become of her, or of her yet unmarried daughter?

If that were the case, it was a sad reflection on her belief in her own son. Did she think Girdhar such a poor example of filial responsibility?

'Nothing, Ma,' he said. 'Nothing of any consequence. I am not going to do anything. I will just sit by his side in case he should wake and want something.'

She looked at him, her eyes dry now as her gaze searched

his face. For what? Duplicity? Lies? All of which she may well see there, thought Girdhar. His mother was very perceptive.

'No,' she said, finally, shaking her head. 'If he were to wake and see you beside him, all his anger will come back. I don't know what it was, and you will not tell me—but perhaps it is better that he does not see you until he is well again.' She rose to her feet, using Girdhar's arm for support. 'I will go to him.'

Badrinath slept for the next six hours, a sleep so deep that had it not been for his breathing, his family would have thought him dead. By the time the sun had set, he had begun to emerge from his stupor, but this was still far from wakefulness. He slept still, the sleep was punctuated by snuffles, by vague murmurs and restlessness. His feet twitched, his hands plucked at the thin sheet that covered him.

Kalyani sat with him through the night, staring fixedly at the wan face on the thin mattress. Girdhar, unable to sleep, watched her, and wondered what was going through her head. Was she still worried? Was it a façade, because a woman was expected to worry herself sick over her husband? Because widowhood was the end of all things, the beginning of a life of ostracization, of being suddenly and completely cut off from all that was even remotely to be regarded as enjoyable?

When he became fully conscious, the first question Badrinath asked Yamini—whom Girdhar had informed and who had insisted on coming—'Where is your brother?'

Involuntarily she looked over her shoulder at where he was sitting on his haunches, just outside the door. Girdhar looked up on hearing Badrinath's voice, and his heart stilled in fear.

'Get him.' Badrinath looked and sounded exhausted.

'Baba, I think—'

'I do not care what you think. Bring him here and leave us alone.'

With a resigned sigh, Yamini got to her feet.

'Tell me,' Badrinath said when Girdhar appeared in the doorway. 'Tell me what you were going to say. Spare me no detail. Tell me all.'

'Baba, I think we should wait—'

'Will you dictate to me? You?' Badrinath's anger was beginning to rise again. For a wild, frantic moment, Girdhar wondered if he should simply turn and run out of the house, out through the dusty little lane outside, out of Yoginipur.

He straightened his shoulders. 'No, Baba,' he said. 'I will tell you. But please listen till the end, otherwise it will never be said.' He paused. 'And it needs to be said,' he added in a flat voice. Had he still been looking at his father's face, he would have seen the anger dissolve into a vague foreboding.

Girdhar did not sit. He stood by his father's bedside and said it all. His voice quivered, but did not stop. He spoke of his visit to the tomb of Qutb Sahib and of meeting Amir Khusro there. He talked of that first trip with Bhushan to the hermitage of Nizamuddin Auliya. He spoke of the baoli there and how the Sultan's attempts to halt its work had affected the men.

Badrinath bristled. 'I know what the Sultan decreed,' he cut in, despite the tacit promise that he would not interrupt Girdhar. 'I don't need you to tell me things every urchin in the bazaar knows.'

'Yes, but you don't know what happened at the baoli when the Sultan banned the sale of oil.'

'You came back. Because you couldn't work any more.'

Girdhar shook his head. 'No. I came back because'—he swallowed, trying to summon up the courage to say what he must—'because what happened after that made me realize what path I must take. I don't think the news had reached Yoginipur by then, when I arrived. And you have been in bed since then; you have not heard the news though it is now common knowledge even here.'

He sensed movement behind him. A shadow moved into the rectangle of light that was the doorway. His mother, he guessed. Badrinath's gaze flickered briefly towards the door, then back to Girdhar.

'We had oil enough in our lamps and some to spare for two days' work, no more,' Girdhar said. 'But after that we would have had to stop.' His gaze softened, his memory travelling back to those moments, to the anxiety and disappointment. 'We knew it would be impossible to continue, and I think most of us had reconciled ourselves to going back and working on the Sultan's fortress until it was completed. And who knew what he would think up next? Most men in Ghiyaspur think the Sultan is being vindictive. He just wants to show the city that he is more powerful than—'

'You said you had something to tell me. If you want to give me a speech on politics, get lost.'

'No, Baba. I'm sorry. That was not what I meant. It was just—just that you can see how deep in despair we all were. We thought we wouldn't be able to work there any more. And then, Hazrat Sahib came.'

'Who?'

'Nizamuddin Auliya Sahib. Khusro Sahib had told him, about the ban and about how worried we all were.' His voice had sunk to a near-whisper; he cleared his throat. 'Hazrat Sahib went down on his knees there, facing west, and he prayed. I don't know what he said. I don't think any of the men did. Perhaps not even Khusro Sahib, for he murmured his prayers, and Khusro Sahib jokes that he cannot understand his friend because his friend speaks Turkish and Khusro Sahib knows no Turkish'—he flinched at the expression on his father's face. 'He prayed,' he said, now nearing the end of his narrative, and feeling a sense of relief at having got this far. 'And the water that lay at the bottom of the excavation lit up. It shone bright enough to outshine a hundred lamps.'

Badrinath looked unimpressed. He said nothing, however.

'Baba,' Girdhar said, 'I cannot continue like this any longer. I—I cannot stay here, I cannot go against my heart.'

A long moment of silence passed. He heard the rustle of clothing as someone shifted outside. The person at the doorway had been joined by another. Yamini, he thought, also come to see and to hear. And perhaps his younger sister. If that was so, it was good. It was good that all his family should hear it at the same time. To walk through the same fire, again and again, to repeat those words—as painful for him as they would be to his parents and his sisters—would take too much of a toll.

'Do you mean that you will go away and live there in Ghiyaspur?' Badrinath's voice was soft. So soft that Girdhar had to strain to hear what he said. So soft too, that Girdhar had no difficulty in recognizing the anger brimming below the surface.

Girdhar nodded. 'That is the only path for me.'

'Because a charlatan hoodwinked you into thinking the moon shone out of a pool of water? Because all of you, gullible and stupid, believed rubbish like that? He waved his hands and poof!—there was light? Did it not occur to you that the moon and the stars are so bright that even the slightest trickle of water will catch their light and reflect it a hundred times? And the amount of water in a baoli—' Badrinath laughed, a contemptuous guffaw that hung in the air. 'What fools.' He stopped, and from the silence at the doorway, Girdhar heard a stifled whimper. His mother, sensing impending doom.

'Whatever it was,' Girdhar said, 'I saw what I did.' Something occurred to him, something that he had not even thought about in all these days. It lent him strength to add, 'And—that is not it, Baba. I do not leave because of a miracle. Or not a miracle, as you think. It is just that I see something there in Hazrat Nizamuddin Auliya Sahib, in Khusro Sahib. They are religious, very religious, but they are tolerant, too.' His throat had gone dry; he swallowed, his gaze moving involuntarily to the terracotta water pot beside his father's bed. 'They are gentle, kind. Their religion makes them better men.'

'And ours does not?'

After a few moments to think over it, Girdhar wagged his head, non-committal. 'It does to some,' he admitted. 'But not—not others.' He rose to his feet, ready to flee. It was, anyway, nearly done. 'You, Baba, use your religion as a means to beat and bully people. You enforce your beliefs until those around you find it stifling. You have beaten all of us because we failed to do something or the other that you thought was our religious duty. I still remember how you thrashed Ma.'

'Girdhar, please,' his mother wailed from the door. 'Stop!'

Badrinath directed a gaze filled with malevolence towards his wife before looking back at Girdhar. 'This is the blood of your great-grandmother,' he said. 'Jayshree, who saw no harm in fraternizing with the enemy, in serving that wretched woman who sat on the throne. I thank the gods that my grandmother died before she could influence my father, turn him as rotten as she was.' His voice faltered. Girdhar could not tell whether it was from emotion or exhaustion. Or both.

'Say what you have to say,' Badrinath said through gritted teeth. 'And be done with it.'

'I cannot live under your roof any more, Baba. I cannot find in myself any reverence for the gods you have thrashed me into worshipping. I leave your home, and I leave your gods.'

Pandemonium broke out behind him. His mother rushed forward, clinging to him, begging him to stay, berating him for being so thoughtless. Her grip was hard enough to be painful, her voice grating and harsh. His younger sister was wailing. Yamini was murmuring, trying to pacify her sister.

'Stop it,' Badrinath rasped. And when it had no effect, he

snapped, 'Shut up, all of you! You, woman, leave him.' When Kalyani did not let go, he repeated in a slow, deliberate voice, 'Let go of him.' Each syllable hung in the air, menacing in its intensity. A shiver ran down Girdhar's spine.

Kalyani obeyed, but to everybody's surprise, possibly even her own, she said, 'Your only son.' It was an indistinct mumble, the words muffled by her terror and her anguish. 'How can you let your only son go?'

'He is not my son.' Badrinath looked up into Girdhar's eyes, his own eyes blank. 'I will have his name expunged from every place it appears. He will not inherit anything I leave behind. And if any of you dare to even set eyes on him from now onwards, you will go the same way as him.' He looked away. 'Go now, all of you. I need to rest.'

Interlude

'Ah.' Nasiruddin sat back with a sigh of satisfaction. 'So that was the connection. I was surprised that you had begun a story that was not connected to the earlier stories. But there it was, the link hidden till the end.' He grinned, his teeth gleaming white in the small fire they had lit in the dilapidated mosque where they had sheltered. 'An interesting tale. I have always been a follower of Allah, I was brought up thus and I continue thus. It never occurred to me how it might be for someone of another faith to approach mine.' The grin had vanished, to be replaced by a pensiveness as he stared into space. 'One thing I do not understand, though,' he said. 'How was it that they were so poor? Jayshree had been a wealthy woman, from what I gathered. The daughter of a wealthy family, and married to a wealthy man. Then how was it that her grandson was no more than a stone carver?'

Shagufta stretched; hours of sitting in one position had left her with stiff, aching muscles. 'Jayshree's father, Nandu, was a stone carver too,' she reminded him. 'Nandu. He had been influential enough while his father-in-law, Sridhar Sahu, was in Qutbuddin Aibak's good books. When Sridhar Sahu's duplicity was exposed, he fell from favour. It was a hard fall, a destructive fall, and Nandu, his son-in-law and protégé, was affected as well. And because Nandu and Gayatri hated Altamash for what they thought was his role in the downfall of Sridhar Sahu, they had deliberately distanced themselves from anything to do with the court.'

'And Jayshree's loyalty to Razia,' supplied Nasiruddin, 'must have seemed even more of a betrayal.'

She nodded. 'Yes. Also, when Razia's short reign was over, with Razia dead and Jayshree dead, the family lost even that unwanted link to the court. Nandu's wealth had trickled away over the years, and he had gone back to being a stone carver long before his death. It was always what he was best at. And Jayshree's husband: well, he was no Sridhar Sahu; his business acumen was next to nothing. His son had even less, and though he made an effort to follow in his father's footsteps, it was no use. He failed, and eventually reverted to the craft of his ancestors.'

'Stone carving. And his son Badrinath followed suit, and then Girdhar.'

'It's not as if they were utterly impoverished,' Shagufta said gently. 'Not as wealthy, of course, as Jayshree had once been, but not piss-poor like me.'

To her surprise, he frowned. 'Don't say that. You aren't.' He looked genuinely annoyed, disturbed by the word she had used to describe herself. 'You are not, you cannot be.'

There was a brief silence, an awkward silence in which Shagufta did not know where to look. Then, finally, with a somewhat strained chuckle, he said, 'But I grant you this, you know how to tell a story well. I know you said you weren't a storyteller, but you should try taking up that profession; you have a flair for it.'

He was smiling, and Shagufta gave him a watery smile in return. 'It might be an easier way to earn a living.'

'Easier than what?' His brows drew together in a frown of curiosity. 'I mean, how do you keep body and soul together? You have no man to look after you, no family—which must mean that you take on some work. What do the women in your land do if they have no man to feed and clothe them?'

'Must a man always feed and clothe a woman?' She got to her feet, stretching to loosen her aching muscles. 'These past few days, I have fed you, quite literally too, with my own hands. I have cleaned you, I have dressed your wounds. Are you a woman then, Nasiruddin Sahib? And am I a man?'

He bowed his head in acknowledgement of the logic, and in admission of his own presumption. 'That was wrongly worded, then. But I am curious: how do you make a living?'

'How does a woman in times such as this and without a family, make a living? I was not brought up to till the land. And while I can scrub my own pots and pans and sweep my hut and mend my clothes, I know I will never be able to do so to any rich woman's satisfaction. What is left, then?'

He looked down, embarrassed, as the most likely explanation occurred to him. Shagufta went to the few twigs that remained of the firewood they had collected. The rest they had added as the night wore on, to keep the little fire going. She had nearly said once or twice that she was tired and would like to sleep now, but watching him, his face intent and his eyes eager, she had not had the heart to do so. So she had talked on and he had listened.

She had picked up those last few twigs when she heard unfamiliar sounds. Boots, the rustling of branches, the occasional voice. Men, approaching in a group, and careless of being heard. To be so unafraid in times like this, the group must be large as well as armed. Shagufta's mind whirled, trying to juggle different fears, different thoughts. Find a place to hide, remove traces of the night spent here, get ready to fight—

A hand pressed down on her forearm and Shagufta swung around, her other hand instinctively gripping the bundle of twigs and raising it high.

'No!' Nasiruddin hissed. 'It's me!' He was already looking around, his eyes searching the darkness of the trees. Dawn was still a couple of hours away, thought Shagufta. Perhaps if they hid, they would not be seen. But they would be better off hiding among the trees, in the undergrowth. Not here, in the only proper shelter around.

'We must put out the fire,' she whispered. 'And we must get away from here.'

With his hand, he gestured for silence. He had straightened up now, and was suddenly looking as alert as a predator that has caught wind of its prey. She wondered what he could see.

She could not see anything in the gloom of the night, but

she could hear, and the sounds were clearer now. Discernible conversation, even if it could be heard only in snatches. A sentence here, a few words there, in a language she could not recognize.

Shagufta scuttled away, scrabbling for dust to throw on the fire. Nasiruddin turned. 'What are you doing?' He looked genuinely surprised. 'Don't be afraid; these are friends, my men.' His voice was still low but the strain, the fear that been lurking in his eyes the past few days, was gone. Magically wiped away.

'Your friends,' she pointed out. 'Not mine.' She moved to throw another handful of dust over the fire, and he stopped her.

'Don't. Let it be. I will stay here, I will pretend I am alone. You hide.'

He tilted his head towards the copse of trees nearby. There was no time to wonder if this was a horrible prank, if he would call his friends and compatriots to join him in attacking a lone woman. Already they were so close she could hear the rustling of garments, the soft curse as someone tripped over a protruding root or snagged a sleeve on a branch. Shagufta grabbed her shawl around her and ran into the trees beyond the mosque. Once in the shadow of the copse, she changed direction, moving away from where she had entered, but staying close enough to see what was happening.

They emerged from the trees on the far side of the mosque, and as they did so, Nasiruddin came out from the shelter of the mosque. She had not seen battle before—not the way soldiers on a battlefield fought—and she was taken aback by the frightening suddenness with which the men went from tired slackness to full attention. Bows were drawn taut, arrows nocked, swords out of their scabbards and on the ready before she had even realized it.

In the light of the torches held by two men at the front of the group, she saw Nasiruddin standing with his arms akimbo, his legs apart. He was saying something to the men in their own language, and she could only imagine what it might be. That he was one of them, that he was glad to see his own countrymen again. Or was he also saying that there was a woman nearby, a woman hiding? A woman who was used to selling her body to men and who, therefore, was prime game for all of them to take their pleasure with? Bile, bitter and sour, rose to her throat. What a fool you have been, she thought. What an utter fool. What could have possessed you to drag an enemy soldier into your house? And then to run away here, far from familiar surroundings, with him? Were you so desperately lonely that you did not care who it was, as long as you had someone to talk to?

They were smiling now, some of them even laughing. The weapons had been put away, the tension dissipated. One of the men—short and stocky, with a stained cloth wrapped about his skull—had taken Nasiruddin's arm and drawn him aside. The deference with which the others left them alone may mean that this was the leader of the troop, Shagufta thought. The two of them had their backs to her now, their heads almost touching.

She watched for what seemed an eternity, waiting for the two men to draw apart, for an unintelligible order to ring out. For the men to come pounding through the trees, heading towards her. Her mind raced, looking for escape. She could not possibly outrun them or fight them off, and how long would she hide? They would flush her out soon enough. The thought crossed her mind that she could kill herself, but she discarded that idea as soon as it arose. Life was too precious.

They had drawn apart now, and the leader of the troop stood facing Nasiruddin. He was once again at the head of his troop, the leader of his men, talking to a man they had come upon in the woods. She wondered what he said.

As she watched, with a few words—she guessed they were farewells—the men moved off. Away they went, the sound of their passage through the trees and the bushes gradually fading. It was only when there was utter silence again, with not even the glow from their torches to be seen, that she heard Nasiruddin call out softly, 'Where are you? Come out, they are gone.'

She did not move.

'Come out. Trust me.' He sounded weary, exasperated. 'If I had to tell them about you, I wouldn't have let them go away.'

There was truth in that. Feeling a little sheepish, Shagufta left the shelter of the trees and moved out into the clearing. He turned when he heard her coming, and a quizzical smile appeared on his lips: he had noted that she had vanished into the trees at one spot but emerged at another.

'You are a clever woman,' he said when she reached him. Shagufta was brushing the dirt and the dried leaves off her clothes and hair; she did not even look at him.

'Why? Had you really thought I would stay there, within easy reach of a mob of men thirsting for my blood?' Her mouth twisted in a grimace. 'After having had their fill of me, I would think.'

'Do you think me such an ingrate that I would hand you over to them in return for all that you have done for me?'

She looked up then into eyes that glittered with anger in the first pearling of grey in the air. 'I don't even know you,' she murmured. 'I know your name, and I know that you are a soldier in the invader's army. But beyond that? A man is not defined by his name or his occupation.'

'Am I so very much an enigma? In all these days that you have been within arm's reach of me, is that all you have gathered?'

It dawned on her that she was being unfair, peevish; she was letting the terror of the past minutes erupt in anger. It was an odd feeling, this realization that she was no longer holding back her emotions. When had this happened, this moment when he had ceased to be a stranger to whom she was merely polite, and had become someone to whom she could show her anger?

He was a soldier, she reminded herself, of an army that had swept into Dilli. They had killed thousands, plundered and burnt her city, reduced it to a derelict ruin. She must not feel any attraction for this man. He was the enemy, and she barely knew him.

'So who were they?' she asked, brushing past him and heading for the shelter of the mosque.

'They were a stray contingent looking for stragglers. The army is heading back.' When she turned to stare into his face, he gave her a wan smile. 'Surely you did not think we meant to stay here? To set up a new dynasty like that—who was the first of them, the Muslim Sultans of this city?'

'Aibak. Qutbuddin Aibak.' The answer came of its own accord, uttered without a thought. Her mind was reeling from the implication of what he had said. He would be gone, she thought. Gone perhaps before the sun set on this day.

She looked up into his face, her eyes searching his. 'Why did you not go with them?'

He looked embarrassed. And unsure, as if he did not know. 'I had some unfinished business to attend to.' Unexpectedly, his mouth curved into a smile, but it was a smile that did nothing to relieve the sadness in his eyes. 'I cannot leave without listening to one last story, can I?'

Shagufta felt the tears pricking at her eyelids, the lump that had risen to her throat. 'That is all I am? A storyteller?'

'I did not say so.' A firm but not ungentle hand grasped her by the elbow, guiding them both into the corner of the mosque where they had sat through the night. He said no more as he sat her down and draped his thin blanket about her shoulders. While she sat he moved about, gathering more twigs and reigniting the fire she had put out so hurriedly. When the flame finally began to lick at the twigs, he said, 'Was that true? That the Hazrat made the water of the stepwell shine at night?'

'They say he did. They say, in fact, that ever since, the water at Nizamuddin Sahib's baoli has had the power to work miracles. People claim to have been healed of deadly diseases just by dipping their hands in it.'

Nasiruddin looked impressed. 'I would dearly have liked to see it for myself.'

Shagufta remained silent. After a moment, he said in a voice so low that she had to strain to hear him, 'You know I have to go. I cannot stay. This is not my city, not my land. Your people are not mine. If I stayed here just for you, do you think your people would let either of us live in peace? We would be tormented day and night because of who I am. I am safe here only as long as I am within reach of my comrades. The day they leave, and I am left alone—'

He shook his head.

Of course he was right. She had known it and yet she had hoped. Hoped too, that he would know how she had begun to feel about him. Hoped and dreaded. Dreaded that he would realize just how lonely she was, how needy.

'I will remember you,' he was saying. 'How can I ever forget you? All that you have done for me. And—you.' There was an awkward pause. He had stilled, sitting there, one bent knee resting on the ground, the other propping up his arm. 'Give me something to remember you by. One more story, that is all I ask. Please.'

The tears were running down her cheeks, and she wanted desperately to run away back to the comfort of her quiet, lonely little hut. To howl out her unhappiness, to rage at kismet or the world, or that ambitious and greedy Taimur, who was not satisfied with what he had, but must come ravaging, unleashing his men on a city that was ill-equipped to ward them off. In every which way.

Her own folly, she thought. If she had stayed in her hut and not ventured out; if she had fled as soon as she had seen the enemy soldier lying bleeding in the street—this would not have happened. She had nobody to blame but herself.

Shagufta wiped the tears off her cheeks. When she was certain her face was composed and her voice would not quaver, she said, 'It is said that when someone remarked that Ghiyasuddin Tughlaq had built such a magnificent fort, Nizamuddin Sahib said, "*Ya rahe ujad, ya rahe gujar*". He prophesied that the fort would remain barren, deserted—or that it would be inhabited by the nomads, the gujars.' Her voice had gathered strength from this matter-of-fact narration of a story that had been bred in her since she was a little girl. 'It turned out to be correct too, for Ghiyasuddin Tughlaq did not get to spend many days in the fort he had built. He died four years later, killed when a wooden pavilion collapsed on top of him. He was returning from a campaign and had stopped to watch a muster of the elephant cavalry.'

'I am sure this is very interesting,' Nasiruddin said dryly, 'but I would rather hear a story about everyday people. About you, for instance.'

'And if I say I am a part of this story?' All of its own, a small smile came to her lips.

'You are?' His left eyebrow rose in surprise. 'How?'

'Are you really interested?' She waited to see his nod, then added, 'If that is so, then let me tell it my way.'

'Meandering? Talking about an old mystic and a Sultan, and the enmity between them?'

She shrugged. 'I won't speak, then. Let it be.' With a sudden change of topic, she asked, 'Where and when will you meet the rest of your men? What did you tell them?'

He looked taken aback by the way she had met his gentle mockery of her storytelling, but he answered. 'I said I had a few things to collect, because I had been lying in an abandoned hut in the settlement, and had left in a hurry. They told me they would be congregating near that large mosque with the tower beside it, by late afternoon. The plan is to camp there for the night, and leave at first light tomorrow.' He paused and drew in a deep breath. 'Tell me your story as you will. Tell me about the Hazrat, about the Sultan, whoever. Just'—his voice faltered and his eyes looked, for a moment, as if he were about to weep. 'Just tell me a story.'

'Come here, then, and sit beside me.' She patted the floor next to her.

'They say that when Sultan Ghiyasuddin Tughlaq was on his way back to Dilli from that campaign—it was in the east, far away from home—he vowed that he would put Hazrat Nizamuddin Auliya in his place when he returned. Someone brought news of that to the saint. And the Hazrat Sahib is supposed to have said just one sentence: "*Hanoz Dilli dur ast*".'

'Dilli is yet far?'

Shagufta nodded. 'The Sultan would have to be back in Dilli to carry out whatever he had in mind.'

'Which was?'

'Who knows? Perhaps the saint knew, perhaps his spirituality allowed him some form of prescience. I don't know. At any rate Ghiyasuddin Tughlaq never made it back to Dilli. That day when the pavilion collapsed, he was crushed under it, and his son Jauna Khan came to power, with the title of Muhammad bin Tughlaq.

'Muhammad bin Tughlaq was an odd man,' she said, shaking her head. 'Constantly wanting to do things. Of course, like nearly all emperors, even the most debauched of them, one of the first things he did was to build a castle for himself, and a fortified city.'

'What happened to the fort Ghiyasuddin had built? The one which caused that furore?'

'Do you not remember?' A rare, impish smile appeared on her lips. 'The Hazrat had prophesied that Tughlaqabad would either remain deserted, or it would be inhabited by the nomads. That was what happened. For a brief while, Ghiyasuddin Tughlaq did live there—he even built his own tomb opposite, while he was alive—but eventually, all that mad haste came to nothing. When Muhammad bin Tughlaq ascended the throne, he made his own city, which he called Jahanpanah.'

She had noticed the impatience beginning to loom again in Nasiruddin's eyes. 'In the same year that Ghiyasuddin Tughlaq died, so, ironically, did Hazrat Sahib. Amir Khusro Sahib was heartbroken; they say he mourned his old friend so deeply that his grief eventually killed him too. He died a few months after Hazrat Sahib.

'But four years had passed since Girdhar had left his own family and come to take refuge with Hazrat Sahib. Or with Khusro Sahib, call it what you will—I personally think Khusro Sahib was more responsible for Girdhar's defection than was Hazrat Sahib. And Khusro Sahib, in those four years, helped Girdhar rise to a level he had never imagined.'

'I thought he had meant to convert to Islam,' Nasiruddin remarked. 'Did he not?'

'He did. Not immediately. Even if you have little affinity left for the religion you were brought up with, it is difficult to change the habits of a lifetime, is it not? How can you believe in millions of gods one moment, and one supreme deity the next?

'A year and three months, that was what I was told,' she said. 'A year to decide, once and for all, that he could not possibly go back to his old life. A further three months to decide what he wanted to do with the rest of his life, and to break the news to his family. His father refused to even see him, but he told his mother and his sisters. And then he went back. After he was converted, he chose his own name: Musa.' She chuckled. 'So appropriate.'

Nasiruddin looked puzzled, so she explained. 'You do not know what Girdhar means. It is another name for the Hindu god Krishna. It literally means "he who bears a mountain". There is a myth about a mountain named Govardhan, which Krishna persuaded the people of his land to worship, because he said that the mountain sheltered them from storms and fierce winds, and its forests gave them life. Till then, the people had been worshipping another deity, the god Indra. So when they turned away from Indra and began praying to Govardhan instead, Indra was jealous, and furious. He showered lightning and thunder and torrential rain down on the people, and to shelter them, Krishna lifted Govardhan on the tip of one finger.'

'The mountain.' Nasiruddin smiled. 'And Musa went up the mountain to receive the Ten Commandments from his god.'

She smiled back at him. 'I don't think Girdhar—no, I should call him Musa, now—ever went to the mountains; he was a Dilli man, Dilli was in his very blood. Khusro Sahib took him under his wing, and in the few years before Khusro Sahib died, even before Girdhar became Musa, he was able to introduce his protégé to some important courtiers. Not as a courtier, not even as a prospective courtier, for Musa had no such inclination or ambition. But as a craftsman who knew his craft.'

She looked at the tiny fire, staring into its white-gold heart. She did not reach out her hands to it, even though they were cold. It was better to warm her hands against her own body, because when the fire was gone—as it would be, soon—she would be left without it, anyway. On her own, again.

Shagufta looked away from the fire, blinking as she did so. 'The wretched fire,' she mumbled, even though Nasiruddin had not commented. 'Even when there is no visible smoke, it irritates the eyes.'

'All fires are like that,' he said, gently. 'For all the warmth they provide, they are dangerous. They can kill and maim. Better, perhaps, to stay away from them.'

'Or maintain a judicious distance. Yes.' She pulled her shawl closer about her, shivering as she did so.

'Two years after Khusro Sahib died, Musa had found

himself a powerful patron, one of the elite courtiers in the court of Muhammad bin Tughlaq. The Tughlaqs were all keen builders, you know; between them they built numerous palaces, mosques, tombs, and the forts, of course. And Muhammad bin Tughlaq's successor, Firuz Shah Tughlaq, was not just a builder, but a restorer, too—' she broke off, shaking her head in resignation. 'I beg your pardon. I am meandering again, and you do not have the time to spare for meanderings. Very well.' She cleared her throat, and in a sudden change of subject, said, 'You have not been south of Dilli, I suppose?'

He shook his head, astonished.

'And I do not suppose you ever will, either, if you are going back.' She said it without bitterness, having reconciled herself to his inevitable departure. 'There is a town many kos away, in the peninsula called Daulatabad. The Hindus used to call it Devgiri. Two years after Muhammad bin Tughlaq became Sultan, he decided to shift the capital to Daulatabad.' She saw the bewilderment in his face, and could not help chuckling. 'I told you, he was an odd man, impulsive and moved too much by his whims and fancies. He had mad ideas. One day he took it into his head to introduce token coins: brass and copper in place of silver. It wreaked havoc with the economy; every other person, they said, became a counterfeiter.

'But,' she continued, 'Daulatabad. That was another mad adventure, and many people were very sore about it.'

'How did he manage it? It is not easy to uproot an entire city and shift it to another part of the land.'

'He didn't take everybody, even though some of his detractors would have one believe otherwise. It was only the court, really, and those who served it directly. The courtiers, their households, the people whose very livelihood depended upon someone who was at court.'

'Ah.' A knowing smile had come to Nasiruddin's lips. 'Musa. So will you tell me now the story of how Musa went to this new city—Daulatabad, did you call it?'

'No, I will not tell you of Musa's trip to Daulatabad or of his sojourn there. It was not for long, not even as long as Muhammad bin Tughlaq was Sultan. A mere eight years, no more. By then, rebellion was brewing in other parts of the land, and the Sultan realized that he would be better off in Dilli.'

Shagufta huddled deeper into her shawl. 'Musa had never really considered staying behind in Dilli. He had nothing left in this city. His father had disowned him and the rest of his family was too scared to go against Badrinath's wishes. And there was his patron, intent on keeping up appearances once they were in Daulatabad, ready to commission one building after another,'—she shook her head. 'It made sense for him to go to Daulatabad, and it proved to be a good move for him. He had considerable skill and undoubted talent; but the stint in Daulatabad also brought him fame. He grew in stature and became the carver most in demand among the nobility. He gained respect.'

'Like that boy in your first story. The farmer's son who fled to Dilli and became a stone carver.'

'Madhav. Yes. Madhav travelled a long way.' Her eyebrows drew together in a thoughtful frown. 'I had never really thought of it, but there is that similarity in their stories. Both literally travelled a long way, and metaphorically too. Madhav from the village in the countryside to the capital city and a completely different occupation. Musa from Dilli to Daulatabad, and back. And from Girdhar to Musa.'

A moment's silence, and then she said, 'I digress. Let me get this over and done with, so that I can move on to the story I have to tell.' As if anticipating what he was going to say, she shook her head. 'No, I cannot leave this out. Because it has a bearing on what I am going to narrate. You should know how it is connected to what has gone before, shouldn't you? Well, Musa came back to Dilli ten years after Khusro Sahib, Hazrat Nizamuddin Auliya Sahib and Sultan Ghiyasuddin Tughlaq had died. He was thirty-two years old by then, and not yet married.'

22

Fourteen Years Later

AH 736 (1335 CE)

He had been away ten years. Ten years had not made much of a difference to the city he had left behind, but they had changed him. Dilli was much the same; Musa was not. When he had followed his patron and the court to Daulatabad, he had been a young man, unsure both of his new religion and of his ability to make a living. The man who returned to the city of his birth bore little resemblance to that one. Musa was not the thin, frightened Girdhar who had once cowered before his father. He was a strong, capable man in his prime, confident, wealthy in his own way, and much sought after.

But he did not know where he fitted in. In Ghiyaspur, where he knew people and where evenings could pass happily in remembering those days when Hazrat Nizamuddin Auliya and Khusro Sahib had been the life of the settlement, its focus and the twin lamps that illuminated it? Or in Yoginipur, where few would recognize him, but which was where his family—even if it had thrown him off—still lived?

Though he did not say so openly, he had missed his mother and his sisters, their children. Even, he realized, his father. You do not throw off the ties of a lifetime so easily, Khusro Sahib had once told him. Your blood will always be theirs as well.

And deep down he knew too, that the religion he had been brought up in would never completely desert him.

Nizamuddin and Amir Khusro, with their warmth and gentleness, had shown him that piety could be very different from the strictures and orthodoxy of Badrinath's idea of religion. Inspired by them, Girdhar had forsaken the gods he had grown up with and adopted the one God of Islam. But sometimes, faced with the stranger tenets of his new faith, he found himself wondering if he had, indeed, done the right thing by converting.

Every time such doubts assailed him, he would go to the dargah of Nizamuddin Sahib. Or if he happened to be in Yoginipur, to that of Qutb Sahib. The easy quiet, the acceptance of all who came restored his faith and reminded him why he had chosen to convert in the first place.

But it was unsettling, he thought, that he should thus need to bolster his faith every now and then. Did this happen to others, too? Hindus and Muslims, equally? Did everybody find themselves torn, teetering between faith and its lack? Once, he might have put the question to Khusro Sahib; now, there was no one whom he could turn to, no one who was both sympathetic friend and wise counsellor.

He went to what had been once his home, and was painfully aware of the stares as he walked through the lanes of Yoginipur. His complexion and features were proof that he was of this land. His attire contradicted that. The fitted pyjamas, the long tunic, the turban tied in its own distinctive style. His close-trimmed beard and moustache. A Muslim, said those eyes, even when they did not accuse. Not one of us.

His father was dead these seven years, said his mother. Kalyani's hair had gone a stark, unrelieved white and her face had hardened into a shell that betrayed little emotion. She did not smile or weep when she recognized her only son. She did not push him away from her doorstep, nor was she effusive in her invitation for him to come inside. When she spoke, her voice was flat and toneless.

She lived alone now; Girdhar's younger sister had been married off, just a year after Badrinath died. She now lived far away in some village beyond the river, and came only once a year to visit, to check that her mother still lived. Yamini, however, was the same. Older now, but otherwise unchanged.

Musa glanced surreptitiously around the inside of the

hut. It looked much the same as it had done the last time he had been there, a lifetime ago.

'Do you need money?' he asked as he got up to leave after half an hour of sitting with his mother.

For the first time he saw a flicker of emotion in her eyes. He was not sure what it was, whether anger or despair, or confusion. Or all of those. He thought he saw tears, but she looked away. 'No,' he heard her say in a muffled voice. 'No, he would not have liked it.'

'Ma,' he said, his voice gentle. 'Baba may have cast me aside, but you gave birth to me. For me, you will always be my mother. How can I see my own mother in need of money and stand by without lifting a finger to help?'

Silence greeted that question. When he repeated it, she said in a voice barely above a whisper, 'Does it give you peace? This religion of yours? Does it make you a happier person than you were?'

He blinked, surprised at the sudden change in topic. 'I suppose,' he said, after a little consideration, 'it does. Yes, it does.' When he saw the stricken look in her eyes, he added, 'I was thinking of that not too long back. Baba'—he swallowed; this was awkward—'Baba was very harsh in the name of religion. What he did and what he said reduced his religion to nothing more than a set of vicious and inhuman rules. It made me fear religion, not love it.'

'And? Does this religion of yours make you love it?'

Did it? Even he did not know. He remained silent.

'I think the gods don't make religion,' his mother said in a flat, dull voice. 'It is people who make religion. A good person who is religious can attract you to his religion. And the other way round.' She sighed. 'Your Baba was not an evil man, Girdhar. He was flawed, like all of us are. I do not forgive him for some of the things he did, but there was a lot I was grateful for as well.'

'What about me?' he asked. 'Am I not your son any more? Baba repudiated me; what about you, Ma? Do I not have a claim on you any longer?'

But she merely shook her head and when he would not go, she turned and went away instead, drawing the flimsy door of the hut shut behind her.

Yamini was less inhibited, less obstinate about retaining the walls that Badrinath had insisted on erecting years ago. 'Look at you!' she breathed, her fingers caressing the fine cloth of his sleeve. 'So fine. And such a big man.'

Musa laughed, embarrassed. 'What did you expect me to be? An adolescent still?'

She grinned. 'No, but—ah, it is good to see you. I thought you were dead, Girdhar.'

He did not correct her, as he had not corrected his mother. For them, perhaps he would always be Girdhar, not Musa. And anyway, they were neither of them really wrong. He was Musa, but he would always remain Girdhar, too.

He asked after her husband and her children. Some names were strange to him; they too, he realized, had moved on in life. Boys had grown into men, the baby he had last seen in her arms was now on the verge of beginning work as an apprentice to a potter.

Musa was wise enough to have noticed the curious glances of neighbours as he approached his sister's hut. A Muslim man, an obviously prosperous one, and coming to meet Yamini when she was alone at home. Speculation would run rife. He could wager that none of them, not even those who had once upon a time frequented Badrinath's home and spoken to Girdhar, would recognize him. So he was careful to remain standing outside her home, in the lane where all may see him maintaining a discreet distance from her. They would undoubtedly come flocking to her as soon as he was gone, wanting to know how she happened to know a Muslim man, but at least he had done what he could to lower the chances of salacious gossip, of people wondering about their relationship.

Yamini knew, too. Even if people were not as vehemently fanatical as Badrinath had been, they would not look kindly upon a Muslim entering a Hindu household. Even if the household happened to be that of his own sister. No, they would say, she was not even his sister any more. By becoming a Muslim he had lost his caste, his family, everything that had tied him to his life as Girdhar.

As he was leaving, Yamini asked, 'Where are you staying? Where is your house?'

'Right now at a travellers' inn. I suppose I shall find a house for myself soon enough.'

'Let me know when you do. Perhaps I shall come visiting.' Her smile was soft, gentle.

'Will your husband not mind?'

'Perhaps he will.' She shrugged. 'But my love for my brother is as deep as my love for him and for my children. He knows that.' Her nose wrinkled up as she made a face. 'I am not Ma.'

'I noticed.' He could not stem the dejection that crept into his expression and his voice. 'Baba commands her even though he is dead.'

Yamini reached up to put her hand on his shoulder. 'It has been many years, you know. Give her time; I think she will let her heart finally decide her course.'

A silence had fallen. Somewhere very far away, someone began singing. He could not hear the words, but he recognized the tune: it was an old song, a lover's song, of heartache and yearning.

'It will never be the same, though.'

She nodded. 'No, it will not.' Her expression was open, honest. 'It cannot be.'

Not with Yamini either, he thought as he wandered back through the streets towards the inn where he had rented a room. The sweetness, the honesty and the warmth had been there, but tempered by a distance that even she had probably not been aware of. As if she held herself back. As if, even though she called him Girdhar, she knew that Musa was not Girdhar, that he could not go back to being Girdhar.

But when he did find himself a house two weeks later, he went to let Yamini know. Again he stood at the doorway, letting the neighbourhood see the distance he maintained. 'If your husband will let you, come sometime,' he said, trying to keep the pleading out of his voice. 'And bring the children.'

Yamini promised, but with a caveat. The festivals would begin soon: Dussehra would come in ten days' time, and after that there would be a string of other festivals, major and minor, culminating in the joyous celebration of Diwali. 'You know how it is,' she said. 'I will not have a moment's respite. There is the house to be cleaned and decorated, new clothes to be made, all that cooking to be done—'

'I know. Come when you are free, when you want to meet me. Not because you feel obliged to come.'

But before she came, there arrived at his threshold a man whom he had not seen before, but who said he was Yamini's neighbour. He did not use Yamini's name, of course, since that would be disrespectful, but he talked of his friendship with Yamini's husband, Hariprasad.

The visitor's sun-darkened skin was thin and dry. His limbs were frail, his back bowed and his shoulders stooped. He walked with the aid of a long, stout bamboo, and when he spoke, his voice rasped. Musa wondered what was wrong with the man, for there was something certainly wrong with him. Perhaps consumption, or some other disease that was eating away at him.

'I saw you the other day outside Hariprasad's house,' the man said. 'When I asked his wife, she told me that you were her brother. She told me what had happened.' He left the statement ambiguous. Musa wondered what explanation Yamini had given him.

'I knew her father and brother had been stone carvers

and'—his gaze wandered appreciatively across the room, taking in the simple but not poor furnishings, the clean plaster and the solidity of the wooden chest that stood under one window—'it seems you have done well.' His look turned thoughtful. 'Unless you have given up that skill? Are you still a stone worker?'

Musa, mystified, assured the man that he was.

'I have something to show you,' the man said, with a small sigh of relief. 'I would have brought it, but I had no one to help me.' He explained. 'It is a piece of carved stone, an old piece. My ancestors too were stone carvers. I suppose one of them made it. I think it is beautiful, but I wanted someone who knows, someone with expertise in matters such as this to see it. Hariprasad's wife assures me that you are such a man.'

'My sister is kind.'

'She is also truthful, or so Hariprasad says. Will you come to my home and see it? I would be grateful.'

ᨒ

His name was Durgadas. Servant of Durga, the mother goddess. A goddess Musa remembered from his childhood as being the embodiment of all that was powerful. She was Shakti. Might, omnipotence, a power that could not be resisted. He did not believe in any of that any more, but that long-ago belief had once made him believe that some of her power would rub off on those who followed her. Even more on those whose names evoked the goddess.

Durgadas was a paradox. A man thus named, but with not a hint of sturdiness in that fragile frame of his. Or so it seemed from the bowed shoulders and the limbs that looked as delicate as a bird's. But look into his eyes, and if you were perceptive enough you might see the strength in his eyes.

And there was strength in the man, a strength of character and of will.

'My son will be here later,' Durgadas explained as

he stepped over the threshold of the dingy little hut and gestured to Musa to follow him. Musa paused, booted foot on the strip of wood, so old that it had been worn down to a concave that sagged bowl-like in the centre. 'Come in, come in,' Durgadas said, realizing why his guest had halted. 'I do not care whether you are Muslim or not.'

Musa raised an eyebrow at that, but stepped in. Durgadas limped over to a sagging rope-bed, a charpai that stood against one wall of the room. The space beneath the charpai had been turned into a storehouse, crowded with bundles, old clothes, odds and ends. Here, in his own house, even though the limp was no less pronounced, Durgadas moved with greater confidence, lighting a lamp, pulling out a stool for his guest, and one for himself.

Having seated himself, he reached under the bed and began pushing aside things to get at something at the back. He spoke as he worked, his voice muffled as he explained why Musa's religion made no difference. 'I have little use for religion, you see. It's not as if my religion can put food in my belly or look after my family when I am gone. All it can do is offer some solace in bad times. Her prayers kept my wife going every time she lost a child, every time the tax collectors came. When a cart ran over my leg. She kept saying it was the will of the gods.' He made a face. 'As if that helps.'

He seemed to have found what he had been looking for under the bed: a large flat rectangular shape, wrapped in sacking. He tugged at it, and Musa could see that it was something heavy. Not terribly bulky, but heavy. Musa offered to help, but Durgadas shook his head. 'No, I can manage.'

But he was panting by the time he had drawn it out fully, and perspiration dotted his forehead when he looked up. 'I have not shown this to any stranger, do you understand? Only my son and I know of it.'

Musa nodded. 'I will not tell anyone.'

Durgadas's hands were fumbling with the strings that

held the sacking closed. He undid one knot here and another there, before pulling aside the sacking and using a rag to wipe whatever had lain concealed within. Durgadas put the rag aside and held up the lamp, high enough for its flame to illuminate what could be only dimly seen through the daylight filtering in between the gaps and chinks of walls and doors.

Musa drew in his breath sharply.

It was a frieze. A scene depicting a woodland or an especially verdant garden, he could not tell which. Squirrels peeped out from amidst leaves, a parrot thrust its head out of a hole in a tree trunk here, a pair of mynahs sat on a bough there. Clouds swirled, glimpsed briefly through a gap in the canopy of leaves. And what leaves, too! The slim, serrated leaves of the neem, the large glossy ones of the banyan. Mango and peepal and the curling tendrils of a vine that crept up the gnarled bole of a fig tree. Flowers, each petal perfect, even when the complete flower was no more than the size of a fingernail.

He drank it in, unable to believe what he was seeing.

'I have never seen anything so exquisite,' he said finally. 'Not in the best of palaces, nowhere. The Sultan himself does not possess anything approaching this.'

'It was made for a Sultan,' Durgadas said. From inside a fold of the sacking he withdrew a folded square of leather, old and cracking at the edges. 'This was written by a professional scribe, I think,' he added, opening the leather and taking out a piece of yellowed paper, the ink on it faded. 'The script is too fine to have been the work of any of my ancestors. We are not men of the pen, but men of tools.' He glanced at Musa. 'Do you want me to read it out?'

'I can read it myself,' Musa said with dignity, ignoring the implication that he was illiterate. It was only later that it crossed his mind that Durgadas might have thought that Musa's years of being a Muslim had made him forget the script of his childhood and youth.

It was a relatively long missive—yes, missive indeed,

though it was addressed to no one in particular and bore no date. But there was a name at the bottom, and there was a story, heart-warming and yet heartbreaking. About a stone carver who had poured his heart and his soul, all his energies and skill and creativity into making this frieze during the last months of his life. It had been made for Her Majesty, Razia Sultan. She had not commissioned it, she had not even known of it. And she had gone to an early grave unaware of its existence.

'I am too confused and too deep in sorrow to know what to do,' said that long-ago stone carver in the writing of the scribe. 'My mind has deserted me, but my hands will work on and complete this, if for no other reason than that my conscience would not allow me to leave it unfinished. You who read this, perhaps you will understand better. Whether to put it on Her Majesty Razia Sultan's grave. Whether to bury it beside her deep in the ground, where only she may know of its existence. Whether to sell it off or take a hammer and destroy it. It was the pinnacle of my work. I leave it to you, whoever you may be, to do with as you wish.'

'Razia Sultan,' said Musa. 'That would have been—what? A hundred years ago?'

Durgadas shrugged. 'Perhaps. I do not know for sure; I am an unlettered man.'

'And this stone carver, this Madhav, whose name is written at the bottom, was one of your ancestors?'

Durgadas nodded. 'Yes. On my father's side of the family, we have been carvers ever since Madhav arrived in Dilli.' He accepted the folded paper back from Musa and replaced it in its leather covering. 'I, too, would have been a carver, had my father lived. He died when I was barely two months old, so I inherited my profession from my mother's side of the family. I am a potter.'

'Madhav was obviously a man of great skill and talent,' Musa remarked. 'And if he presumed to create something like this for Razia Sultan herself, he was probably a fairly important man too. Not a nobody.'

Durgadas nodded. 'Many years ago, my grandmother had told me that Madhav had once been the most respected stone carver in Dilli. Under Altamash, and under Razia Sultan too. There are many mosques, many tombs and pavilions and gateways, which Madhav had a hand in not just carving, but in supervising, too.' He looked again at the frieze, his fingers wandering over its edge almost reverently.

'Why did you show me this?' Musa asked when Durgadas had rewrapped the frieze in the sacking.

The other man did not answer immediately. It was only after he had rewrapped it and pushed it under the charpai that he asked, 'Do you want it?'

'Want it? What do you mean?'

'Just what I say. Do you want it? You have seen it; and given that you are a skilled stone carver, you can probably assess its worth.'

Musa stared at where the flat package lay under the charpai, half hidden by the debris of a lifetime—perhaps several lifetimes—that Durgadas was piling back onto it. 'It is beautiful,' he conceded. 'But what would I do with it?'

'I do not know.' Durgadas sighed. 'It seems such a shame that something like that should remain hidden, unknown, unappreciated.' He looked up, his eyes sad. 'Only I and my son have seen it in all these years. And poor people like us, what do we know but to say it is beautiful? You are the only man who can appreciate it truly. You can put a value to it.'

There it was, the real reason behind this visit. Musa nodded his understanding. 'That I can. But who would buy this? A nobleman? If you wish, I can ask around among courtiers who I think would appreciate this and might want to buy it—'

'No,' said Durgadas. 'No, I do not want to sell it, please.'

Musa stared, astonished. 'Then what? What is the point of that if it is not to be sold?'

Durgadas shook his head slowly. 'I do not know if you will understand. I am a poor man. All I have of any worth is this. You may not have known outright poverty, but you understand what it means to know exactly how much down to the last jital you own. To value it, to mourn over every break, ever scratch, every rip.' His gaze wandered to the charpai, as if he could see beneath it, to the package that lay there. 'That is my treasure. Not just because it is valuable, but because it is also a matter of pride that one of my ancestors could have made something so beautiful. I cannot sell it. Perhaps my son will not have such qualms.'

'What do you want of me?'

'Keep it for me.'

It was simply said, but it was not so simply done. That was not all, for Durgadas did not merely wish Musa to be safekeeper for him. He wanted, in exchange, a promise.

'Just that you will return it when I or my heirs ask for it back. And till that happens, you will keep it safe. Away from public eyes. A secret.'

'And what happens if I should die tomorrow? I am not even married yet, let alone a father. I have no heirs. Who will honour my promise then?'

'You will marry,' Durgadas said with certainty. 'You are skilled, and well-respected, you have wealth. There will be many who would be eager to form an alliance with you, now that you are back in this city.' He paused. 'If you decide not to marry, nominate another to take your place after you. I ask only that he be trustworthy, and a skilled stone carver, a man who can truly prize it.' He looked around at the wattle-and-daub walls of his hut, the cracks in the dried mud, the splinters of exposed reed and the worn, sagging wood of the doorframe. 'A man with a proper house, not this ramshackle excuse for one. I cannot sleep at nights for fear that some thief will break in and steal the only thing of worth that I possess.'

Musa did not have the heart to point out that it would be a foolish thief who would break into a house as poor as this.

'Take it, Musa Sahib,' Durgadas said. 'Please, do me this favour. Take it and keep it for me and my family. Someday we may ask for it back; till then, guard it, if you will.'

23

Thirty-three Years Later

AH 761 (1368 CE)

Everyone said Dilshad Khan was a lucky man. Lucky to have been born to a father who had earned the respect of the court and of the Sultan himself, even though he was neither a soldier nor a scholar but a man who had used his hands to make his wealth and a name for himself. Dilshad Khan, they also said, was lucky that his father had married a woman from one of the most esteemed families in Dilli. Not wealthy any more—and that, said those in the know, was almost certainly the reason they had been willing to accept as son-in-law a man who had not even been born a Muslim, but had converted. A convert, but one who possessed both substantial wealth and the ability to continue to go on adding to his coffers.

Yes, Dilshad Khan had been born with a silver spoon in his mouth, and it was hardly a surprise to anybody that by the time he was ten years old, he had not just the finest horse of any scion of the aristocracy, but was also being asked after with deferential affection by men with little daughters still in their cradles. When he turned twenty, he was married to one of these, a genteel girl who brought with her both wealth and breeding, making Dilshad Khan even more envied.

On this day, with winter just beginning to set in over Dilli, Dilshad had further reason to be proud. He was the father of a son, pink-cheeked and plump. It had been a week since the child had been born and today was the day of his circumcision. The house, large and grand, had been especially cleaned, decorated with flowers and fine porcelain and a splendid carpet in the main courtyard. The women—Dilshad's mother and wife and their many female relatives, friends and neighbours—were like a flock of excited mynahs.

Rushing here, rushing there, laughing, gossiping, taking full advantage of the occasion to enjoy themselves.

In the more public part of the house, well away from the secluded quarters of the zenana, the men talked of politics, of the intrigues at court, of the Sultan Firuz Shah Tughlaq's enthusiasm for building. Citadels, a madarsa, his own tomb. Someone laughed and said, 'Musa Sahib, had you still been a stone carver, you would have had enough work to last you several lifetimes.'

Musa, grey-haired but still unbent, smiled complacently. 'I will always be a stone carver,' he said. 'Dilshad does not like to think of me as one, but that is the truth.'

Some men smiled knowingly, and one murmured something in a quiet, conciliatory tone, reassuring their host. But the fact was that most of them were aware that Dilshad was embarrassed that his father had been a stone carver, and that Musa did not think it anything to be ashamed about. He had not taken on any commissions for the past several years, but it was no secret that Musa still carved. The rooms of his house had the most exquisitely carved niches in all of Dilli. The pillars in the courtyards were masterpieces, and it was impossible to ignore the beauty of the gateposts, carved with a pattern of flowers and geometric designs. Yes, Musa's love for the stone that had been his companion since his birth would be a part of him till his death.

The conversation moved to other topics, to a young man who was getting married, another who had been sent as emissary to the eastern provinces. The gathering consisted largely of men who had known each other most of their lives—or at least, in the case of Musa himself, for the better part of the past thirty years. They knew each other well, they fitted together well. Their conversations flowed with the ease and comfort of long acquaintance.

In the midst of it all, a servant came to Musa, bending to murmur a message from the gatekeeper. A bullock cart had drawn up outside the house and in it was a man—he looked to be very ill—who was asking for Musa Sahib. 'He said to say his name was Durgadas, and that you had last met him when you had just returned to Dilli.'

'Durgadas?' Musa, initially puzzled, quickly placed the man, and was disturbed by the news. 'You say he is ill?'

The servant nodded. 'It looks like it. There is,' he offered, 'a baby lying in the cart beside him.'

'A baby?' Musa stared. 'Why would he bring a baby—?' Without finishing the sentence, he got to his feet, slowly and with the support of the servant's arm. Dilshad, hearing his father's apology to his guests as he excused himself, hurried to Musa's side, wanting to know what had happened. Some of the guests, who thought more highly of themselves than the others, were looking affronted at their host's sudden departure.

'Stay with our guests; it is unseemly for neither of us to be there,' Musa said when Dilshad reached his side. 'Offer my apologies again, and say I will be back as soon as I possibly can.'

'But what is it?'

'A man has come, a man I briefly knew. And yes, send someone for the physician. Quickly.'

The gatekeeper was standing in the lane, peering into the back of the cart with his torch held high. Beside him was a stranger, a stocky young man with a thin stick tucked under his arm. 'Did you drive him here?' Musa asked briskly, and the man nodded. 'He said I would be paid here.' There was a question in his tone, an implication that he would like to be given his due and allowed to leave.

'Soon.' Musa turned to the servant who had accompanied him outside. 'Go in and fetch others. Bring a charpai or something so that we can put Durgadas on it and take him inside.' A muffled wail from inside the cart made him pause. 'And fetch one of the maids. A woman with experience of looking after children.' He turned away and indicated to the cart driver to stand aside.

'You wasted your money getting that physician,' Durgadas breathed. 'I told you it was no use.' His thin chest heaved, each breath an effort. The skin stretched, shiny and scaly, across cheekbones, eye sockets and a jaw prominent enough to make his face look more a dead man's than that of a living one. Only his hand, clutching Musa's beside him on the charpai, seemed to have some strength left in it.

Musa shook his head. 'Let us say it was for my own satisfaction, then. I do not turn away a man who comes to my doorstep, not even to hand him over to Death.' He paused, aware that Durgadas's life hung by a thread. 'Who is the baby? Why have you brought it here?'

'She, not it.' A faint smile brought out laugh lines on either side of his mouth, making him look more alive. 'My granddaughter. I brought her because there was nowhere else I could take her. My son died of smallpox six months ago, and my daughter-in-law died giving birth to this little one.' He swallowed. 'I have tried to look after her these past few months. What will become of her now?'

A servant entered, carrying a jug with a small handleless earthen cup. He placed it in the niche next to the charpai, and beside it put a small drawstring bag made of rough cotton. He poured out a cupful of liquid from the jug—lukewarm, its smell faintly floral. Opium, thought Musa, as the servant handed the cup to him. The physician, while taking his leave, had murmured that there was little he could do except perhaps lessen the pain.

Durgadas shook his head when Musa offered him the cup. 'Let me finish what I have to say. Then I will be able to rest easy.'

'Why subject yourself to unnecessary pain?'

'No. This will blur my mind if I drink it now. Later, Musa Sahib, when I am done.'

Musa put the cup on the stool beside the charpai. 'Very well. Tell me, then, and quickly.'

'I have no one left in this world,' Durgadas said. 'No one

except my granddaughter. There is nobody to look after her.' A cough, dry and hacking, wracked his frame.

Musa waited for it to die down before asking, 'Is there nobody from your daughter-in-law's family to care for the child?'

Durgadas shook his head. 'You have been one of us too, even if you are now rich. You will understand. My daughter-in-law has a brother and a sister, but they are so poor, they can barely look after their own children. To hand her to them would be to kill her.'

Musa held the tired hand in his own and felt the pulse fluttering erratically against his fingers. This man could be dead between one flutter of that pulse and the next. 'I will take her in,' he said, 'but you do realize the implications, do you not? This is a Muslim household. I was once a Hindu, but—'

Durgadas did not allow him to finish. 'That does not matter. Her life is more important than her faith. Bring her up to know the difference between good and evil. That is the same in both religions, is it not?'

Somewhere in another part of the house, laughter rang out. In the men's quarters, where the party was in full flow, musicians had begun tuning up. Musa could hear the tinkling of a dancer's ankle bells as she hurried down a corridor.

Dilshad was taking good care of their guests. Dilshad, he thought, suddenly remembering that his son was a different man than him. He had grown up Muslim, and—perhaps because he was painfully aware that his father was a convert—Dilshad did all he could to make amends for what he saw as a shortcoming. He did all he could to prove that he was a good Muslim, and more than a good Muslim.

He would not look kindly on Durgadas's granddaughter being brought up in this house. But that, decided Musa, was a bridge he would cross when he reached it.

'I will bring her up as best as I can,' he said. 'I promise. While I am alive, she will not want a grandfather. I cannot promise other relations, but a grandfather, no.'

The hand holding Musa's loosened, as if in relief. 'I knew I could trust you,' Durgadas breathed.

They stayed there in that small, sparsely decorated room, with the sounds of dancing and singing now coming to their ears.

'I pulled you away from your celebration,' Durgadas murmured. 'What is the occasion?'

Musa shook his head, brushing off the implication that this man's arrival had been a disturbance. 'My grandson's circumcision. His father is the one who must be there; no one will take it amiss if I am away for a while.' He smiled fleetingly. 'It is too noisy for my liking. You give me a good excuse to get away from it.'

When Durgadas merely gave a tired smile and said nothing, Musa said, 'That frieze is with me, still safe. I will give it to your granddaughter when she is old enough to understand.' He saw the tired nod, the faint smile of gratitude. 'I still do not understand why you chose to entrust it to me, though,' he added, 'there is no lack of skilled stone carvers in Dilli, men who would have been as suitable, perhaps more, than me.'

Durgadas was quiet for so long that Musa thought he was too exhausted to answer, too close to death, perhaps, for the question to have registered. Then, in a whisper so low that Musa had to lean forward to hear the man's words, Durgadas spoke. 'Do you remember,' he asked, 'the few times we met, years ago? After I had first met you to offer you the frieze? The long conversations we had?'

Musa nodded. Durgadas and he had indeed met several times after that first meeting. Mostly, it had been Musa going to visit the other man in his hut; Durgadas had baulked at the thought of visiting Musa's much larger, grander home, where he had been certain he would feel out of place. Sometimes they would sit under a tree and talk, at other times they would walk on the bank of the Hauz-e-Shamsi. Musa had told Durgadas his own story, and that of his forebears: of Jayshree and her fierce but ill-fated loyalty towards Razia Sultan, and of her mother Gayatri, and how Gayatri's parents had brought her to Yoginipur years ago from Agroha. In turn, Durgadas had spoken of his own ancestors, beginning with the child who had fled a destroyed countryside, and who had come to Yoginipur along with an ageing and half-blind stone carver from whom he had learnt the craft that had continued in his family for several generations now.

'Perhaps, if things had been different, I might have been a stone carver too,' Durgadas said. 'Like Mahesh, and like his father Madhav, who carved that frieze.' His tongue wandered out to moisten dry lips and Musa offered him water. He refused. 'Let me finish. Your sister said your great-grandmother died in the service of Razia. Where better to place the frieze in safekeeping than with you? My ancestor carved it for the woman your great-grandmother died for. It was appropriate.'

His voice was thin as a wisp of smoke now. The words had been said haltingly, with many pauses to draw breath. He was going, slipping away before Musa's eyes.

'Give her the frieze,' Durgadas whispered. 'And tell her what I told you.'

'Of course I will. I will give her the letter, the one that Madhav left along with the frieze.'

The dimming eyes twinkled for a brief moment. 'For her to be able to read that letter, you will have to teach her to read the script.'

'I have not forgotten it. Even if I do by the time she is old enough to begin learning'—a thought struck him—'or if I am dead, I will instruct my son. She will be brought up the way you would have wanted, and I will tell her everything about her ancestors, all that you have told me.'

They called her Chhoti. Little one, an ambiguous enough name that assigned no fixed religion to the bearer of it.

Musa's wife and daughter-in-law, who obediently followed her mother-in-law's views on everything connected with the household, disapproved. Musa's daughter-in-law silently; Musa's wife vociferously. The child of a heathen, dumped so unceremoniously on them? What good would come of that?

'I was a heathen for nearly twenty years of my life,' Musa pointed out to his wife. 'Do you mean to say that no good came of your marriage to me?'

That made her even more furious, but Musa eventually had his way. Every argument she posed, he countered. The child would be a burden on them, she said, and he replied that weighing about a tenth of a sack of wheat, she could hardly be called that. And if Begum Sahiba spoke heatedly of the expenses that would be incurred, the clothes and toys, the wet nurse, and countless other, ever-increasing costs that go into raising a child: well, Dilshad's little son was already being brought up. And he was the same age as Chhoti. They would grow up together. They could share a nurse, or not. If clothes were stitched for the baby boy, they could as well be stitched for the baby girl. 'I will pay for all of it,' Musa said, with finality. 'You need have nothing to do with any of it.'

A maid named Meera was entrusted the job of looking after the baby, and she continued to be nanny and foster mother to the toddler, and then to the girl as she grew older. Musa's wife and daughter-in-law, and the drifting female population of the household—sisters and cousins, nieces and aunts who came visiting and stayed on, sometimes for months, sometimes for years—showed Chhoti no affection. They did not push her out of the zenana for fear of Musa, but they were quick to admonish her for the smallest of infractions, and to criticize, berate, and discriminate against her.

But there was one person from whom Chhoti received nothing but love, and that was the benevolent old patriarch whom Chhoti regarded as her grandfather.

'You must remember that I am not your grandfather,

child,' Musa—an older, more shaky Musa—said when Chhoti was old enough to understand. 'Your grandfather was someone I knew.'

'But you are the only grandfather *I* know,' Chhoti said simply.

And that was that.

So Musa, who had never planned otherwise in any case, took it upon himself to be the grandfather he supposed Durgadas would have been. He was as affectionate to Chhoti as he was to Dilshad's son—more, in fact, said his resentful wife—and whether it was a kiss to soothe a bruised knee or an answer to some niggling question about where the sun went at the end of the day, Chhoti would be certain to find Musa more than willing to comply with her every request. He was patient and kind, stern when he had to be, and with a never failing supply of good humour.

On the day she turned five, he called her into his room. When Chhoti had accepted the gift he had got for her—a little musician, made of carved and painted wood, and holding a drum which could actually be played—he smiled and said, 'Sit down, my child.' She stared at him, eyes wide in the round little face. 'What is it, Dadu? Do you have another gift for me?'

She grinned, well aware that this grandfather who was not really her grandfather but doted on her as if he were, always gave her more than one gift for her birthday. Or for Eid, Diwali, Holi, any occasion to celebrate: Chhoti was always the happy recipient of Musa's generosity. True, the rest of the family did not celebrate Diwali or Holi or many of the other festivals that marked the passage of the year, but Dadu made sure she did. He would instruct the cook to make special sweets, and Musa and Chhoti would have their own festivities, their private celebrations. If it was Holi, Dadu would take her out into the little courtyard at the back of the house, and they would play with colour, Dadu's white hair turning a hundred shades of red and yellow and orange in the process. If it was Diwali, he would have dozens of little earthen lamps lit, and there would be garlands of flowers decorating the arches leading into the courtyard. And, there would always be gifts for Chhoti.

'Yes,' Musa said, with a smile that mirrored her own. 'Yes, there is another gift. It will last you a long time, long after I am gone. Through all your life.'

Chhoti's eyes grew wider. 'What, Dadu?'

'Come,' he said, taking her hand and seating her on a low stool. 'You will see.'

That was the day Chhoti's education began. Musa had spent the last month not just buying ink and paper and reed pens for her, but also finding whatever manuscripts he could, so that he could reacquaint himself with the script of his youth. His tongue had not forgotten the words, and after an initial period of slow and faltering reading, he regained the momentum he had once known. He had never been much of a reader—who expected a stone carver to be a scholar, after all?—but now, as teacher, he had to set a good example.

'Dadu,' said Chhoti one day as they sat at their lesson, 'why does Ibrahim not read with us? I asked Begum Sahiba, but she didn't say.'

Begum Sahiba, the name by which Chhoti called Dilshad's wife, did not like Chhoti. Like her now-dead mother-in-law, she had made up her mind to dislike the child from the moment Chhoti had become part of the household, and with her mother-in-law dead, she had doubled her efforts to make Chhoti realize how unwelcome the girl was. Chhoti, too young yet to understand this abhorrence, remained unfazed, and her refusal to be deterred by Begum Sahiba's coldness infuriated the woman even more.

In a house full of people, Chhoti had ended up with only two true friends. One was her de facto grandfather. The other was his grandson, Ibrahim.

Ibrahim, the same age as her, was the darling of the family. He had cousins, all of them older than himself; he had two younger siblings, twins born when Ibrahim was three years old. And yet his status as Dilshad's firstborn accorded him privileges. The rest was a result of Ibrahim's own nature: open, irrepressibly buoyant and prone to mischief. The type of mischief that endeared him to people, and made them laugh: turning his clothes inside-out, kissing doting adults with honey-smeared lips, repeating every single thing he overheard—including embarrassing epithets overheard amongst the men of the house. They loved him.

And Ibrahim loved Chhoti. All his free time, and there was plenty of it in the early days before lessons began, was spent with Chhoti. He brought out his toys for her, he concocted games for them to play, he joined her on exciting expeditions through the guava and mango orchards behind their house.

'Children should be free to be children, they must be allowed their play,' Musa had said one day, when Dilshad, coming into the courtyard and finding Ibrahim and Chhoti playing together, had protested. 'They are of the same age, son,' Musa had added placatingly. 'All of Ibrahim's cousins are older than him, and the twins are too young. Chhoti is exactly the same age. They are perfect as playmates.'

'Playmates today, Abba,' Dilshad had grumbled. 'What of tomorrow? This can take on unseemly proportions. It is not as if she is his sister, that either of them will know that there is a precise definition to the relationship. This is so amorphous.'

'They are too young for it to be anything more than amorphous,' Musa said gruffly. 'For the love of Allah, Dilshad, they are children. Little children. Do not make their play a sordid thing.'

Although Dilshad said nothing, it was obvious from his silence that he was not convinced, and that he never would be.

Musa's love for Chhoti did not, however, mean that there was any corresponding lack of love for little Ibrahim. Ibrahim, after all, was family, his own flesh and blood. And Musa knew, from the painful experiences of the past, that one could not sever oneself from family. Even now, years after they were dead, his parents appeared in his dreams, and he saw again the anguish in his mother's face, the anger in his father's. He had gone, very occasionally, to visit Yamini when she was still alive, but after she had died two years earlier, even that connection to his natal home had snapped. Thinking of them, his sisters and his parents, only filled him with remorse and made him even more aware of his duty towards his son and his son's son.

So when Ibrahim was old enough to begin more formal lessons, Musa himself chose a tutor for him, a young man but with the solemnity of a much older one. He was strict with his pupil, and Ibrahim's lessons were closely regulated. Even though Ibrahim did his studying in a secluded room within the house, he was, for all practical purposes, away from home. Every morning, well before the day's lessons were to begin, a servant would clean the room. Shortly before the tutor was to arrive, a little salver with the barest of essential refreshments—a pitcher of water with a tumbler, a paan, a few sweets—was placed in the room. On most days, the tutor only had a few sips of water. Once, because it was the day after Eid, he consented to have a laddoo. He believed with a near-fanatical fervour that for the mind to be clear and receptive of knowledge, the body must be removed from all temptation, whether it be food and drink, or comfort and company. The austerity did not sit well with Ibrahim, but he was too young to oppose it and too much in awe of his grandfather to voice his resentment.

By the time Chhoti was old enough to ask Musa why Ibrahim did not study with her, Ibrahim was spending three hours of every day with his tutor. The following year saw that duration rise to four hours and by the next year, while he was spending four hours ensconced in the room with his tutor, Ibrahim was also spending a further three hours studying on his own: poring over books, learning things, completing work that the tutor had assigned.

Despite that, he always found time to ferret out Chhoti from wherever she might be. Even if it was for a mere quarter of an hour, even if it meant they could talk only briefly, and that too, mostly about whatever each of them was learning—and it astounded Chhoti to realize that the subjects Ibrahim learnt were so very different from what she learnt. Her studies were increasingly focused on literature and on the scriptures of Hinduism, because Musa thought it important that she should grow up aware of her heritage.

Dilshad's wife, much though she resented the presence of this orphan in their lives, realized that whether they liked it or not, Musa would not let Chhoti be discarded even after his death. The thought that when Chhoti grew to be of marriageable age, they would have to find an eligible Hindu man for her to marry, was too much to stomach. But perhaps, thought Dilshad's wife—though she dared not voice the idea before her father-in-law—perhaps Chhoti may be trained to be a good maidservant.

So, as Musa grew older and more forgetful of what was happening around him, Begum Sahiba took Chhoti in hand. 'What will become of you?' she asked. 'If you don't know what a maidservant is supposed to do, how will you supervise her work?' Chhoti was set to doing chores that maids handled in the house: sweeping and mopping floors, dusting, cleaning, scrubbing utensils. She hated it, and she made no effort to hide her hatred, which only served to incense Begum Sahiba even more. 'You have to learn, Chhoti,' she would say. 'You have to learn, otherwise what will you do?' And Chhoti would be given another task to perform. 'Don't tell the men,' Begum Sahiba would say. 'They don't understand such things.'

Though she was resentful, Chhoti knew that telling either

Musa or Ibrahim would only make things more difficult for her. They might intervene on her behalf, but it would cause acrimony, and Begum Sahiba would vent her spleen on Chhoti. The zenana was hemmed in by rules and strictures more rigid than any walls could ever be; for Chhoti to antagonize Begum Sahiba would be most unwise. So when Ibrahim asked her why she looked so sweaty, she evaded the question and asked him what his tutor had taught him. Instead of telling him of her day, she listened with glowing eyes to his recounting of his. 'How fascinating it sounds,' she said wistfully one day when he had been telling her about the poetry he was reading. 'I wish I could read Persian, too.'

'I will teach you.'

Chhoti gave him a look that was both doubtful and mocking, yet at the same time with the faintest glimmer of excitement. 'Hah!

'No, you wait and see. I will,' replied Ibrahim, with quiet confidence. 'I study very hard, so I know.'

24

AH 779 (1386 CE)

It was Eid, and the house had been lit up for the festival, with hundreds of little earthen lamps glittering in neat rows along the parapets, in niches and at the edges of garden paths. Hordes of servants had been sweeping, dusting and polishing for all of the past week, and every carpet, every rug and every bolster had been beaten and brushed until it could not possibly hold a single speck of dust.

The cook, along with a battalion of assistants, had spent the past few days hard at work, and on the day of the festival, the kitchen had been a hive of frenetic activity from well before dawn.

Ibrahim made several stops at friends' and neighbours' homes to greet them for Eid on his way back from namaaz. When he finally got home, he stood in the first courtyard of his house and looked around. A smile hovered on his lips, a smile that was not reflected in his eyes. Those eyes, so uncannily like his grandfather's, harboured the frustration of a man who did not know where to turn, who knew that his desires were at odds with the demands of those around him. What he wanted, and what his mother wanted, were two diametrically opposite things.

As if on cue, his mother came, bustling out of the room in front.

'What are you doing here? As it is, you're late,' she cried. 'Hurry up and wash. I have put out fresh clothes for you, new clothes. What took you so long?' Even as she spoke, she was tugging at his elbow, steering him towards his room.

She had put out a long tunic and coat, both ostentatiously embroidered, with pantaloons and turban to match. Ibrahim blinked. 'Must I wear these, Ammi? They are'—he groped for an adjective that would convey his reluctance to don such clothing, yet without hurting his mother's feelings—'they are a little too grand for me.' He laughed, a little shakily. 'Our guests will wonder what sort of scholar I am.'

Before his mother could answer, a servant came in with an ewer of hot water, a thin towel over his shoulder. Begum Sahiba instructed him to place it in the corner, and shooed the boy out. She turned to take the coat Ibrahim had taken off, and said, 'These clothes may be grand, but a prospective bridegroom must be shown off, not hidden beneath the ink of your madarsa.'

'Bridegroom? Me? But—'

With slow, deliberate movements his mother spread his old coat across half the bed. She straightened the sleeves, smoothed out the panels, and set the seams neatly. 'You are eighteen years old,' she said in that quiet voice of hers that had been deceptively docile when she was a young woman, but which had revealed over the years an assertiveness that had made even Dilshad bow to most of her wishes through all his married life.

'Eighteen is hardly an age to be married.'

'Most men are married by the time they are eighteen. Many at a much younger age.' She finished folding the coat, and looked up at him. 'It gives one more time to set up a proper household, to have sufficient heirs.' She did not say more as she turned her attention to the turban he had removed, but Ibrahim knew what she meant. Dilshad had married when he was twenty, and had sired only three children, of whom the eldest, Ibrahim, had been the sole survivor into adulthood. Six years it had been since Dilshad had died, at less than forty years of age, of tetanus. With Dilshad's death had died out his resentful wife's last hope of having more children. More sons, dutiful sons. Not sons who were wilful and heedless of her distress at the path they insisted on choosing.

Ibrahim knew and understood, but he harboured too many grudges of his own to be sensitive to his mother's worries. 'I have no wish to marry and you know that, Ammi. You have known it since—' he broke off.

She snapped, so suddenly that it startled him. One moment she was standing, carefully folding the length of cloth that was his turban; the next, she had flung it across the room and had whirled on him, her grey eyes blazing with fury. 'Since that hussy began making eyes at you!' She saw him go white with shock, but she was too angry to care. 'Did you really think you would be allowed to carry on, the two of you? Your father and I had warned your grandfather of this when he took her into this house. I knew she would come to this! I knew it. She should have been a servant; she should never have been allowed to think of herself as anything better!'

That was the crux of the matter; her resentment was not so much directed at Chhoti as it was at her late father-in-law. Musa, though he had already been an old man when Chhoti had washed up at his doorstep, had asserted himself in no uncertain terms. He had made Chhoti a member of the family, not merely of the household. No one, while the old man was alive, could have dared to suggest that Chhoti should have been a servant.

But Musa had been dead these past ten years—he had gone in his sleep, quietly and peacefully—and his going had not eased matters for Dilshad's wife. The resentment that had burgeoned in her towards Musa had transferred itself to Chhoti, and with every passing day, week, month and year, it had grown greater.

She stopped to draw breath, gulping the air deep into her lungs. It served to soothe her, to still that temper that could be so violent but so short-lived, too. Ibrahim, watching her warily, knew that this sudden tranquillity was no more than a thin veneer, so fragile that it was like the finest muslin wrapped around her anger. One tug, one pull at it, and it would rip right away.

'She is gone, Ibrahim,' his mother said in a quiet,

controlled voice. 'Gone forever from this house and our lives. Forget about her.'

ଓ

There was little time then, or through the rest of the evening, to go searching for Chhoti. Ibrahim made a feeble attempt at a protest by dressing not in the clothes that his mother had put out for him, but in an altogether more subdued coat and pyjamas. Of the guests his mother had invited to the feast, there was just one family whom he did not know: a robust and red-cheeked gentleman with two sons, one a boy and the other a youth whose voice was just beginning to break. Accompanying them in two well-curtained palanquins were unseen figures that disappeared inside the zenana without stopping. The family, thought Ibrahim, for whom he was supposed to be on exhibition. He wondered if it was his imagination or whether the old man was already looking around with a speculative and unashamed eye at the mansion.

He did not throw them out of his house, but he made it clear to them that he did not seek their company. His friends were there, as were relatives whom he had not seen this past year. They wanted to share news, they wanted to know how it was to study at the most splendid madarsa in all of Hindustan—no, perhaps in all the world, for did it not attract scholars from as far away as Baghdad? They wanted to know if the fruit trees in the gardens of the madarsa bore fruit all the year round, as some awestruck visitors had claimed, with mangoes filling the air with their sweetness even in the deepest of winter?

Ibrahim laughed. 'Of course not. The Sultan is an energetic man, but even he cannot work wonders with the seasons.' He grinned. 'But when the time is right, yes, the trees are laden with fruit. And the gardens are full of flowers.'

'It must be wonderful to look out of your classrooms to see that vast lake,' a distant cousin remarked wistfully.

'It is huge. Imagine all that shimmering water, just at your doorstep.'

The conversation wandered on about the madarsa, its masters—among them the greatest scholars of the East—and their students. About the Sultan himself, who was so proud of the madarsa he had established that he was even having his own mausoleum built right in the midst of the madarsa buildings.

Since Ibrahim's mother could not possibly have appeared in front of the male guests, one of her brothers had been given the task of introducing the ruddy-faced gentleman to Ibrahim. Ibrahim nodded, offered greetings and his wishes for the festival, and left it at that. 'You must come to our house sometime soon,' the gentleman said with a meaningful look. Ibrahim gave him a weak smile and made a non-committal remark about how difficult it was to get leave of absence from the madarsa.

It was a wearying evening. More than once, a restless Ibrahim found himself wishing his guests were gone, and that he could leave the stifling environment of the chamber to look for Chhoti. My dear, he thought, what have they done to you?

As soon as the last of his guests had gone—even before the clip-clop of the horses' hooves had been muffled by the night—Ibrahim hurried through into the depths of the house, searching. Not for Chhoti—that would have been pointless, because he knew that his mother would not have lied about something like that. Instead, he went looking for someone who might know where she had gone. Meera, he thought. Meera, who had brought her up and who had been the closest Chhoti had had to a mother.

Meera would know.

❧

Meera looked into Ibrahim's eyes, her own flat, lacking emotion. 'Why do you ask for her now, sahib?' Her tone was bitter and accusatory, and Ibrahim was taken aback. The Meera he had seen now and then had been a cheerful, smiling woman with a youthfulness that seemed to defy the passage of time. The Meera who used to bring a three-year-old Chhoti to Musa's room to play had looked almost exactly the same—except for a few more grey hairs and some extra flesh—as the Meera who used to hustle a reluctant sixteen-year-old Chhoti to the temple every week.

That Meera, it seemed to him, was gone forever. She was thinner, and a crop of wrinkles pulled her face down. But no, that was not it. It was her expression, the look of deep anguish and anger, that made her look so much older and more weary than when he had last seen her.

'Why do you call me "sahib"? I was always "Ibrahim" to you,' he said, countering her question with one of his own.

'Because that is what you have become. You are the head of this household now. Not a child any longer, but a man.'

Ibrahim could not help the snort of laughter, bitter and sarcastic, that burst from his lips. 'I am no more the head of this household than you are. Do you think Chhoti could have been sent away without a word to me if I had actually been the master here?' He shook his head. 'I am the master only in name. Now tell me please, where Chhoti has gone. Was she'—he swallowed, suddenly frightened of what he may discover—'was she sold off? As a slave?' He dare not think worse: as a concubine? No, surely his mother would not have been so brutal, no matter how much she had despised Chhoti. One woman could not do that to another.

Meera shook her head. 'No, not sold.' She turned her head away, her eyes fluttering shut with pain. 'No. She was married off.'

'Married?' He stared, unable to comprehend. 'To whom? When?'

'Shortly after you left to study in the madarsa. To a man chosen for her.'

'Of course it would be a man,' Ibrahim snapped, irritated,

and then realized that the emphasis had been not on *whom* she had married, but *how*. 'Chosen by whom? My mother?'

Meera nodded. His heart sank. 'Who?'

'Would a man of any worth marry a girl like that? No,' she had seen the anger that flooded his expression and she held out a hand to stall him. 'No, I do not mean that there was anything wrong with her; you know how much I love her. But a Hindu girl brought up in a Muslim household? A girl, too, of whom so little was known? Your grandfather had said often enough that her father had been a potter and some other ancestors were stone carvers, like your grandfather himself was. But who will take a dead man's word for something like that? It is a matter of marriage, after all. One can lose one's caste by marrying the wrong person.'

A knot, painful and throbbing, had formed in his chest. 'Please tell me,' he murmured. 'What happened? Whom was she made to marry?'

'The first man who was willing to marry her. Not anybody finicky about his caste.'

'Who?'

'A beggar,' Meera said. Her voice broke on a sob. 'A beggar!'

He had not expected that. A rich man, no; he would not have dared to hope for that, but at least a man capable of looking after a wife? Anger surged through him against his mother. Surely, if it had been so important to remove Chhoti from the house, she could have been sent to one of the many relatives his mother had in houses across and outside Dilli? Not to be cared for, but perhaps to be taken on as a maid? There was always room for one more servant.

No. Begum Sahiba's hatred of Chhoti had been more virulent than he had guessed. The blow must be complete, Chhoti must be given the harshest punishment possible for having dared to impose herself on this house for so many years.

'Thank you for telling me,' he said, when he could finally trust himself to speak. 'Do you know where this man lives, her husband? I would like to visit her, see if there is any way I can help.'

Meera wiped her eyes and shook her head. 'Do not go, Ibrahim,' she said. 'Please, have pity on her. How do you think she will feel when she sees you? I cannot speak for Chhoti, but I am a woman too, and I can understand how she must feel. Betrayed.'

'I didn't betray her.'

'You went away to the madarsa.'

'I had to! Even Chhoti knew that. Ever since the Sultan built the madarsa, Abba had said that I would go there to study someday. We all knew that when I was old enough, I would seek admission.'

'True.' The look in Meera's eyes turned defiant. 'In which case would it not have been kinder to let Chhoti be? Was there a need to teach her Persian, to lend her books to read? To give her hope? She thought this house would be her home for as long as she lived. And who gave her that hope? You. You did, not your mother and not your father. If she had not had that hope she would not be in this situation today.'

She shook her head in a gesture of futility. 'Let her be. Leave her to live her life as she can. There is nothing you can do except cause her more pain. If she sees you, all she will remember is what she has had to leave behind. What could never have been in the first place.' She turned and moved away, but stopped after a few steps and said over her shoulder, 'Please. If you love her, leave her alone.'

Although he hated to admit it, Ibrahim, as he paced about in the courtyard, had to agree that Meera was probably right. His meeting Chhoti would be painful for her; it would remind her of all that had been, and of all that had been snatched away from her. The comfort, the indulgence of

Musa. Ibrahim's friendship, and the love neither of them had expressed in so many words, but which both knew and acknowledged. She would be reminded of all their times together, and the hope that he had let her cherish.

What would she be thinking? That with his going away to study at the madarsa, he had put her behind him. That she had been a mere amusement, someone to keep him occupied before he went on to other things, other pursuits.

But if he did nothing, he would suffocate under the weight of it. Married to a beggar? Chhoti, married to a man incapable of providing for himself, let alone for a wife?

His chest contracted with the agony of it. If he could do nothing else, at least he could make sure she had enough to eat and wear, a roof over her head. What his mother had done was reprehensible and irreversible. He could only try to make amends.

Meera would never tell him where Chhoti lived, so the only course of action open to him was to follow her surreptitiously the next time she went to meet Chhoti, as she must surely do. Perhaps even today, when his questions had upset her, and reminded her of Chhoti's plight.

Ibrahim hurried into his room. When he emerged a few minutes later, he had removed his turban and changed his clothes, swapping the fine coat for a dull brown shawl, changing the pyjamas for an old pair that he usually wore only to bed. He glanced about, making sure he was unseen, before he made his way around to the back of the house, where usually only the servants ventured.

Meera, he should have realized, would have a myriad tasks, and little freedom to go about as she pleased. Ibrahim found himself lurking in corridors, hiding behind columns and curtains, trying to keep an eye on the woman as she went about her work. Fortunately for him, the aftermath of Eid—the tidying up and cleaning to set the house in order after the celebrations—was sufficient to keep most of the servants occupied. Nobody noticed him and wondered why the young master was flitting about in places he was rarely seen.

It was late afternoon before he finally overheard Meera say to another maid, 'I need to go out, Nikhat. It will not be long.' To this was appended a list of instructions—of chores that had been completed, of other less urgent chores that would be attended to when Meera returned. Of chores that had been partly completed and would need another, presumably Nikhat, to complete them.

'Always running off,' Nikhat said sourly. 'Where are you going this time? To meet that—'

'Nothing.' Meera cut her off. 'I will be back soon.'

It was easy to follow her, because she did not seem to suspect she was followed. Ibrahim slipped out through the wicket gate that led into the mango grove beside the house. He made his way quickly through the trees and onto the path which joined the lane in front of the house. She was moving swiftly, too swiftly for a woman of her age and seeming fragility, but he was young and strong, and it was not difficult to keep up.

The first shiver of foreboding went through Ibrahim when Meera stepped off the road and onto a winding dirt track that led past a stagnant pond and through a scrubby field. What lay beyond, he did not know, but he could guess. Meera had hurried on, and Ibrahim followed in her wake till just past the mango tree, where he stopped short. The scene that met his eyes was one of such desolation and dire poverty that it made his stomach lurch.

The huts here were not the wattle-and-daub of much of the rest of Dilli; this was an accretion of debris. Splintered wooden doors, long discarded by a wealthier household; stones, probably filched from ruins. Branches, straw, a little mud here and there.

The stench, the combined odour of sweat, excrement,

urine and rotting garbage, had hit him even as he had walked through the field, and now that he was standing here with nothing to shield him, it made him feel sick. Chhoti lived here? In this squalor? Even the servants from his home, those who did not live in the mansion but had their huts nearby, lived in comparative luxury.

Chhoti, he thought. Allah, Chhoti. What has Ammi done to you?

Meera had stopped next to a woman who was sitting on her haunches, mixing cow dung with chaff to make dung cakes. The woman's face was hidden behind her odhni, but her ghagra revealed a slim ankle, youthful and surprisingly elegant for a woman whose hands were wrist-deep in dung. Ibrahim watched as Meera sat down beside the woman and began a conversation. A neighbour of Chhoti's, he thought.

He wondered what Meera was talking to her about. About Chhoti, perhaps? He edged closer, taking shelter behind bushes and a heap of rubble, until he was close enough to overhear.

25

Ibrahim sat in a corner of the courtyard at Qutb Sahib's dargah. Around him was the whirl of daily life at the shrine: men coming and going, offering flowers and incense at the tomb of the saint, the womenfolk keeping well away but within benedictive distance of Qutb Sahib. The murmur of prayers and of muted conversation ran on in the background, filling the air—as did the incense and the fragrance of jasmine.

Ibrahim heard none of it, smelt none of it, saw nothing that made an impression on him. He had hurried here from the slum, his feet seeming to move of their own volition, hurrying to seek shelter and solace. More, to find anonymity. He was just another supplicant here, a man seeking peace and comfort, one of countless others.

The woman Meera had been talking to had been Chhoti. A Chhoti reeking of cow dung, her faded and patched ghagra a hand-me-down, the hem of her odhni frayed. The rubble behind which Ibrahim had hidden had allowed him to get within half a dozen yards of the two women, and it was then that he had heard her voice, a muffled murmur obscured by the distance and the odhni. It had sowed the first seed of doubt, of a horrible suspicion, in his mind.

But it was not till a few minutes later that his suspicions had been confirmed. Ibrahim, crouching low, his clothing little protection against the thorns and gravel beneath him, was beginning to feel every little prickle and twinge when he had heard a man's voice call, 'Where are you? I need water. Where have you gone off to?' A whining voice, the voice of a man laid up in bed with a disease or an injury, and who had no qualms about ordering those who had to care for him.

Ibrahim had glanced towards the woman, who was laying out the dung cakes in neat rows on the stubbly grass beside her. At the first breath of the summons, her hands had stilled, her spine suddenly gone rigid.

By the time the voice had died away, she was shaking her head, rising to her feet with an unhurried and resigned air. Meera too, had stood, and this time her voice had carried to where Ibrahim huddled. 'Will you be all right? Is there—is there something I can bring for you?'

The other woman had said nothing, but she had shaken her head in a way that confirmed what he had feared, because it was a familiar response: the Chhoti he knew used this same shaking of the head to turn away help. Defiant, clinging on to her independence even at her own expense: that was Chhoti, his Chhoti. When it had been a Chhoti stuck in the branches of a mango tree she had climbed impulsively and would accept no help in descending, it had been a matter of exasperation and laughter. Now it broke Ibrahim's heart. He had had to make a great effort to stop from running forward and begging her to forgive him, his mother, even his grandfather, who had made a blunder by bringing her up to be someone he could not ensure she could be for the rest of her life. He had held back, a lump in his throat and tears in his eyes.

He had watched and waited as Meera had murmured a farewell and patted Chhoti's shoulder. Only when she was gone, the same way she had come, had Ibrahim hurried after Chhoti.

The man who had summoned Chhoti had cried out again. This time he demanded not just water, but for Chhoti to press his aching legs. The pain, the agony—and oh, this stupid woman, gone so long.

For a moment, Chhoti had stopped. Ibrahim, ducking swiftly behind a tree, had noticed the way she suddenly came to a halt, her neck straightening up and her chin lifting. He had recognized the emotion; he had seen it often enough in Chhoti. It had always reminded him of a mare rearing her head to throw off the bridle, the saddle, the rider and all. A thrill of joy had shot through him at the realization. There was hope after all; Chhoti was not utterly broken in spirit.

But he had been mistaken. The pause had been momentary. The next instant, she was moving again, this time more swiftly. Ibrahim had followed, puzzled.

The path emerged from between a straggling row of thorn bushes on one side and a pool of green water on the other. This was the heart of the settlement, where its huts nestled. The air was heavy with the stink of unwashed bodies, of dirt and sweat and excrement. He had instinctively raised his sleeve to his nose to block out the stench, and had, with a surge of remorse, lowered it in almost the same movement. If Chhoti could live amidst this, he could bear it.

And there she was, disappearing through the open door in a sagging hut off to the left. A dilapidated dwelling, the gaps in its thatched roof patched together haphazardly with heaps of twigs and grass. The walls were dotted with rows of drying cow dung cakes stuck on them. More cakes, already dry, stood in rows, leaning one against the other on the ground in front. Uniformly round, the diameter of a large melon, two fingers thick. Neatly ridged in a pattern of fingermarks. The cow dung cakes were the only element that was neat and orderly in the chaos around. The rest, from the scrawny mongrel dozing in front of the doorway to the worn walls with their peeling mud plaster, was poverty at its worst.

He stared, appalled. He waited, too, in the hope that Chhoti would emerge. Perhaps her errand would be short. She would give her husband some water, press his legs a while and then come out to do other chores. Ibrahim knew next to nothing of how a household, big or small, functioned, but logic told him that someone would have to cook, clean and wash. Without a servant to help—the very thought was ridiculous—Chhoti would have to do it all herself.

He waited for a while, but then other people started

appearing. Older children, staring curiously at this relatively well-off stranger. Women, bearing loads of cut grass on their heads, staring with less curiosity and more hostility. An old man, his eyes rheumy and one leg missing at the knee.

Ibrahim could have borne their stares, he had thought, but when one of the women stopped to ask him what he wanted, he turned and fled.

'Are we here to amuse you? Eh? You come here with your fancy ways and think it's very entertaining to see how we live, yes?' The woman's voice called out after him. The other women burst out laughing, and one added, in a loud cackle, 'Oh, I wouldn't mind him staring if he gave us something for it. What do you think, sahib?' Her voice raised itself to a shrill, sharp yell. 'Pay us if you want to watch!'

Now he sat against the cool clean wall of Qutb Sahib's dargah and, through closed eyes, relived his shame. The shame of that ignominious retreat from the settlement, and the shame of knowing that there was little he could do to help Chhoti if he could not even get to her.

A man, down on his knees, curled into a ball, was praying in an inarticulate but desperate murmur a few yards away. His voice rose every now and then into a wail of despair. Qutb Sahib, intercede for me. Qutb Sahib, you are the refuge of this beleaguered soul. Qutb Sahib, help me. Help me, Qutb Sahib.

If only he could have such unswerving faith, thought Ibrahim. If only he, too, could summon up the piety to believe that all he had to do was pray, and that the rest could be left to the power of a being infinitely more powerful than himself. But even his prayers, when he said them in silence, fell into a void that left him as disturbed as before. His prayers brought him no relief, and showed him no way forward.

He knew, deep down, that if Chhoti had to be helped out of the morass into which his mother had flung her, he would be the one to help her.

But how he would do that, he had not the slightest notion.

Finally, after the lamps had been lit at Qutb Sahib's dargah and most of the crowd was gone, he rose to his feet, gathered his shawl about his shoulders and left.

And there, in the lane outside, beside the Gandhak ki Baoli, was Chhoti. He did not notice her at first; she was sitting, a shapeless figure wrapped in the gathering gloom of the evening, with her back against the outer wall of the stepwell. As he came up the road, she stood up. At first, he mistook her for a villager, getting up after a brief rest. It was only when she stepped out, right into his path, that he looked into her face. She had lifted the odhni off her face, and the glow of a torch burning in a sconce outside a nearby house washed over her features.

Earlier that day, having seen the squalor in which Chhoti lived, he had begun to half dread coming face to face with her. No one could live like that and emerge unscathed, he had thought. An existence so poor could ravage the greatest of beauties, put wrinkles where there was not yet time for them. More than he feared the decline of Chhoti's beauty, he feared that when he saw her as she no doubt was now, he would not be able to hide his reaction.

The face that looked up into his had not changed, at least not its features. Chhoti's complexion was as clear, her face as lovely and unlined as when he had seen her last. What had changed was her expression. The optimism, the cheerful insouciance of the girl from a wealthy household—even if she knew herself to not be entitled to that wealth—was gone. In its place was a hardness, a mask he did not recognize and which frightened him. She had grown up. And the woman she had turned into was a stranger.

'Why did you follow Meera?' she asked without preamble.

'I—' He swallowed. The events of the day had stripped him of his peace of mind; this sudden encounter robbed him of whatever composure was left. His mind whirled, from stunned recognition of her to embarrassment at her condition, to trepidation at the look on her face and the accusation in her voice. 'I wanted to know where you lived,' he blurted out, finally.

'Why?' she snapped. 'What did you hope to achieve?' From somewhere further up the road came the sound of approaching feet, of people talking. Chhoti glanced about, before hurrying to the small gate that led into the Gandhak ki Baoli. Without her summoning him, Ibrahim followed.

It was dark inside the enclosure, the lamps of the nearby houses and the weak light of a thin crescent moon barely filtering through the trees that stood around the gate and just inside. The smell of sulphur, which lent its name to the stepwell, hung heavy on the air. Chhoti shifted beside him and there came to his nostrils the smell of cow dung and sweat. It made his nose wrinkle in disgust. A fleeting emotion, for the very next moment he was cursing himself for it.

The men, their voices now loud enough for whole sentences to be heard within the baoli, passed by. They were talking of everyday things: a man looking for work, the others recommending this man or that as a possible employer. Ibrahim and Chhoti stood silent in the darkness surrounding the baoli until it was quiet again.

'Well?' She said out of the gloom. Her face was a blur in the darkness.

'I was worried about you. I hadn't known what had happened, what my mother had done—'

She cut him off. 'And what do you plan to do, now that you have seen for yourself? Go home and thank your Allah that you live in better circumstances?' The bitterness had changed her voice, he thought. Not just the tone, her voice itself. The sweetness of a year ago had gone, coarsened to a harshness that jarred.

'Chhoti.'

It hung in the air, that single word. The name by which he had called her from when they had been toddlers together. The name which had been sweetest to him all his young life and which he now uttered with all the agony that had been ripping his heart apart all through the day.

Chhoti, he wanted to say, you know how much I love you. You know I would never have let this happen to you if I had been there. Chhoti, I cannot live without you.

He only uttered her name, and hoped she would understand all that he had left unsaid.

After a long while, she heaved a sigh. When she spoke, the anger had gone out of her voice. 'It is useless,' she murmured. 'What can you do? Will you murder my husband and marry me? But no, even that would not work, would it?' The bitterness was back, making her voice a sibilant hiss. 'You would be ostracized by your family and your community if you were to bring me home, wouldn't you? A Hindu, and a beggar's widow, to boot. You would never be forgiven.' She paused to gather breath. 'Of course, there is no need for a wedding either, is there? I can just be your concubine.' Her voice was acid, and he could hear the betrayal and pain swamping everything else. 'And you always knew it, you knew I could never have been your wife. At the most, a concubine.'

'Stop it, Chhoti.'

'You stop it,' she snapped back. 'You should never have come. Didn't you think how I would feel?'

He hung his head in shame. 'I couldn't breathe,' he whispered. 'I had to see for myself. That was why I—' a thought struck him. 'How did you know I had followed Meera? I was careful.'

In the darkness, he heard her draw in a deep, shuddering breath. 'You were not careful enough. I saw you, from inside the hut. That's why I followed you back here.' A sob burst from her. 'Why did you come, Ibrahim? Why couldn't you have left me alone? There is nothing you can do. Nothing, do you hear!'

They stood there, two figures wrapped in the gloom surrounding them. He wondered why, if she was so inimical to his presence, she did not leave.

'What is your husband like?' he asked.

She was quiet for so long, he thought she would refuse to answer his question. When she finally replied, her voice was devoid of emotion. 'He is nearly fifty. He has trouble walking.'

'How—how do you manage?' He had visions of Chhoti resorting to begging. Or worse, selling herself. He tried to push the thought away, unsuccessfully.

'You don't need to know.' Her voice was cold and hard once again. 'I am going now. Don't try to see me again. We happened to have been brought up together, but that is all. A tie that no longer exists. You are not obliged to look after me and I expect nothing from you.'

With that, without even a goodbye, she was gone. A few heartbeats more and even the sound of her feet hurrying away down the lane was gone.

The very thought of meeting his mother nauseated Ibrahim. In his eyes, what she had done was inexcusable; she had undone all the good that Musa had done by fostering Chhoti. If he came face to face with her, he might forget all the lessons of filial devotion he had been taught. He might see only the ruthless, selfish woman who had married off an unwanted orphan to a crippled beggar old enough to be her grandfather.

Ibrahim wandered about for a while, through the lanes and bylanes around the Gandhak ki Baoli. When every last lamp in every last house had been extinguished for the night, he sat down under a tree. There was a vague thought in his head that he should try to sleep, but slumber, he soon realized, was impossible. The cold bit into his bones. His hands and feet were as ice and the wind whipped about his ears. More than that, though, was the turmoil that raged in his head: the anger, the despair, and the sense of defeat.

The moon rose, travelled across the sky and began its descent. The howling of the jackals rose, dropped, rose again and died down. Other than the occasional shout from a faraway watchman on patrol, there was nothing. Nothing but Ibrahim and his thoughts.

No matter how much he hated it, he had to admit that Chhoti had been right. There was no way out. If she was married, married she would remain. It did not matter that her husband was a crippled beggar who needed a servant rather than a wife; Chhoti, with that irrational sense of duty that was so intrinsically a part of her, would still think herself honour-bound to remain with him. There was nothing Ibrahim could do; even if he—an audacious thought, this—kidnapped her, they would never be happy. Her conscience would not allow it, and her unhappiness would not allow him to be happy.

And who knew how long the old man might live yet? It could be years before he died. He may even outlive Chhoti and Ibrahim.

He must have fallen asleep out of exhaustion sometime during the early hours of the morning, and the aazaan from a nearby mosque startled him into sudden wakefulness. Despite the shawl, he was stiff with cold.

Aching and stiff in every limb, Ibrahim got to his feet, his mind now made up. He would go back to the madarsa. If for nothing else than that the constant round of studies and discourses, discussions and reading of books long into the night would occupy his mind, preventing it going down paths there was no point in frequenting.

Those who belonged to Dilli and had gone home for Eid were not yet back. But there were scholars and masters aplenty from faraway lands, and they had celebrated the festival within the madarsa. Garlands of flowers still decorated the mosque and the halls. Rows of sooty earthen lamps still decorated the parapets overlooking the vast water tank that spread at the foot of the school. The students who sat talking and laughing in the sunshine were enjoying a holiday, not studying. Ibrahim passed by them without a second glance.

That evening he went out on an errand of his own. He found a boy in the village outside the madarsa, and gave him a sealed letter. It was addressed to his mother. Inside was a brief and impersonal note, explaining that he had decided to cut short his holiday and return to the madarsa. He did not know when he would come home again. She would understand that, he thought. She was perceptive; she would have known that the acrimonious note of their last conversation would not be forgotten so quickly.

'And this,' he said, handing another sealed note to the boy, 'you must give to Meera. Ask for her, and make sure you give it only into her hands, and only when you are alone with her. Nobody must know of it, do you understand? Tell her that whoever she goes to, to have it read, must be someone she trusts'—he paused, wondering how to phrase it—'someone she trusts with what she told me.' It sounded lame, but it would have to do.

There, he thought, as he made his way back into the madarsa. It was done. Meera would know, and perhaps she would tell Chhoti too, the next time they met, that he had retreated into the sanctuary of the madarsa and may remain inside its academic seclusion for years to come.

He breathed deep of the scents around him: the grass underfoot, the flowers in the parterres and on the trees. Incense that someone had lit at the entrance to one of the halls. It was clean here, clean and quiet and beautiful. It was a world so far removed from Chhoti's that they may well be two different worlds. Heaven and Hell.

Would she be relieved that he would no longer be near

her? That he had accepted her desire to be left alone? Or would she despise him for giving up so easily? Would she ever forget? Ever forgive?

Ibrahim squeezed his eyes shut. Tears leaked out and trickled down his cheeks. His shoulders shook, and when he groped on the shelf for a book—something to distract him, anything to give him a sense of direction—it tumbled from his hands and fell to the floor.

He had to work, thought Ibrahim, his mind suddenly filled with a near-panic. He had to work hard, fill every minute of every hour of every day with ceaseless occupation. It was the only way he could maintain his sanity.

Ibrahim had never had to labour with his lessons before. Now he struggled, his mind wandering, his focus falling apart at the slightest distraction: a word uttered, a whiff of a fragrant flower, an obscure memory evoked by something so mundane that it was laughable.

The change in Ibrahim did not go unnoticed. Most of his fellow students—there were none, really, whom he could call his friend—were too busy with their own studies to realize there was something wrong. The handful who noticed either rejoiced that their own chances of excelling were increased because Ibrahim fell behind, or contented themselves with asking him, briefly and with little sincerity, if all was well.

It was the masters who noticed. They had noted and appreciated Ibrahim's diligence and commitment, his aptitude for debate, his coherence and intelligence. Now they saw, instead of the worthy scholar, a man who was absent in spirit even when he was present in body. His work fell away; his arguments, when he was forced to provide them, lacked logic and conviction. He would sit in the study room, his books open before him, but his gaze would wander out over the shimmering waters of the hauz outside.

'Do you draw inspiration from water, Ibrahim?' one of

the more acid-tongued masters had said in exasperation. 'If that is the case, perhaps you should go down and fill a bowl to bring up here. Put it in front of you. Who knows, in looking down at it you may accidentally look at your texts too!'

'You are like a son to me,' said Abdul Latif, the kindly master who had taught Ibrahim mathematics since the day Ibrahim joined the madarsa. 'All the masters worry about you, child. What is it? What preys on your mind?' He placed an affectionate hand on Ibrahim's shoulder, and the younger man came close to breaking down.

But this was too deeply personal a thing to confess. Al Khwarizmi's algebra was something Ustad Abdul Latif knew in all its ramifications and details; the heart of a very young man, in love with the Hindu wife of a beggar, would probably be a puzzle to him. Ibrahim shook his head and mumbled that it was nothing.

'I can see that it is something,' the master said with a sigh. 'Because you were never like this. But I will not compel you. I will just give you a word of caution. Remember that the madarsa holds its reputation very dear. It is, after all, the Sultan's. If you do not go back to your studies ...' he left it at that and Ibrahim understood. It was not a threat; Ustad Abdul Latif was a mild-mannered man, not a man to threaten. It was a word of caution. Ibrahim would be asked to leave before he brought disgrace to the madarsa.

Two days after Ustad Abdul Latif spoke to him, Ibrahim left the madarsa of his own accord and for reasons he could not have foreseen.

☙

It was evening when a student, a youth not yet six months in the madarsa, came to Ibrahim. Ibrahim had been sitting at the foot of the building on the grassy bank of the hauz, when he heard the boy calling his name as he descended the stone steps from the students' quarters. 'I've been looking for you everywhere,' he said. 'There's a woman come to meet you. She's at the gate.'

Ibrahim froze at those words. His mother, he thought. His mother, come to tell him that she had found a bride for him and decided on the date of his wedding. His stomach knotted in fear and anger.

'Aren't you going?' the boy asked, confused. 'She's at the gate.'

Ibrahim shook his head. 'I don't want to meet anyone. If anybody asks, say you couldn't find me.'

'I don't think she's going to go away,' the boy muttered. 'She's come with a great big bundle on her shoulder. A Hindu woman. Pretty, too. Maybe a servant? Perhaps your family sent something for you?' A glimmer of animated anticipation came into his voice and his expression; if fine sweetmeats had arrived from Ibrahim's home, it may well be that he, as the messenger, might be allowed a sample.

But Ibrahim was already gone, racing around the hauz and up the flight of stairs that rose to the mosque and the gate nearby.

It was Chhoti, of course. She was standing outside the gate, just beyond one of the gateposts. The guard at the gate and a handful of young men—most of them students—were watching her with undisguised interest. Some had perhaps passed a comment, for Chhoti's face bore a look forbidding enough to discourage any further overtures from strangers.

'Master,' she said before he could say anything. 'Your mother has sent some things for you.' He saw the expression in her eyes, the plea to not reveal their secret in front of the curious audience that hung about. 'Not this,' she added, as he glanced at the bundle that lay on the ground beside her. Of course not, he thought; nobody could believe that that shabby and dirty sheet could have been sent by Ibrahim's mother. 'There is a cart at the end of the road.' She inclined her head, gesturing towards the dirt track that led away from the hauz and the madarsa. 'The cart driver was unwilling to come all the way to the gate. If you will come with me ...'

As soon as they were out of sight of the group at the gate, she stopped under a tree. 'My husband is dead,' she said, 'and I could not bear to stay there any more. I am sick of that place.' She sounded stifled, suffocated. Ibrahim did not know whether to commiserate with her or to congratulate her. Had she felt anything for her husband? She had been married to him a year, after all. But she sounded so bitter.

When she stood there, saying no more, as if waiting for him to speak, he finally asked, 'What happened? How did he die?'

'Of old age. Poverty. Hunger. A fever. Oh, I don't know!' Her voice rose to a strangled cry, a near-shriek of dismay and helplessness. 'I killed him!'

Those three words, damning and awful, rang in his ears, echoing till he almost believed they had been a figment of his imagination. She was crying now, her sobs heartbreaking.

'What do you mean?' His mind was racing, already beginning to plan. The law would be after her. Her neighbours would have reported the murder by now. It would perhaps be a matter only of hours before she was traced to her original home, where it would be discovered sooner or later that Ibrahim and she had been in love. They would come to the madarsa then. He must get her away. He had to get her away.

She was speaking, hiccups and sobs intruding on her words, her teeth chattering as she clutched her arms about her. 'I—I used to pray every waking moment that he would die,' she was saying. 'I prayed and hoped, with all my heart. I dreamed about him dying. I even,' her voice fell to a strangled whisper—'I even planned what I would do. I thought of setting fire to the hut and running away while he was sleeping. Or poisoning him.' The tears were now streaming down her face, but her voice, paradoxically enough, had steadied. 'I killed him,' she said in a quiet, level tone. 'I killed my husband, Ibrahim.'

The relief that washed over him was so great that he

chuckled out loud as he caught her wrist and pulled her into his arms. She smelt of sweat and cow dung and smoke and other unpleasant things, but the only thing that mattered was that she was here, she was innocent, and she was free. No longer another man's wife. 'Oh, Chhoti,' he laughed. 'My poor Chhoti. Do you truly imagine that your prayers and your plotting make you a murderess? If that were the case, we would all be guilty of not one but many murders.'

She looked up into his face, an injured expression in her eyes. 'I meant it, every time I thought of it. I have never prayed so fervently in my life before. The gods know. Your Allah knows. They know how earnestly I wished to be free of—of him.' She shook her head, looking away. 'Oh yes, I killed him. You may laugh at me for it, but I know.'

She had drawn away from him even as she spoke. He still held on to her wrist though, and even as their arms stretched, he said, 'I was not laughing at you, Chhoti. I would never make fun of you so cruelly.' That made her pause, and he took advantage of her hesitation to add, 'No. I did not mean to make fun of you, or to belittle your anxiety. The law cannot punish you for what your mind thinks or your heart yearns for, can it?'

She did not turn back to look at him, but some of the stiffness seemed to leave her body. For a long moment they continued to stand thus, and then she turned and walked the two steps back to him. Her odhni had slid down to her shoulders and when she turned her face up to him, he could see every detail of it: the finely arched eyebrows, the tears on the lashes.

'You don't understand, Ibrahim,' she said softly, shaking her head. 'Do you remember when we were small and we were playing in the garden? The gardener told us to stay away from the pink-flowered bushes that grew along the eastern wall.'

Ibrahim blinked, disconcerted and puzzled by the sudden and inexplicable change of topic.

'He told us that they were kaners, oleanders. That every part of the oleander, from seed to flower to leaf to bark—was poisonous. I remember him squeezing out some of the sap onto a twig. White and sticky it was, and he said that that was where the poison was its most concentrated; a few drops of it could kill a child. A little more and an adult, if already ill or injured or not in the very best of health, could die. He said we were never to touch it, no matter what.'

A chill crept over Ibrahim.

'That lesson stayed with me a long time,' Chhoti said. 'And oleanders are not hard to find in Dilli, are they?'

From somewhere down the road, in the dusk that was fast turning to night, someone began to cough. A hacking cough, dry and loud and unceasing. Chhoti looked over her shoulder, as if she would be able to see whoever it was. When she turned back, she shook her head. 'I used sap. It's very bitter, do you remember—that was what the gardener had told us?—so I put as much lime and ginger as I could manage, to mask the flavour. I told him it was a new recipe for a pickle, which I had just learnt.' She was wringing her hands now, her fingers twisting the edge of the odhni. 'I put a lot of it on his plate, you know. And then I left.' She swallowed. 'I could not summon up the nerve to sit there and watch.'

'And?' Ibrahim asked. His throat felt constricted.

'And he died. When I returned, an hour later, he was dead.'

'What about the others? Your neighbours? What did they say?'

'Nothing. It came as no surprise to anyone that he had died. Some of them offered their condolences. Perhaps it was out of a sense of form.' Her mouth twisted in a smile that held no humour. 'He was cremated this morning. I had my things packed before then.' She glanced back at the bundle that lay against the trunk of the nearest tree.

'Tell me, Ibrahim,' she said, her eyes glistening with tears, 'do you think you might be able to find a place for me in your home? As a maid? If nothing else, I have acquired a certain proficiency in sweeping and scrubbing and making do with very little.'

'My home? The one where my mother lives? I do not consider that my home any longer.' He looked back over his shoulder at the lights of the madarsa. For a moment, longing came into his eyes: a longing for the world he was probably leaving behind forever.

'I have no home,' he said, turning back to her with a smile, and bending to lift her bundle. 'But come, let us go, shall we? We will make a home for ourselves.'

Epilogue

'That's it?' Nasiruddin said, when Shagufta fell silent.

She gave him a small smile. 'Why are you surprised? Did it not seem like a logical end?'

He shrugged and made a face. 'No, it isn't that. It's just—just that I would have thought you would have more to say.' He shook his head, suddenly and vigorously, putting her in mind of a dog shaking off drops of water. The image in her mind made her smile widen. He did not notice, however, and carried on. 'But I suppose it is a satisfying end, in some way. The hero and the heroine finally come together, after all the obstacles have fallen aside. Or been made to fall aside.' He grinned. 'I must hand it to Ibrahim, though. It takes courage to marry a woman who's killed her first husband.'

'Or who thinks she's killed her husband.'

'Thinks? Why? Did she not, then?'

Instead of answering his question, Shagufta rose to her feet.

Sometime during the course of the past few hours, the fire had died down and Nasiruddin had had to build it up again. While he had foraged amidst the trees for dry twigs and broken branches, Shagufta had gone looking for water, carrying with her an old broken-necked water pot she had found lying in the undergrowth behind the mosque. When the fire was once again blazing, she had carefully balanced the pot atop the twigs and slipped in a handful of mulberry leaves. Nasiruddin had looked askance at it, taken one sniff of the infusion, and refused to drink any of it. She had nursed it, though, while she spoke: the liquid was hot and soothing, good for an aching throat.

She now got up and placed the pot back on the fire. It was nearly out; only the embers were left, and they would soon be gone, sunk into ashes, within a few minutes.

'Well?' he asked. 'What did you mean?'

'Childhood can be so busy,' Shagufta replied, after a moment. She shook her head slowly, a smile of amusement playing on her lips. 'There is the entire world to be explored. So much to be learnt, so much to be seen. It is hardly surprising that something that is learnt will be forgotten.' She picked up a twig and stirred the embers beneath the pot. A tiny burst of orange-yellow shone for a moment, before settling into a dull red beneath the grey.

'A gardener taught a little girl a name for a poisonous plant, and showed her that it had pink flowers. What did that little girl remember when she grew up? Pink flowers, and poison. Nothing else. Not the shape of the leaves, not the shade of pink. Not whether the flowers grew singly or in bunches. Nothing except the colour.'

'You speak in riddles.'

Shagufta shook her head. 'No. It is simple, really. I remembered nothing but fragments. And I was too desperate to think straight.'

'You? You—you were talking of yourself? *You* were Chhoti?' He stared, aghast.

She looked at him, and smiled as she did so. 'Why not?'

'How? Chhoti was a Hindu, and you are not.'

'Why? Does a name make so much of a difference? What is in a name, after all? And Chhoti? Chhoti merely means "small". It really has nothing to do with my being Hindu or Muslim, or anything.' She shrugged. 'When we got married, the imam at the mosque asked me my name. The first name that came into my head was Shagufta, a maid I had remembered from my childhood. So I told him that was what I was called. Shagufta. I am Shagufta now, Chhoti is long dead.'

She had said it without rancour, without any semblance of regret. But when she saw the wariness that had come into his eyes, she looked away, saddened. 'What? Do you not like the idea that I grew up a Hindu? Or is it—could it be that

I am suddenly not quite so attractive? Do you now wonder if I have been trying to poison you all these days? Do you wonder if my hands still have traces of oleander?'

Involuntarily, Nasiruddin glanced at her hands where they rested in her lap, and then glanced away quickly. 'No. No, of course not.' Then, a moment later, he added, 'But you were saying it wasn't oleander, was it?'

She shook her head. 'It wasn't. A few months later, I saw the same bush growing near the fort. I suppose I must have looked guilty, or awkward; uncomfortable, at any rate, because Ibrahim asked me what was wrong. When I told him, he burst out laughing. Because that wasn't oleander at all. It was something completely harmless. Jarool, I think, it was called. Or something like that. I don't remember.'

'Then your husband didn't die at your hands.'

She shrugged. 'Who knows? Perhaps all those prayers did have some effect. I prayed so desperately to be rid of him, that perhaps even the sap of the jarool killed him.'

He sat still, staring at her as if seeing her for the first time. 'I cannot believe it,' he said, after a moment. 'You. You, Chhoti? The picture you drew of Chhoti was so different from what you are. I would never have imagined that you and she were the same.'

She lifted the pot to her lips and took a small sip from it before placing the pot in her lap, atop her crossed legs. 'Perhaps we are not,' she said. 'That seems like a lifetime ago. I have changed since then.' When he did not react, she added, 'You should know that I was never much of a Hindu, despite all the teachings Meera tried to impart to me. And I was never much of a Muslim either, despite having grown up in a Muslim household. I was neither here, nor there. Never really a part of Ibrahim's family, but never really able to separate myself from them. Like a shadow, perhaps. Always there but always unnoticed.'

She sat still, staring into space. Only her hands moved, her fingers curling over the rounded shape of the water pot, warming themselves on it. 'His mother, and the rest of the family, could never have accepted me. We both knew it; we were bound to be outcasts from his world. So from the madarsa, we went away, just the two of us.'

'Where?' he asked, when she fell into another reverie.

'Here and there. He took me to a mosque and we got married. The imam looked askance at me, I remember. He must have seen my ghagra showing under the edge of the shawl I wore—but he did not say anything. My Persian was good, my understanding of the religion perfect. He must have thought I had been in some calamity and been forced to wear a Hindu woman's clothes.'

'And where is Ibrahim now?' Nasiruddin asked. His voice was low, as if he had guessed the truth and guessed too that it was painful.

He was looking at her with gentle, understanding eyes. Shagufta gazed back at him, the pain that she had called up out of the past wrenching at her. It had been painful to recall those days, but it had also been cathartic; for all these many years, she had been alone with those memories. And memories, whether they are of happy times or sad, need to be shared in order to attain their correct proportions. Memories that are too sad must be spoken of, to blunt their edge and to relieve the pain they cause. Memories of happiness too, must be shared, for only then can the happiness spread. And some memories, compounded of both sorrow and joy, must be shared if only to help one understand them in their entirety, to be able to discard the agony and hold the joy closer.

Shagufta shook her head. 'He died, seven months after we were married. It was cholera. I fell sick, too, but I survived. When I came to, I found that he had died while I had been unconscious. They took him away and buried him—I don't know where.' Her self-composure cracked, and she bent her head, cradling it in her hands, her shoulders shaking with her grief.

Nasiruddin looked on miserably. He moved once or twice, unsure whether to wait for her to recover on her own, or to make an attempt at comforting her.

Before he could do anything, though, she straightened up and wiped her eyes with the edge of her shawl. 'I am not usually so weak-hearted,' she said, with an embarrassed laugh.

'It is not a sign of weak-heartedness to mourn someone you loved.'

She said nothing.

A silence fell over them. An awkward silence, broken only by the sounds of the copse around them. Squirrels chittering in the trees, a pigeon cooing in the overhanging dripstone of the mosque, the heavy flapping of wings as a pair of hornbills swooped down into a tree. 'You should go now,' Shagufta said.

He nodded, but reluctantly. When he made no move to rise, she lifted an eyebrow. 'What is the matter? Do not say that my tale has affected you so deeply that you cannot wrench yourself away from me and go back home to your own people?' Her voice was teasing, but not entirely.

'Why not? Would you not like me to stay?'

'I would like a lot of things. I would like to live in a grand house, like Musa Dadu's. I would like to wear fine silks and to never know hunger. I would like an army of servants to wait on me hand and foot.' She laughed, dismissing her fancies with a shake of her head. 'But I know I would never be truly happy even if I had everything. Happiness is an odd thing. You can have everything, and be miserable. Or you can have nothing, and be the happiest of God's creatures.'

'You are a philosopher.'

'And you are a soldier. An enemy soldier.' She reached out a hand and touched his, her fingers lingering over his knuckles. 'A soldier who listened to my stories and who shared my memories. Thank you for that. But it is enough. I will not hold you back; I do not even wish to. Because this is not your home—your home is elsewhere, and your people wait for you there. The people you love, and who love you.'

'How about you? Who loves you? Whom do you love?'

Shagufta shrugged. 'Whom do I love? That is a question easily answered. But he can never love me, for he lies two yards deep in the earth. And who loves me? I don't know.' She looked up. 'Do you? Do you love me, Nasiruddin, of the army of Taimur?'

He pondered over the question, turning it about in his mind, mulling over it. 'Yes,' he said finally. 'In the way I interpret love, yes.'

'There you have your answer, then.' She smiled, her face luminous for a moment. Then, just as suddenly as she had smiled, she stood up. 'Come, I will take you down to the nearest path from where you can get to your rendezvous with your companions.'

'No—wait—I just said that I loved you.'

She looked at him, her eyes clear and her gaze honest. 'Yes. Do you wonder why I do not ask you to stay? Because perhaps a year from now, two years, or maybe far less, you will begin to miss all that you hold dear. You will miss your land and your people and your friends. You will miss the food your mother cooked and the birds that chirp in the trees near your home—you do have birds, don't you? And trees? You will miss those. You will miss the little things. I know, Nasiruddin; I know. When I was thrown out of the only home I had ever known, I realized that the things you miss most are the small things.' She was smiling, but her smile was sad. 'No. Go, Nasiruddin. Someday, if Allah wills it, you will return. I will be grey-haired and you will be bent, and we will sit and reminisce over these days.'

He sat, watching her silently as she gathered up the few things she had brought with her. She hesitated over the broken water pot; she had finished every last drop of the tea she had brewed from the mulberry leaves. It was broken, but it had served its purpose. It may well serve her again sometime. And it would remind her of this day. Shagufta picked it up too, and straightened up.

'Come,' she said. 'Let us go.'

'Wait,' he said, reaching out to halt her. 'There were two things I wanted to know, two things that puzzled me.'

She nodded, waiting for him to ask.

'First, how is it that your family became so poor? I mean,' he looked a little abashed, but persevered, 'If I have traced your lineage correctly, you belong to Madhav's family. Madhav had been a stone worker of great repute, he even got to work for the Sultans. With that fame and honour, there must surely have been a certain amount of wealth too. But from what you said—'

Shagufta had begun shaking her head even as Nasiruddin was speaking, and now she cut in before he could finish what he wanted to say. 'No,' she said. 'No, it wasn't like that. Madhav was never really interested in wealth, and from what Musa Dadu told me, for Madhav and for his son Mahesh, life was more about being content. They were comfortably off, never rolling in wealth.' She paused, rubbing her hand absently against the knot in the bundle she carried. 'Those who came after them, their descendants—including Durgadas, my grandfather who left me in Musa Dadu's care—they didn't have the innate talent or the ability to work hard, as Madhav and Mahesh did. They took whatever wealth they had for granted, and so it went.'

'How did you come to know of all of this? Your grandfather died when you were a baby.'

'Do you not remember? When my grandfather first came to offer Musa Dadu the frieze, he did talk of Madhav and of Mahesh. And of how Madhav created the Garden of Heaven for Razia Sultan, for whom my ancestor Jayshree gave up her life. Musa Dadu later told me that that touched him so much, it made him curious to find out about Madhav. So he went to meet Durgadas, several times, just to listen. To learn more.' She looked down, a roving fingertip having found a tiny hole in the edge of her shawl. She pinched it between forefinger and thumb, as if doing that would close up the hole.

'I think Musa Dadu was lonely, too,' she added. 'He was a Hindu converted to a Muslim, no longer considered family by those with whom he shared ties of blood, and without any other family, yet. Perhaps he yearned for human company, the company of those who reminded him of his own youth. Of simpler times.'

She looked up. 'When I was a girl, Musa Dadu made it a point to tell me every single thing he had learnt from Durgadas about my family, about Madhav and Mahesh. In turn—and perhaps that was because I wanted to know all I could about Ibrahim's folk—he told me also about his own family. Sridhar Sahu, Ratna, Gayatri. Jayshree. Badrinath. And, of course, Girdhar, who became Musa.'

Nasiruddin nodded. 'The Garden of Heaven. I was wondering about that. Where did it go?'

Her lips twisted in a bitter smile. 'Did you think I was given it as my dowry? When Ibrahim's mother married me off to that old man, all she gave me as a wedding gift was a coconut and the clothes I was married in.' She turned her face away, as if unwilling to let him see that remembered pain. 'And I had forgotten all about the frieze, anyway. Musa Dadu had shown it to me years ago, when I was a little girl. He had told me it was mine, and he had shown me where he had kept it for safekeeping. But I forgot then, when I was leaving the house. I suppose I was too busy thinking of other things.'

'Later? Did you not remember later?'

She shook her head. 'I did not. I was too preoccupied with maintaining my sanity.' He was still sitting, looking intently up at her. 'Come on; it is getting late.'

'But later?' he asked, as he got to his feet. 'With Ibrahim? Could you not go with him?'

'We were too busy being deliriously happy,' she said,

with the quietly amused smile of an older woman looking indulgently on at the romance of a young couple. 'Nothing else mattered. In any case, I knew that Ibrahim did not want to ever go back to that house again. If I had thought of it and told him I wanted to go, I suppose he might have considered, but I never did remember. I didn't need to. And after he died, I did not have the nerve to go back. I was too scared.'

She had begun walking, making her way down the narrow path that wound through the bushes. He fell into step beside her. 'Now? You are your own woman now, you have nothing to fear. And it is your property, after all, you have a right to it.'

Shagufta shook her head. 'I have no need of it. Perhaps someday, but not now.'

The path was a forgotten one, meandering through the trees and passing only occasionally near habitation. Now and then, they passed what had perhaps once been habitation: old stone walls, collapsed and crumbling under the weight of weeds and saplings, some already growing into trees. When they passed near settlements, the fringes of the town, they heard the inevitable sounds of human habitation: people talking, a child crying, the creak of a pulley as water was drawn from a well. Only once did they cross paths with another human being, a skinny boy guiding a meagre flock of goats. He gave them no more than a passing glance; in the gloom, one saw only a man and a woman, not that the man was one of the invading army that was now going back.

Shagufta said nothing all the way. It was only as they emerged from the trees into the vast space dominated by the Jami Masjid that she stopped and said, 'Go, then.'

Nasiruddin stopped. 'It is goodbye? Are you sure?'

She nodded.

'I—I will come back,' he said, on an impulse.

She smiled at him with something akin to affection. 'That is gratitude speaking. And the heat of the moment.'

She noticed the crestfallen look that came into his eyes, and murmured, 'Yes. Come back. Someday. And if I am not here, there will be another. Another to tell you stories.'

She watched him until he had been swallowed up by the shadows of the mosque and the Qutb Minar. Then, with tears flowing down her cheeks, she turned and made her way back to her own life.

Historical Note

In 1192 CE, Muizuddin Muhammad Ghuri, then Sultan of the Ghurid Empire, invaded India. Ghuri had attacked the region several times previously, in the process annexing important towns such as Multan and Lahore. At the decisive Second Battle of Tarain (Tarain is today known as Taraori, in the Karnal district of Haryana), the Ghurid forces defeated Prithviraj Chauhan, who ruled much of western and northern India from his capital at Ajmer. Chauhan was taken prisoner, and later executed. Delhi, which was part of Chauhan's domain, came under Ghurid rule.

Muhammad Ghuri continued to rule from Ghur; for his newly acquired Indian territories, he appointed his trusted general, Qutbuddin Aibak. Aibak had been sold into slavery as a child and had been eventually bought by Ghuri; his abilities and prowess had so impressed Ghuri that he had elevated Aibak to one of the highest positions in his court. On Ghuri's death, Aibak claimed Delhi and the other Indian territories that had been part of the Ghurid Empire. The dynasty which Aibak founded was known as that of the Mamluks, or the 'Slave Sultans'—so named because of Aibak's past.

Several of the earliest and most impressive Indo-Islamic monuments still extant in Delhi were begun during the reign of Aibak, including the Qutb Minar and its neighbouring mosque, the Quwwat-ul-Islam, then known as the Jami Masjid, the 'congregational mosque'. Aibak's son-in-law and sometime successor, Iltutmish or Altamash, added to these structures and built some more of his own. Altamash had declared his daughter Razia as his successor, but she was able to ascend to the throne only later, having to overcome bitter opposition from the Chahalgani, the forty-member elite of Turkish nobles who held sway in Dilli. Razia's reign was sadly short; a little over three years after becoming Sultan, she was deposed and eventually killed after being ousted from Delhi.

A series of mostly ineffectual Sultans (barring some exceptions, like Balban) followed Razia, until the rise to power, in 1290 CE, of Jalaluddin Khalji, founder of the Khalji dynasty. Of the Khaljis, Allauddin Khalji (r. 1296–1316 CE) was the most prominent, and left his mark on Delhi in the form of several important monuments, including the Alai Darwaza beside Qutb Minar.

The Khaljis were succeeded in about 1320 CE by the Tughlaqs, a dynasty whose name has become almost synonymous with that of its second ruler, the mercurial Muhammad bin Tughlaq, who introduced a new coinage (setting off a spate of forgeries) and shifted the capital from Delhi to Daulatabad in the Deccan, only to return to Delhi after less than a decade. As interesting as Muhammad bin Tughlaq was his predecessor Ghiyasuddin Tughlaq, who had founded the dynasty and carried on a long-standing war of words with the Sufi mystic Hazrat Nizamuddin Auliya. Auliya, along with his dear friend, the famous poet-musician-statesman Amir Khusro, was a contemporary of Ghiyasuddin Tughlaq's, and there are several apocryphal stories surrounding Auliya, Tughlaq and Khusro.

The last of the important Tughlaqs, Firuz Shah Tughlaq (r. 1351–88 CE) instituted several administrative and economic reforms, and contributed a good deal to the built heritage of Delhi. Besides building his own citadel (Firuz Shah Kotla) and several other important structures (the madarsa at Hauz Khas is one of the important ones), Firuz Shah also carried out repairs to existing monuments like the Qutb Minar.

Firuz Shah Tughlaq died in 1388 CE, and the Sultans who succeeded him were unable to retain a hold on the empire. Ten years after Firuz Shah's death, in December 1398 CE, Taimur—Amir Timur or Tamerlane—attacked

Delhi. Taimur's sack of Delhi left many thousands dead; the city was plundered and ravaged, and Taimur carried away not just a lot of riches, but artisans and craftsmen to enrich his own capital at Samarqand.

Much of the historical background in this book is accurate, or close to it. The interactions of my characters with the real, historical characters—Razia Sultan, Amir Khusro and Nizamuddin Auliya among them—are, of course, completely fictitious. I have tried, however, to make the historical characters as true to life as I could.

Lastly, in a city as old as Delhi, along with all the facts, there is bound to be some lore as well. Delhi has its fair share of legend, which includes the story of how the name 'Dilli' was derived from the 'dheeli keeli'. Or the many stories about Hazrat Nizamuddin Auliya and his tussle with Ghiyasuddin Tughlaq. The baoli at Nizamuddin (in Central Delhi, centred round the dargah of the saint) is still revered by the devout, who believe in the miraculous healing powers of its water. Auliya's tomb complex next door houses not just his tomb—which attracts thousands every week—but also Amir Khusro's as well as many other prominent royals from the centuries since.

Razia Sultan, however, lies interred far away, her tomb a nondescript one near the Turkman Gate (named for Hazrat Shah Turkman Bayabani) of Shahjahanabad.

Acknowledgements

The writing of a book can be a difficult task, but it's made easier by friends and family who offer inspiration, support, encouragement and feedback in much-needed and regular doses. I have several people to thank for their help along the way in the development of this book. Development, not merely the writing, because there was much that came before the writing.

My cousin by marriage, Yogam Datta 'Yogi Didi', who has an enviable collection of books, was the one who introduced me to Edward Rutherfurd's brilliant Salisbury saga, *Sarum* (Ballantine Books, 1987). *Sarum*, over a quarter of a century ago, first made me wonder if it was possible to write a story about a set of families in Delhi. When, ten years or so back, I decided to take the plunge, several family members obliged without my needing to ask. My father Andrew Liddle and my sister Swapna Liddle, lent me books to help my research along. My father, who is a renowned numismatist, answered questions on coinage, and Swapna (a historian who specializes in the history of Delhi) read through the entire manuscript to weed out any historical inaccuracies.

Another person who, completely of her own accord, offered valuable help is Ramya Sarma. Ramya edited an initial draft of the manuscript and in the process gave me valuable inputs about my writing as a whole. (Yes, Ramya: I now make a concerted effort to *not* put in commas at the drop of a hat. And I use a calculator.)

Many thanks are due to the good people at Speaking Tiger: to Renuka Chatterjee and Ravi Singh, whose faith in this book I will always be grateful for. And to Aruna Ghose, who did such an excellent job of editing it.

As ever, I have my husband Tarun Bhandari to thank.

For support, for ideas, for exuberant excitement (how much that counts for, only a writer struggling with self-doubt knows) and for being, as always, my very first reader and very first editor. And, last but by no means the least, my daughter, who is known in public to those who don't know her personally, as the Little One, the LO. The LO turned seven this year and has taken to peering over my elbow and watching as I type. While I was reworking sections of *The Garden of Heaven*, the LO noticed Razia Sultan mentioned. Her eyes immediately lit up, and she ran off to fetch her *Amar Chitra Katha* book about India's great queens. I have now been appointed editor-when-it-happens to the story the LO has said she will write about Razia.

Thank you, everybody.

ALSO BY MADHULIKA LIDDLE IN SPEAKING TIGER

SPEAKING TIGER

WOMAN TO WOMAN

STORIES

Madhulika Liddle

Category: Fiction/Short stories
Format: B
Page Extent: 184 pages
Binding: Paperback
Territory: World
Pub: November 2017
ISBN: 978-93-86702-58-6
Price: ₹299

BISAC Category:
FICTION/Short Stories (single author)
FICTION/Women
FICTION/Literary

Praise

'Detailing, empathy, and irony shine through these stories... Madhulika brilliantly explores the lives of her heroines with twists that add to the impact... real life meets a superior storytelling skill.'—Hansda Sowvendra Shekhar

Stories that span emotions from pathos and despair to hope and even humour, bringing alive the world of women: Women losing, women winning; women being women.

Description

A young girl finds herself looking on as her mother listens to the woes of the world, always offering a sympathetic ear and a shoulder to cry on—while harbouring a bitter secret few know of. A woman and her brother try to come to terms with the knowledge of their mother's infidelity. In a flood in Assam, a family is ruined and their daughter finds herself sent off to an unseen bridegroom in faraway Delhi. In a colonial bungalow in the heart of rural India, a lonely old woman notices the stark difference between her privileged life and that of the poor around her. But who, really, is more privileged? In the span of a bus journey, a prostitute and a nun find they have more in common than they had imagined. And in the snowfields of Kashmir, a young widow takes her revenge on the man who killed her husband in the only way she knows...

Written with sensitivity but unafraid to explore the hidden secrets and dark corners in ordinary lives, *Woman to Woman* is a collection of twelve beautifully crafted short stories by award-winning writer Madhulika Liddle.

The Author

Madhulika Liddle is a novelist and award-winning short story writer. Although best known as the author of the Muzaffar Jang series, featuring a seventeenth-century Mughal detective, Madhulika also writes short stories in various genres. Her story, 'A Morning Swim', won the Overall Prize in the Commonwealth Broadcasting Association's Short Story Competition in 2003. In 2016, she became the first Indian to be longlisted for the prestigious *Sunday Times* EFG Short Story Award for her story 'Poppies in the Snow'. In addition, Madhulika blogs about classic cinema, travel, food and history, at www.madhulikaliddle.com.

Speaking Tiger Publishing Pvt Ltd, 4381/4, Ansari Road, Daryaganj, New Delhi 110002. Tel: +91 11 47472630
Email: customerservice@speakingtiger.com **www.speakingtigerbooks.com**